the
Gift Maker

the
Gift Maker

MARK MAYES

urbanepublications.com

First published in Great Britain in 2017
by Urbane Publications Ltd
Suite 3, Brown Europe House, 33/34 Gleaming Wood Drive,
Chatham, Kent ME5 8RZ
Copyright ©Mark Mayes, 2017

A CIP catalogue record for this book is available
from the British Library.

ISBN 9781911331773
MOBI 9781911331797
EPUB 9781911331780

Design and Typeset by Michelle Morgan

Cover by Michelle Morgan

Printed and bound by CPI Group (UK) Ltd, Croydon, CR0 4YY

urbanepublications.com

FSC
www.fsc.org
MIX
Paper from
responsible sources
FSC® C013604

To my parents

Term parents

the
Gift Maker

Sometimes only a stranger
can give the gift of hope...

MARK MAYES

THE GIFT MAKER

one

THOMAS WAS WOKEN by a loud, insistent knocking on his door. At first he thought the knocking was part of a dream he was having. He was back at school, in a cupboard, hiding from the metal-work teacher. He had broken one of the tools, and the teacher, Mr Kohl, who had a thick red neck and the face of a pig, was manically searching for him, clattering files and rasps across the room. Mr Kohl began pounding his sizeable fist on the cupboard door Thomas sat trembling behind.

Suddenly sitting upright and breathing heavily, Thomas mumbled, 'Yes? Who is it?'

No answer. The knocking came again, this time in what seemed to Thomas to be a bossa-nova rhythm. He peered at the luminous green hands of the clock on the bedside table.

'Hello?' called Thomas.

'A package for you, Mr Ruder.' The voice belonged to his landlady, Mrs Senf. Thomas wondered how she knew about bossa-nova rhythms. And he also wondered why she was delivering him a package at gone two in the morning.

'I'm not dressed, Mrs Senf. I'm in bed. Please can you leave it outside the door.'

'The gentleman said to give it to you in person. He made me promise, Mr Ruder.'

'Okay, Mrs Senf. I'll just put something on.' Thomas felt for his t-shirt and, in the dark, struggled into his jeans. He did not bother with socks. En route to the door he tripped over his guitar. It fell hollowly to the floor. Cursing under his breath, he unlocked then opened the door a crack. 'It's so late, Mrs Senf. Surely there's no post at this time.'

The small bright eyes in Mrs Senf's wizened old face stared into the dark space behind Thomas. She did not meet his gaze, which was unusual for her. She wore a purple nightdress with a rather large white bow at the neck. Thomas wondered if he was indeed still dreaming. Mrs Senf licked her lips. She brought up her hand, in which she held a small blue box. This, too, had a white bow. It was slightly bigger than a watch box, but smaller than a box that may contain a single book. As Thomas was a student, he assumed it was one of his colleagues returning a borrowed item. But in such a box and at such a late hour? Mrs Senf did not appear to want to actually give the box to him. She held it close to her thin chest.

'The gentleman said you would understand. He was very polite. It's a good thing that I have trouble sleeping or else I would have been put out by so late a call.'

The hall lamp gleamed weakly behind Mrs Senf. The smell of boiled beetroot from supper still hung faintly but resolutely in the air.

'What did the gentleman look like, Mrs Senf?' Thomas had opened the door a little wider, and Mrs Senf stared bleakly at his long bony feet. He had feet somewhat too big and hands somewhat too small. God had been playing a trick, his uncle Gustav said.

Mrs Senf cast her rheumy eyes to the ceiling and chewed her bottom lip. She rubbed her wiry-haired chin elaborately. This all

THE GIFT MAKER

seemed rather dramatic to Thomas. 'Well now, he was a substantial man. Not fat, but substantial. Very large hands, like a navvy. And hairy. The hands, I mean. But so well dressed. Not like many of today's youth. I say youth, but he was maybe about forty. Well, that's young to me. I asked him his name and he tipped his hat at me and said that "Mr Ruder would know all about it." She looked down at the blue box then back at Thomas as if they shared a secret. 'Do you know what's inside?'

Thomas put out his hand, paused, then took the box from her light grip. 'Ermm...yes, I think it may be something from my professor. To do with my studies, I'd say.'

'Oh, I doubt that somehow,' said Mrs Senf, with a sour expression. Then she spun round and Thomas watched her small yet strangely imposing form stride away down the corridor and turn where the stairs were. He softly closed the door, went to the bedside table and switched on the night-light with the turtle base, the one his cousin had given him for his twenty-first birthday.

The description of the man Mrs Senf had given meant nothing to Thomas. He sat on the bed, looking at the small blue box with the white ribbon, oddly afraid to open it. He brought it to his ear and shook it. Nothing rattled. It was of what Thomas would describe as medium weight for its size.

There were no words on the outside of the box, no name or address. But on the bottom side, the side opposite the elegantly-tied bow, was a series of neatly-written numbers in black ink. Two digits followed by a dot, followed by two more digits, then another dot, finally followed by four digits. For several minutes Thomas tried to puzzle it out. Of course! He shook his head. For a university student he often considered himself somewhat slower than average. It was a date. And more than that, it was a date Thomas now recognised. It was his own date of birth.

This young, wispy-bearded history undergraduate with pretensions to be a songwriter was not ordinarily of a superstitious nature. In fact, along with his fashionably cynical friends, he enjoyed poking fun at the recent rise in fortune tellers, Tarot readers, and *alternative* healers that had set up shabby booths in the market place and placed small hand-made cards in shop windows. He had even boasted to Ulli, one of his closest friends, that he, Thomas, could learn any of these "methods of deception" in less than a week, so as to supplement his meagre government grant, and the small and irregular cheques his father sent him from Schlunkenfurt.

So it was with no little surprise that Thomas felt an unnameable dread when considering the blue box in his hand, the box that bore his date of entry into this world. So much so, that he suddenly opened the bedside drawer, placed the box inside (among the cigarette papers, plectrums, and unfinished love notes to women he had never even spoken to) and shut it with a force that, along with possibly waking Mr Lutzig below, attempted to obliterate its existence from Thomas's conscious mind.

'I need rest,' he thought out loud. The next day harboured a tutorial with Professor Halloumi, and Thomas had barely sketched out his ideas on the "Causes and ramifications of the Lipnitz Affair in relation to the Yulma Crisis" (that had followed the very next year). At this rate, he would have to sit the term again. His father would once more call him a hopeless dunce, who "squandered money made by the sweat of my brow" and insist Thomas return to the faraway smallholding, to the rusting carts, dark lumpy fields, and scrubby woodland of his youth. In short, to give up all hope of what Thomas dreamed would be a brighter and better future.

'I'll wake early tomorrow,' he thought, 'and go over my notes.' So putting aside the strange entry of the blue box with the white ribbon into his otherwise easy-going life, he climbed, still dressed in jeans and t-shirt, back into his hard narrow bed and fell asleep.

❦ ❦ ❦

Thomas caught the usual tram, got in the same carriage he always did, and sat at the back on the left, as he always did. He was, however, only a creature of habit in certain things. When it came to food, the kind of girls he liked, or what he should wear, he would often find himself utterly perplexed, sometimes considering himself a "person without a centre", as he had heard the condition described at an open debate with the fashionable psychologist Boris Matzolleck, one night recently at the Municipal Halls.

At Glocken Street he was joined as usual by his two henchmen, as others dubbed them: Ulli and Jo (short for Johann). Ulli's beard was the cause of much envy from many of his fellow students. It surpassed even Professor Braunkniesel's for both length and thickness. Ulli would absentmindedly stroke and play with this luxuriant growth, giving him an air of someone in deep contemplation of exceedingly esoteric matters. His close friends knew otherwise. Whether in a lecture or debating politics on the street corner, he was invariably wondering how soon it would be before he could repair to one of the many taverns that were dotted around the student district, to quench his unquenchable thirst on a jug or three of hock or umpteen tankards of malzbeer.

Jo (short for Johann) was a very different kettle of fish, and often smelt like one. His prematurely grey hair was very thin and receding. He cared nothing for personal hygiene nor the nasal sensibilities of others. His mind was above all that, and he would coolly dismiss any suggestions, or sometimes outright demands, that he pay attention to his social responsibilities. He dressed in an impersonation of a factory worker from thirty years ago. The only concession he made to his true identity, that of a philosophy student at a small and somewhat politically-reactionary provincial university, was the occasional moonflower in his rough serge lapel. Why he wore these strange blooms he would never answer. 'It is a personal matter,' he would say, and gaze obliquely into the middle distance. Jo was the only student of the three worthy of the name. He actually studied. Indeed, some of his tutors were even a little in awe of him. Before a class with Jo they made sure they did their homework.

'Ah, comrade Thomas Ruder,' boomed Ulli in a sonorous bass, making the old ladies and young mothers turn.

'Greetings, oh bearded one,' intoned Thomas, in a somewhat lacklustre voice. It was the pair's customary mode of greeting.

The two newcomers sat either side of Thomas. Jo gave Thomas a half-hearted upward flick of a hand. The philosopher had not slept a wink. He had been revising for his end of term exam. Everyone knew he would breeze through it, yet he wore a constant expression of worry and a genuine sense of emotional strain emanated from his slender frame.

'I see you've forgotten your books again,' said Thomas to Ulli. 'Too busy trimming that monstrosity, no doubt.'

Ulli grinned. There was something green stuck between two of his large, uneven front teeth. 'I study society, my friend. Every street corner is a book. In every alleyway lie the secrets of the ancients. I see an essay on human travail in the unintelligible bark of the newspaper seller. My eyes are my pen. My heart, the exercise book of eternity.'

'You left them in the tavern?' said Thomas, unimpressed.

'I think so,' said Ulli, shrugging. 'Will need to check at lunch. Could be one of several places. Will you come with?'

The tram rattled across the oldest bridge in the city, St Hermann's Bridge, which straddles the venerable and habitually grey-brown waters of the Launz. Wooden-shuttered shops lined either side. This was the beginning of the jewellery district. The shops hung precariously over the river like ornately-carved limpets. Plenty of glittering riches here, but mere trinkets to the seekers of a deeper shining.

Thomas yawned. 'Not this time, fuzzy face. I'm going to meet Liselotte.'

'Not a chance,' said Jo. This sudden interjection surprised the other two friends. Jo had been so quiet for the last three stops that they had all but forgotten his existence.

'I beg your pardon, boffin?' said Thomas, turning to the aromatically-challenged youth on his right.

Jo continued to stare through the smoke-stained window as the tram threaded the southern environs of the city, past large department stores, government buildings, statues to The Fallen. 'Saw her with Franz the other day, by the fountain. Very much in amour, I would postulate.'

Ulli gave a laugh more akin to a shout. 'And you know precisely what about love, my speccy brethren?'

Jo ignored the teasing. '"It is precisely in each man's failure does he find the seed of his growth."'

The other two exchanged a look. 'He's quoting Vogel again,' said Thomas. 'It's Vogel this and Vogel that, ever since he won that essay prize. In any case, she agreed to meet me. I sent her a note.' Thomas knew he was blushing and that Ulli would be merciless if he spotted it, so he pulled the collar of his coat up around his burning cheeks.

'She's a kind soul,' droned Jo. 'Probably let you down easily.'

'We'll see,' said Thomas.

All three grew silent, falling back into their private worlds, eyes closed, or staring listlessly at the passing city. The tram climbed through narrower streets, past shops selling incense, abstract paintings, privately-printed books, and all manner of bric-a-brac. Dotted between the shops were cafés and taverns, where the likes of these would-be thinkers and world-changers hung out in a fug of cheap tobacco, weak coffee, and stale beer fumes.

'Damn, it's our stop,' said Thomas suddenly. 'Ring that bell, Ulli!'

The tram came to a squealing halt and the three friends stumbled out onto the frosty morning pavement. Satchels were slung over shoulders and hands were dug deep into pockets as the trio slouched into Ganz Street, making for the hallowed groves of academe, otherwise known as Schwalbenbach University.

two

THOMAS STOOD STAMPING his feet beneath the third lime tree along from the Bauerbŭmmel Gate. He observed the steam of his breath fan out, curl, and disappear in the raw and darkening air. The tutorial had not gone well. Professor Halloumi had called Thomas a man of no little potential, but with an equal facility for loafing and muddleheadedness that would inexorably lead him to a minor civil service position somewhere in the Grauben Territories, at best. Thomas had promised to do better. To, with no trace of irony, forego the indolent pleasures of youth. He ended the encounter by offering his hand to the venerable scholar who gazed at it witheringly as though it were a bowl of four-day-old fish-head broth.

Liselotte was late. Exceedingly. Thomas began to wonder whether Jo had been right and she was indeed letting him down gently by avoiding their assignation. The enamoured student had hoped to invite the dark-haired beauty down to the Orchid Rooms for rum-coffee and zimmelcake. And, if things went swimmingly (and why would they not?), he hoped to accompany her back to her lodgings, to discuss, among other things, the state of contemporary poetry, rumours of war in the East, and, with a bit of luck, become enmeshed in the finer intricacies of a young woman's lingerie.

Thomas bit his reddening knuckles. He was on the verge of sloping off to join Ulli in a probable alcoholic-therapy session, when he spotted that familiar high-collared, cherry-red coat and the shiny black boots he had seen Liselotte wearing around the quad earlier that day.

'I had to post a letter,' said the full-lipped, cat-eyed young woman as she approached. She was a little out of breath, which surprised Thomas, as he knew her to be captain of the middle cohort's planzball team, and no mean goaltaker was she.

'It's fine and dandy. I like the cold. In fact, I thrive on it, as my landlady will testify. Never anything for the meter.' He rubbed his thumb against his first two fingers, and winked, expansively. Things had not begun well. This sort of clownishness would never impress a girl of such high thoughts and neo-romantic aspirations. Indeed, a tiny vertical frown line appeared above the bridge of her exquisite aquiline nose.

'I've come to tell you something,' she said. 'But let's get into the warm first.'

Thomas's mind spun twenty to the dozen. This *thing* she had to tell him could either cast him back into the deep well of his despondency, or might lift him heavenward on gossamer wings made of pure iridescent joy, and so on and so forth. Such power does the female of the species possess. Or such is she given.

The Orchid Rooms was a drafty, cavernous place. Once a church, raised in the name of a now-defunct sect long since driven beyond the city walls, it nestled imposingly between the Old Tannery and a foreign bank. The young could-be couple entered through an impressive archway and were met by a sour-faced woman of about sixty, who sneered a 'good afternoon' to them in a thick country dialect.

'For two, is it? Not just coffee, mind. You've got to *eat* something. New rules. Keep out the one-cup-for-an-afternoon's-warmth-mongers. New manager, you see. New broom. We're not a doss house anymore.'

From her broken-toothed gob came the reek of onions riding on something nebulously sweet. Death, perhaps. She gave them each what passed for a menu (but which was in actuality a greasy piece of yellowing paper) and gestured to a small round table near one of the columns, about four down from the inevitable statue of Wolfram Von GrohlenFürz. These edifices to the *Great Man* had sprung up everywhere in the country, and more so now than at any time in Thomas's memory. The government's cynical appropriation of this long-dead, bulbous-nosed 'Hero of the Nation' led to many a student, or disaffected worker, daubing the Hero's face with paint, sour cream, or worse.

Thomas and Liselotte sat down. The chairs were hard and rickety. The table was stained and rickety. There was a distinct paucity of orchids in the Orchid Rooms.

'So, here we are. Luxury on every side,' said Thomas, with a spreading of his child-sized hands. He motioned to one of the ancient waiters, who tottered over to take their order. The man stood there, blankly, not looking at either of his two customers. With each tubercular breath, his slack mouth formed tiny bubbles of greenish spit at one puckered corner. This was service of the highest order.

'What will you have, my dear?' said Thomas.

'Do you still offer the chocolate mandolins?' asked Liselotte, trying not to look into the waiter's vacant yellow eyes. His ruffled shirt-front was stained with a century of tobacco, egg, and sauces diverse and various.

'No mandolins. Boss take them off,' said the waiter, whose absurdly large name badge, pinned to the left epaulette of his oversized black jacket, announced to the world that he went by the name of Kaspar.

'Perhaps the Bombolinis?' said Thomas to his would-be paramour with a barely restrained leer.

'No Bombolinis,' muttered Kaspar. Then adding, more to himself than to the customers in his presence, 'Boss no like them.'

Thomas felt the need to be assertive, which never boded well, and often proved disasterous, especially concerning matters of the heart. 'Two rum-coffees, my good man. And a whole zimmelcake. Sod the expense!' Thomas grinned at Liselotte, then looked expectantly at the waiter.

'Language! Bad language not permitted. New boss...,' mouthed Kaspar.

'Yes, new broom and all that jazz. I know. Look, we're hungry. Need brain food, old man. We, believe it or not, are the future of this country.'

The waiter snorted, wiped his sleeve across his bubbling mouth and hobbled off, presumably to locate the beverages and the zimmelcake.

Liselotte gazed at her palm as if something shiny and expensive lay there. She was clearly elsewhere. With lantern-jawed Franz, thought Thomas, allowing himself an inward sigh. Yet there was hope. Although Franz possessed the body of a klempball champion, and owned a face straight out of one of those *Youth for the Future* magazines from the 'seventies, he was somewhat short in the noodle department, as Ulli could testify, having roomed with him for several months during their first year. This Franz

THE GIFT MAKER

fellow could not boil an egg, and would not know where one came from either. Yet the girls mooned over this athletic birdbrain, as is their wont.

'What did you want to tell me, my sweet?' said Thomas, attempting to break through the shell of Liselotte's apparent indifference.

'Thomas Ruder, I am not your sweet, your dear, or your little poppet, or any other such psychologically and emotionally belittling name you care to bestow on me. I am a fellow colleague, a fellow student, and most likely your intellectual superior. Times are changing, Thomas. It is time you changed with them.' She said all this while staring at her purple-varnished fingernails, occasionally smoothing an uneven edge with her thumb.

'I'm so sorry...sorry,' stammered Thomas. 'I didn't mean to offend you. I was just having a little joke, pretending to speak in the old-fashioned style. It's not my natural way at all. I promise you it stops here, my...my *friend*.' He winced.

She finally looked at him, her almost-black eyes searching his face for any trace of irony at her expense. When she was finally satisfied she looked around her (rather too affectedly, Thomas thought), and said in a low, purring voice that sent a tingling to Thomas's extremities, 'I don't want to be overheard, Thomas. I need to tell you something. It's serious.'

Thomas saw the decrepit and halting waiter wending his unsteady way over to their table with what passed for a tray, but which consisted of a stiffened piece of cardboard. He slammed down the rum-coffees without the merest sense they were to be drunk by fellow human beings, and slid the dense sugary cake into the centre of the table without a jot of style or ceremony. He waited for a moment, expecting a gratuity, no doubt. The two young people stared into their steaming mugs. Kaspar cleared the phlegm from his throat and spat ripely into a dingy handkerchief, which he had retrieved and now replaced into the top pocket of his jacket. He oozed away leaving a palpable sense of human misery in his wake.

When the coast was clear, and there remained only half-a-dozen or so other patrons in the establishment, all several tables' distance away, and clearly lost in their own interminable chattering or the late-afternoon edition of the Feldschrauber (that putrid organ in snivelling service of the industrial elite of this soul-worn country), Liselotte leaned over to Thomas, her small round breasts nestled in a maroon sweater, slightly flattening the zimmelcake beneath them. How Thomas would have loved to have been that cake at that moment. She cupped a hand to her mouth and whispered, 'I've been given a box, Thomas. A very strange box. I have absolutely no idea who it's from, who made it. I don't know why I've been chosen. But I had to tell someone, I had to, although I really shouldn't. No one would believe it, Thomas.' Her eyes caressed his face. 'I've always thought you to be an open-minded person, and somehow I trust you. I need you to see it. Will you come to my room after we've had our coffee? Please?' Her brow furrowed in expectation.

Thomas instinctively took one of her long-fingered hands in his. It was surprisingly warm. The skin on the back of the hand was rather dry and flaky, but he disregarded this detail. He nodded gravely. 'Yes, Liselotte. I will come.'

He thought of the blue box, still unopened in his bedside cabinet, so mysteriously delivered to him the night before. The box with his birth-date inscribed on the outside. But about all that he said nothing.

He squeezed her hand, which was noticeably larger than his own, and repeated, rather unnecessarily, but with all the solemnity he could muster, 'I will come.'

three

LISELOTTE LIVED JUST off Linzen Square, on the third floor of a smart-looking apartment building of the King Ludwig period. The silver plaque by the entrance announced that the building had won an award for the quality of its restoration. Her family were considerably better off than Thomas's, her father being an assistant bank manager in Jarleskunk, that delightful if slightly staid seaside town one hundred or so miles to the south.

As they climbed stairs that smelled of polish with an undertone of mint, Thomas, who was behind Liselotte, watched puppy-eyed, as her statuesque form (she was only half an inch or so shorter than he was) fluidly ascended the six flights, offering him a glimpse of smoke-coloured stocking with every stride.

From flat 2b on the second floor a violin could be heard. The player was obviously no slouch, but the sound was discordant to Thomas's ears. Aggressive, one might say. He was very much one for sweet airs and honeyed melodies, so unlike the majority of his contemporaries, who affected to relish the brutal throbbing of bass guitars and rasping vocals that spewed a pumped-up rage against everything from their parents to the State Employment Department.

Liselotte came to a halt outside a cream-painted door and rummaged for the key in her coat pocket. The key fob had a little metal cat with bright green eyes attached. Emeralds perhaps. 'She is like a perfect cat in human form,' thought Thomas. Liselotte let them both in, giving a quick glance down either side of the gloomy corridor before she shut the door behind them.

'Would you care for some wine, Thomas?'

Thomas nodded, thinking he would have done well to have brought a bottle himself, as a gift. A drop of something heady to loosen up the possibilities of the evening, so to speak.

'What I'm soon to show you may require a little fortification.'

Thomas wondered why Liselotte used such old-fashioned language. He decided it was due to her literary studies. She, like himself, was clearly possessed of a deeply romantic soul. It could not be doubted. If only he could rival Franz in abdominal muscles and biceps, he, Thomas Matheus Ruder, and the raven-haired beauty in front of him would be a match made in heaven, or somewhere close to it.

How trivial and unnecessary his comparisons to Franz would come to seem in the ensuing days, but as yet, neither of these youthful seekers of the world's joys and mysteries could possibly guess what part each would play in the other's life-story.

They stood in a dim entrance hall where coats were hung and a miscellany of shoes and boots were ranged on a wooden rack on the floor. For an instant, Thomas considered reaching out to the girl to stroke that glorious mane of jet-coloured hair. All he did, though, was to clear his throat rather too loudly, an habitual and somewhat bizarre tendency he displayed when nervous. Other anxiety-induced tics included a prodigiously loud sniff, which had been known to win him stares of affronted horror, especially when performed in the public or university library, or at a chamber concert.

THE GIFT MAKER

Liselotte ushered Thomas through a further door, turned on the light at the wall, and revealed the main room of the apartment to be furnished in the Count Friedrich style. There were several pastoral watercolours hung along the picture rails: a bridge over a brook in the late afternoon sun, a cow drinking from a pond, a shepherd leaning on a crook as his sheep cropped the mountain pastures behind him. Thomas looked up and noticed a cobweb coating part of the ceiling rose.

Long beige drapes were pulled across a window at the far end of the room, and Thomas became aware of a sharp ticking from a carriage clock on the mantelpiece. Its tick, he was certain, would have driven him to drastic measures had he owned such an article. Jo short for Johann had told him, just before the Feastday of Klauschen von Freinuss, of Holderbauch's famous aphorism: *In the ticking of clocks is revealed our necessary mediocrity.* Thomas did not pretend to understand this apparently weighty dictum, but it had made him vaguely suspicious of any sort of timepiece since hearing it.

A thick, blue oriental rug lay in front of the fireplace. It had a grey symbol at its centre that made Thomas think of a maze. This was repeated in smaller versions around the edges of the rug. Ever since Thomas was an infant he would find his gaze, and thence his mind, drifting into and growing ensnared by the patterns on carpets, tiles, walls, anything almost. This dreamy activity took him to a place of temporary serenity, while he wove his way around spirals and whorls, in and out of boxes or swirls, as if he had been an ant or a bee in a former life, and this pursuit was the atavistic remnant of the dance of some long-dead drone, informing its colleagues of the location of good pollen.

Liselotte removed her coat and tossed it casually over the pale-gold two-seater settee. She then went to a small cupboard and retrieved two purple-tinted crystal glasses and a slender bottle containing an amber liquid. Ah! Sweet Dauben wine from the Southern Territories. It had been several months since Thomas had got his bum-fluffed chops around such an aromatic treat. Liselotte uncorked the bottle and poured a generous amount into each glass. She handed one to Thomas, lightly brushing his fingers with her own. This sent a jolt of fizzing pleasure mixed with exquisite pain through the young man, that only the truly lovelorn can understand.

They drank in silence. The wine sent a summer warmth coursing around Thomas's insides. It rendered him instantaneously a braver soul. Liselotte wiped her mouth with the back of her hand.

'Oh, sorry, Thomas. Please take your coat off. Yes, put it there.'

Thomas laid the threadbare, dark-blue army-surplus greatcoat rather preciously over Liselotte's own. Near to swooning, he gazed at the two garments, imagining them fleshed out by their respective owners.

'Thomas! You're off somewhere again. Head in the clouds. I brought you here to show you something. Something very important. Just sit over there and don't move. I'll be back directly.'

Thomas did as he was told and sat obediently, sipping his wine. Liselotte was his junior by a good half a year and yet she took it upon herself to talk to him as if he were a snivelling five-year-old in short grey trousers, face smeared with a favourite aunt's chocolate pudding. She swept out of the room leaving a trail of jasmine scent and an intolerable absence in Thomas's heart. He heard her beyond the wall, opening a cupboard, so he thought. Then he heard her mutter something to herself. Or was it to another? Was this some ghastly and cruel trick? Could a creature so beautiful and fragrant really be so cold and pitiless? That must be it. Franz was there, in the very next room, and would be produced presently to utterly humiliate his potential rival. Thomas would of course be polite, even shake the big oaf's hand, risking it being crushed by the buffoon's idea of bonhomie. Then he would slink out like a whipped dog. He would leave the university, naturally, possibly even the country, if he could borrow the train fare. On second thoughts, suicide would be the only decent (and romantic) gesture left to him. Thomas was just considering by which method he would slip from this mortal coil when Liselotte returned, clasping across her impossibly lovely chest a squarish item wrapped in dark cloth. She placed it, reverently, on the table under the window. Thomas got up and went to her side.

'Now, before I unwrap this, Thomas, you must promise never to tell a soul about anything you witness here tonight. Not even your two henchmen, Ulli and whatshisname, the smelly one? It must be our secret. You must swear to it.'

Thomas assumed his best, most grave and responsible face, the one he used in front of his mother when she was angry with him, which was not often now, as she was dead these last two years. It was the face he displayed to any authority figure, from teacher to country policeman. A face that could be trusted unreservedly, a face that was clearly incapable of any misdemeanour or irresponsibility.

Thomas nodded, slowly and with no little gravity. At length, he said, in a slightly sibilant whisper, 'Yes, I swear, Liselotte. I swear on all I hold sacred.' What exactly he held sacred he was fortunately not pressed to say.

Liselotte, apparently satisfied, reached out to the cloth-ensconced item on the table and quickly divested it of the material.

'There it is,' she said. 'Now you've seen it, I don't think things will ever be the same again. For either of us, Thomas.'

The box lay there, nestling on a sea of black. Its ivory colouring emitted a strange luminescence, or perhaps this was a trick of the light in the room, thought Thomas. The box was slightly bigger than a watch box, but smaller than a box that may contain a single book.

'Did it…did it come with a ribbon, maybe?' Thomas stammered.

'How did you know that?' said Liselotte.

'Oh, just a guess. I mean, many boxes have ribbons, don't they? It's the done thing.' He wilted under Liselotte's quizzical gaze.

'Open it,' she said, at last.

'Me?' said Thomas, placing the flat of his hand against his chest. 'Are you sure? I mean, if it's personal, what right have I got to…'

'Just open it, Thomas.'

He moved closer to the table. Now he was more than ever struck by the the glow coming from the ivory box. Thomas knew how ridiculous his next thought was, but he was unable to suppress the notion that the object in front of him pulsed with an indefinable energy, as if there were an electric current passing through it, or more incredibly, as if it were somehow alive.

Thomas looked at Liselotte, then back at the box. He reached out a trembling hand. There was a delicate gold clasp on the side that needed to be unhooked in order to free the lid. Thomas tentatively flicked it open with one of the long fingernails of his right hand, especially grown, if often broken or half-chewed, for mournfully plucking his tarnished and invariably out-of-tune guitar strings.

He carefully lifted the lid a fraction, and peered inside. He opened it a little further. Then he saw something of the contents. Letting the lid fall back shut, his mouth suddenly as dry as the northern plains of Lainz, his heart began throbbing wildly. Without knowing how he got there, he found himself back by the two-seater settee, the wine glass at his lips, held by a tremulous hand.

'You saw?' said Liselotte, coming to him, her arms reaching out to take him by the shoulders. Amazingly, he was oblivious even to

THE GIFT MAKER

her touch, which under normal circumstances would have sent him into a thrill of delight. But now he was intent on uncorking the Dauben wine and fulsomely replenishing his glass, before rather uncouthly gulping down the sweet tawny liquid.

'You saw inside?' she repeated, pouring herself an abundant glassful.

At last he turned his eyes to her. He wrestled with some vague inclination to cry, or perhaps to laugh. His knees had grown watery weak as he allowed himself to flop down onto the settee.

He placed his now empty glass on a small octagonal table. 'It's some illusion, isn't it? A joke, no? Very clever, of course, but a toy, yes? Liselotte?' He paused for a moment to read her face. 'Please, tell me it is.' He gripped his head in his hands, rubbing his thumbs across his eyes.

'You've only seen the beginning, Thomas. Come back to the table.' She tugged lightly at the cuff of his dark-grey shirt.

'No, you must get rid of it, Lise. Burn it. Throw it in the river or down the toilet even. I don't care. Just lose it. I'm not a superstitious person normally, as you know, but that…that cannot be good, Lise. It cannot be natural. It's…'

'Evil, Thomas? No, it's both more and less than you think. You're in shock. I was too, at first.' A wistful smile played around her wide mouth. She seemed eager to convert him to some secret rite. 'Come back, Thomas. Let me show you.'

He rose unsteadily and accompanied her back to the table where the box lay. She lifted the lid clean off, and placed it to the side.

There it was, surrounded by a cushioning of pale-pink cotton wool. A tiny glass coffin, no longer than four inches. And inside it, swathed in a white wrap, lay a figure. Thomas saw once more the jet-black hair draping luxuriously over the slim yet toned shoulders.

The face was at rest. Not dead, only sleeping. The aquiline nose was faultless. The cat-like eyes lightly closed, the hands held in a loose crossing over the midriff, purple nail-varnish perfectly covered the tiny nails. The bare calves and feet lay slightly apart.

'I think I can see movement…the chest, Liselotte. It's the wine, surely. Please tell me I'm dreaming.'

'No. She is breathing, like you or I. She's only asleep. Later, she'll wake, and then you'll see something. It's early yet.'

'You mean it's alive? Impossible! It's a trick, something mechanical, Liselotte, or some illusion, or witchcraft. It cannot be real. Such things are not in the world. It must not be.'

'Not an *it*, Thomas. A she. And you know very well who she is.'

Thomas tried to ignore Liselotte's last words. 'My God, it's breathing! It's alive.'

'You know who she is, don't you?' Liselotte's eyes widened.

'Yes, of course I do.' Thomas studied the tiny figure asleep in the glass coffin, then looked back at the warm and lovely girl beside him, the object of his long-held desire. 'It's you, Liselotte. It's you in the coffin.'

Without a word, Liselotte picked up the lid, and as if fearing to disturb the sleeper within the ivory box, she ever so gently replaced it.

✂ ✂ ✂

They sat at the table eating toasted muffins spread with cream cheese, which Liselotte had prepared for them in the small red-tiled kitchenette. They each had a mug of Balarna tea, the taste of which Thomas did not greatly care for, but stunned as he was, he sipped at without complaint. Neither spoke. The box now lay on the rug with the maze patterning. It was once again draped and hidden by the thick black cloth.

THE GIFT MAKER

'Did you see who left it?' said Thomas, his voice suddenly loud and coarse to his own ears.

Liselotte wiped a few crumbs from her lower lip with a napkin, which she then purposefully folded into a small square as she spoke. 'No. I found it left outside my door when I returned from the theatre on Monday evening. A neighbour, Mrs Grau, told me, when I asked her, that no one had called on me while I was out. And she'd know, the nosey beast.'

'So you've had it for three nights and you've not told anyone? How could you possibly keep this to yourself? It should be reported…or something.'

'You'll see why when she wakes up. Just one more hour, Thomas. Be patient, please. It will be worth it. That I can guarantee you.'

Thomas looked at the carriage clock, whose tick had previously faded into the background, but which now returned insistent and brittle, like a nagging voice or a trapped insect. 11.05pm. One of the last trams rattled along a nearby street on its way to the terminus. Then, in the distance, winter geese honking forlornly as they traversed the sky over the quietening city. A whisper in his head told him repeatedly to make some excuse and leave, to have no truck with this bizarre and disturbing phenomenon, to forego the possible affections of Liselotte if need be. It was clear enough already that she saw him merely as a reliable friend and confidant, no threat or enticement did he hold for her. He had been cast as the dependable type, happy with his sexless role in her life, always obliging with a cheering joke, to play the fool for her amusement, to offer a brotherly shoulder in times of distress. Indeed, Thomas knew only too well that once this friendship role was fully embedded in her mind, and even his, the chance of a way back or forward on to more romantic territory was negligible, if not impossible.

He swallowed the last of his muffin. 'Any more wine?' he pleaded.

Liselotte shook her head, sending the ends of her softly curling dark hair swinging. How it still pained him to suffer her effortless beauty, the more potent for the fact that she was in no way attempting to attract or tease him with her considerable charms.

Then he thought again of the blue box that lay unopened, unexplored, in his bedside drawer. And the numbers written on the base. 'Liselotte, I was wondering if maybe there is some writing on the box. Underneath, perhaps?'

'Not writing, no. But something else,' she said, once more turning a shining and suspicious eye on him, seeking to uncover his motive, his secret understanding. 'You seem to be exceptionally good at guessing things this evening, *comrade*.' She added the unmistakable flavour of scorn to the last word.

Thomas looked down, biting his lip. There was stillness between them. Then Thomas said: 'The truth, Liselotte, is that I've been given one as well. A box. A blue one with a white ribbon. A man, I have no idea who, delivered it to my landlady at around two o'clock last night. And on my box, Lise, there are numbers written in black, on the base. Those numbers match my date of birth.'

Liselotte stood abruptly and noisily cleared the plates and mugs from the table before stomping out of the room with them into the kitchen. Thomas winced as he heard her banging and clattering about. Soon came three dull thuds from below. A neighbour had been disturbed, no doubt. Sound carried surprisingly easily in these older buildings.

Liselotte returned, slightly flushed. She avoided his gaze. She extinguished one of the lamps on the sideboard, leaving only a single other lamp burning. It barely lit the far side of the room with a diffuse orangey glow. The black shape lay on the oriental rug.

THE GIFT MAKER

Thomas fancied he saw an unearthly luminescence permeating the dark material that enfolded the box.

'When were you going to tell me?' said Liselotte, in a whisper that scarcely hid her continued annoyance. She spoke louder. 'You let me go on and on, as if you knew nothing, pretending to guess this and that. Are you behind this in some way? What are you, Thomas Ruder?'

She sat back down, her arms folded across her body, as if for protection.

'I haven't opened it, Lise. I have no idea what's inside my box, and seeing yours, I'm certain I don't want to look. I left it in my drawer. No one knows about it at all, except my landlady, and I told her it was just something to do with my studies.'

'Weren't you curious? How could you not open it?' Liselotte said, in a marginally kinder tone.

'Something about it bothered me. The birthdate numbers, the late hour, and please don't laugh now, my landlady told me how a man with large hairy hands had delivered it. He told her she had to give it to me in person.'

'You didn't see him? You don't know this man?

'No,' said Thomas. But look, Lise. It's twelve. As he said the word the carriage clock softly chimed once, then returned to its interminable beetle-like ticking.

'Now you'll see something, Thomas.' Liselotte went to the box and unwrapped it carefully. She removed the lid. Thomas sat rooted, afraid to see what would happen next, yet painfully curious.

'Come over here, scaredycat,' she said. He walked over like an obedient, if reluctant, child and kneeled by her. With great delicacy and gentleness she lifted the miniature glass coffin from its bed of tissue paper and placed it on the oriental rug. The tiny figure lay within, still sleeping, yet now Thomas noticed that she lay on her side, her head cradled in the crook of her arm, black hair draped across her face, all but covering it. This was proof that the being could indeed move, and Liselotte had not lost her senses. Thomas breathed deeply and slowly, trying to steady his nerves. The skin of the figure was alabaster-white, yet had the sheen and suppleness of life rather than of some marble or porcelain model.

It surprised Thomas that he was not excited by seeing the object of his desire covered in a strategically-draped sheet, albeit a four-inch version of her. If anything, he felt protective of the diminutive being, the way a father might feel towards a helpless baby. He keenly perceived its vulnerability in the giants' world that surrounded it.

'Is it actually you?' he said.

'I don't know,' answered Liselotte. 'We are something to each other. But not the same. Now watch.' She opened the lid of the coffin. Two miniscule hinges supported it as it folded back. 'Wake up, my darling. It's time to play. Wake up now,' said Liselotte, a peculiar light in her eyes, her voice deeper and more hoarse than usual.

Then the figure moved. It turned and stretched sumptuously in half-sleep. A tiny tongue poked between the lips and moistened them. Then the eyes opened, first a fraction, then fully. And they were as dark and glowing with intent as those of the grown woman that looked down lovingly from such a height. A broad grin broke out on the being's face, mirroring that of her larger sister above. The figure sat up and smoothed down the sheet that preserved its modesty. This drapery must have been pinned at the back in some fashion, presumed Thomas. She then climbed lightly and gracefully out of the coffin and dropped onto the rug, her feet sinking down into the pile as if she were walking in long lush grass.

THE GIFT MAKER

'Wait, my treasure,' said Liselotte. 'I'll fetch your board. I'm sorry, I nearly forgot.' She hurried over to a tall slim cupboard at the semi-lit end of the room. The figure on the rug appeared to emit its own light from within, which allowed it to be clearly seen, animated as it was amid the gloom.

'Board?' said Thomas, unable to tear his gaze from the uncanny and miraculous sight before him. He shut his eyes tightly, then opened them. And yes, she was still there, small as life, a perfect image of Liselotte, yet the length of a small cigar, and probably the weight of one, too.

Her hips described expansive arcs, first one way, then the other. Next, her slim arms windmilled slowly backwards, then forwards, then each circled in opposite directions. She lunged forward on the thick-piled rug, alternating legs as she progressed. Now, standing perfectly straight, her head moved in elegant circles. 'Yes,' thought Thomas, 'she is limbering up for something, as a gymnast or athlete might.' He noticed two faint patches of pink at her cheeks, which had not been there before.

'Here it is, my little one.' Liselotte placed an old-looking chessboard, devoid of pieces, down near the figure. It appeared, to Thomas, a hand-made board, the sides crudely finished, but with a top worn smooth by countless games and brushes of hands now long dead, as he supposed. The darker and lighter squares were made of two distinct types of wood, the grain being markedly coarser in the lighter one. *Pauzen wood*, Thomas considered, vaguely remembering an off-the-cuff and inevitably fruitless carpentry lesson his father had attempted to give him when he was still of elementary school age. So, he had remembered something, despite his father's obvious disdain for his son's lack of practical ability.

'You have a brain, but it doesn't reach your hands,' Ruder senior had occasionally remarked to his thoughtful yet manually awkward eldest boy. So very unlike his younger brother, Karl, who could make anything from wood, furnished with only the barest instruction, and a heap of innate ability. Karl, his father's clear favourite, who could break horses without a trace of bullying, who could fix cart wheels and windlasses, and who knew the names of a hundred country flowers without recourse to a single book.

The figure clapped her hands and it made the same slight sound as a matchstick breaking. She skipped, somewhat awkwardly, through the deep fibres of the rug and stepped up onto the board. Here, all trace of stiffness or hampering of movement disappeared. With her upper body quite erect, her hands floated out on either side, as if attached to invisible strings. They were raised slowly and majestically above her head into a pose that reminded Thomas of an Indian statue. She lifted one foot from the board, toes pointed down like one of the State Ballet dancers, then gradually, with supreme grace and balance, she raised her leg higher and higher, taking her foot with one hand, to eventually bring her leg fully extended above her head, so that her grounded and raised leg formed one almost perfect vertical line.

Thomas could not help but notice that as the figure executed this pose, the hem of the toga-like wrapping rose to her upper thighs, then slightly above. What he glimpsed beneath was startling for its absence. There was no trace of hair, and more importantly, no trace of any sexual organs whatsoever. Where they might have been, the pale skin was unbroken and smooth as a doll's or artist's maquette might be. What kind of creature was this? Was she indeed alive, as Liselotte believed, or was she in some way mechanical? Her movements were undeniably as natural as any human being's, and there glowed the vivacity of life about her creamy flesh. The miniature face, as a human's is,

THE GIFT MAKER

was capable of portraying a thousand shades of emotion. The eyes carried purpose and intelligence behind them.

Liselotte was lost in contemplation of her small-scale self, as now it leaped, pirouetted and span around the board, black hair flying, white wrap whipping and flapping vigorously with each turn. With the simultaneous abandon and willed precision of each phrase of the dance, flowing like wind or water, the figure travelled the circumference of the chessboard, then diagonally across it, from corner to corner, sometimes taking great strides, even at times cartwheeling or somersaulting through the air to land steady and rooted, before moving off once more to describe marvellous arabesques and dizzying spins, ornamented with elaborate snaking gestures of arms and hands.

Thomas had never seen a dance so passionate, so powerful, so elemental, as though the dancer moved to some great melody beyond human hearing, for some intent beyond human reason or will. So focussed and expressive was every gesture, from her fingertips to her perfectly arched feet. And the story she told through her body was further transmitted by the near-ecstatic, subtly changing expressions on her lovely face.

Suddenly the dancer stopped and fell down in a swoon of what Thomas supposed was exhaustion. She did not move and her eyes were now closed. Thomas was relieved to see her chest rise and fall with each breath.

'Ah, she's tired herself out,' said Liselotte, as if considering the playful antics of a toddler.

'Does this usually happen?' asked Thomas. They were both sat on the floor, before the rug, Thomas's hand less than an inch from Liselotte's. He fought against the temptation to touch her.

'Yes, always the same. Each of these last three nights. She needs to rest now.'

'Back to the coffin?'

'I let her curl up on my pillow.' Liselotte reached out, and with minute care and painstaking slowness, she used an index finger to roll the once-more sleeping figure onto the palm of her other hand. The figure's head turned from side to side, a look of some discomfort on her tensed features at being so touched and moved, yet her eyes remained defiantly closed.

Liselotte stood, cradling the tiny woman in her relatively giant palm, and left the room without a word. When she returned, her hands were empty.

'She looks so peaceful on my pillow. I always check on her regularly.' She said this more to herself than to Thomas. He remained sitting on the floor.

'Lise, I don't understand any of this. It's supernatural, isn't it? Ungodly? I think we need to tell someone.'

'Who should we tell?' Liselotte looked down at him, frowning.

'Someone who'll know what to do with it, who'll know how to take care of this...thing.'

'Thing? I beg your pardon!'

'You know what I mean. You don't know what to do with it, do you? How to care for it properly. Does it eat? Does it talk? What does it want, Lise? What is it? And who brought it to you?'

'She is not an it. And yes, she does talk.'

'She does? Well, what does she say?'

Liselotte picked up Thomas's coat by the collar and held it out to him. 'I'm thinking I made a big mistake showing you. I'm not sure you're worthy of the gift.'

'Gift? What gift? What are you talking about?'

'Open your own box, Thomas. If you dare. Perhaps it's better that we do not see each other again.'

Thomas got to his feet and took the proffered coat. He could not meet her eyes. 'I didn't mean to offend you. Or the other person. Your little dancer-toy. She can't be kept as your pet, surely? For your entertainment.'

'I suppose you'd have me turn her over to science, would you, Ruder? Or worse still, to some grubby-fingered impresario in a checked suit. Make some money out of *it*, should I? No. You understand nothing. You look with the eyes not the heart. You'll end up some pedant history teacher in the suburbs, sour and shrunken like the ones you pretend to despise. She's told me things. Things I need to do. Things only I can do. Foolishly, I had supposed you might be a part of the journey. But I'll make better progress alone. Tonight was a mistake.'

Suddenly Thomas felt worried. He knew he had handled things badly. 'But where are you going, Lise? What is this journey? And what about your studies? Your love of poetry? Are you going to abandon all that? Are you going to abandon me?'

'You?' said Liselotte, 'What is there to abandon with you? I have simply mistook you for a friend. That's all. She can't be with me long. As she told me herself, she's only a signpost, a temporary companion.'

The bewildered and near-to-tears history student struggled awkwardly into his coat and walked to the door that led to the small entrance space. He turned. 'I'll see you in the refectory tomorrow, no doubt. Or at the evening debate? Schnürrer is to speak.' His voice rang hollow with false enthusiasm.

'Schnürrer has nothing to teach me,' said Liselotte.

Thomas, stalling for time, said: 'I can see you here tomorrow, then. Aren't you eager to see what my box contains? I promise to show you. We could open it together.'

'That's your affair,' Liselotte shrugged. She had grown entirely cold to him in the few short minutes since the dance had ended.

Thomas wanted so much to hold her at that moment, to clasp her to him, regain her trust and their former intimacy, and to understand what she meant by the journey, and the gift. Did she say these words in the literal sense, or was this something more esoteric, a journey of the heart or soul? A spiritual journey, perhaps. He feared for the balance of her mind. And his own. Why had these infernal boxes come into their lives to upset them so? These had been unwanted gifts which had ruined their friendship.

'I will see you tomorrow,' he said, in a trembling voice. He half stepped into the entrance hall. She followed him to the inner door and made to close it. 'Please…tomorrow,' he said. She remained side-on to him, her face betraying no emotion, blank as a porcelain doll, her lips set hard against each other. He thought of the tiny creature, her double, fast asleep on a mountainous white pillow. Dreaming of what?

'Tomorrow,' he whispered, before letting himself out the main door and softly closing it behind him. The hollow click of the latch engaging struck him to the heart.

THE GIFT MAKER

four

KASPER'S WAS HEAVING with students, revolutionary-hearted filing clerks, the terminally unemployed, and the preternaturally parched, not to mention several of the city's lower-end prostitutes masquerading as off-shift factory workers.

Unnecessarily heated and veritably screamed conversations were in interminable flow as Thomas threaded his way, malzbeer in hand, through narrow, elbow-ridged avenues of beards, corduroy, caked make-up, and the almost palpable stink of under-washed bodies, to the marginally less crowded and quieter snug, where Ulli usually held court in a fug of blue-grey smoke.

From an ancient jukebox Xavier Faust was belting out his latest. A dirge in honour of the tin miners from the last century, forced to eat grass and potato peelings in their search for nutrition when the mines closed. The ironic and inconvenient fact that it was Xavier's father, an absurdly wealthy industrialist, who had inherited much of the land that was once mined, and had turned the area over to sheep-farming to extract some meagre profit from it, was conspicuous by its absence in the minds of Xavier's diehard fans. Two funeral-faced young men, adorned incongruously with dark eye-makeup and peasant shirts, appeared to be straining to decipher the dense lyrics, nodding grimly as verse gave way to turgid verse: *I gave my best years underground. A subterranean heart unfed by greedy claws that grasp my last.* Then the less than rousing chorus: *Who would live the life of a tin man? Bereft with a belly empty as a tin can,* Xavier groaned glumly, as the fiddles and bagpipes skirled their intricate and maddening patterns, and a soft drum pulsed like a weakening but insistent heart.

'Hey, Tommy,' called a thick-tongued and throatily familiar voice. Ulli was wedged comfortably between two young women, who both sported denim dungarees and viciously short haircuts. Thomas recognised them from one of the university societies that he had sporadically and half-heartedly attended during his wide-eyed, slack-jawed, first year. Now had it been the Student Affiliation for the Rights of Women Meat-Packing Workers (open to supportive, mild-mannered males), the Worshipful Association of Voluntary Virgins (a quasi-religious group), or the hiking club? Thomas considered that it did not really matter, as he had no particular desire to know them better. Their attire and fashionable scowls put paid to any interest he might have had.

'Good evening, my irrepressible chronicler of the ages,' Ulli slurred, moving his coat from a small round stool and patting its top as encouragement for Thomas to sit. Flecks of ale froth and what appeared to be particles of dried egg speckled the dark mass of hair that almost obliterated the lower half of Ulli's face. His thick moist lips parted and his mouth opened cavernously wide, in a paroxysm reminiscent of lockjaw, as a low coughing rumble, as that of a fuel-starved engine, came forth, which Thomas identified as the pointless and unfocussed glee of the seriously inebriated.

'Sit down, Comrade,' said Ulli, with an oily leer. 'You know Marieta and Bilma? Rhizomes of the new political consciousness

THE GIFT MAKER

that is soon to engulf this sorry country.' He had an arm around each of their bony shoulders. Their faces were stoic, empty, studiedly grim. They peered hard at Thomas as if he were a strange mythical beast, caged and harmless, and of no importance to their lives, incurious as they were about the past, as most people were, Thomas concluded. Then they turned their blank eyes on each other and shared a secret look, the meaning of which, derision, was not entirely lost on Thomas. These two specimens, who affected an air of bored nonchalance, attempting to outdo each other in their practiced indifference, in perfect unison picked up their tall green wineglasses and brought them, in a sterile fashion, to their thin rougeless lips.

Torn-up beermats and two empty wine jugs littered the table, along with several dead beer bottles. The evening, thus far, had been bizarre, to say the least, and was continuing in the same vein, thought Thomas. 'Yes, I think we've seen each other around,' he said, coolly. 'How are your studies progressing?' he asked neither one in particular.

'So-so,' they responded, almost as one.

'Good, that's good, then. Religious studies, isn't it?' said Thomas, before taking a deep draught of his own malzbeer. He did not normally drink malzbeer, but this specific variety was guaranteed to create the necessarily desired oblivion by about glass six.

'We prefer to see religion as a socio-cultural manifestation rather than a numinous phenomenon,' said Bilma, with what could reliably be described as a sneer.

'Well said, Bilma,' said Ulli, belching fulsomely into Marieta's left ear, to which she gave no reaction. Again the two women, across the oblivious Ulli, exchanged a brief, meaningful glance, after which Marieta stood. Ulli's arm flopped down from its previous resting place.

'We need to go to the ladies' room. Excuse us,' she said, in a tight voice. Now Bilma stood, and the dungareed duo edged their way around chairs, tables, and the backs of bar-room philosophers and bores, most matching both nomenclatures, to be wholly swallowed up in the morass of sound and smoke that was *Kasper's* on a typical Thursday night.

Thomas slid into the three-seater booth next to Ulli, and sat in the space so very recently occupied by the scrawny bottom of the sneering Bilma. The seat had been left surprisingly warm by such a cold fish. Ulli bashed his pewter tankard, usually kept especially for him behind the bar, against Thomas's thick, dimpled ale-glass.

'So, how did it go with the charming *Lisechen*?' Ulli winked, archly, and ungently dug Thomas several times in the ribs with his elbow.

'Oh, you know…we had a pleasant time. I helped her with some research,' replied Thomas, casually.

'Research, eh? Is that what my Tommy-boy calls it? So you *did* get somewhere, after all. Jo will have to eat his words, the little bookworm. Ach, it's always the quiet ones you've got to watch, eh Tommy?'

'It's not what you think, Ulli,' said Thomas, with feeling. 'Liselotte is not your usual country girl. My intentions were merely to understand her a little better.'

'*Understand* is it now?' guffawed Ulli, spattering beer across the table. 'I've never heard it called that before.'

'Ach, let's change the subject. I'm determined to get good and blotto tonight. Things have been getting on top of me lately, Ulli. I've imagined I've seen odd things, impossible things. It's just thinking to much. The "heat-oppressed brain" and all that. I'm going to take a leaf out of your book, or even a chapter.' Thomas grinned at his own, rather weak, joke.

 THE GIFT MAKER

'What kind of odd things?' said Ulli, sounding relatively sober.

'It's nothing. Just an empty box. A chessboard fantasy. A folie à deux, I'd say.' His brow furrowed. 'Some kind of mirage or trick of the light. Best left alone.' Thomas began to feel that he was saying too much. He attempted to cover this by banging the sturdy wooden table with his palm. 'Race you, Ullichen,' he said, raising his half-full glass. 'Loser has to buy the next round, and kiss the marvellous Bilma.'

'I'll drink to that,' boomed Ulli. The students drained their drinks in short fashion, Thomas slamming his empty glass on the table a fraction before Ulli's tankard.

And so the night followed, as so many had done previously, with Thomas and Ulli buying drink after drink for each other. Spending money like air, that would have better been spent on books, new winter boots, or even the train ticket home to see their families at Christmas. With other soused carousers and ale-house intellectuals they grew involved in various fiery debates and pointlessly abstruse philosophical discussions, one about whether fish feel pain. Not a syllable of any of this could Thomas remember as he found himself urinating, mostly against a wall, yet partly over his shoes, in a dark and dank alleyway, and now obviously but inexplicably separated from Ulli. He knew he was somewhere near the river, for he could hear the rushing water of one of the many weirs from beyond the grim, gloomy tenements and warehouses that loomed either side of him.

A cat jumped out from under a dustbin lid. It was pale-grey, and its green eyes caught the muted light of the half-moon, which could be glimpsed in the narrow strip of cloud-blown sky, directly above Thomas.

The lid clattered to the cobbles, and the cat shot past Thomas, who urinated on his lower trouser leg in surprise. It disappeared around the bend into the alleyway that was lost in blackness. Its tail held high was the last thing Thomas saw.

Thomas was not in the least aware of how drunk he was, so when he lurched forward, without a plan that he could clearly formulate, to follow the cat's vanishing tail, he fell headlong into a pile of rubbish heaped by another bin. It was made up predominantly of rotting vegetable matter, empty jagged-edged tin cans, and a milky thick gunge that stank violently of sour milk mixed with decomposing fish. The combination of odours hit the back of Thomas's throat and caused him to retch abundantly. He pushed himself up on all-fours, like an exhausted mongrel, and blindly crawled out of the mess, his hands finding puddles of dingy cold water as he made slow and intermittent progress along the alley. Now he could smell his own vomit, which had spilled onto his shirt and coat front. This was topped off nicely by the sour-sweet acridity of the rotting vegetable ooze and the milky gunge, which coated portions of his clothes, hair, and face. In falling, the edge of a rusty can lid had sliced his cheek, and warm blood now dripped steadily over his jaw and down his neck. The gallon or so of malzbeer and the six shots of korn had so befuddled his senses that he was more or less impervious to pain, and felt nothing from his wounded face but a dull, wet throbbing and a warm trickling around his neck, which was curiously not without pleasure.

With the help of some steps that led to a padlocked metal door, he hoisted himself up to a vaguely standing position, gripping the rough stone balustrade as if it were a floating lifeline in a high and raging sea, which in a sense it was, as now his head began to pound mercilessly, as though a champion boxer was relentlessly beating his beer and spirit-drenched brain from within Thomas's paper-thin skull.

THE GIFT MAKER

He peered into the utter blackness at the end of the alley. Some yards away, a pair of tiny green lights, two inches or so apart, flashed at him, then went off. They came on again and moved to a higher position. Such was the impermeable darkness around them, it seemed that they floated in mid-air. At the moon's emerging from behind a cloud, Thomas saw, as the faintest of silhouettes, a cat's shape atop a parapet, tail snaking out. Then a swift leaping, and the black outline with the green fire eyes, which Thomas fancied was temporarily frozen in flight, was abruptly and disappointingly no longer there. Something else moved in the darkness a little distance away. There came to Thomas's ears the sound of chuckling, like that of a small child.

'Who's there?' said Thomas.

There were tiny footsteps to be heard. They were moving away. The chuckling died, then came again. Thomas thought he heard a high-pitched but hushed voice say, 'The gift horse has no teeth.' Absurd, thought Thomas. This is some waking dream, some drink-induced auditory hallucination.

A cold wind sprang up of a sudden and cut through Thomas's back as well as his drunken reverie, bringing him to a state of sobering self-disgust.

He did not know what subconscious sense of direction brought him, foot and head-sore, back to his lodgings. He had been aware of the need only to put one foot in front of the other, to not stumble, and to avoid the late-night, infrequent yet speeding cabs as he had traversed this street or that boulevard.

And there he stood, blinking in miraculous contemplation of his hand reaching out with a key, of the key entering the lock, and the pure satisfaction of the key turning, allowing the door to open. Never had he even considered the possibility that the little rented space on the second floor of this plaster-cracked building could warrant the name of *home* until now.

The stairway was unlit, although a line of weak light showed under Mrs Senf's door. He did not have the energy to care whether she came out to confront him, and thereby notice the state he was in. He thought only of that narrow haven of bed and the coarse, woollen blankets, and the expected bliss of his head hitting the duck-feather pillow, all of which lay a mere forty-eight steps away.

He closed the door of his room behind him as softly as he could. In the dark, he undressed completely, then wiped his face and hair on a towel wetted with cold water from the sink by the window. Shivering and quietly cursing his reckless expenditure and the deserved throbbing in his head, he climbed like a burrow-scurrying animal beneath the cold covers. Within the minute, he was on the border of sleep. His cut cheek no longer hurt, unless he moved his jaw, but the skin there was tight and felt puffy and tender to the touch.

At some point during that endlessly fitful and mouth-parched night, he got up, in semi-slumber, and groped his way to the sink, to fill his cupped palm time and time again from the tap, and swallow the chilly, metallic-tasting water. Yet somehow the moisture was never enough to regain the soft flexible palate, and dampen the tongue so that it did not feel like it was made of dessicated wood shavings. Turning back to the bed, he heard a very light and sporadic scratching sound. It would not be the first time a mouse had got into his room. One morning in October, he had deliberately left a lump of stale cheese on his desk, by way of an experiment, to find upon returning from his classes later that day that it had been severely nibbled at. Crumbs of cheese led a trail away from the main chunk, which finally petered out by the skirting board, just behind the headboard of his bed. He had pulled the whole bedframe away from the wall, but had found no hole nor any other trace of the rodent.

This time, though, the scratching came from his bedside cabinet. And as Thomas listened by the bed, ears cocked like a hunting dog, waiting for the slightest sound and its exact location, the scratching came again, and it came, Thomas now realised, from the drawer into which he had placed the unopened blue box of the night before.

He curled trembling fingers around the handle of the drawer, and was about to pull it open assertively, when he stopped and turned on his bedside night-light, the better to see the innards of the drawer and to identify whatever was causing the scratching, and whether or not it had anything to do with the box's contents. Would he find a miniature version of himself in a glass coffin on lifting the lid of the box? Was the tiny doppelgänger scratching at the covering of its glass tomb, desperate for food, water, or air? These questions, and others less distinct, crowded his mind as he once again gripped the handle. With a quick jerk, he snatched the drawer fully open. Two mothballs, Mrs Senf's own, rolled to the drawer's near side. He took out the cigarette papers, plectrums, and love notes to women he had never even spoken to. The back portion of the space was still mostly unlit and Thomas reluctantly placed his hand inside and reached deeper, groping about for the box or anything else that he might find. There was a sudden brittle tapping and scurrying of movement within, and Thomas felt a sharp pain in the ball of his thumb. He quickly pulled his hand out with a stifled curse, and immediately saw in the lamplight two thin lines of blood running down from his thumb over his palm. 'It bit me!' said Thomas. 'The thing bit me, damn it!' Not in the least knowing what exactly the *thing* was to which he referred.

Then, at great speed, a small bundle of white, trailing a pinkish string, leaped over the edge of the drawer. It landed unperturbed on the carpet, and without a moment's pause continued its journey, to finally disappear around the back of the sink, where the rusting, paint-flaking pipes descended into the floor. 'So it was you,' Thomas said, in a whisper, to the now-vanished mouse. 'You little monster. I'll set a trap for you in the morning. No more free cheese for you, you brute.'

A further realisation began to seep into Thomas's alcohol-addled brain. There had clearly been no box in the drawer. In fact, apart from the two scentless mothballs, his odds and ends, and the erstwhile mouse, the drawer had been completely empty. Thomas double-checked to make sure. The box was gone. But where? Had Mrs Senf taken it? That would be going too far, to meddle with his personal possessions merely because she had happened to accept the delivery of it from the hairy-handed, if polite, stranger. Or had one of the other lodgers entered his room during the day? He must check all his valuables at once, of which there were admittedly few, the principal one being a rolled-up wad of notes that was to last him well into the new year, certainly at least until the end of January, and which was stuffed into a sock, that was in turn wrapped in a college scarf at the bottom of his wardrobe.

Thomas quickly retrieved the scarf and took out the sock. He pulled out the stash of notes from within, immediately relieved that there were any in there at all. Having counted them carefully three times, he was satisfied that there were exactly the correct number of notes as he had expected there to be. He sighed deeply and slumped onto the dishevelled bed. The banknotes, each depicting in a different colour Princess Filomena's tight-curled, rather elongated head, lay in three distinct piles of denomination on the ruffled blanket.

THE GIFT MAKER

He went back to the apparently empty drawer and once again groped inside. Throwing the mothballs at the wall in frustration at finding nothing else of substance, he continued to quite redundantly feel across the base of the drawer, minutely inspecting the sides, for what, he was not sure. The result of this search yielded precisely nothing but a patina of dust, which now coated his fingertips, and half a shirt button, that he supposed must have been left by a previous incumbent of the room.

Finally, ensured of the absence of any box, blue with a white bow, or otherwise, he once more returned his money to its hiding place, sufficiently satisfied of its continued safety. Wearily, he climbed back under the blanket, which now felt very cold against his body, and, switching off the night-light, he resolved to speak to Mrs Senf in the morning about the missing, indeed stolen, box. If required, he would move out. In fact, he had heard there was a small room available in the building where Jo short for Johann lived. A little more on the rent, admittedly, but the area was more desirable and tastefully Bohemian, very close, in fact, to the Klinken Park, where students from the prestigious Ladies' Academy took their lunch, or strolled in twos and threes, practicing the graceful walk they had been taught at this exclusive finishing school, not the least unaware of the effect this would have on any passing male.

It would be a room, slightly smaller than his present one, but superiorly furnished, and where a hard-working scholar might keep an unopened blue box in a bedside drawer, free from any care that it might be stolen from him before he had even a chance to peruse its contents. It was in this state of righteous anger, amid the after-effects of serious alcohol abuse, that Thomas attempted to get at least a portion of a night's rest.

five

'MORE SCRAMBLED EGG, Mr Ruder?' Without waiting for an answer, Mrs Senf ladled another helping of the golden, fluffy, not uneatable mixture onto Thomas's plate, and added a further thickly-cut wedge of greybread and butter, for good measure. 'You look like you might need it after your...*escapade* last night.' She intoned the word escapade as if it denoted the nadir of all things dissolute, licentious and morally corrupt.

The slightest sound echoed through Thomas's head like a jackhammer. He sipped his whole-bean coffee, and did not have the strength, either physical or emotional, to resist Mrs Senf's obvious mothering of him this morning. He had heard recently, via Luigi, who occupied the basement room, that she had a grown-up son of whom she was ashamed for some reason, and once, when somewhat tipsy on the Feastday of Saint Rummelstauber of Bergfurtz (a highly unusual state for Mrs Senf to be in), she had confided in Luigi about her son, Egon, who was "Many miles away, so far I could never make such a trip, an old woman like me". She had pulled from a jade-coloured purse, which habitually hung from the waistband of her dress, a tiny black-and-white photograph of a rather vacant-looking young man with extravagantly thick black

THE GIFT MAKER

eyebrows, and a crooked nose – surely the result of some brawl. Gazing at the image, she had wept copious tears, burying her head, at one point, in Luigi's chest, while bemoaning: "Oh, why did he have to do it? Didn't I give him everything? Didn't I scrub steps until my fingers were raw? Oh why, why, why!?"

Luigi had gently pressed her for further details, at which her mouth grew thin and tight, and she wiped her face energetically on a dishcloth, and went about her business without uttering another word on the subject.

'Mrs Senf,' said Thomas, in a husky whisper, staring down at his egg and bread as if it were a puzzle he had to solve. 'There is a certain issue I need to take up with you.' He cleared his throat. 'I am glad only yourself and I are at the table.' Mr Lutzig, Luigi, and a hatchet-faced young woman, whom Thomas rarely saw, and knew only as Teresa, had gone to their respective places of work, none of which Thomas had the slightest clue about, so incurious could this youth be concerning matters that did not involve him directly.

Mrs Senf put down her cup, rather too loudly for Thomas's liking, as well as the Mildenfunk Weekly Chronicle she had been flicking through. This organ limited itself to reporting the banal doings and non-doings of the so-called "celebrity class": band leaders, fashionable singers, second-rate actors, and minor members of the now largely-defunct First Family. She raised her eyebrows and pursed her lips in a mask of alert and haughty expectation.

'Mrs Senf,' Thomas continued nervously, 'I have some reason to believe…I would say I was justified in thinking that…in fact, I can come to no other conclusion than…'

As Thomas stumbled on, trying to confront his small but fearsome landlady with the unpalatable fact that there may very well be a thief in the Senf household, the icy winter rain drummed on the corrugated iron roof of the small shed abutting the house. And although it was nearly eight o'clock in the morning, it was still dark outside.

'Mr Ruder,' said Mrs Senf, cutting into the young man's broken, one may say derailed train of thought. 'Please spit it out, would you? I have several duties to attend to this morning, the least of which is to go to Kraussmann's to get the chops for this evening's dinner. I was sorry, and a bit offended, to tell the truth, that your meal of spicy meatballs with swede mash had last night to disappear into the neighbour's dog, Lulu, but there can be no reduction on this week's rent. It is about fairness, Mr Ruder. Our arrangement is clear: seven breakfasts, seven evening meals. I believe I have fulfilled my side of the bargain, except those two days I was in hospital, for which I allowed when calculating your weekly charge. So if that is what all this is about, you can...'

'No, no, no, Mrs Senf. Not at all. Your meals are uniform in their culinary excellence.'

'You what? Are you making fun of me with your clever words? I might not have a degree but...'

'On the contrary, Mrs Senf,' said Thomas, in a tone of such mildness and conciliation that would surely placate the angriest of bears. 'You are a magnificent cook. Second only to my mother.'

'That's as it should be,' answered Mrs Senf, with a decisive nod.

Thomas had never told Mrs Senf that his mother had passed away six months before he left his home town to attend university. He feared that divulging this fact to his landlady might cause her to mollycoddle him all the more.

'It's about my room. I mean something that was in it which is, how may I put this, no longer enjoying the space that it once inhabited.'

'Don't talk in circles, boy.'

THE GIFT MAKER

'My box is missing, Mrs Senf. The blue box with the white ribbon that the gentleman delivered to me, via you, the night before last. I am sure you remember it. And the man who brought it to the house at such a strange hour. The hands, yes? Well, it's no longer there, Mrs Senf.' Thomas was growing breathless with emotion. 'In other words, Mrs Senf, someone has taken it. Stolen it!'

'You think I…?'

'On my father's best horse, no! Not you, of course not. But someone has been in my room and removed it.'

'What did it contain, Mr Ruder? Was it very valuable?'

Thomas thought quickly, and assumed a somewhat pious expression. 'The value was wholly personal and sentimental, Mrs Senf, but none the less dear for that.'

'I am certain none of the other boarders could have taken it. I insist on two references from each, as you know. All my guests are of good character.'

'Perhaps, Mrs Senf, if you were to merely slip a small note under each door, enquiring whether anyone has seen a blue box? This would not amount to an accusation.'

'I shall do no such thing. Your property is your own responsibility, Mr Ruder. I will not insult my other lodgers just to satisfy your silly curiosity.'

'But I have had something valuable stolen. In your house, Mrs Senf!'

Mrs Senf stood up, clutching the newspaper in one hand and her half-finished cup of coffee in the other. 'I thought the value was merely personal?'

Thomas did not reply.

The landlady continued: 'As I said earlier, I have a number of things to attend to.' She sniffed, then went to the door. Turning, she said, in an artificially polite voice: 'Please put your plate and mug on the draining board, as usual, Mr Ruder. And if you are not happy living here, you know the term of notice, as set out in the signed agreement. I can think off-hand of several working people, not layabout students, who would bite my hand off for your room, and be very glad of it. They would certainly give me less trouble, that's for sure.' She went out, muttering to herself. The only words Thomas could make out were, 'Drunken bum…coming in at all hours'. Then he heard Mrs Senf's private door shutting, significantly louder than normal.

Thomas was stunned, though not altogether surprised at his landlady's lack of co-operation. Ever since he had moved under her roof it had been a battle of wills, and he had felt himself regarded more as a recalcitrant teenager, than the thoughtful and serious-minded scholar he knew himself to be.

He left the kitchen, deliberately not putting his plate and mug on the side, as he had been instructed. It was some small act of rebellion, done in order to strengthen his resolve for the larger step of seeking alternative accommodation.

It was with new-found vigour that he mounted the stairs to the room which he instinctively knew he would not spend another night in. Even his hangover took back seat to the renewed sense of purpose that decisiveness can bring. He packed his clothes, books, night-light, journal, and various small useless items into the two large holdalls that he had brought with him on that long and circuitous train-ride to Schwalbenbach. The room in Mrs Senf's house he had seen advertised on the first-year student noticeboard, and he had moved in that very first day, merely dumping his luggage on the bed, and after paying the first week in advance, strolling out into September evening sunshine to explore the myriad intersecting streets, alleys, and small ornamental squares of this old part of town. He had never felt so charged with

THE GIFT MAKER

hope, brimming with the irrepressible sense of so much life and adventure laid up in store for him. There would be new friends, new experiences, new ways to think and feel, and there would undoubtedly be – love.

So it was, that a long-legged, somewhat pale and greasy-haired young man was seen struggling out the door of 43a Faulen Gasse into the frosty morning air, guitar slung over his back, a large green army-surplus holdall in each hand, wearing two overcoats, and making his way, with occasional pauses for breath against one of the ornately-carved lamp-posts, to his usual tram-stop. He did not know if Mrs Senf had seen him go, nor did he care.

Thomas arrived at the stop a minute too late for his usual tram, thereby missing his friends on the journey, but caught the next one. A vinegary-faced man on the seat opposite glared at him and his worldly possessions as if he was some criminal or dangerous anarchist. The man had sprouts of white hair emanating from his ears and nose. His face was haughty with disgust. Then Thomas realised he had not left Mrs Senf the final week's rent, and wondered if this stranger's palpable opprobrium for him was the universe's way of pricking his conscience.

At the university gate lodge he tipped Gustav, the continually whistling keeper, a schilling, so that he might stow his belongings under one of the long wooden benches until the day's lectures were over. At lunch, he would seek out Jo, and arrange to bring his luggage round to the vacant room in his friend's apartment building that evening. He felt sure that Jo's landlady would be only too pleased to have him under her roof.

It was nine twenty-seven, and with no little consternation, Thomas realised he had precisely three minutes to get to the Jauss Lecture Room, which lay on the fourth floor of the Freidenlaube Building, some distance away. He grabbed a notebook, pen, and a half-eaten bar of chocolate from one of his holdalls and raced through knots of students, who were ambling about the quad, lounging against pillars, and perambulating along the corridors at a more scholarly pace. If he was a second over nine-thirty, the formidable Professor Lipschnitz would admit no entry. In fact, the door would be securely locked.

He reached the door at the exact moment that Professor Lipschnitz was closing it.

'Apologies, Professor, please may I be admitted?' Thomas panted.

The professor, a short, slight man, with gold-rimmed glasses and a large wart, like a third blind eye in the centre of his forehead, gave Thomas a withering look. Then he opened the door wide, and said in a surprisingly powerful voice for such a small man, 'Enter, Ruder. You are most fortunate that you find me in a patient humour today.'

Thomas dashed to his desk, acknowledging with perfunctory nods and hand gestures, several of his cohort. The professor took his position at the front of the class. He was in the habit of staring intensely over his glasses into the middle-distance until the room was in a state of absolute silence and stillness. The slightest of noises or any extraneous movement would throw him off his stride, be it a hushed cough, the squeaking of a chair, the falling of a pencil to the floor, or, and woe betide the wrongdoer, the sucking of a boiled sweet. The latter variety of offender against the requisite quiet would be advanced upon by the warted academic, tissue paper in hand, for the partially sucked bonbon to be deposited into the paper, which would thence be enfolded and stuffed neatly and rather delicately into the shirt or jacket pocket of the erstwhile sucker of the sweet.

'Now,' said Professor Lipschnitz, 'who would like to offer us an overview of the political and social machinations that led to the attempted Coup of the Feather Lancers, and if you please, some background on Heinrich Baulz et al. would be appreciated, so to contextualise the reasons for failure at that point? Ah, and of course the barbarous repercussions on the guest-workers of our own fair country, cannot, nay, *must* not be skirted over.'

Thomas glanced up, fearing to catch the Professor's gimlet eye. All other heads were bowed, seemingly studying the text in front of them, or more likely, the wood grain patterns and dried ink stains on the surface of their desks.

'No one? Hmm? So you wish all to be scholars, do you? You wish to take a government subsidy so to improve yourselves, and thereby increase the general cultural capital of our nation? I suppose you thought you were in for an easy ride; that you need do no more than turn up for three years, at the end of which you are given a nice piece of paper that guarantees you a civil service position, or a job at Kraussfelz. And yet no one can offer me a rudimentary explanation of an event that we covered last semester. You, Ruder. Since you have deigned to bless us with your presence this morning. And do not think I have not noticed your face. I never had you marked for a brawler, young man. Perhaps you can take us through this particularly shameful chapter in our neighbouring state's history. Hmm?'

Thomas fussed with his note book, tapping his pen on the desk, before realising this noise would only incite Lipschnitz to greater apoplexy. He did not look up, and delicately covered his bruised and cut cheek with his palm. 'Sir,' he bagan. 'Sir, I have had several personal problems of late…and it is with regret that I have not prepared notes for this lecture. I am of course aware of the Coup, and of Baulz, but feel I could not do my fellow students justice, nor indeed History herself, to give so unprepared an account of the matter we are speaking of. I do beg your, and the class's, pardon.'

'Nicely done, Ruder. I see a potential politician in our midst, ladies and gentlemen. Your father was not a weasel farmer, was he?'

'Sir?' said Thomas, his face reddening, an unfamiliar anger mounting in his chest. Yet still he did not look up at the waspish intellectual whose eyes he could feel boring through his thick mop of mousey-brown hair.

'I ask you again, Mr Ruder. Please will you outline the failed Coup of the Feather Lancers. You are keeping your colleagues and myself waiting.' It was so deathly quiet in the room that dust could be heard falling through the air. Minute specks of chalk from the board made their huge floating journeys down to the reddish tiles of the floor. A crab-spider in the far upper corner of the room could be deafeningly perceived, as lines of silken thread emitted from the tip of its abdomen, to be woven round and round in meticulous creation of an orb web, so particular to this variety. Thomas himself could hear the blood gushing through the finest capillaries of his wrist.

Finally, the young man, whose nerves were already somewhat frayed, stood, and without addressing anyone directly, muttered, 'I am not well. Not well…excuse me, please.' With this, he bolted for the door, and upon finding the key on the hook nearby, he swiftly unlocked it, and was seen hurriedly progressing down the waxed-floored corridor by Jo, who had just delivered an essay on *The Subjective Object: A Discussion on the Phenomenology of Prudlebaum's Metaphysical Imago Studies* to his tutor's office.

The stentorian tones of Professor Lipschnitz boomed after Thomas: 'Ruder…Mr Ruder, come back here at once!' then faded, as the fleeing student turned the corner, and descended the marble stairs, then pushed through the heavy, glass-panelled doors, finally to emerge into the now brightened winter morning.

THE GIFT MAKER

He leant, panting with anxiety, against a walnut tree in the Silberschwanz Quad, named after the famous, if morally dubious, moral-philosopher, who had been chancellor of the college some one-hundred years previously.

'Needed some air, did you, old fruit?'

Thomas looked up. Jo short for Johann stood there, a wry expression on his young-old face, a brown leather satchel, bursting with books and folders, slung over one slim shoulder, and what looked like half a bienenstich cake in his left hand.

'Jo, it's you.'

'Quite possibly,' said Jo, setting down his satchel on the path. 'Then again, perhaps I am merely a pigment of your imagination, or perhaps another version of the Jo you know, having slipped, via a time-bend, through a portal in the cosmic veil from an alternative universe where I am your long-lost brother, or more likely your confessor.'

'What?...oh, yes. It's a joke, I see. Look, do you have a few moments? I need to ask you something.'

Jo, taking a large bite from the bienenstich, gestured to the bench that stood by the stone fountain with the leaping dolphin, which only seemed to work now and again. Today, a mere trickle emanated from the dolphin's half-grinning, half-grimacing mouth.

'Old Lippy didn't sound too pleased with you. He was fairly apoplectic. He slammed the door so hard when he went back into the class that the glass broke.' Jo was in a jovial, light-hearted mood, which was very unlike him. He also sported a smart new blue blazer, set off by a gold tie, crisp white shirt and amber cufflinks, all very much out of character. He looked like the head boy at a minor public school rather than donning his usual faux proletarian mode of dress, which had become something of a joke between them. Thomas resisted his urge to comment on these radical changes in style, his mind brimming with more pressing matters.

'I'll send him a note of apology,' said Thomas. 'Perhaps I'm not cut out for study anyway. I should most likely go back to my father's farm and toil the soil like generations of our family have done, world without end. I'm the first ever to break out of that little world of seed bags, chicken sheds and local gossip, the first to want to explore what lay beyond the hills, the first to…'

'Enough,' said Jo, putting up both hands. 'You're feeling a bit sorry for yourself, I reckon. What was it you wanted to ask me, Yeoman Thomas?'

Thomas smiled at his friend and clapped him heartily on the shoulder. 'Yes, you're right, comrade. I need to pull myself together. And I also need a new place to lay my hat. Is that attic room still available at Mrs Wierbach's?'

Jo's face dropped. 'I'm afraid not. Was taken two days ago by a big fellow named Daumen. Odd chap. Met him at breakfast this morning. Inordinately large hands, and hairy as a wolf, the hands I mean. Polite enough when I met him and dresses quite nattily. Speaks in a very measured tone with an odd sort of diction, almost like someone from the past, or how you'd imagine they'd talk. And he doesn't look you in the eye, which I find peculiar for such a large person. But he's a noisy individual in his room. I don't like to complain, but he's banging about up there late into the night. It's like he's building an ark or something. And there have been some eerie noises in the small hours, almost animal. No one has visited as far as I'm aware. It's just him, but there is talking. I'm wondering if I need to have a word. Not sure what his metier is. Something about him I just don't like.' Jo stuffed the last of the sticky cake into his mouth and licked the sugar from his fingers. 'You're still at old Senf's though, aren't you?'

THE GIFT MAKER

Hairy hands? It can't be, thought Thomas. Too much of a coincidence. He shook the image of the hirsute deliverer of strange boxes from his mind. 'I walked out of there this morning, all my worldlies on my back. I've left them with whistling Gustav. I'm homeless, Jo. Homeless!'

'Don't be so dramatic. You can stay a few nights with me, as long as you don't snore or come back drunk with our friend Ulli and disturb my philosophical musings. You'll find another room soon enough. Plenty about.' Jo stood and swung his satchel back over his shoulder. He sagged a little under its weight. 'Must get these back to the library,' he said, tapping the bulky collection of books. 'Meet you by the main gate at four.' With a wave of his hand, he began to move off in the direction of the cloisters.

'Just a minute,' called Thomas. Have you seen Liselotte, by any chance?'

Jo turned. 'No one has. I met Cristiana, her pal, on the tram this morning. She seemed worried about her, as they'd planned to go for early morning planzball practice before lectures. Cristiana called at her flat and got no answer. Your paramour seems to have vanished into thin air. Eloped with that meathead Franz, is my guess. See you later, homeless wanderer.' Jo strode away, bag swinging, along the colonnade, and turned into the library building.

'Vanished into thin air,' Thomas said aloud to himself. 'My God, she *has* taken the journey with her tiny dancer. I must find her.'

six

AT JUST AFTER seven p.m. that evening, having left his belongings with Jo, Thomas found himself looking up at the dark window of what he was sure was Liselotte's apartment. He stood at the back of the building, where the grey rubbish cans were lined up neatly, each with their respective flat number painted on them in white paint. The communal washing lines on the small rectangle of frozen grass were, naturally, free of clothes. Thomas dug his hands deeper into his overcoat pockets and wondered how he might obtain entry to the block of flats so as to reach Liselotte's door. Perhaps she had not gone anywhere, and lay there ill or injured in the dark. Perhaps she had been left tied up, or worse, by the man now living in Jo's apartment building, who had used the strange box and its supernatural contents as a bait to lure poor Liselotte into some heinous trap. Thomas had rung the bell to flat nine several times, and rung it protractedly. That soft yet self-possessed voice, which had so charmed him, had not answered. No one had.

In the short time that had elapsed between Thomas witnessing the miniature Liselotte dance upon the chessboard, he had convinced himself that it had indeed been some illusion or mechanical trick. He had not wished to question this revised assumption too deeply, for fear of his sense of reality once more giving way. If a tiny living creature could climb from a three-inch glass coffin and dance on a chessboard before falling down in a swoon of exhaustion, what else might there be in the world? What certainties could he any longer trust in? And who but Liselotte and he had seen the creature, the double, or whatever it was? Who else could, or would, possibly believe it?

Then he remembered: Mrs Grau, the all-seeing, all-knowing neighbour. Surely she would have noticed anything odd in Liselotte's movements that day, or heard something unusual coming from her rooms. Possibly she had seen the young woman leave (if she *had* indeed left) and knew something of her whereabouts.

Thomas went to the front of the building, located the bell for *Grau*, and pressed it.

'Who is it?' demanded a thin quavering voice.

'Mrs Grau?'

'I'm not expecting anyone. Go away or I'll call the police. I have a big dog here as well.' There came a harsh crackling through the small metal speaker before the intercom went dead.

Thomas tried again. 'I've called the police,' said the reedy voice. 'My husband will also be home soon, and he is a very jealous man.'

'Please, Mrs Grau,' said Thomas. 'I don't mean any harm. I was just looking for Liselotte. Miss Hauptmann? I am her friend. She told me what a good and kind neighbour you are.'

'She did?'

'Oh, most definitely. I am a little worried about her, you see. We attend the same university. And she has not been seen by anyone. Please, if you know anything…'

There was a pause. 'Come up to the door. I will keep my chain on. A woman can't be too careful these days. And remember, I have a large dog.'

The door made a buzzing sound and Thomas pushed it. He began climbing the several flights of stairs. The violinist was playing the same piece of music as the evening before, only faster and more manically this time. Thomas's nose caught whiff of a variety of meals being cooked or enjoyed. Turning down a gloomy corridor, he came to Liselotte's door on the right. He was tempted to knock on it immediately, but a little further along, on the left, a slant of light was thrown out across the carpet from a fractionally open door. As Thomas approached he saw thin, white-knuckled fingers, one bearing a large red-stoned ring. A brass chain prevented the door from opening further. Thomas could see half a face. It was old, neither distinctly male or female, yet not wholly unpleasant to look at. It wore thick, black-rimmed glasses, and had bright red lipstick on, that extended in places beyond the boundaries of the lips, giving a somewhat grotesque and clownish aspect to the mouth. The hair was short and browny-grey.

'Mrs Grau?' Said Thomas, flashing his most winning and trustworthy smile.

'Don't come any nearer. Schtupsee is sleeping. But if I give him the word, he will tear your leg off. Or worse!'

'Your husband?'

'No, the dog, silly.'

'Mrs Grau, it's about Liselotte. Miss Liselotte Hauptmann, as I said. Do you happen to know where she might be? We had arranged to meet at her apartment this evening.' Thomas almost convinced himself of the truth of this last statement.

The elderly woman opened the door a fraction wider. Now Thomas could see a good three-quarters of the face, and a little of the room behind. A smell of almonds and of baking wafted from behind Mrs Grau. And he could see china ornaments arranged along a shelf. There was a goose reaching for grapes which was very

THE GIFT MAKER

similar to one his mother used to have in her corner cupboard. His father had smashed it to smithereens against the stone floor the day after his wife had died. For a few weeks Thomas had kept the goose's head, then one night he had buried it in the woods.

Mrs Grau clearly noticed Thomas's nostrils quivering. 'I'm cooking mandel-biscuits for St Grünwald's Day. The orphan children seem to like them. I have done this every December for over forty years. What do you think of that?'

'It's very…very decent of you, Mrs Grau,' Thomas nodded. 'Did you happen to see Liselotte this morning, by any chance?'

Mrs Grau's bejewelled hand rose to her forehead, and she rubbed her palm across it, as if trying to conjure memories and images from an opaque and intransigent crystal ball. 'Yes, young man. Yes, there *was* something odd. Oh, my biscuits!' She let the door fall to with a bang, which did not quite cause it to shut. Thomas could hear her in the kitchen, cursing and clattering about with what he took to be baking trays.

When she returned, she unlatched the chain and opened the door wide. 'I think you may come in. You have an honest face, and I set a lot of store by faces.' She appeared flushed from her exertions as she studied the young man in front of her. It was as though she remembered him from long ago. She bade him inside. 'Here, we will go into my little sitting room. Oh, and take your shoes off, will you. I have been cleaning all day.'

The place was indeed spotless. No trace of dust could be seen. The paintwork gleamed, as did the brass fittings of the wall lights ranged along the short passageway. Thomas followed Mrs Grau into a dimly lit room densely furnished with overstuffed settees, wing-backed armchairs, pouffes, maddeningly-patterned rugs and seemingly redundant footstools. Nothing matched with anything else. The walls were taken up with very many paintings and photographs, of all sizes. Some of these Thomas imagined to be members of Mrs Grau's family and scenes from her youth. There was a black-and-white shot of a young woman in a coming-of-age gown, her features and build reminiscent of those that Thomas observed in the somewhat shrunken form of the elderly lady in front of him. Some kind of dance was going on in the background of the photograph, and the look on the young woman's face could only be described as pained. There was a large chalk-pastel painting of a beady-eyed black poodle on the wall facing Thomas. From where he sat, deeply ensconced in a yellow floral-print chair, the poodle's eyes glinted at him menacingly. Mrs Grau now sat on a green velvet settee opposite him, beneath the painting of the pooch.

'Is that Schtupsee, by any chance?' Asked Thomas, feeling obliged to make some small-talk before getting to the matter of his missing friend.

'Ah, yes, my Schtupseelein,' she turned her head and said with a sigh. 'Never before have you seen such a clever animal. He knew when I was sad. He felt it. This was when my husband was alive. And when I cried, my Schtupsee would come to me and rub his curly head on my leg. That dog had a big heart. It had feeling!'

Thomas now realised that both husband and Schtupsee had gone through the long grass, so to speak. Mrs Grau was clearly a lonely and frightened old woman, which probably explained her excessive interest in the doings of her neighbours, and her hollow threats to unwanted visitors. He nodded sympathetically. 'I'm sorry to hear about your husband, Mrs Grau. Was it a long time ago?'

'Not long enough. The bastard gave me a hell of a life. I should have married Schtupsee, if only he were a man instead of a poodle. That would have brought me more happiness. Men are not trustworthy, Mr...'

THE GIFT MAKER

'Ruder,' said Thomas, feeling a little embarrassed by the intensity of emotion that the elderly woman now exhibited. It made him sad and fearful of old-age. *Is this what it all might come to?* he thought.

'Ruder…Ruder…yes, I think Miss Hauptmann may have mentioned you,' said Mrs Grau, closely observing him, as if he were more than likely an impostor.

'She did? When? I mean, when might that have been, please?' Thomas was being more than usually careful to mind his manners.

'Hmm…this morning. We met on the landing. She said she was going away for a short while. To see a friend, she said. Women have so many *friends* these days, and that can only bring problems.' Mrs Grau smacked her lips. 'I noticed she had a small bag with her, like an overnight bag. Very nice leather, it looked like. I used to have one similar. But this had tassels. I do not care for tassels. She had her red coat on, and black boots. A nice outfit. I just happened to notice these things, you know. I wasn't looking especially. Oh, and she also carried a box. Or at least it looked like a box, but it was wrapped up in black cloth. I have no idea what *that* was. Young people these days are so secretive, Mr Ruder. But what do they have to be secretive about? We were much more innocent. And happier. We did not know how to be so complicated.'

Mrs Grau interlaced her fingers and began twisting them to and fro. 'I do this to keep the arthritis at bay. Age will come to you one day, young man. Don't doubt it. Age will come.'

'Did she say anything else, Mrs Grau? Anything at all?'

'Would you like a tea, perhaps, Mr Ruder? And a biscuit to dunk in it? I do not have so many guests these days. Not that I mind. I like my own company. And I have my memories.' She waved loosely at the numerous pictures and photographs on the walls. The ruby on her ring flashed in the light from a standing lamp.

'No tea, Mrs Grau. Thank you. Please, if she said anything else, I *need* to know.' Thomas shifted uneasily in his chair.

The elderly woman sniffed, stood, and went slowly to the door, resting her hand on the brightly polished knob. 'I see that I am keeping you, young man. Always in a hurry, the young. Always chasing after this bright thing or another. Your friend, Miss Hauptmann, said that if a Mr Ruder should come asking for her...and see, I do have a good memory, despite what my sister says...she told me to tell you to look in your pigeon hole. I did not understand her. Are you a bird fancier, by any chance, Mr Ruder?'

'No, it's the place where our letters, returned essays or notes from tutors are put. At the university,' replied Thomas, putting on his shoes.

'I do realise that. I'm not senile yet. It was my little joke. I see you do not have a very good sense of humour. Neither did my husband. May his soul never rest in peace.' She gave Thomas a rather charming grin and opened the door.

'Thank you, Mrs Grau,' said Thomas, standing once again in the communal hallway. 'And goodnight.' He moved off with a wave of his hand. As he reached the head of the stairs, he heard a now familiar voice at his back. It spoke just before a door was smartly shut.

'Some things are better left unopened, aren't they, Schtupsee dear?'

seven

THESE GIFTS I give do not come for free. Gifts ought to be free, but they never are. They tie you to the wishes of others. To your own sad expectations. To the penitentiary of your dreams. The beneficiaries are not random. I watch them, as I am told. I listen to their thoughts. I know their reveries and their nightmares. They have to be worthy of the gift that is bestowed. For it is sourced from their innermost core. I am merely an artisan. A contractor.

The girl with the black hair and the cat eyes is one such recipient. As a child she longed to dance more than anything in the world. Yet she wilted under the doubtful attitude of a mother who mocked her daughter's efforts to copy the dancers at the theatres and ballrooms she would be taken to. 'You move like some strange bird,' her mother would tell her. 'Ah, my poor Lisechen, your legs are doing different dances. Not everybody can do everything. You are very good at reciting poems. It is best to do only what you are good at. Or people will laugh at you.'

The young Liselotte would suffer great pangs of jealousy over her pretty blonde cousin, Katrina, who joined the state ballet at a very young age, and was encouraged by everyone. Katrina was groomed to dance the greatest roles: *Irina, Petronella Von Dorn,* even the *Ice*

Maiden in that great work by Hausen. 'There is a natural,' Lise's mother would say, nodding at the cousin, then looking back at her daughter with a smug expression, as if her opinion represented a compliment to her own tastes and knowledge.

This dark-haired girl locked her passion away in a small box inside her head. She grew tall, long-limbed, too tall certainly to partner most male dancers of the day. Instead, she developed a facility for language and poetry, and for some sports, those that required running and stamina, but at dancing, even the most rudimentary kind, even folk dances on feast days and holidays, she felt herself stiff, awkward, her body fearful of its natural delight in movement. The box was locked and placed in some deep cabinet of her mind, containing something she could never be yet always was. Now the box has been opened, and the dance, whether it proves to be a dance of hope or a dance of despair, has begun.

The other project was far more difficult, more contradictory and knotted. And so the refusal, or more correctly the reticence to accept, by this guitar-strumming, callow youth, hurt the maker. Yet it is not for me to take these rejections personally. The contents were engineered. The box was delivered, as I was instructed. It was shunned, or more exactly, feared, and so removed, the contents let loose to do what it will. To do what it must. All this was done as I was instructed. The gift will find the receiver, whether he wishes it or not, for it is part of him and cannot be denied.

Liselotte begins her journey. Only she can decide when and where it will end. I often wish to know the outcome of my involvement in such disparate lives. These poor monsters. But that is neither my role nor my responsibility. It would be an abomination. Playing God. And who am I to play him?

The young would-be historian is enamoured. He is her faithful spaniel. Yet he is now dogged by another.

I sit in this rented room. My tools, substances, and designs scattered across my worktable and around my feet. Exhausted, the wine bottle empty as my heart. I am tired, yet there is work to be done. Other gifts to bestow. I neither seek nor wish for thanks. My hands are coarse, large-boned, hair sprouting from the knuckles and even at the palms. Hands of a street fighter, a stevedore, an oaf. No. Hands of an artist. Of sorts.

Somewhere in the night an owl has caught its prey. I hear the owl's mad screech, and the crying of its quarry. Then deep silence.

eight

THOMAS WALKED BACK to Jo's room, where he had left his belongings. On the way, he considered whether he should confide in his friend. This was all becoming too much to bear alone. If Liselotte was missing, surely her parents, the university, and no doubt the police should be informed.

Letting himself in with the spare key he had been given, he found Jo in the kitchen, vigorously stirring a very large pot on the two-ring stove.

'You've never had my soup before,' said Jo, still with his back turned. 'I chuck everything in. It usually works. It's sort of an antidote to my over-ordered mind. "In the teeth of chaos, we find the crucible of our clarity". Know who said that? *Luniette*. Very much underrated.'

'I don't get it. It's one of those things that are meant to sound profound, but are probably just a load of kugels,' said Thomas, helping himself to a slice of the buttered bread that lay in a heap on the cutting board.

Jo turned. 'You'd do well to read him. Interesting life. Professor at Cholmeau. Ended up shooting his wife, convinced she was working for the secret police and spying on him. Evading justice,

THE GIFT MAKER

he was hit by a bread van not two miles from the house I grew up in.'

'Crumbs,' said Thomas, through a mouthful of bread.

Jo shook his head and went back to stirring the bubbling cauldron, the contents of which, Thomas concluded, did not look or smell half bad.

Thomas observed that Jo's body-odour issues were conspicuous by their absence. Whenever he was physically close to his friend the faint but pleasant aroma of rose water would greet his nostrils. Jo's nails were carefully trimmed and clean. Also, his thinning grey hair had been newly washed and a sweet-smelling oil had been recently combed through it, giving it more wave and volume. All this was more than significant when added to the recent alterations in dress. This evening Jo wore an emerald-green silk shirt and beige slacks. He padded noiselessly around the kitchen in dark-brown moccasin slippers over bony bare feet. Had he met someone special? Had he come into money? Had he dumped the erstwhile pose of the disenfranchised worker as an adolescent ruse? Thomas pondered the likelihood of each rationale.

'Any luck with the lady?' said Jo.

'Liselotte? Oh…well, she seems to have gone away.'

'Bad timing. She has an exam next Monday, doesn't she? Perhaps she's visiting family. I met her father once. Very stout fellow, spat when he spoke. I was quite drenched after our little conversation. The mother was as tiny as he was fat, and she seemed to have a stultifying effect on her daughter. I remember, whenever the girl tried to speak, the mother would break in with a contradiction or a change of subject. It was quite painful to witness.'

'When was this?'

'At the beginning of term, when they invited that arch-charlatan and poetaster Schmuck to read from his ghastly new book:

Wind-chimes of Fortune. Why the literary establishment go gaga for him is beyond me.'

'Yes, Schmuck is bad. Not even knowing Lise was there could induce me to sit through that. Not even the free wine and nibbles.'

Suddenly there was a very large thud above their heads. The two students looked at each other. Several more bangs followed before a loud groan was let out.

'He's started,' said Jo, slamming down the wooden spoon he had been using, and turning off the gas. 'It's not so bad from the other room,' he gestured through the half-open door. 'God knows what he's doing up there. I've even been having dreams he's cutting up bodies. Very odd individual. I'll dish this up. Please, go through.'

Thomas sat down at the small square table. The room was neat, and tastefully furnished. Surfaces were free of dust. This was the first time he had been to Jo's lodgings, aside from hastily dumping his belongings in the hallway earlier that day. It was far more ordered and cleaner than Jo's previous tendency to ignore his personal hygiene would have suggested. A folding bed had been made up for Thomas and pushed to one side. The blankets were turned back tidily, the pillow was fantastically white and ironed to perfection. Jo had books. A *lot* of books. Mostly they were text books on philosophy, and potted and not so potted lives of the great thinkers, both of the day and antiquity. A bronze bust of bushy-eyebrowed Graulitz surveyed the room imperiously from the top of a chest of drawers in the far corner. But there were also atlases, novels by obscure foreign writers, slim volumes of impenetrable verse by minor poets now most likely languishing in county asylums, all the books of the world religions, both mainstream and obscure, psychological case-studies and political manifestos, numerous cutting-edge science books and periodicals, even several large volumes on modern art. It was as if his friend were trying to assimilate all knowledge, to reach toward a final and sublime theory of everything. Beyond the many tomes that filled the bookshelves and glass-fronted cupboards, piles of them were neatly stacked on the floor around the room. Thomas reached down and picked one at random. *Being and the Ontology of the Void,* by someone called Herbert Felchnoir. He opened a page and a line immediately stood out from the text. "Stepping out of the box of being can prove disasterous to those of a nervous or weak-minded disposition." He shut the book and replaced it on the pile when he noticed the door opening to reveal Jo bearing two very full and large bowls of soup. These were then positioned on the table and Jo returned to the kitchen to get the bread. 'Shut up, you moron,' Thomas heard Jo shout, in a very uncharacteristic tone.

Returning to the table with the bread and two bottles of dunkel beer, Jo said, 'Apologies for that outburst, comrade. This new tenant above is driving me crazy with his banging and his moaning and groaning at all hours. It's like he has some workshop up there. I never actually see him, except for that one time at breakfast, although I hear him creeping down the stairs at night. That usually wakes me up. He seems to be very much a night owl.'

'You said about his hands?'

'Yes, hairier than a baboon. He's at the top of the building, and doesn't seem to bother anyone but me. It's really interfering with my studies. I've tried cotton wool, and something makes me nervous of approaching him or knocking on his door. He's like that character in Geiser's novel. A man who is part wolf and cannot live easily in the company of others. A nocturnal beast of the shadows.'

Thomas wondered whether to speak his heart to his friend as he dipped his bread in the thick tasty soup, which was crammed with succulent pieces of lamb and various root vegetables. 'This is very good, Jo,' he said. 'Are there butter beans in here?'

'Indeed there are,' said Jo. The banging had stopped. Jo looked up at the ceiling. 'Perhaps if we could both go up, in a friendly manner, of course, and sort of try to explain the situation. I'm sure with two of us it would be fine. He might even invite us in, and we can see what he's been making.'

'Boxes, do you think?' said Thomas, without thinking.

'Boxes? Why should you say that?' asked Jo, before taking a swig from his dunkel beer.

'Oh, just the idea of the banging. First thing that popped into my head.'

'Boxes…hmm.' Jo began to chew his way energetically through a particularly resistant chunk of lamb.

The two young men sat in silence eating their soup and sipping their beer, seemingly lost in their own thoughts. Finally, Thomas put his spoon back in the empty bowl. 'Okay, I'll go up with you. Do you think we need some protection? A stick or something?'

Jo laughed silently, his mouth full of soup that he strove to swallow rather than spray over the table and possibly his friend. At last, he said, 'I believe in the power of reason and gentle pursuasion. To reach out to the humanity in each person, their sensitive side, as it were. And if that doesn't work, we use this.' Jo had leapt up from the table and reaching behind the tall bookcase, now brandished a slim, dark wooden cane with a golden tip and an arching silver handle. 'Just a little twist here, and a quick pull, and we have it: The Equaliser.' Jo had drawn from within the body of the cane, which he threw to the side, a thin yet vicious-looking tapering blade.

'My God,' said Thomas. 'This is so unlike you, Johann. Surely this is a joke.' He stood and cautiously approached his friend.

'Sharp as a razor. Sharper. I used it as one to test it the other day.' Jo ran his finger lightly along the blade's edge, making Thomas wince.

THE GIFT MAKER

'Please, put it away,' said Thomas. 'I have a thing about blades and knives. They make me very nervous.'

'Some latent desire you are obviously repressing,' said Jo, eyeing his friend with a mock quizzical expression. Niftily, picking up the wooden component from the floor, he sheathed the swordstick and placed it back in its hiding place. There came a harsh and insistent tapping from above their heads as if someone might be beating metal with a small hammer.

'No time like the present,' said the philosophy student.

In semi-darkness, for there was no light on the top landing, they climbed the steep flight of stairs that led to the neighbour's door. Neither student spoke or seemed prepared to knock. In the gloom they stared at each other. The air where they stood was significantly colder than it had been outside Jo's own door. They both felt a sense of foreboding rather than naked fear. Something permeated through the shut door of Mr Daumen. It was akin to an energy or force of will pushing them back, dissuading them from disturbing the man working within. Thomas looked at Jo and shook his head. It had been much more comfortable eating soup and drinking beer in the warm room below. Yet this character might indeed have a connection to his missing blue box, and more importantly, so Thomas felt, the missing Liselotte. Surely he was man enough to brave knocking on a door in a respectable rooming house, or were his penned protestations of love and adoration just so much self-indulgent blather? Was he indeed a coward, as he had often suspected? Confident of the passionate words and rarified feeling safely expressed into a diary or a maudlin song. But what or whom had he ever stood up for? What had he ever risked, for another or for himself? Jo was biting his lip and raising his hand to knock when the handle was turned violently on the other side and the door was flung wide open. The two young men jumped back. A cold wind rushed into them, pushing them as flat against the wall as was possible, then it drew away, and Thomas sensed that same pulsating field of energy hovering on the threshold of Mr Daumen's apartment. Not daring to breathe, the two students stood frozen.

The room beyond the open door was unlit. No one was standing in the doorway. From the dark space emanated a pungent chemical smell. Jo was immediately transported back to chemistry lessons at school. Yes, it was surely iodine. To Thomas it resembled nail varnish remover. He had once liked to unscrew the tops of the strange glass or ceramic bottles and jars lined up on his mother's dressing table, and sniff at their contents, perhaps even dip his finger into this cream or that coloured substance. But that was so long ago. The last time he had seen the dresser it had been cleared of everything except a single photograph in a gilt frame.

'Hello?' said Jo, immediately feeling foolish, but not knowing what else to say or do. He cleared his throat and tried to deepen and steady his quavering voice. 'It's Johann from downstairs.' His mouth had gone dry. 'We met at breakfast briefly the other day, Mr Daumen. My friend and I just wanted to…to mention…' He faltered. 'Do you think he's there?' he whispered.

'Of course he is. Who else would have opened the door? And we just heard noises from his room before we came up,' said Thomas in a very low voice, recovering a minute proportion of his composure. 'Excuse me, sir' he said, more loudly. 'My friend here is studying for an important exam. My name is Thomas Ruder, and…'

'I know who you are.'

The voice had come from very close by, as though the speaker were standing in the doorway. But he clearly was not. It had been a man's voice, deep and resonant, with a slight accent that Thomas could not place. And had the speaker put a slight emphasis on the word you? He could not be sure.

'Mr Daumen,' said Jo, tremulously. 'I…I mean we've only really come up to ask you if you wouldn't mind perhaps being a little quieter. I don't like to complain, but thought it best to say it to your face rather than tell Mrs Wierbach. I mean I'm sure you don't realise how the…the work you are doing travels…the sound of it, I mean.'

There came no response. Neither student wished to go nearer the open door, yet they were backed into the wall and must cross the doorway if they were to get back to the safety and warmth of Jo's rooms. The air around them had grown even more chill. Thomas tugged at Jo's sleeve and said, in a whisper, 'Let's go. Something is very wrong here.'

Before Jo could respond, the voice spoke again. 'I am barred from meeting recipients. It would be problematic. I keep the necessary distance, to remain objective, an impartial craftsman fulfilling a commission.'

'Who is he talking to?' said Jo. 'The man is deranged, surely.'

Thomas finally allowed his growing suspicions to surface. Ignoring his friend, he took a step nearer the gaping door. His questions came in a flurry: 'I have to know. Was it you? Was it you who delivered the box to my landlady, to be passed to me? The box with my birthdate on it. The blue box?'

'Ruder, what on earth are you going on about? Do you know this man? Or are you cracked, too?' said the bewildered Jo, now gaining courage from some unknown source. He boldly approached the open door but was thrown back violently against the wall as if he had been physically pushed. Yet there was still no one to be seen. Jo half crouched against the wall, not daring to look up into the blackness beyond the door, seemingly unable to speak.

'As you ignored your present, it yearned to open itself,' said the voice. 'The box was collected. Its content is now in the world, and neither you nor I have any control over it.'

'And Liselotte?' said Thomas. 'Her present also came from you?'

'Via me, yes. I am merely the artificer.'

'I don't understand any of this,' said Thomas. 'Who or what you are, whether this is all some bizarre dream or the beginning of madness. But where has she gone? Is she safe? Is her dancer any danger to her? Please, tell me.'

'She is following her road, as you may have done yours. She is following her will. Now your road may be following you. Unwanted gifts can distort from their original purpose. I bear no responsibility in this. My work with you both is done. I have said enough. Too much.'

And with his last word the door began slowly to close, ostensibly untouched by any human hand. It shut gently, and a key was turned on the other side.

nine

WHEN THOMAS SPOKE to me I longed to reach out to him, but I am forbade. The boy is more than he knows. The other, with his books and lofty thoughts, is in actuality walking in a ditch, a brain on a stick. I longed to show Thomas my work, my soul-work, to let him understand that he *had* been chosen for a fine purpose. The ordinary man most extraordinary. Yet in his callow rejection is the waste. And the wasted are never contented.

I am lonely in my room, in the world of my room. I rarely sleep for the dreams that wake me hurt my memory. Dreams of a once life. A child's face, blossom, fine clothes, bunting, some haunting music on a terrace, and her devastating smile. So many lost names. Now I wish to be nothing. And when my duty is done, He may find it in his will to release me to nothingness. To sweet non-feeling.

On my worktable is a face. The mouth moves but the eyes are blind. I am working on the eyes. They are always the most difficult. These happen to be blue-grey. When such creatures are connected to themselves their need for their worldly shadow grows with each day. They are so winsome in their vulnerability. But if ignored, they are fierce of heart. Yet when I make a heart, I make a blank. Sometimes I stare at the blood droplets on my fingertips, how they turn to blue on contacting the air, some odd reversal. I could squeeze such a heart, make it pop like a berry. Instead, I find the cavity. Make the necessary connections. Voilà.

Thomas will follow her. How far he will follow will be his test. Why do we not choose kings, magnates, the absurdly beautiful, those drenched in riches, charm and power? Would be like shooting fish on a plate, fish already dead. For all their material and bought scope they are but puppets of history, of their own greed. The hunter, if he is true, has respect for the prey. And his prey must be worthy of him. We look for the pure, if hidden, desire. The love of the love for its own sake, not for gross gain. A rare thing in this and other worlds. I say we, but as I have conveyed, I am indentured. It is He, that pale whisperer, that knows, by heart, the suitable candidates. To capture goodness is a formidable apprenticeship. Older than oceans. Many are groomed, many fail. Yet I long for redundancy. I long for the end time.

It is necessary to leave these lodgings. To leave this city. All cities are, eventually, the same. All towns, all rooms. The tools and substances of my trade are easily found. Their combination is the darkest alchemy.

The new bottle is opened, as her present has been. The intoxicating liquid flows into my glass, as she is now intoxicated with her own possibilities.

I raise my glass to you, Liselotte. I had some pleasure in your making. Not the obvious sort. Though I drew from your innermost wish, the fleetness of your leaping form, I like to think there is somewhere in all my work, the maker's mark, the unreadable signature in the burnt umber.

Going to the window, I look out over the sad city. Those blue and orange lights. Their winking hope. I can hear the young men whispering in the room below, their minds pregnant with stalled action.

This drunkenness keeps me going. This liquid, somewhat like blood, balms my mind.

ten

SINCE BOARDING THE train, she had, now and then, closed her eyes for a few minutes, merely to rest them after the sleepless night that was so unbearably long. Yet always was she careful not to loosen her hold on the object wrapped in black cloth, which lay pressed tight to her side. She pulled the collar of her red coat up around her face, as if to shield herself from potential hostility or recognition. Choosing a window seat, she had allowed her mind to wander as the city gave way to the endless parade of soullessly modern tower blocks and the near-identical, rabbit-hutch housing of the suburbs.

This was her first train journey in many years, having been used to the privacy and comfort of her father's sleek and expensive sedan, that had always smelled of newness and security. Scarcely a tree or shrub could be seen amongst the concrete shells dotted with innumerable windows, many fronted by a line of dingy washing strung out across a narrow balcony. Deadness and uniformity pervaded the view. People got on at the various stations, and those who alighted disappeared beyond the barriers into the hard grey and dirty-beige world beyond. People, Liselotte noticed, with blank or harsh faces, drained of colour and vitality like their surroundings, their spirit guttered out. Even the children were sullen, or glared at her with a barely concealed aggression.

As the suburbs gradually thinned and gave way to dark-brown fields and hedges, interspersed with stands of dense woodland, the carriage emptied until there were just Liselotte and one other passenger. He sat on the left side of the train, and she on the right. She became aware of quick glances in her direction. She noticed the movements of his head in her peripheral vision, although he might merely be looking out the window on her side, she considered. Tightening her grip on the box, she sensed the faint tingling warmth that pulsed through the black cloth in which it was wrapped, as if the box itself were living, as well as its contents.

'Excuse me, miss,' he said.

She turned her head and he was looking right at her. He was not smiling, yet there was a twinkle of humour in his eyes. They were kind brown eyes, she observed immediately. The lips were full, more like a woman's. Older than her, certainly. But not so much.

'I don't wish to trouble you. I know how pleasant it is to drift away in thought, in a kind of reverie, I suppose, as a train moves through countryside. As the darkness approaches and lights come on in far-off farmhouses and cottages.' He spoke casually, with no trace of anxiety or hurry. His voice was lighter and higher in tone than she had expected from a man of his build. He wore a dark-grey suit with a diamond-patterned black and silver tie, and she noticed the thickness of his limbs. His thighs looked particularly muscular beneath the tightly-stretched material of his trousers. She made an effort to withdraw her attention from such observations.

'I don't mind,' she said. 'It's nice to talk on a journey. It helps it along sometimes.'

'As long as the other person is not a bore. As long as they can listen as well as talk, eh?' Still he did not smile. His eyes danced with hers, without mockery, without guile. Or so it promised. His stare was not an affront, it was more like the open gaze of a young child, brimming with unadorned curiosity.

'That's true,' she said. 'Are you going much further?'

'To Grenze.'

'No. Really? I am too. We have at least another four hours, if that old timetable's correct.' She gestured to the yellowing piece of paper behind a smoke-stained covering of glass on the wall of the carriage.

'Do you play cards, perhaps?' he said, this time the faintest of amused smiles on his expressive mouth.

'Only children's games,' said Liselotte. My sister and I used to play for hours. I usually won. But the thing is, I don't care for games of chance.'

'Is there such a game as chance?' he said, his eyes widening as if he really believed she had the definitive answer.

Liselotte shrugged. 'I wonder, would you like to sit here, opposite me? I think it might be easier for us to converse.' She blushed at her own boldness. Then something made her think of Thomas, and a vague guilt pricked her. Had she needed to be so hard on him? Of course he was painfully in love with her. She knew. At least she had left him a note. How *annoying* love could be, unless it came from the right source, the *one*. The *one* that might appear only once in a lifetime. On a train journey, perhaps.

The man stood and stepped across the aisle. Steadying himself on the back of the seat, he slowly and deliberately sat down opposite Liselotte. There was something about all his movements, the lack of any jerkiness or suddenness that gave the impression of a body moving under water, or as though the air was thicker about him. He crossed his legs and loosened his tie a little. 'Fleisher,' he said, holding out his hand. 'Horst Fleisher.'

THE GIFT MAKER

Liselotte was unsure of what to do. Shaking hands had become unfashionable with young people of late, or at least with those whom she considered her social equals. She reached out tentatively and allowed her fingers to be enclosed by his. His skin was warm, smooth, and she experienced a sense of deep reassurance, as though nothing bad could ever happen to her while this man was present. He smiled broadly now, showing slightly uneven yet very white teeth, a slender gap between the two front ones. A sign of good luck, she remembered.

'And you are?'

'Oh, I'm sorry,' she stammered. 'Lise…Liselotte. I'm a student.' Then she added: 'At the university,' and felt foolish for the unnecessary explanation. He surely must think her a fool already, and any moment now would get up and move to another carriage, making some polite excuse.

'What makes you want to visit Grenze?' he asked. 'Not so much there. Except a rather lovely theatre. Do you know it?'

So, he was a *questioner*. For Liselotte, it seemed that everyone she met had their own conversational style, which either irritated or endeared her to them within minutes. The type who would ask countless questions while giving little away of themselves, endlessly, desperately proving how much they were focussing on her, often made her uneasy, suspicious. They were the tryers, and their effort was an effort to encounter. But with Horst it was different. Already. She *wanted* to tell him things. Trivial facts, something of her background certainly, the first thing that came into her head. Though some subjects would be out of bounds. She relaxed her hold on the box, so as not to draw attention to it. She did not yet wish to know too much about him. She wanted the initial mystery to last. For now.

'I have a cousin there. In Grenze,' she said, and wondered if he could tell by her face or body language that this was not so.

'And I,' he said, allowing his soft brown eyes to wander vacantly over the passing view, 'I have a funeral to attend.'

'I am sorry,' said Liselotte. They sat in silence for a long minute, both staring at the landscape. Imperceptibly, they had come to this higher country, neither remembering the point of change. They were now aware that the train had slowed in the effort of its gradual climb. The flat arable land had given way to slopes and valleys, fast-running streams, and outcrops of bare rock. Sheep dotted the hillsides, stepping between the scrubby trees and patches of dark gorse, whose gold-yellow flowers were still noticeable through the evening gloom. In the distance were great masses of pine, coating the hills, and beyond these were the majestic Vogel Mountains: dark forbidding rock ascending to whiteness. In the fading light, Liselotte saw a bird of prey hovering motionless in the air, before it dropped like a falling stone to reach something on the pale grass below. Her heart fell with the bird.

Turning, she saw that the man was looking right into her, wearing a melancholy expression that made him even more attractive, if anything.

'I am not sorry,' he said quietly. Then he violently threw back his head, baring his muscular throat at her, to emit a high-pitched uncontrolled laugh. She put her hand to her mouth. The ugliness of his delayed response and the manic yelping noise he had made, and continued to make, shocked her deeply, disgusted her. She knew at once that something was not right with this man, and nothing else of his apparent charm and physical attractiveness could ever make up for this display. The yelping continued, descending a scale and growing quieter, becoming more like a feeble bark from deep within Horst's broad chest. His eyes were almost closed, as though experiencing some private bliss. Then he began moving his head from side to side, as if to shake the last of the mad giggling from his mouth. At last he grew almost silent, and breathing slowly and deeply, like a worn-out runner, brought up his thumb to wipe a thread of spittle from the corner of his mouth. This thumb was then unselfconsciously smeared over the seat next to him.

'Excuse me,' said Liselotte. 'I need to go to the bathroom.'

'I'm afraid there are no *bathrooms* on this train.' He had come back to himself, and resumed his slow, carefree manner of speaking.

'The toilet then. I didn't wish to say it.'

'We all go, my dear,' he said.

Liselotte now disliked him intensely, and knew she must find a way to escape his company.

'By the way,' he said, 'I tried the one at the end of this carriage when I got on. Blocked, I'm afraid. Stinking like a byre. I believe there is one three carriages down the other way. He jabbed with his finger. He wore a faint look of challenge. The brown eyes were no longer kind. They were dead brown marbles.

She looked out the window, considering what she might do. Taking the cloth-covered box under her arm, she stood. 'I suppose I will have to use that one then. Excuse me, please.' She tried to place a cold note into her voice, as she did sometimes when speaking to her sister or rude shop assistants. His knees blocked her from moving into the aisle.

'Surely you don't need to take that with you?' he said, jutting his chin in the direction of the box. 'I can look after it.'

'Excuse me, please.' His legs still stretched out across her path. She would have to step high over them in order to get out. She glanced at her overnight bag in the luggage space above the seats.

The tassels swinging with the movement of the train. Could she not simply grab the bag and leap over or push through this man's legs and find another carriage? Find an elderly couple to sit next to, or the guard of the train. To make a complaint. Yes. But what could she tell the guard? That a man had offered to look after her luggage, and had made an off-colour joke about a funeral? She would be laughed at. Be that as it may, she knew she had to get away from Horst Fleisher.

'Leave the box here, Lisechen,' he said, appearing not to notice or care that he impeded her progress. He had used the diminutive of her name, as if he knew her well. Only family members or intimate acquaintances may do this, as he was surely aware.

Confused and becoming more agitated and angry by the second, Liselotte sat back down and stared fixedly out the window, pretending he was no longer there.

'I thought you needed to...you know. Lost the urge? It can happen.'

There was an emergency cord above her head. Next to it was a sign printed in thick red letters, stating that unnecessary use of the cord would lead to a fine. She longed to pull it, and keep pulling it, until an army of guards came and bodily threw this intimidating man from the train; hurled him into that darkening ravine down there, among the rocks and bushes and brown-water streams.

Fleisher was the right name for him, she thought. *Butcher*. For beneath the expensive suit, the studied urbane manner, was an uncouth small-town butcher's boy. A man used to cutting up meat all day, cleaving through bones. She had heard that butchers in the country still drank a mug of warm pig's blood each morning. Some throwback tradition or ritual. It gave them strength, apparently.

'It probably doesn't work,' he said. 'They never do on these cross-country trains.'

THE GIFT MAKER

She glanced at him and saw that he was gazing up at the cord, with a strange wistful expression, as if genuinely bemoaning the state of the railways.

At that moment, they entered a tunnel through one of the hills, and after a few seconds the weak light of the carriage faded down until it was nearly out. She could barely see his face, and hunched into herself as if to create a protective screen. She gripped the box with both hands. Then the carriage light went out altogether, leaving them in total darkness. She heard him clear his throat. He began humming a tune, something like a folk song she remembered from long, long ago. She pressed herself back in the seat, trying to get as far from him as possible.

He sang snatches of a song, repeating lines over and over, in a low, soothing voice, as if attempting to lull a baby to sleep. *Two little maids, two little maids…they bring the milk, they bring the milk.* The voice changed and reminded Liselotte of her mother's, yet her mother had never sang to her. Her eyes were growing heavy and she felt her fingers loosening their grip on the box. *Two little maids, two little maids…they climb the hill, they climb the hill.* She shook herself to alertness once more. How easy it would be to fall, she thought, to drift down to sweet unknowing. The seduction of the tunnel of sleep as the train rattled on, rocking her softly, taking her deeper and deeper inside the hill. Down and through. Nothing to fear, nothing to need, to simply let go, let go. Ahh. *And the cows wander home…and the night falls on the house…and the night falls, and falls, and falls…and the maids bring…* He sang with the voice of a crone of centuries past, pacifying a baby in the dark. Like it had always been.

She felt something on her leg. A hand? A steadying hand, comforting and reassuring. She reached down to the warm pressure on her thigh. She felt it. The fur covering the tendons. She caressed the almost retracted nails, barely poking out from their hiding places, and underneath she felt the pleasing roughness and springiness of the pads. How large and heavy it all was. Seeing through a portal in the dark now, it was all there. The muzzle where his mouth should be. The high pointed ears and black rubber-like nose, twitching. And the pale green eyes, pulsing at her, with their pupils black and hard as the night around. There was a smell of the forest, of gently rotting wood, insects, of dry leaves and mushrooms and broken birds' eggs, of fern and pine and new-turned earth. Then the lips drew back like an awful smile and the teeth were bare, for they glinted on account of their sharpness. And the long salmon-coloured tongue lolled and dripped.

eleven

JO PACED UP and down the room, shooting glances at the ceiling. He accidently knocked over a pile of books. 'Damn it,' he said. He seldom swore.

From the chair by the dining table, Thomas attempted to tell his friend the story of the boxes from the beginning. Of his own now missing and unopened blue box, delivered late the previous night by the being upstairs who represented himself as Daumen; of the miniature chessboard dancer who slept in a glass coffin: Liselotte's double. He paused, caught on the ribbon of his words, and of the bizarre nature of what they told. *No one could believe this*, he thought. 'You must think me mad,' he said to his feverishly pacing friend.

'Go on,' Jo kept saying. 'I want to know it all. I'm part of this now, whether you like it or not.'

As Thomas neared the end of his tale, Jo sat down across from him. 'She's left me a note, apparently. Her neighbour told me,' said Thomas.

'I don't know whether to call the police or a priest,' Jo answered. 'What happened upstairs…it was unexplainable. I literally couldn't move when that…that force threw me back. Look at these.' He waved a hand at the books that lay around. 'These proclaim the power of reason, of logical dispute and analysis. The allegedly supernatural may be evaluated, as a burned-out superstition certainly, a testimony to our psychological development and progress, and in our scientific age…'

'I saw it all, Jo. And you felt it, upstairs. Books don't hold all the world. *Those* don't. There are older, more abstruse texts of course. There are…'

'Oh, so you're an expert now?'

'I'm not saying that. It's just that there are more things…'

'Than are *dreamt of in my philosophy?* Very amusing.'

'I've got to read her note. Now. She may be in danger.'

'We could let the authorities handle it,' said Jo, uneasily. 'Her family will surely become aware of her being missing, as well as her friends, and the university, of course.'

'And I thought *I* was a coward.'

'What?'

'You heard.'

'Right,' said Jo, going behind the tall bookcase and once more retrieving the swordstick. 'I might seem a bit of a harmless boffin to you all. I know how you snigger when I try to explain life from a more rational aspect, taking all objective and subjective evidence into account, but I *do* have a sense of honour, and I *do* have a belief in boundaries that may not be crossed. I'll sort this fellow out.' He quickly approached the door, which was immediately blocked by Thomas leaping in front of it.

'You mustn't. This isn't the way. What do you think you could achieve with that thing, anyhow? Can't you see the man…the whatever he is upstairs has powers beyond the physical? You can't go around stabbing at shadows.'

'Out of my way, Ruder.'

THE GIFT MAKER

'And we can't tell the police or your landlady. They'll think we've gone off our chumps. I have a feeling our Mr Daumen will be soon to vacate, to move on to some other anonymous room in an anonymous rooming house; some other city perhaps, now we've discovered his lair. I don't know what he is and I really don't want to know. We simply need to focus on Liselotte. At least I know I do.'

Jo deflated like a balloon. 'I'm not really the avenging hero, am I?' He dropped the swordstick to the floor and went and sat heavily on the couch. 'You know, Thomas,' he said, staring at his knees, 'I've never once in my life been in a physical fight. Not once. I always found a way to avoid them, to talk myself out of them. To take down an enemy with clever words. But sometimes the power of debate and reason and all the weighty quotes in the world simply won't cut it. And it's the ancient game of kill or be killed. That's never really changed, and perhaps it never will. And in the teeth of that challenge you are revealed for what you actually are.'

'Look, let's think positively here.' Thomas tapped his fist against his forehead. 'Is the university open now? I mean, do you think we can get access to the pigeon holes? I'm sure she'll have given me some sense of where she was going. Remember what I told you about the *journey* she mentioned?'

Jo stood up and gazed at his reflection in the mirror that hung above the fireplace. It was as though he did not recognise himself. He slowly shook his head, then turned. 'There's a connecting door, via the refectory. They always leave it unlocked. Old Müller should be on the gate. He'd do anything for a few schillings.'

Thomas threw on his overcoat and checked for the wad of notes in the inside pocket. It was safe. 'Well, what are we waiting for?'

As Jo was lacing up his suede boots, Thomas added, 'By the way, comrade. I've never been in a fight either. Unless you count my brother when I was five and he was two. Hardly a testimony to my valour.'

Jo looked up at him and smiled, but there was pain in his eyes. Thomas realised he knew nothing of his friend's family background, or indeed if he had any close family at all.

They descended the wooden stairs two at a time, not caring for the noise they made, to emerge onto the frosty street, their breath feathering into the sharp air.

'This way will be quickest, along the river,' said Jo. They both rubbed their hands against the cold and moved off down Lametten Street, which would bring them to the black and freezing waters of the Launz. From there it would be a good two-mile walk.

'I've been meaning to ask you,' said Thomas, as they passed under a row of bare plane trees. 'What's with the change of style?'

Jo cleared his throat but did not answer.

'The clothes, the threads, old man. You've gone all debonair on us. No longer the champion of the proletariat, eh?' Thomas attempted to lighten the mood.

After an awkward silence, Jo responded. 'Like you said. We need to focus on Liselotte.'

The two young men trudged along the glinting pavement. Beyond a low stone wall on their right was a twenty-foot drop to the dark, fast-moving river. To their left were the endless government buildings, their anonymous heavy-stoned faces, blank and unforgiving, their sentry-like windows grey-shuttered for the night. Few knew the exact purpose of them all, or indeed, the true purpose of any.

As they turned away from the river, crossing the Gustav's Boulevard, they cut through a small park. They had not seen a soul since leaving Jo's building. A sheet from a discarded newspaper blew across their path, entangling itself in Thomas's legs. He

THE GIFT MAKER

brought the sheet up to his face and read out the headline under the lamp by the park gate. '"Women are warned not to travel on late-night trains alone. Third assault in as many weeks."'

'Scaremongers,' Jo said. 'They want us to be frightened all the time. So we never question anything. Never question their unquestionable right to decide what is best for us.'

Something rustled in the bushes a few feet away. A fox, thought Thomas, but he caught his friend's alarm at the sudden noise.

'Come on,' let's go. 'I'll buy you a mutton pie at *Alphonse's* after we get the note. He's open all night for the print workers, the cabbies, the night nurses, the waifs and strays.'

'Like us?' said Jo.

'Like us.'

They exited the park and began walking up Augusta Street, past the Military Museum and the Centre for Tropical Diseases.

One hundred yards behind, something struggled out of the thick bushes by the park gate. It was the height of a ten-year-old child. Proportionally, its hands were a little too small and its feet were a little too large. It wore a dark-blue army greatcoat, and its hair was long, greasy and unkempt. Around its top lip and chin sprouted a wispy beard and moustache.

It heard the footsteps of the two students ring out, yet grow more distant, on the hard cold air. It breathed deeply through its nose. *That's the one*, it thought. The other's scent was on the chill breeze. Smiling to itself, it began a vigilant and noiseless passage up Augusta Street.

twelve

CLUTCHING THE BOX, she stumbled along the darkened train with the sound of a dog-like padding close behind her. There came also a throaty animal breath, warm and acrid, sometimes distant, sometimes inches from her ear. Tearing through numerous connecting doors, she rushed along one unlit carriage after another as the train thrust itself deeper and deeper into the hill. Bumping into seats and partitions, she once reached out and touched something wet in the dark.

Pushing desperately against one door she was propelled into bright light, causing her to shield her eyes. The door closed behind her as of its own volition. A violin played a delicate minuet, but she could not see where the music was coming from. There was a faint scent of apples in the air. This carriage, much to Liselotte's relief, was half-full of travellers. They all looked perfectly ordinary. Older men and women, dozing children, young couples, and what might be businessmen, lost in their newspapers. She was aware of the sticky wetness on her hand from before. Looking down, she saw that her palm and fingers were coated with what was surely blood. Quickly and vigorously she wiped her hand on her coat, thinking the red would not show. She thought about the

THE GIFT MAKER

handkerchiefs she had packed in her overnight bag. But then – oh – it had been left behind in her panic. In her frantic attempt to escape that creature.

She sat down across from a respectable-looking couple who were in late middle age. The man, who had thick reddish eyebrows that curled up at the ends, which reminded Liselotte of an owl, was neatly dressed in a wine-coloured waistcoat and yellow tie, and appeared to be asleep, his head tipping now and again to the shoulder of the lady next to him, whom Liselotte supposed was his wife. She, buxom and rosy-cheeked, smiled at Liselotte and nodded gracefully, before her almost black eyes became dreamy once more, lost in memory or untroubled vacancy. Further down the carriage two young women were discussing something in hushed tones about another person called Lena, at which one of them would suddenly laugh quite childishly, to be instantly shushed by the other. Liselotte caught the line, 'And she never even asked permission.' Then the other retorted, 'She deserves everything that comes to her'.

Further down still, a baby cried quietly and persistently, hushed by the deep tones of an older female voice speaking in a language unknown to Liselotte. The owner of the voice she could not see, but merely caught sight of an iron-grey bun of hair visible over a seat top. The soft delightful music continued and Liselotte, still weak and shaking from her ordeal, breathed slowly and deliberately, letting her eyes rest, grateful for the normality and security of her new surroundings. She hid her stained hand in the deep pocket of her coat. The box lay on her lap, once more tightly wrapped in the black cloth.

A man in his fifties on an adjacent seat, some commercial traveller Liselotte had supposed, coughed into a red handkerchief. When Liselotte looked at him, he winked at her. She noticed ash marks on his black trousers. Two large suitcases gently shook in the luggage rack above his head, a financial newspaper lay, neatly folded, by his leg.

'Must give up the cigars, my dear.'

Liselotte smiled politely.

'Would you care to give us a little dance, my dear?' he continued. He looked at her beseechingly, his expression cartoon-like, in what seemed to Liselotte a parody of earnest supplication.

'What do you mean?' she said. 'We're on a train.'

'I know that my dear. Not as green as I'm cabbage looking. But you have the aisle. All great dancers can dance anywhere. Think of Nilla, or the great and sadly missed Seleszny. Listen! That music is for you, didn't you know?' He coughed again, more violently, into his handkerchief, then appeared to convulse before coming to himself. 'Look my dear, look what I've found,' he said, glowing with unabashed pride. He opened the red handkerchief with some reverence for Liselotte to see, and there amid the sputum and smears of phlegm lay a tiny blue egg. A bird's egg. 'Now what do you think of that, my poppet?' he said. 'Surely that is worth a little entertainment. A country gavotte or a pirouette or two from such a delicious young thing as yourself?'

Liselotte turned her face away. The egg was certainly attractive, and such a pretty pale blue, and so perfect, but to be situated among that oozing mess, that discharge. 'No,' she said, shaking her head like a wilful child. 'No, none of this is right. I am simply going to Grenze. I have an appointment. I do not know you. Any of you. No, this is all wrong. This is not my story.'

'What is wrong, my child?' said the woman across from her, her husband gently snoring on her shoulder.

'I'm not your child,' said Liselotte. 'I simply want to be left alone. To make my journey in peace.'

'But you came and sat here. Is this any way to behave?' said the woman, adding a harsher note to her voice. 'Is it any way?' she asked the businessman, who had folded up the egg in the handkerchief and tucked it carefully into his breast pocket.

'It most certainly is not!' he said, with puffed-up propriety.

'It's not decent or obliging,' muttered the husband, still with his eyes closed, and apparently asleep. A trickle of drool slid down his chin onto his starched collar.

'She wants her journey in peace,' mimicked one of the two young women who had been discussing the unfortunate Lena.

Once more, Liselotte rose from her seat, box tucked under one arm, seeking refuge, seeking calm. As she went along the carriage they all stared at her as if she were some curious bloom, or long-dead species suddenly returned from a forgotten world. She felt herself blushing with anger and fear. She wanted to tear at their stupid animal faces, their stock expressions, their shallow eyes that betrayed no warmth nor fellow feeling. They were mere machines with sour blood for fuel, children and adults all. Eating and excreting. Waking and sleeping through featureless lives. Judging and busying themselves with pointless tasks and gossip. Mouthing received ideas, dead to mystery and wonder and love - their own and anyone else's.

'You're evil,' she said, in a shaking voice. 'Why do you look at me so? Why do you stare at me? I'd turn you all to stone. I would *disappear* you.'

At the end of the aisle was the reason for the scent Liselotte had noticed when she first came into the carriage. The iron-haired matron, who had cooed over the restless baby, was peeling a vast quantity of apples, of various sizes, both red and green. Piles of unpeeled fruit lay in her copious lap and at either side of her. The skinless fruit heaped up in a large wicker basket in front of her, while mad spirals of skin lay inches deep around her thick-stockinged feet. The music stopped. Iron bun looked up as Liselotte reached out to the connecting door in her bid to escape.

The peeler's face was pink with exertion and natural aggression. Sweat glistened in the many folds of her neck and chin. A bulbous wart on her cheek shot out long curling grey hairs.

'Kascha, Neekasch. Kascha Neeman,' boomed the apple peeler, wagging her small but observably sharp knife at Liselotte.

'I don't understand you. I don't know what you're saying,' replied Liselotte, seemingly unable to make her exit through to the following carriage.

'Nabda, funil, se me szashui Foi. Foi Foi Foi!' yelped the woman, still shaking the knife, but now at the swaddled form on the seat opposite. 'Foi!' she wailed in a long note of enraged despair.

The scent of apples, some obviously rotting, made Liselotte feel drunk. She longed to swoon, to fall to some impossibly soft, clean, safe, and blissfully white bed, to sleep. Sleep for thirty years. She turned her head to the baby on the seat, which the woman continued to gesture at. It could not have been more than eighteen inches long. Its body, arms and legs were fully and tightly swaddled in dirty off-white bandages. Some parts of the bandaging showed sickly yellow stains. The head also was bandaged, but for an oval of freedom where the face pushed out, doughlike. And that face. 'Oh, my sweet God,' said Liselotte to herself. That face was crawling with maggots. In and out of the nose, the mouth, the eyes. It was a mass of maggot activity, like a second constantly moving skin. Yet the mouth appeared to move, as if attempting to cry. Yet now no sound came as it had before. Not even a whimper.

'Foi,' shouted the woman with the knife, and stood up and over the baby, sending apples rolling down the aisle, knocking over

THE GIFT MAKER

the near-full basket, to then bring the juice-dripping knife high in the air.

Liselotte screamed as she tore her eyes away. The box slipped through the black material and fell from her grasp to the floor, and in her shock she did not realise it had fallen. Hands, unseen by her, picked up the box and hid it under a shawl. She screamed as she wrenched the connecting door open and stepped out into the dark. She continued to scream and the sounds she made were far-off, as though coming from another person, or another time. Here was a ledge. She knew somehow that beyond the next step lay nothing. The brutally rhythmic sound of the train on the tracks was very loud, and a sharp cold wind cut into her cheek and blew her hair over her eyes. She could smell smoke and oil. In the flash before she made her decision, she saw in the distance to her right a bright mountain top, like a beacon of possibility and hope, picked out by moonlight against the black-blue sky. With a desperate unknowing leap she threw herself headlong into the rushing night.

thirteen

'I COULD LOSE my job for this,' said Müller, pocketing the three silver coins that Thomas had reluctantly handed him. Thomas had thought one would have sufficed. It was important to conserve money.

Müller, noticeably tipsy, wiped his flaring, red-veined nose with the back of his hand. With the other he unclipped a large ring of keys from his belt, and inserted one of them into the lock of the rivet-studded wooden door. It squeaked as it turned.

'Just get what you've come for, and no playing the fool with me,' said Müller.

'Keep your hair on, old man, we'll be in and out,' said Jo to the perfectly bald nightwatchman, who merely grunted in reply.

Thomas flicked a metal switch on the wall and the corridor was semi-lit. They paced along the heavily-waxed floor, and passing through the refectory door, despite the gloom within, they noticed that all the tables had already been made up for breakfast for the following morning. Cutlery, bowls, plates and empty water jugs were set out in regimented fashion over neatly-pressed white tablecloths.

'For the boarders,' whispered Jo.

 THE GIFT MAKER

'I don't know why they bother escaping their parents only to end up institutionalised here, obeying a thousand petty rules, having their rooms cleaned for them, their bottoms wiped, no doubt. They obviously don't want to grow up,' said Thomas, with a sniff.

'Come on, we've got no time to pontificate,' said Jo, trying the handle of a door near the serving hatch. It creaked open. 'Through here.'

'What was that?' said Thomas.

'Nothing. The place is empty. The boarders are in the Schwanz building.'

'I thought I heard footsteps. Light ones, like a child or something.'

'You're still in a funk after that nonense with Daumen.'

'Nonsense it was nonsense! Are you getting your rational head back on, by any chance? You know exactly what you saw and felt.'

'Wait…there was something,' said Jo. 'Listen. Is that breathing?'

The two young men stood deadly still in the gloom of the refectory.

'It's nothing. Just our nerves, I'd say,' said Thomas. He pushed past Jo, and found and flicked a light switch, which illuminated the common room reserved for his year. Along the far wall, beyond the tatty sofas and a miscellany of chairs and coffee-stained tables, was a large wooden construction of student pigeon holes. He quickly found his name and retrieved a returned essay, liberally scribbled over in red by Professor Halloumi. His eyes caught the phrase "Very weak argument". Underneath the essay lay a small white envelope with *T. Ruder* written in green ink on the front. Instinctively, Thomas smelt it. There was a trace of something flowery, but not the perfume that he had hoped for, the one she always wore. *Kismet*, he remembered. A month earlier he had resolved to buy her a bottle, but when he saw the prodigious price, he decided on a box of violet cremes, which he left anonymously in her pigeon hole along with a card signed, *from a respectful admirer.*

'Well, open it then,' said Jo, impatiently.

'It may contain something private.'

'Look, either we're in this together, or we're not. I promise not to poke fun at you regarding your finer feelings.'

Thomas delicately peeled opened the envelope and slipped out a single piece of cream-coloured paper. He began to digest the words greedily, barely stopping to make sense of them.

'Read it out, for goodness sake.'

Thomas cleared his throat. '"Dear Thomas, firstly allow me to apologise for my harshness last night. My trust in you remains intact, and I know in my highest thoughts that you would not divulge anything you saw, nor pass on to curious or idle ears the contents of this note. This is what friends are obliged to do for each other."' The word *friends* cut deep into Thomas's chest. He paused.

'Get to it. Where has she gone?' said Jo, attempting to snatch the note, which Thomas pulled smartly away.

'All right, why do you have to rush everything? "We, my friend and I, have embarked on an indispensable journey to a town called Grenze. I doubt you would have heard of it. I am to meet a man named Reynard, an impresario and theatre manager, who, my friend has assured me, can open the necessary doors so that I may awaken my long-repressed dream."'

'Why do these literature students write as though they were from the last century?' said Jo, rolling his eyes.

Thomas ignored his friend. '"I tell you this because I must tell someone, and in you I perceive a similar idealism and desire to

THE GIFT MAKER

follow your soul's chosen path. There is a steeliness in you, Thomas Ruder, that would not accept the common life, the common run of things. It is like we are brother and sister in our hearts' longing, and, in truth, I had always wished for a brother."'

'Oh brother, where art thou?' said Jo.

'Will you shut up!' said Thomas, with uncharacteristic vehemence. He steadied himself. 'She ends it with, "I will write to you, or perhaps you may hear of me by other means. Wish me luck! Your sister/friend, Lise x."'

Thomas slowly folded the piece of paper and put it back in the envelope, which he then tucked into his inside pocket.

Aware of his friend's raw feelings, Jo said, gently, 'We should go now, old chap, or that sozzled fool Müller will be kicking up a fuss.'

'Yes, we should go,' replied Thomas in a low and somewhat mechanical voice. 'To Grenze.'

Just then, from the refectory, came a sound of something metallic falling to the floor. Thereafter was heard further clattering followed by the sound of breaking plates. Then a huge crash as of a table being turned over.

'My God, he's finally lost it. He'll probably blame us, the sot,' said Jo.

'Let's turn this light out and creep around him,' whispered Thomas. 'He'll probably fall down in a heap at any moment.'

Jo flicked the switch and the common room was in darkness. Another table was turned over accompanied by the sound of smashing glass and crockery. The students edged their faces around the door that opened on to the refectory. They caught sight of a table being upended, followed by the awful din. A metal water jug slid several feet towards them. Behind the activity they could make out a shadowy figure, but it was certainly not Müller. It could be no more than four feet tall.

'That's not Müller,' said Jo.

'It's a child, isn't it? I can't make out the face. It seems to have longish hair.'

'We'll get the blame for it, no doubt.'

Thomas stepped forward. 'Hey, what do you think you're doing?'

The figure stopped moving. It was wearing some sort of long coat, similar to Thomas's own. Yet the face was indestinct in the low light. There came a small eerie chuckle that echoed around the dining hall.

'It is a child. Some little ruffian,' said Jo. 'This is a result of not teaching ethics to the masses. This country is turning into a moral sewer, and all because of a lack…'

'Shhh…' said Thomas. 'He's waving at us. No, wait a minute, he's motioning with his finger for us to come towards him. The cheeky rascal.'

'I've dealt with his sort before,' said Jo, moving forward. 'You stop that right now or the police will be called. Your parents, if you have any, will be given a big fine. Do you understand?'

Still the figure stood motionless except for a curling index finger, beckoning the students forward.

'It seems to have hair on its face,' said Thomas. 'Or is that dirt?'

Jo took a few more steps towards the figure, at which it picked up something shiny from the trestle table to its side and flung it with enormous speed and power.

Thomas watched helplessly as Jo's head shot back and his hand went automatically to his eye. He let out a shout of pain and shock. The butter knife clanked to the floor.

The figure turned and, effortlessly leaping a table, sped from the room. Light footsteps receded down the corridor beyond.

'Are you all right?' said Thomas. 'Did it hit you in the eye?'

THE GIFT MAKER

Jo still covered half of his face with his hand. 'No, I think it missed. But I'm injured. Look.' He brought his hand down and Thomas could make out a red welt emerging a fraction below the left eye.

'You were lucky it was just a butter knife. It might have blinded you otherwise.'

'Yes, I'm so very lucky. I mean I could be sitting by my fire reading an engrossing book on ancient civilisations, while munching a piece of buttered toast and sipping tea. But instead I have the great good fortune to be here with you in a dark and cold college refectory at God know's what hour, having just had a knife thrown at my face by some evil little thug. I should count my stars, I really should.'

'I don't think it will scar,' said Thomas.

'Stinging like I don't know what,' said Jo, once more placing his palm over his eye.

'We better tidy this up as best we can, or old Müller will report us,' said Thomas.

'Any good at sticking plates together, are you?' said Jo, witheringly, as they surveyed the disorder.

'I'm surprised Müller didn't waddle in with all that commotion going on,' said Thomas. 'And why did he let the little brute get through in the first place?'

'Probably comatose,' said Jo, picking up a glass which had survived its fall intact.

In the near dark, for they could not find the light switch, Thomas and Jo righted the upturned tables. They cleared pieces of broken plate and glass into a bin. They rearranged the knives and forks and spoons into a semblance of their previous order.

'It'll have to do,' said Thomas. 'Maybe Müller will forget we've even been here. Why they let that old wine tub keep the gate, I've no idea.'

They left the refectory and passed down the hall once more to exit through the heavy main door. They crept cat-like towards Müller's hut. Through a smoke-stained window they could see the glow from a small coal brazier. Then they noticed a black shape on the floor in front of the hut.

'Is that him?' said Jo.

'It looks more like a couple of sacks dumped together,' said Thomas.

As they drew nearer they saw that it was not a couple of sacks at all. It was, in fact, Müller.

'He's lying at a very strange angle,' said Thomas, as they stood over the prone body. 'Look at his arm, it's all twisted.'

'Might even be broken.'

'Do you think he's had a fall? We ought to help him or he could choke on his vomit. I started a first-aid course once…'

'You *started* it?' said Jo.

'Yes, back in high school. I was a bit partial to the instructor taking the classes. Very tall and muscular she was, a javelin thrower. I liked them like that in those days, but my taste has changed. I was always first to volunteer for mouth-to-mouth.'

'Why didn't you finish, then?'

'I caught the mumps, and by the time I was better the classes had ended and she, Ludmilla, I think her name was, well, she'd joined the Officer Training Corps. I heard through my cousin that she won the St Bischoff's Medal 2nd Class for her bravery during the Orlitz mining disaster.'

'Yes, I remember that one. Terrible loss of life. But what about this chap here? Give me a hand, will you?' Jo kneeled down and began trying to roll the heavy torso of Müller onto its side. Thomas joined him and they struggled to finally move the nightwatchman onto his back.

THE GIFT MAKER

'He's a dead weight,' panted Thomas.

'Heavens! Look at his face. It's almost black. His tongue is sticking out,' said Jo, moving back a little.

'And there's something around his neck. It's cut right in. I can't hear him breathing, Jo. His hands are very cold. Get me a light, quick! Look in his hut.'

Within a few seconds Jo had returned with a small battery-powered torch that shone a yellow light on the man's severely discoloured face. And the two students could now see that cutting deep into the flesh of his neck was an extremely tightly-wound length of bronze-coloured wire, the ends of which were twisted together and stuck out over his jumper.

'He's dead, isn't he?' said Jo.

'Yes,' replied Thomas. 'And unless I'm mistaken, that's a guitar string wrapped around his throat. Most likely a low E, heavy gauge. I believe I use the same make.'

fourteen

'BE CAREFUL, DON'T give her too much at once.'

'I know what I'm doing, woman.'

'I truly thought she was dead.'

'Another hour and she would have frozen. Or the wolves would have got her.'

'Such a beautiful girl. My little ice maiden, her hair black and flowing, just like our Gisela's when she was that age. And there's something about the shape of the eyes, too.'

'Don't mention that girl's name in my house.'

'She's still our daughter, Aldo. And it's my house as well.'

Liselotte twisted her head away from the spoon, soup dribbling down her chin. Her eyes had been half-open and heavy since Aldo had roughly shaken her awake to try and get something warm into her. She had not spoken, other than to intone the words 'peeling apples', over and over, in a melancholy drone. She closed her eyes once more.

'Come, let me wipe that away,' said the woman with the round glasses. 'You need to sleep again, I'm thinking. Yes, that's it now, just lie back, and I'll tuck you up a bit.'

'She's not a baby, Gerda,' said Aldo, shaking his head before leaving the room with the barely-touched bowl of chicken broth.

 THE GIFT MAKER

His wife listened as his heavy boots clumped down the stairs of their small cottage. 'I know you're not a baby, but you're our guest,' said the woman, stroking Liselotte's sleeping face, and smoothing back her hair. 'Still so cold,' she muttered.

Gerda had been returning home from the village after buying cooking oil and sausage, some two miles walk, when she spotted the figure lying at the bottom of a bank not far from the railway tracks. The aging couple often told themselves, and each other, that this would be the last winter they would stay in their lonely and somewhat ramshackle cottage on the edge of the great pine forest, known as the *Dichtenwald*.

When Liselotte awoke, it was to the heavy warmth of the goose-feather duvet. She stretched out luxuriously. The bed and the pillows were perfectly white, with delicate embroidery along the edges, and she had a sense of having slept for a very long time. Thirty years, perhaps. For a drowsy moment she imagined herself having woken from a troubling yet now distant dream, into the familiar safety of her own room. But that wardrobe wasn't right. No, indeed, it was a rough-hewn country-style of wardrobe, quite unlike her own. And where were the prints of Hegler's ballet dancers on the far wall? And why was there a pewter water jug by the sink? Why, in fact, was there a *sink*? And, when she looked up and turned, she was shocked to see a large wooden cross hung above the bed. This was not her bedroom. She had never been here before.

In her mind she conjured up two distinct rooms as a series of pictures. She knew both had belonged to her at some point in her life. The first, which had several stuffed toys ranged along the bed (including a hedgehog with a forester's hat and a pipe in its hand), and a window opening out on to an ornamental garden with a fishpond, and beyond that, yes, that's right, out of sight but known, the end of land and the blank expanse of the sea.

The second room was the one with the pictures of ballet dancers. Here there were many books, mostly poetry, and an old typewriter on a dark hand-smoothed desk. This room was surely in a city. From that high window she could see a busy street below with trams and people passing. She struggled to comprehend the repetitive but indistinct cry of a newspaper seller.

Now, from somewhere below, came the smell of cooking. Sausage, and fried potatoes with onions was Liselotte's guess. And there were hushed voices. A man and a woman.

Liselotte pushed back the heavy quilt. The effort of so doing forced her to realise how weak she was. When she attempted to stand on the patterned rug by the bed, a stab of pain shot through her ankle. She sat back down, and saw that it was red and badly swollen. There was also extensive bruising on her legs and upper arms. Instinctively, touching her face, she felt her right cheek and eye to be puffy also. 'What's happened to me, and where am I?' she wondered. She wore a pink nightgown, patterned with cabbage roses, which was several sizes too big. 'How absurd all this is,' she thought. She did not know whether to laugh or cry. Thinking proved difficult.

Then she heard footsteps coming up what she presumed were stairs beyond the door. Without knowing why, she got back under the covers and pretended to be asleep. The door opened and someone came in.

'Are you all right, my dear?' said a kindly voice. 'I thought I heard you get up. You really need to rest that foot. Dinner will be ready soon. I'll bring you some up.'

Liselotte turned and opened her eyes. A bespectacled woman, whom Liselotte judged to be in her early sixties, was smiling down at her. She had a roundish, childlike face, yet it was imbued with a sense of purpose and dignity. She was dressed in a red peasant

THE GIFT MAKER

blouse with white lace at the neck and cuffs, and a long, flowered skirt that almost reached the ground. Her grey hair was worn in a thick braid that hung halfway down her back. On the ring finger of her left hand she wore a simple gold band. Those hands surely belonged to one who had spent a lifetime washing clothes and bed-linen without the aid of a machine.

'Where am I?' said Liselotte. 'I remember being on a train. I don't know you, do I?'

'My name is Gerda. Pleased to make your acquaintance. And that's Aldo bumping around down there. The *old man*, as I call him.'

'I seem to have hurt myself. My foot and...'

'Yes, you were in a parlous state when we found you, half covered with snow. Another few hours and you'd have left this world, so Aldo reckons. I told him you may have fallen from a train, and he just laughed. You'd be past all concern,' he said.

'I don't remember falling anywhere. I just remember being on a train but I don't know where I was going. I remember something to do with apples.'

'Ah, yes, the apples.'

'You know about them?'

'Well, last night you kept talking about them in your sleep. Couldn't make head nor tail of most of it. Seemed to distress you, my pet.'

'How long have I been here, then?'

'Two nights...no, three. That soup you just had is the first you've eaten, though we did manage to get some tea with brandy into you yesterday. What's your name, my duck?'

The young woman thought for a moment, her brow furrowed. 'Lise...Liselotte,' she said at last, and tried to think what that name meant, where and how that name fit into the world, for although she could remember both her old rooms, as clear but disjointed pictures in her mind, she could not remember other people associated with them. She must have a mother and father. And siblings, perhaps, and friends, surely, but who and where were they? And how had she come to be travelling on a train away from them all? Or had she been going back? She felt the prick of tears.

'Try not to tire yourself,' said Gerda. 'I'll bring you up a little plate of something in a wee while.'

'Thank you,' was all Liselotte could think to say, as the kindly woman stroked her hair and turned to leave the room. 'Thank you,' Liselotte repeated.

She lay there, staring at the ceiling, the cracks therein forming mountain ranges, river courses, long jerky paths leading nowhere. Her thoughts could not grasp anything except the present moment. At least she knew her name. That was a start. Surely someone she knew would soon come to collect her, to explain everything that had happened. They would laugh, no doubt. And in later years say, 'Remember that time when…'

A little later, as promised, Gerda brought up the meal, with the sausage cut into small pieces, as if for a child. Liselotte allowed herself to be fed, propped up against the pillows.

'So, you can't remember anything else?' said Gerda.

'Oh,' said Liselotte, and her face was a mask of puzzlement. 'I remember a man. He was kind at first. I think I liked him…and then he changed.'

'That sounds familiar,' said Gerda, with a soft chuckle.

'No, I mean he changed into something. But then it went dark.'

'I've heard about these things before,' said Gerda, offering Liselotte another forkful of the delicious fried potatoes. 'In time, your memory will come back. Just in fits and starts at first; then

THE GIFT MAKER

you'll start joining everything up like a jigsaw, and before you know it…'

'I feel I'm a burden to you.'

Gerda shook her head.

'Can I meet Aldo, your husband?'

'Just try not. He'll soon be telling you tales of his army years and boring you silly with his woodcarving.'

'Woodcarving.' Liselotte smiled. 'I can see an eagle made of wood. It stood on…or in…oh, I don't know, I don't know.' Her eyes filled with tears, and when they fell Gerda wiped them away with the napkin.

'That's a good girl,' said Gerda, when the plate had been cleared. 'Oh, pardon me, I'm on strict instructions from his lordship not to baby you.'

'It's all right,' said Liselotte. 'I do feel rather like a baby. It's like I've started life again. Everything is curious, because apart from the pictures I have in my head of other rooms I think I've lived in, there's nothing else.'

'Where are those rooms, do you think?'

'I don't know, Gerda. But I need to hang on to them.'

'That's right, Lisechen. You hang on to those rooms, and those pictures will grow into something more. I'm sure of it.'

'You called me Lisechen. Someone else used to do that. Once.'

Gerda nodded. 'I have a daughter, you know. Gisela. I'll tell you about her after you've had a little rest. Shall I turn this light out?'

There was no answer.

Gerda went to the window. 'It's getting dark out there. And cold, so cold. I'm glad I spotted you, dear. I'm so glad. If you hear a howling, don't you worry. There are wolves in the forest but they can't get in here. You're safe and sound now. Wolves are mostly shy of people, anyway. They don't really want anything to do with us.

And who can blame them, eh?'

But Liselotte had already succumbed to a great tiredness. Gerda turned down the wick in the oil lamp, which sat on the chest of drawers, until it gave out only a small but comforting glow. *In case she wakes and is frightened of the dark,* thought Gerda.

fifteen

'WE NEED an alibi.'

'Why? Nobody saw us, Jo.'

'How can we be sure? And they'll have fingerprints from the plates and glasses we touched. The police will know that someone was let in.'

'Do you think that boy did it? How could he, though? I know Müller was sozzled, but still, he's a grown man, and by no means weak.'

They turned down a cobbled alleyway. High in a tenement window a pale blue light shone. Thomas glanced over his shoulder. He half expected to hear sirens at their backs. 'I'm not sure it was a boy,' he said quietly.

'What then? Some dwarf? I suppose there must have been two of them, or more. The others did for poor old Müller while the young one caused havoc in the dining hall. But why?'

Thomas shrugged. 'Things are falling apart in this godforsaken country. They don't need a reason. Just out of their minds on home-brew. Powerful stuff that, sends you crackers. The masses are turning, Jo. The uneducated, the unemployed, and even some of the war veterans, are seething. They feel there's nothing left for them. No future. Just like in that novel by Frinkel, the barbarians are at the gates once more. But these barbarians are a home-grown variety. History moves like this, in repetitive cycles. We develop an apparent stability, a so-called civilisation, but it's merely a fragile carapace, a chimera, a naïve and temporary illusion, while always from below…'

'*We're* not much better,' Jo interjected. 'We should be reporting this to the police right now.'

'And who would the number one suspects be? Are you mad?'

Jo remained silent as they crossed Engel Street. The huge white letters of the Secken Brothers store glowed from across a vacant Drachen Square. 'My face is damn sore,' he said at last.

'I feel partly responsible,' said Thomas. 'If I hadn't dragged you into all this…'

'We're both in it now. Up to our necks. No point in regretting anything. Let's sit down here for a moment and work out what to do.'

They sat huddled into themselves, collars pulled high around their ears, on the steps of the public library.

'It's just after two a.m.,' said Thomas, squinting at the gold pocket watch that had been his grandfather's. He shivered. He had a particular memory of his grandfather, that of trying to pull the grizzled old man's long black leather boots off. Thomas was in a kitchen with a stone floor dusted with flour, and something was bubbling away on a double range. Chickens wandered in and out of the doorway. The four or five-year-old Thomas pulled and pulled, and suddenly the boot came free, causing him to fly back at speed and land on a sack of potatoes. The old man had laughed like a castrated goat, and when he died of pneumonia the following year, he left the boy the gold pocket watch in his will. There had been a little buff card, now lost, tied to the watch: *To my flying boot boy.*

'Where might Ulli be this time of night?' said Jo.

'Either trying to sober up in some late-night coffee house, or slobbering over some unfortunate girl.' Thomas stood and stamped his feet for warmth. 'I'm wondering if there's a train to Grenze.'

'What, now?'

'Why not? Maybe it would be best if I were out of the city for a while. And I desperately need to know if Liselotte's safe. They'll put that down to another random, pointless murder.' He jerked his thumb over his shoulder. 'No particular motive. There'll be another Müller or Hansi or Grauben on the gate before the month is out.' He sniffed loudly.

'You really can be a heartless individual, can't you?' said Jo, also standing. 'Just because Müller liked a drink, as most of us do, he's expendable, is he? I've heard you call our government a dictatorship, a parcel of venal thugs in moth-eaten brocade, but you'd fit in very well among them, I reckon. Do we know if Müller had a wife, or children, ageing parents, a dog or parrot who loved him, small or big dreams and hopes of his own? Do we care? I, for one, do.'

Thomas looked at his friend. 'I'm terribly sorry for the man. But what good will it do us to get involved? He's beyond all pain, as they say. We couldn't recognise that lout if he sat across from us in a restaurant, and we didn't even see the others.'

'It's odd,' said Jo. 'Don't take this the wrong way now, but despite the darkness, he reminded me of a miniature version of you. The coat and hair and all.'

'Rubbish!' But Thomas remembered Daumen's odd pronouncement: *Now your road may be following you.* And something about unwanted gifts distorting from their original purpose. He shook the notion from his mind. 'He couldn't have been more than ten.'

'Not a dwarf then?'

'Enough,' said Thomas, making a swiping movement with his hand. 'At least walk me to the station. I have a train to catch.'

Their steps rang hollow in the great hall of Schwalbenbach Central Station. A few tramps dozed fitfully on the benches, some covered with yesterday's newspaper, or a dirty and torn blanket, empty beer bottles littering the floor around them. A thin man with a drooping moustache was sleepily mopping the floor in one corner. He kept going over the same area, mechanically. Only one of the many ticket windows was open.

'Where to?' barked the thick-set man behind the window. A tinny radio played a silly dance tune in the background.

'Are there any trains going to Grenze before morning?' said Thomas. Behind him, Jo was tenderly feeling his bruised face.

'Grenze?' The man gave a sour expression. 'Leaves at three. Platform eighteen. Won't be one back till Monday. I s'pose you know that.'

'No…I mean I don't mind. Is there a restaurant car?'

The man rolled his eyes. 'No, matey, and there ain't a band neither. Nor a four-poster bed.'

'There's no need to…'

'Sixteen schillings return. I s'pose you do want to return, do ya?'

Troubled by the dent the train fare would make in his dwindling finances, Thomas reluctantly handed over three five-schilling notes and a single coin.

They walked in silence to the platform, Jo attempting to dislodge from his mind the image of Müller's dead face.

'I'll be back next week, Jo. I have a lot of work to catch up on. Don't want to re-sit another term.'

'Work is the last thing on my mind. I'll be waiting for that heavy knock on the door.'

'There's no reason why we'd be suspected. We'll just cover for each other, yes? At yours all night. Easy.'

Jo looked gloomy. 'You do realise how far Grenze is, don't you? It's a tiny dot at the edge of the world. And if Lise has jumped ship from university and wants to follow her dream, whatever that is, some theatrical bent, I'm imagining, then why try and stop her?'

'I'm not. Remember all I told you about the box. The contents? And Daumen. Be careful of him, Jo.' Thomas reached out his hand, which his friend took half-heartedly.

A whistle blew, startling the two young men. There was a black locomotive, hissing steam, in front of three dark-green coaches. Thomas was the only passenger evident on the platform. A guard in a black uniform with red piping down the arms and legs and a red peaked cap stepped out of the nearest carriage doorway.

'You haven't even got a toothbrush,' said Jo.

'I was gonna shout all aboard,' said the guard in a nasal voice, while sidling up to them. He had long reddish sideburns and was chewing something. 'But it's just you two, I expect. Don't get many on this run, not this time of night. I'd go for that next carriage, lads. It's the only one with heating.'

'Not me,' said Jo. 'My friend here is going to Grenze.'

The guard laughed in a dead sort of way. 'Now why anyone should voluntarily go to such a place is beyond me,' he said, and wandered off down the platform, whistling tunelessly.

'Sounds like the trip of a lifetime,' said Jo. 'Do send me a postcard, care of the Pizny Gaol, cell 4357.'

'It won't come to that, comrade.' The two men hugged each other without embarrassment. 'This is just something I need to do. A matter of honour. Don't laugh, I mean it. I've never truly followed my heart, and it's about time I started learning to.'

'I don't like station goodbyes,' said Jo. 'Ever since…' he stopped.

'Ever since what?'

'Oh, nothing.' Jo shook his head vigorously. 'Just make sure you come back, with or without your damsel in distress. If anyone asks about you, I'll say you've gone to visit a sick aunt or you're on a quest to find the Lost Island of Mandelbrot.' And with that, he strode off, not looking back once.

Thomas ambled down to the next carriage, as advised, and had no problem finding a seat, for there was no one else there. There were still fifteen minutes before the train was due to set off. The windows were grimy and the carriage cloth stank of tobacco and sweat. On the seat across from him, rolled into a corner, lay an apple. It was pale green with patches of pinkish blush on the sides. It looked very fresh. He smelled it. It reminded him of his father's orchard. Smiling, Thomas picked up the apple and pushed it deep into his overcoat pocket. *Something for later*, he thought.

The relative warmth of the carriage, and spongy softness of the seat when Thomas stretched out along it, his long legs dangling into the aisle, and his rolled-up overcoat for a pillow, were all that were required for the young man to fall almost immediately into a deep and dreamless sleep.

sixteen

FROM THE WINDOW she could see part of the lake surrounded by fir and pine trees, patches of holm-oak. Ice blue and dark green against a world of white and grey. Her ankle was improving but still weak. The bruises had mostly faded. Each morning, a watery winter sun woke her and each time she was baffled by the unfamiliar room.

Gerda had given her some of the daughter's old clothes, which certainly fitted her better than Gerda's own. Opening the pine wardrobe, she gazed at herself in the mirror on the inside of the door. She was Liselotte, that much she knew. But what did that name mean other than the four syllables that comprised it? She once had books and a desk of her own. She once lived in a city, but the city was not her childhood home. Further back was the sea. A warm sea in summer, but always so windy on the beach. She remembered a red and white spotted hat with a wide brim. Someone was pushing it down onto her head and she was laughing. When she looked down, her legs were those of a child, and damp sand clung to them in patches which she brushed off.

Gisela's dress was of grey cotton. It had long sleeves and was cut low in the front. It had a wide banding around the waist and the hem fell to just below Liselotte's knees. She also wore a dark-blue knitted cardigan with duffel coat style buttons, and pockets. Gerda had provided her with thick bed-socks and an old pair of once pink slippers that were a little to large. In these her walk became more of a shuffle. She did not remember what her own clothes looked like, or indeed, where they were. She would have to ask Gerda.

What had her style been? Had she preferred loose flowing garments or fitted bodices, diaphanous silks or practical woollen skirts and tweeds? Muted autumnal colours, or daring pinks, mauves and lemons? Had she smoked? Had she drunk cocktails on verandas and at garden parties? Had she played the viola, or the flute? She had no idea. Her mind was not a map but an uncharted territory, flickering with grainy disconnected pictures, smells and sounds, and fragments that would not coalesce into narrative. Since coming to this place, or rather, *coming to* in this place, she had accepted the couple's concern and hospitality without question, too vague in her mind, or too fearful of facing the full extent of her unknowingness of herself or who she had been.

Aldo had brought up an old electric fire, which gave out a reasonable amount of heat if you sat near enough. There were three bars. Above these was a plastic covering made to look like glowing coals, under which a fan frantically blew strips of paper that gave an unrealistic yet charming effect of flames dancing.

'Excuse me, Lise.'

Liselotte jumped in her skin and quickly closed the wardrobe door.

'I'm sorry, Aldo, I was just looking at Gisela's clothes.'

'We both want you to treat this room as your own. And you're welcome to use anything you find in that cupboard. They're as good as yours now.'

'Why don't you like to talk about her?' said Liselotte, sitting down in the armchair by the fire.

Aldo stood awkwardly in the doorway. 'I know it sounds hard to you, but I prefer to think of her as dead.'

'But Gisela isn't dead. Gerda said she was going to tell me all about her, though she never does.'

Aldo dragged his palm across his lined brow. He seemed lost in thought for a moment, then he said: 'I used to carry her on my back from this cottage to that lake.' He moved slowly to the window and stood there, motionless, staring out. Light flakes of snow were falling, caressing the glass, turning clear on impact. Liselotte noticed the pine needles that had attached themselves to his bottle-green jumper. The jumper was thickly woven with scuffed leather patches at the elbows. Aldo's grey hair curled at the back, and in it were strands of a weak yellow.

'She always wanted me, never her mother. Of course she loved her mother. She's a good woman, as you know. It sounds silly but she'd always say, "Daddy, can I marry you when I'm big?". I told her that one day, when she was older, she'd meet a kind and handsome young man, and if all went well he'd become her husband. He wouldn't have to be rich, that's not what's important, I told her. The main thing is that he'd be gentle, not a boozer or card-player, and he'd have something in the way of brains, and he'd be able to protect her if he needed to.'

'But what happened to her? Where is she now?'

Still he stared out the window, at the meandering snowflakes that were growing in number and size. 'I told her never to take the job. She didn't need to work while she was under our roof. She wanted to save up, she said. For a trip to the capital. To stay in a hotel for the first time in her life. Go to the theatre, the ballet, all that malarkey. Read about it in some silly book. She wanted finer clothes than we could afford, finer than were truly necessary.'

Liselotte felt the material of the grey dress between her thumb and fingers. 'What job did she take, Aldo?'

'She'd done reasonable in her lessons, and she could sew and cook as well as her mother. Gerda will tell you that herself. And she could read better than me, and do all sorts of calculations in her head, without paper. We wanted her to go to the college in Freistadt. She might have been a teacher, instead of working in that tavern.'

'So, she was a barmaid. Surely that's not such a bad thing?'

Aldo turned quickly, causing Liselotte to sit further back in the chair. His face had reddened and there were the beginnings of tears in his pale blue eyes. 'I should have stopped it. It's where she met *him*!' he said, his face twisting with pain and deeply-locked anger.

Just then, there were footsteps coming up the stairs. Aldo's face resumed its usual phlegmatic and untroubled expression, as if he had not been talking about his daughter at all. As if he had not been dredging up jagged emotions and the sourness of regret, merely chatting about the weather or the best type of wood for carving, such was his customary bland conversation with Liselotte.

It was not Gerda, as Liselotte had expected, but a boy of about fifteen. She stood up and nodded at the youth, the chair scraping loudly on the wooden floor. He was short and wiry, with curly black hair and a large mole high on one cheek. His skin had a darker hue than that of both Aldo and Gerda, as if he had grown up in a warmer climate.

'This is Mabon,' said Aldo. 'We call him Mabe.'

The boy looked at Liselotte with a slightly puzzled expression, as if he had seen her before but could not remember where or

THE GIFT MAKER

when. He put his hand out, and Liselotte, stepping forward, took it. It was warm and soft in hers. His dark and questioning eyes drew her in.

'That's an interesting name you have,' she said. 'Is it from another country?'

The boy shook his head and smiled faintly.

'He doesn't speak,' said Aldo. 'He might be able to, for all I know. He just doesn't.'

'Oh, I see,' said Liselotte, though she did not really see anything. This new life of hers, a life without a history, without a background, without the necessary intimacies of being known by someone, anyone, was growing stranger by the minute. It created within her a sense of vertigo, an uncomfortable fragility of being, as if her fledgling personality were an image drawn into sand that an indifferent wave might at any moment wash clean away.

It struck her that she could decide to be anyone she wanted to be. Yet there must be innate qualities and sensibilities within her, and such behaviours and mores as she had internalised from others, her family and social world, both now unknown to her, that caused her to act and think in the way she did.

'He's Pesha's boy,' said Aldo. 'Helps me out with the firewood, tending the goats, other bits and pieces.' He looked tenderly at the boy, who lowered his eyes. 'I never had a son,' he added, more to himself than to Liselotte or the boy.

'Come on, lad, we've got that wall to mend.' Before leaving the room he turned to Liselotte. 'Gerda will be back from the village soon. Probably best you don't go out in those.' He nodded down at her slippers. 'There's some washing needing doing if you feel like keeping busy.' He gave her one of his sad smiles then trod heavily down the stairs. The boy stood in the doorway for a moment, looking back at Liselotte.

'Nice to meet you, Mabe,' she said.

The boy narrowed is eyes. 'Be careful,' he said, in a low breathy voice.

'Come on, lad!' called Aldo from below.

'Wait...' said Liselotte, but the boy was already halfway down the staircase.

She went to the window and saw Aldo, with the boy trailing a little behind, trudging through the snow in the direction of the lake. Mabe turned his head once, and he seemed to be looking up at the window where Liselotte stood. She could not be sure but she thought he put his finger over his lips. Liselotte watched them until they disappeared into a stand of pine trees.

She sat on the bed, wondering what the boy had meant, and why he had chosen to speak to her when he was usually mute. She sat there for a long time, desperately trying to fix the gesture that the boy had made into a reliable memory in her mind. Had he in fact spoken? Why should Aldo lie to her? Had the boy given her a sign that she herself must not speak?

Then a disturbing realisation struck her: she did not know how long she had been at the couple's cottage. Her sense of time had become distorted. Most days were spent in the same way. She would wake to the lessening shock of the unfamiliar room, then pass the morning in superficial conversation with Gerda or Aldo, sometimes helping with household chores. Other times she would be in her chair by the small electric fire reading one of Gisela's "silly" books: invariably an overblown and gaudy romance, featuring naïve yet wilful young girls from small towns and rural backwaters, longing to find their fortune and their *true love* in far-off places; undergoing innumerable perils along the way; falling for charming and dangerous would-be suitors, yet eventually finding their *prince*, be he a wealthy aristocrat or an esteemed surgeon.

    THE GIFT MAKER

Gisela had evidently been inspired by these plots, and sought to emulate one of their wispy and winsome heroines. But where was she now, and who was the *him* that Aldo had mentioned with such bitterness? Liselotte resolved to ask Gerda about her absent daughter the next time they were alone together. She had up until now felt reserved about pressing what was an obviously painful issue, preferring to let the burdened woman speak her heart when she was ready.

Evenings, when Liselotte felt like being alone, she would come up to the bedroom, saying she felt tired, and move the chair to the window. There she would sit, under a blanket, for what might be several hours, seemingly hypnotised by the dark woods beyond the carpet of undulating white, by the dizzying flakes of snow that struck the window silently, the endless falling flakes, all distressingly unique in design, stretching out beyond her sight and understanding. And past the woods the frozen lake. On a clear night, she would gaze at the great rolls and sweeping spirals of stars, such as she had never seen. And the moon rose massive and imposing in the sky, sometimes pale gold, sometimes silver, sometimes blood-red. Often it appeared alarmingly near, and its light bathed Liselotte's watching face, transfixing her.

She no longer dreamed.

It may have been a week or a month that she had lived at the cottage. The meeting with Mabe, or of Aldo telling of carrying his young daughter on his shoulders to the lake might have occurred five minutes ago or five days. And the belief that she could not be certain which, startled her. Despite Gerda's optimism, nothing more of her previous life had returned to her memory. All her recollections now were of the indistinct period of time she had spent with the couple. And these gave the impression of a flat unchanging present.

Even the detailed and coloured images she had treasured, of the two rooms she felt sure had once belonged to her, had begun fading into pencil sketches, one by one the particulars becoming generalised, bleaching out to non-existent lines on a white background. Now those rooms were arbitrary rooms someone else had merely told her about, and she carried no sense that they had any claim on her, nor her on them. And the conviction of having once been on a train, travelling somewhere necessary, had likewise been reduced to a random detail that may very well have happened to someone else.

There came the sound of the front door latch opening. Liselotte smoothed down her dress and hair in the wardrobe mirror, and prepared a face to meet Gerda. A face that she hoped would not betray her growing sense of unease.

Gerda knocked lightly at the door and entered without waiting for an answer. This habit had grown to become the source of some annoyance to Liselotte, but she felt she could not make her feelings known, since the woman and her husband had been so kind to her, had saved her life in fact.

'You remind me so much of my girl,' said Gerda, stroking Liselotte's arm.

'I understand she worked in a tavern in the village. And she met someone…' said Liselotte. Gerda's face clouded. 'I'm sorry, I didn't mean to speak out of turn,' Liselotte continued.

'It's all right,' said Gerda, smiling tightly. 'Come downstairs. I've bought some pastries. One with apricot, one with cloudberries. I'll tell you something while he's out.'

They were seated around the sturdy kitchen table, steam rising from their mugs of coffee, which Gerda made very strong, so strong in fact that Liselotte often felt a little light-headed after drinking it. There was also a strange but not unpleasant aftertaste to the brew,

 THE GIFT MAKER

which Gerda assured Liselotte with a shrug was the way it was drunk in this region. "Our secret blend," she would call it.

And then Gerda began her tale.

'When she first brought him to the house, we were both impressed by his manners, his soft voice, barely above a whisper, yet it carried – carried right into your head, as if his voice was on the inside of your skull. Very odd, but not unpleasant. Nearly always in white he was, but never a stain on it, and with that white hair, turned early like it does for some men, he was quite a picture. I remember he had such smooth, smooth hands, long fingers, like an artist or a poet, I used to fancy. Aldo now says he never trusted him from the beginning on account of his his lips being too thin. A silly country saying. But I remember well how he enjoyed the man's sophisticated conversation, full of quotes that old fool pretended to recognise. How Aldo glowed when his woodcarvings or fences were praised. He was like a little boy, Aldo was. Puffed up, like they get sometimes. Of course, we knew he was perhaps a little old for our Gisela, but what a catch.'

'Do you mean he was rich?' said Liselotte, brushing the pastry crumbs from her dress.

'He certainly made out that way. Said his father was a count, that they owned trout farms, a mill, had a score of servants. He said it casual, not boastful, as if he was a little bit embarrassed by it. I liked him for that. At the time.'

A log split noisily in the grate, sending up a shower of sparks. Gerda stood and poked at the fire with a blackened tong. She sat back down. The kitchen had grown darker, and Liselotte could hear the whining of the wind that had risen up outside.

Liselotte looked at the door, as it rattled now and again in its frame. 'Do you think Aldo and Mabe will be safe out in this weather?'

'Don't worry on their behalf. The old man will be at Mabe's father's place, testing out his plum brandy, if I know anything about anything.'

The two women sipped at their mugs, staring into the fire.

Liselotte broke the silence. 'And did your daughter, did Gisela fall in love with this man?'

Gerda sniffed and took a mouthful of the pastry. She spoke while chewing. 'She was a fool. But then women often are, aren't they? He took her away to the big town. I don't like to use its name as it brings back black memories, a place I've been less times than there are fingers on this hand, and never want to see again. He bought her expensive wine, fancy cakes, silk scarves, a bracelet with blue diamonds on it.'

'Blue diamonds?'

'Yes,' said Gerda. 'We mine them around this area. Or at least we did a few generations back. They are very rare. It turned the girl's head, as well he knew it would.'

'Did they…?'

Gerda frowned. 'They had separate rooms. At least that's what they told me. And I believed her. That girl couldn't lie to me. Then. I'd see it in her eyes, mother's can. He'd been the perfect gentleman, apparently. Just one kiss on the cheek when he left on the train back to Grenze. Damn, I said it! Oh, she was dead with the heartbreak. Couldn't get her up in the mornings; she'd lie there like a corpse staring at the ceiling. Wouldn't eat more than a few crumbs, wouldn't help with the chores. A real case of the heebie-jeebies. But when our postman would come up the lane she'd race down those stairs like a wild thing and fling open the door and run barefoot to meet him in her nightdress. It would terrify poor old Jasper, so he'd nearly drop his sack and scarper.'

THE GIFT MAKER

Gerda chuckled, but there was no humour or joy in the sound.

'Did he ever write to her, then?' asked Liselotte.

'I should have burnt it and buried the ashes. That's what I should have done.'

'Why, Gerda?'

The older woman's face grew harsh. She got up and threw her coffee dregs into the fire, making it hiss. 'He sent her a train ticket. To Grenze. For a little *holiday*, he said. I should have suspected something. He also wrote some claptrap about getting my girl into the theatre, told her she was a natural, that she could be another Diese, that she had the same "shimmering grace", that's the expression he used, and she kept repeating it to me, her eyes full of daft dreams. I heard that letter read out a hundred times if I heard it once. She told me this man was an *impresario,* that he had many contacts and powerful friends. I didn't know what the word meant, but she'd read about such a person in one of her daft books. Since she was a tot she always liked to recite, bits of poems and folk-stories, and the like. And she did have a sweet singing voice, that's true.'

'Is that so bad?' asked Liselotte. 'Did Aldo and you not want her to go into the theatre? I imagine it to be a wonderfully exciting and glamorous place.' In Liselotte's mind had risen the image of a thick red curtain opening on a sumptuously-lit country house scene, while she herself sat in the dark, waiting for someone to enter onto the stage. Whether this was a memory or imagination, she could not tell.

Gerda snorted. 'Oh, she got glamour all right, and plenty of it.'

'What do you mean?'

'While she mooned over this swine he began introducing her to his friends, insisting that she be *kind* to them, if you get my meaning; convincing her that each one could help her up the ladder, so to speak. One was supposed to be some famous producer, another was a theatre manager. All lies, of course. He never took her out himself, never spent a penny on her. And these friends were all as old as Aldo, or even older. She wrote telling me how shabby this so-called impresario's rooms were, how coarse his habits were compared to when they first met, how even his voice changed when he grew angry. How he gripped her arm once so as to leave bruises. She told me he was like many people in one. And sometimes the original one would appear and she would fall in love with him all over again. She had this dingy old put-me-up bed in a tiny box room. Had to cook and clean for him, too. I begged her to come home. I begged her.'

Gerda's eyes began to shine and she quickly wiped the back of her hand across them and shook her head.

'I still don't understand,' said Liselotte, feeling foolish. 'Why didn't she just leave?'

'He controlled her, can't you see? He had some hold on her. And she didn't have a schilling of her own. Nothing for the train fare back. She didn't know a soul there. He'd turned her into a common prostitute and kept all her earnings, that's what I believe, anyway. My poor sweet baby, she'd never even kissed a boy before she went there. Her letters got more and more desperate, but she never blamed him in them, always said it was her own choice. That was part of his control, I reckon. I knew the innocence and joy were being drained out of her. Then the letters stopped altogether. We wrote to the Grenze police insisting they help us, and to the mayor at the Rathaus. They wrote just two lines back saying that Gisela was an adult and that she may follow any profession she wishes to. Profession! I ask you. Grenze is a very terrible place.'

Liselotte bit her lip. Then she said, 'Well, couldn't you and Aldo go and collect her, bring her back?'

THE GIFT MAKER

'We certainly did,' said Gerda with some passion. 'He wouldn't let us see her. Her own parents! We were made to stand in the street like tradesmen rather than family. He had one of his thugs bring down a note that said that she no longer wished to see us, that she had another life now, and that she was happy. He couldn't face us himself, the coward. Pah! Happy?' Gerda paused to calm herself. 'I think he made her write it. It was her handwriting, all right. But he must have threatened her into writing and signing it. We called up her name and I saw a curtain moving above. A face peered out. I couldn't be sure, but I think it was my Gisela. But the face was thick with make-up, and older looking, like some cheap music-hall singer, or a you-know-what. It wasn't a natural face. I've seen it since in my dreams, and in one dream I rub away the make-up with a towel and my little girl's face is underneath, and she's crying.'

'And Aldo?' said Liselotte, 'Didn't he try to do something?'

'I've never seen him so angry. He demanded us be let in to see Gisela alone, to persuade her that she should come home. This thug just laughed in our faces. Then my husband went for this animal, this hired bully, with a great yell he went for his throat, but the man kicked at my husband and he fell back into the road. Then the door was slammed. We went home, and a week later we received a letter from this man's lawyer threatening us with legal action if we go anywhere near him or his house again, or harass his "staff". My God, that's not a word I would have used.'

'So awful,' said Liselotte, reaching over to gently brush away a tear from Gerda's cheek.

'I'll never give up, though,' continued Gerda. 'I still write, every week. Never a reply. I've even thought of hiring some men to help us. They can always be found for the right price, but we are so short of money now, and we're getting on. Though he still looks strong,

Aldo is not in the best of health. In any case, this was all nearly two years ago now, and Gisela might no longer be in Grenze. Heaven knows what's become of her.'

Liselotte glanced down at the grey dress and dark-blue cardigan she wore, and realised for the first time that she had become a replacement for the couple's daughter. That she was a blank slate upon which they could write an alternative future for their missing child, a future they themselves had wished for her. Then she remembered how Gerda had several times called her Gisela, and had quickly corrected herself, red-faced and smiling to cover her error. Liselotte now wondered if these had indeed been innocent mistakes, or the secret will and wish of a heartbroken mother revealing itself.

Gerda took the mugs and plates to the sink, leaving Liselotte sitting at the table, stranded in thought, stroking her hand over the smooth wood, tracing around the dark oval-shaped knots with her fingertip. Then she spoke: 'Gerda, you've not mentioned the man's name. The one who took your daughter from you.'

The woman turned, dishcloth in hand, and stared at Liselotte. 'Reynard,' she said. Then she made a face as if she was going to spit. 'I don't like to think of that name. If I could I would rip it out of the world.'

'Reynard,' Liselotte repeated quietly, more to herself than in answer to Gerda. The name meant something to her. It had something to do with a journey she once took, but like a fleeing dream, the more she tried to grasp any associations, the more cloudy and evanescent they became, until she was left with the name alone.

She sat there in the darkening kitchen staring into the dancing flames, whispering that name to herself in a seeming trance, as the older woman busied herself at the stove.

'Reynard…Reynard.'

seventeen

'END OF the line!'

Thomas was woken by a hand roughly shaking his shoulder. The hand belonged to the guard with the long red sideburns, and he was still chewing something.

The groggy student became aware of how cold his body was. He sat up, shivering. 'Where are we?' he muttered.

'Like I just said, end of the line. Get lively.'

Thomas unravelled his coat and stood to put it on. There was a lump in one of the pockets. Then he remembered the apple. Through the smoke-yellowed windows he saw the sign: *Grenze*. A fine drizzle was falling from a gunmetal sky. 'Do you know a good place for breakfast? Something cheap and filling.'

The guard looked at him oddly and said, 'You've really not been here before, have you?' before walking off down the carriage, picking up discarded newspapers and other detritus, to push them into a large paper sack he carried. He whistled a tune Thomas remembered from somewhere. *Yes*, it was the same tune the radio had been playing in the ticket office in Schwalbenbach.

The guard turned. 'Why did you keep moving about the train last night? A real jack-in-the-box you were.'

'What do you mean?' answered Thomas. 'As far as I know I've been here asleep all the while.'

'Well, that is queer. Either you're a sleepwalker or you've got an identical twin.' And with that he passed through the connecting doors into the next carriage.

Thomas listened until the whistling faded. He had no idea of the time, but supposed it was still early in the morning. He got off the train and walked down the wet platform, collar turned up, aware of the stiffness in his back and legs after a night stretched out on a seat. He took the apple from his pocket, went to take a bite, and noticed a small bruise near the stalk. He stopped, and put it back. Feeling queasy and weak through lack of food, he knew he needed something hot and tasty. A bacon and cheese sandwich would do the trick, accompanied by a steaming mug of very sweet milky tea. The platform was deserted, as was the small ticket hall. The shutters were pulled down over the ticket booth windows. The place was spotlessly clean, and smelled faintly of detergent.

A poster by the telephones caught his eye. It was an illustration of a powerful-looking brown horse staring over a fence. The eyes looked right at you and the expression of the horse was more akin to a human expression. Thomas could not decide whether the horse conveyed humour or subtle malice. In the background of the picture was a wildflower meadow and three oak trees that stood some distance apart. The sky was pale orange. Underneath the picture were the words, in large black capital letters: *STAY IN YOUR OWN FIELD.* There was nothing else to suggest what the poster was advertising, or whether it might be some government or educational notice.

Just then, there was a ringing sound behind Thomas, which made him jump. He turned and saw that it came from one of the telephones. He stared at it for a few moments, expecting it to stop. When it did not, he approached it cautiously, and lifted the surprisingly heavy black receiver.

'Hello?' said Thomas.

'Hello?' said a male voice.

'I just heard the telephone ringing in the station. I picked it up,' said Thomas.

'So did I,' said the voice.

'But you must have rung this number,' said Thomas. 'There's no one about though. I've just arrived here.'

'So have I,' said the voice. 'The phone was ringing and I picked it up. There's no one here.'

'Are you being serious?' said Thomas, beginning to wonder if this was some kind of childish prank. He looked around the ticket hall. It was empty. In the distance he heard what he thought was a car breaking hard.

'Who are you?' said the voice, which Thomas now realised had something familiar about it.

'I'm Thomas,' said Thomas, then wondered if this had been wise. At least he had not given his full name. Perhaps Jo had been right, and the police were on to them already because of poor old Müller. 'Who are *you*?' asked Thomas.

There was a pause. Thomas could hear the breathing of the other, followed by what sounded like a stifled laugh.

'I asked you who you were,' said Thomas, now losing patience.

'I'm Thomas,' said the voice, followed by more stifled laughter. Then the line went dead.

Thomas stared into the receiver in the way that actors do, as if expecting some enlightenment by way of this activity; then he replaced it.

Warily, he stepped through the arched doorway into the street. The drizzle was of the fine but soaking kind. The street, too, was deserted. On first impressions, the town struck Thomas as more like a film-set than an actual town; there was an air of expectancy and a sense of void, as if the space were waiting for a cast and crew to set up and begin shooting scenes. Thomas had not seen many films, or plays, come to that, as he was disinclined to feel *trapped* in a space for the duration of the supposed entertainment. His inbuilt good manners would restrict him from leaving halfway if the thing proved turgid or irritating. He remembered being taken, when quite young, to an opera by his father's brother, Gustav – the only other *cultured* one in the family, and referred to as "the professor" by Thomas's father, in a withering tone. The piece had been some nonsense about a knight who had lost his love to an evil prince, and the knight had various trials to endure in order to prove his worth. Thomas was more attracted to the evil prince, on account of his sword skills, but did not mention this to uncle Gustav. It dragged on for an eternity, with Gustav, who wore a pencil-thin moustache that made him look something of a dandy, repeatedly imploring the young Thomas to refrain from kicking the seat in front of him, or wiping his sweet-sticky hands over his trousers. When the boy was released once more into the night air, amid the aroma of sausage stands and frying onions, it was as though he had been unshackled from the darkest dungeon of boredom. That had been the first and last opera Thomas had allowed himself to be subjected to.

Judging by the hand-painted signs, some of the two or three-storey buildings in the street appeared to be shops, but Thomas had no idea what they were selling because all the uniformly dark-red shutters were drawn down and padlocked to the floor. Every house had its curtains closed. It was as if there had been a mass exodus, or else the town was in mourning, or under curfew. He trudged on, flicking his head to release some of the rainwater

THE GIFT MAKER

from his bedraggled hair. It dripped into his eyes and down his nose. The telephone conversation, if one could call it that, had greatly unnerved him, and he began to wonder if he was indeed going mad. He silently debated whether the discovery of a man's murdered corpse the night before had unhinged his mind.

As he turned into another street, which bore the strange name of *Gehenna*, written in red on a makeshift sign nailed to a wall, he had the acute sense of being followed. He stopped, and strained his ears to catch the sound of footsteps, which he was certain had been there an instant before. The fine drenching rain fell unabated. Thirsty, he turned his face to sky and allowed some droplets to fall into his mouth. The rain bore a bitter taste, as if the water were from a stagnant pond, or the run-off from some factory yard. Thomas spat into the gutter and wiped his lips on his wet sleeve.

Just then, something flitted across the road and disappeared under the body of what Thomas supposed was a bread van, due to the picture of a loaf of bread crudely painted on its side. The moving thing had been grey, the same grey as the sky, and travelled with a jerky motion, snaking across the glistening cobbles. A cat, Thomas supposed at first; but it had been too elongated, and in his recollection it had more than four legs; at least six. Too large for a rat, certainly. And who ever heard of a six-legged rat? The muzzle had also been extended, and the ears had been triangular and pointed. In all, it did not match any creature of Thomas's acquaintance.

Instinctively, the student walked to the middle of the road and got down on his knees. From several feet away, he attempted to peer under the van. Something moved beneath but he could not be sure what. There came a sudden, very loud rasping of a horn close by. Thomas looked up and saw that a white car with a blacked-out windscreen was heading directly at him. He clambered to his feet and leapt to the pavement, the side of the car missing his trailing leg by no more than an inch, and soaking him utterly from a puddle of brown water at the roadside. The car drove at excessive speed over the bumpy cobbled road, and appeared out of control as it skidded round a corner, again blaring its horn. The side-windows were also of darkened glass so that neither driver nor passengers, if there were any, could be seen. Before the car had turned, Thomas caught sight of the number plate. It consisted of only three letters: *R I P,* or possibly *R I B,* he could not be certain either way.

Thomas looked down at his soaked and muddied clothes. 'What kind of place is this?' he whispered. He longed to shout after the driver, but the moment had passed. Following the road for several minutes, his shoes squelching with each step, he finally stopped by a house with a sign hanging in the window: *Rooms and Food.* He approached the porch, and just as he was about to knock on the door, it opened wide, leaving Thomas with his fist at eye-level to a small, bespectacled man, who stood in the doorway, grinning. Thomas smiled and made a belated attempt to smooth his hair. It dripped onto the red porch tiles.

'I was wondering if…'

'You're in luck, sir,' said the man, with a further grin that revealed yellowing uneven teeth. 'Just came free this morning. Nasty accident. No luggage? No matter. I see you've already had a shower. Lovely weather for the time of year, isn't it just?' He beckoned Thomas in out of the rain.

The hallway was dingy and smelled unpleasant. Sour, like dirty and wet clothes pushed into a drawer and forgotten. The brown flock wallpaper was peeling. Thomas followed the man, who moved quite nimbly, up a flight of creaking wooden stairs. The man had a split in the back of his grey trousers and Thomas was offered a repeated glimpse of pale goosepimpled flesh.

 THE GIFT MAKER

'This is it,' said the man, extending his hand, as if showing off some marvel. The door of the room was only slightly ajar, so the man unceremoniously kicked it further open. It revealed an area so tiny that you could easily touch both walls if your arms were outstretched. A battered, lumpy-looking mattress took up most of the floor space. There was no pillow, just a tatty beige blanket decorated with a selection of dubious stains. There was a delapidated chest of drawers, and a pocked diamond-shaped mirror on the wall. The pale-green curtains were closed, suffusing the space with a sinister greenish light.

'I'm not sure,' said Thomas.

'You won't get another as good in this town, I can promise you that. Not with it being opening night!' The man picked something from between his two front teeth, then wiped his hand down his shirt front.

'Well…I've only just arrived, there might be another…another,' Thomas stammered, already feeling curiously beholden to the man. 'How much did you say it would be?' He fleetingly wondered what the man had meant by "opening night", but events were moving too quickly for him to ground his thoughts.

'I didn't, sir. We can talk about that after we've gotten a good breakfast into you. You look half starved. Students have to keep their strength up, don't they?' The man was so eager to please, so bizarrely cheerful, that Thomas felt he had to acquiesce to everything and anything the man said. To deny him would be discomforting to the point of pain. The man's intense and frenetic good humour acted out a blithe tyranny over Thomas's weary body and mind.

'How did you know?' muttered Thomas.

'Can always tell. You've got a brain, all right. I can tell a brain when I meet one. Aha, yes. You're one for the books, aren't you?

I no longer bother with them. Memory's going a bit. And the old concentration. I've lost the *art* of concentration, 'fraid to say. But you must see my little collection, you really ought. Just a hobby, you understand. Still, you might be impressed. Indeed you might. But that can wait, sir. That can wait.' The man gabbled at an alarming pace, punctuating his outpourings with sudden manic grins.

The man pulled the bedroom door closed with a bang. 'Let's get the old stove cranked up, shall we? Wiemel left some sausages, so he did; he won't be needing those where he's gone.' He chuckled, slapped his skinny leg, then beamed at Thomas before practically skipping down the stairs. Thomas followed meekly.

'In there, sir.' The man jabbed his finger. 'The parlour, said the spider...' He giggled childishly, then danced off down the low-lit corridor.

Thomas entered the parlour as directed and sat on a wooden banquette which was set against the back wall. An orange formica table lay before him, stained by innumerable cups and glasses and the remnants of dried food. It was sticky to the touch. A gas lamp flickered weakly on a shelf. A few droplets of water fell from Thomas's hair onto the table. He could hear the man clattering about behind the wall. The room was not warm and smelled of dust and old cooking oil.

'Won't be a tick,' the man shouted. 'We've got to keep our guests fed and watered, haven't we?' This last line was said as if to someone else. Perhaps the man was not alone in the kitchen. 'Oh, yes we have,' said the man in a harder tone, as if contradicting someone.

Under the table, something brushed against Thomas's leg. He jerked away and looked down. It was a large brown rabbit, pink nose twitching.

'Hello,' said Thomas. 'Hello there,' he repeated, then reached down to stroke the creature. Quick breaths pulsed through the rabbit's body. As Thomas's hand was just about to touch the fur, the rabbit's head made a side to side movement. A clear gesture of *no*. Then it edged away from Thomas, its little eyes glinting. It flipped around and bounded out of the room, white undercarriage flashing. A smell of sausages frying wafted in.

Before long, the man entered the parlour, carrying a tray. On the tray was a plate with three long curved sausages, somewhat overdone. There was a blob of what Thomas took to be mustard and a dark-coloured roll cut in two. There was also a mug of tea. The man placed the tray in front of Thomas and gave a little flourish with his hand. 'I shall wend my way back to the hot stove. I'm sure you don't want to be gawped at while you eat. We've plenty of time for conversation after.'

'Thank you, sir,' said Thomas, picking up the rather heavy knife and fork.

'Call me Günter,' said the man, giving Thomas a lop-sided smile. 'I go. I come back.'

'I'm Thomas,' said Thomas, but the man had already gone and resumed banging about in the kitchen. Thomas could hear him speaking to himself, through the thin partition wall, or perhaps it was to another. It was hard to make out all the words. Günter seemed to say, 'He *must* enjoy, he *must*', again as if contradicting someone.

The sausages tasted good but the sharp mustard hit the back of the student's throat, causing him to cough. The tea was strong and sweet. The roll was stale.

The meal was having the desired effect and soon Thomas began to feel a little more human. He was working his way through the final sausage and mopping up the grease with the last of the bread roll when he became aware of the man observing him from the doorway.

'Healthy appetite, eh?' said Günter with a leer.

'Hadn't eaten since yesterday,' replied Thomas with his mouth full. He wiped the back of his hand across his mouth. 'Erm…about the room. Is it the only one available?'

'You don't like it?' said Günter, straightening up. 'He doesn't like it,' he continued, addressing this down the hallway. He turned back to Thomas. 'It's reserved for you now. I could have let it go to someone else, you know. Rooms are gold dust on account of tonight's performance.' He made a bitter face. 'You try and help a person out and look where it gets you.'

'Yes…all right then. I didn't mean any offence. I'm only here for one night as it is.'

A slow smile spread across Günter's face. 'Others said the same, and they stayed for years. Grenze isn't a town for everybody, mind you. It's not really for the sensitive types. Are you a *sensitive*?'

Thomas thought for a moment. 'I suppose I have a sensitive side, yes. But about this performance you keep mentioning. What's that all about?'

'Don't you know? You are a green one. Surely you've heard of the Sheol Theatre?'

'Can't say I have,' replied Thomas.

Günter had sat down opposite him, and began scratching at the table top, making a noise that set Thomas's teeth on edge. He gave the student an under the eyebrows look.

'It's Monsieur Reynard's latest offering: *The Statue in the Park*. Sure to be a massive hit from here to the Gelsen Territories.' Günter grew more expressive with his hands, and his voice took on a preachy tone. 'It will be translated, of course. Into a dozen languages, possibly more. School children will learn pieces of it by heart. Everyone who is anyone in Grenze will be there. And some will have travelled many miles to make sure of a seat, paying

THE GIFT MAKER

through the nose for it, too. Everything Monsieur Reynard touches turns to silver. Silver coins that is.'

Thomas remembered Liselotte's note. 'This Reynard person…'

'He is more than just a person, he is *the* person.' Günter waved his finger in the air, and put on a serious face, which Thomas found somewhat comical. He quelled the desire to laugh.

'I've really come here to find someone, Günter. A young lady, and she was going to meet…'

'Many a gilded dream has broken on those shores, sir,' replied Günter. 'The name?'

'Oh, I doubt you'd know her. She can't have been here very long. A day at most.'

'Some days last a very long time,' said Günter. 'Especially here in Grenze,' he added, lowering his voice as though they might be overheard.

Thomas bit his lip. 'Lise…Liselotte…she has long, black hair… green…'

Günter sliced his hand through the air. 'Stop! The best thing you can do, young man, is get on the next train back from whence you came.'

'What do you mean?' cried Thomas. 'She's a dear friend of mine…more than a friend. I need to find out that she's safe and well. She left Schwalbenbach so suddenly. And she left to meet a man here called Reynard.'

'Exactly, sir.' Günter shook his head gravely. 'She is his latest protégé. His latest *amour*. His latest toy.' Günter's eyes narrowed. 'It's the talk of the taverns.'

'But she only would have arrived here yesterday. How could this have happened so quickly? He was only meant to help her realise her dreams…or something. Open doors for her.'

Günter sniggered. 'He'll do that, all right. He'll open very special doors.'

Not allowing Günter's cryptic comment to throw him off his stride, Thomas continued, 'She wanted to dance or act or whatever. It's just a fad, I'm sure. She really needs to come back to the university. She might be throwing everything away.'

'For what shall it profit a man…' But Günter stopped and stood up. 'I did warn you, sir. You can't say I haven't. Just stay here like a good pup, and I'll sort you out a bottle or two of country wine, and you'll sleep the sleep of the innocent; then back home, eh? It would be much safer for you. For all of us.'

Thomas shook his head and banged the table. 'I'll go to this play tonight. I'm not frightened of some half-baked fool in a fancy waistcoat, swinging a gold-topped cane. I'm determined to see Liselotte, and if she wants to stay with this…*individual*, then there's nothing I can do. But I'll at least have tried, or my name isn't Thomas Ruder.'

'That is something of a cliché, Thomas,' replied Günter, casually, as if he had known the student for years. 'The waistcoat and cane caricature. Reynard is not like you might expect.'

'And I might not be what he expects,' said Thomas, in a voice that did not seem to him like his own.

Günter looked at the young man pityingly. 'Right you are then, sir. There's a spare key to the front door hanging on a hook by the stairs. Perhaps you'll want a little nap before your big adventure.' He pointed upwards.

'Thank you,' said Thomas, unsure of whether to follow the man's suggestion, although he did feel suddenly very tired. He thought of the grimy mattress and shuddered.

Günter stared at the student, as if waiting for him to say something else, then he turned smartly on his heels and

THE GIFT MAKER

disappeared down the corridor. After a moment, Thomas could hear the landlord whispering: 'He ate it *all* up, he did. Despite your fluffy-headed doubts. He took it all inside himself. Now who's a clever Günter? Who's a clever boy? Who was right?'

There was silence. Thomas listened intently. Then a reply came, if indeed it was one. It was like the last scream of a dying animal as its throat is cut, and with it came a wild thumping of small feet against wood, which died down to an intermittent bumping, then nothing. On the shelf in the parlour where Thomas sat, the gas lamp went softly out.

eighteen

THOMAS WOKE IN the dark. He thrashed out blindly to each side, fighting off the red bloated hands that gripped and pawed at him. It was just the room, the tangled blanket and the close air. He was low on the floor on the stale mattress. He caught his breath. The curtains became visible as his eyes adjusted. He stood stiffly and went to the window. Outside it was dusk. There was a half-moon low in the sky. A number of dark-clothed people trudged along the road. All separate, none in pairs or groups. They moved at an oddly even pace as if they were part of some turgid dance. Now and then a car came over the cobbles and all the people stopped in unison until the car had gone past. Then they would move off again, seemingly without spirit or direction. Watching them with a rising disgust, Thomas had the sense that they were none of them going anywhere, so lifeless and automaton-like was their gait.

He drew the curtain across once more and picked up his coat, which had been used as an extra blanket. He delved in the pocket for his gold watch. It was nearly six. Had he really slept all day? He had no memory of electing to go to his room. He vaguely remembered Günter's suggestion but he did not recall climbing

THE GIFT MAKER

those wooden stairs for a second time. His mouth was dry and there was a griping pain in his lower stomach. 'What on earth am I doing here?' he said to himself.

Thomas went over to the small mirror on the wall. Above it was a dilapidated light-fitting, which he had not noticed on first seeing the room. A thin cord hung from it. Thomas pulled the cord, and with a click a weak yellowy light lit up that corner where he stood. He gazed at his image with a growing sense of unease. It was his face, certainly, but it was less defined, less himself than it used to be; more of an approximation, as if he were now observing it across time or in mere memory. It was not just the frail light that caused this, no, it was the *structure* of his face – it had degenerated. As they say, we know something like the back of our hand, but who would really know the back of their hand with any certainty if shown a picture of it? One's face is another matter. The pained and sallow visage that stared bleakly back at the student was in some way indistinct, diluted in a way that Thomas could not readily identify. It was surely a paler copy than he was used to seeing, as if the mirror was subtly refusing to reflect his totality.

He turned away and struggled into his coat and shoes. He avoided glancing at the mirror again as he left the room.

A key did indeed hang from the hook at the bottom of the stairs, as Günter had said. It was swinging ever so gently, as if someone had just that moment hung it there and walked away. The house was silent.

'Günter?' said Thomas, quietly.

Down the hall, the door to what Thomas supposed was the kitchen was shut, as was the parlour door. The hallway was in semi-darkness. Through the bubbled glass portion of the front door, Thomas watched as the twin lights of a car arced across. Then footsteps passed outside and diminished down the street.

'Excuse me?' called Thomas, more forcefully. No answer. He reached into his inside pocket and peeled off a five schilling note from the wad, then placed it under a purple glass ashtray that stood on a little table against the wall. Thomas jumped at a sudden thumping against the kitchen door. He looked at the door, his breath frozen. It had been very like the sound of that morning, the thumping that had accompanied the animal scream. But no scream came this time, just an irregular thumping and thudding against the door, which now continued, like something eager to get out, to escape, or else to get at something.

Thomas reached for the key, then thought better of it, and walked quickly to the front door. He turned the knob. It was locked. He rushed back for the key, returned to the door, and fiddled with it in the lock. The lock was loose in the door and the key failed to grip. The thudding and bumping behind him grew much louder and more frantic, like some insane, arrhythmical percussionist. Whatever was in that kitchen was growing more desperate, as long scouring and scratching sounds now accompanied the banging, as though of thick claws being dragged down a hard surface. Thomas felt a chill run down his body. His hand trembled as he attempted to finesse the key into the exact position to turn the barrel of the lock. *What if it isn't the right key?* he thought. *No, it must be. It must be!* 'Come on! Come on!' he muttered, glancing over his shoulder every few seconds to make sure the far door remained closed, as if by so doing he might prevent it from opening, and stop whatever sought to be released from that kitchen from suddenly springing upon his turned back.

At last the key turned. Thomas flung the door wide, just as a great crashing and splintering of wood occurred behind him. The next thing he heard was a thunderous pounding along the hallway, and he was aware of a vast and dense shadow descending upon

THE GIFT MAKER

him. He dared not look back, but jumped outside and slammed the door shut as fiercely as he could. Something hit the front door from inside with great force, causing it to shudder and bulge in its frame. The glass somehow held. As Thomas stumbled down the path, he looked back, and caught sight of a twisting, pulsing vortex of black shadow behind the bubbled glass.

He ran and ran, through a maze of dark and slick cobbled streets until his lungs and legs were on fire. At last he stopped by an old horse trough. He retched into it, bringing up some of that morning's breakfast. As he stood there coughing and spitting into the dry trough, he became aware of eyes watching him. He spun around, ready to fight whomever or whatever it was.

'Hey, hey…all right, young man. Put those fists down. I was just a little concerned.' The voice was very soft, silky one might say, and although barely more than a whisper, it carried clearly and plangently across the twenty feet or so from where the speaker stood.

Thomas wiped his palm across his wet mouth, and still panting from his exertions, he spat, unashamedly, on the floor. There, across the road, leaning nonchalantly against a lamp-post stood a rather diminutive figure, dressed all in white. White trousers, jacket, waistcoat and tie, white gloves and shoes, and yes, even the hair, the hair appeared to be pure white, although the face looked relatively young and virtually unlined.

Life had become so odd, so out of kilter, since the blue box was delivered to his lodgings earlier that week by Daumen, that Thomas suppressed a nervous laugh at seeing the queerly-dressed, half-smiling man, whose velvet voice had thrilled through him like ice, or like a long-awaited kiss.

'Something you ate, perhaps?' said the man. 'You haven't been eating unripe apples, have you? We used to do that as boys. Scamps we were, but meaning no harm. But I see you're not a boy at all. You're clearly on the threshold.'

Thomas cleared his throat. 'What? Oh, I'm sorry. I was running from…I was running to get…oh…' He began to lose his way. 'The theatre. Yes. The Sheol Theatre. Do you happen to know it please, sir?' Thomas felt light-headed and stumbled back a little, steadying himself against the trough. 'I'm new here, you see.'

'I do see,' said the man in white, with a wry smile. 'But we all have to be new at some stage. When we were new we were bright, the brightest they all said. But then it oftentimes goes downhill. The ineluctable tarnishing.' He paused, as if lost in contemplation of something. Then he shook his head slightly. 'No matter.'

The speaker's words seemed to originate from within Thomas's skull rather than from the man's barely moving mouth and his somewhat thin lips. At other points the slightly sibilant tones played so delicately around Thomas's ear, it was as if that mouth were tenderly pressed up against it.

'Yes, yes you're right,' replied Thomas, barely sensing that he had spoken, rather that something other had spoken through him. The man's face, as much as could be ascertained beneath the streetlight, which served further to blanch him, was neither old nor young. Only the milk-white hair was at odds. It looked, Thomas thought, like the face of innocence. That was the phrase that kept reverberating through his mind: *This man is the innocent one.*

The man raised his hand and pointed along the street with a slim forefinger. He moved noticeably slower than the average person and appeared excessively aware of all his movements, of every micro-gesture or tilt of the head. To Thomas he appeared choreographed, so much so that Thomas wanted again to laugh, but bit his lip to stop himself. 'At the bottom of this road is Sacker Street,' whispered the man in white. 'There you will find the theatre. I shall be attending the performance myself, as a matter of fact. But I must beg your leave now, as I am due to meet someone rather special this evening. Someone I do not wish to disappoint.'

Again the man's words emanated from within Thomas's skull, to the extent that the student was unsure whether he mistook them for his own thoughts.

The man performed a small bow. It was courtly, graceful, inherently speaking of all time past, of centuries of service, honour and hierarchy. He stared at Thomas for a moment before speaking. 'As long as you are well. And by the way, it *is* acceptable to laugh. Do not be afraid of your impulses. Perhaps we will meet again, at the interval.'

Then the man blew Thomas a delicate kiss, and gave an ornate flourish of his long-fingered hand, all of which, strangely, did not seem out of keeping, indeed it seemed the necessary thing, the only thing the man could have done. Thomas watched him move off down the road towards the now flickering and coloured lights of what was Sacker Street.

When Thomas had first encountered the man, the end of the road had been in near darkness. Now, as well as the spangled and softly fibrillating lights, came a jumble of music from different sources. Not loud, but muted and confused, as though many instruments and singers were competing for attention from different parts of the street, and in so doing their music and voices created a river of pulsing, skirling sound. The overall flavour, however, was of great gaiety and the tang of hedonistic abandon. It drew Thomas forward like the edge of a terrible cliff.

nineteen

WHEN JO SHORT for Johann returned to his room, he pulled a chest of drawers in front of his door. He lit a candle by his bed, quickly undressed, and slipped under the covers. The house was quiet, and despite the extra blanket, his body was cold. He moved his legs around, and rubbed his sides to generate warmth.

No matter how he tried, he could not banish thoughts of the evening's events. He thought about his friend, fitfully sleeping perhaps, on an empty train, travelling deep into forested country, passing frozen fields, rivers and ravines, under an indifferent moon, in search of a young woman who had made the same journey the day before. Both travelling in hope to a dot on a map at the edge of their world; a place few people knew nor cared anything about.

He thought about Daumen and gazed at the cracked ceiling, upon which shadows from the candle leapt. No sound came from above. Perhaps Thomas had been right, and the man, if that was what he was, would soon vacate. Müller's dead face emerged. The deep welts in his neck where the guitar string had bitten, the purple lips and bloodshot eyes. Jo shook his head but still the bloated, lifeless face remained in his mind's eye. The body

THE GIFT MAKER

would be found in the morning, most likely. Another motiveless piece of brutality to be put down, in certain media outlets, to *our discontented youth*. The usual voices would blare: *we need a good war to instil some discipline*, or *it's surely the influence of the incomers…this once beautiful and proud country is sinking under their filth, their backward creed…send the migrant workers back to their mire*. Some would listen. Some would act.

The story Thomas had told him about the miniature dancing Liselotte was surely a step too far. His friend must have taken some sort of drug, or else was mentally breaking down. A case of over-sensitivity. Jo would need to see such an impossible thing for himself, or he could not accept its likelihood, let alone its reality. And yet, he *had* felt that force-field of energy thrust him back against the wall outside Daumen's room. He had heard the disembodied voice, and seen the door close without human agency. All this talk of boxes and doubles. No. It was not rational. It could not be explained by reasoned argument, or the laws of science. The mind objected, as did the heart; everything objected from the *Weltanschaung* into which Jo had placed his faith and intelligence, since the life-changing event that had occurred one midsummer's day, a year before he came to the university.

His parents had brought him to Lauten station in their little Meizler car to see him off. He was to spend a week by the Kostensee with his mother's half-sister, Frinka. It was the beginning of what was to be a long hot summer, and he had performed well in his high-school exams. Surely the university would beckon the following year. Perhaps he might even try for the Reizler Conservetoire, where his father, Bernd, had won a scholarship, ensuring that he would not go down the mine like *his* father, like so many generations of their family had before.

Jo's mother, Jasmina, who came from a family of guest workers that had stayed, was a violin teacher in their little village, teaching the privately-schooled girls who boarded in the castle by the river. The school had once been a *residenz* that belonged to Count Dieter, that old rogue and roué.

As Jo kissed his mother, a small-boned, shiny-eyed woman, with a thick mass of dark hair exquisitely plaited down the length of her back, and a moonflower pinned near her ear to remind her of her home country and sunnier climes, he had the nebulous presentiment that he might be staying with his aunt for more than a week. His father, balding and broad-shouldered, sporting an upwards curling and waxed moustache, that his wife hated, pressed Jo's hand firmly and touched him briefly on the shoulder. He was not one for displays of emotion. Always immaculately, if a little ostentatiously dressed, choosing silk shirts in vibrant shades, suede shoes, cravats or the occasional bow tie, all of which pleased his wife's tastes but made him the butt of family jokes. "Here comes the silk purse," his elder brother would say, "I better wash my hands first," he would remark, at seeing Bernd's outstretched arm. "Don't want to get oil or coal dust on those lovely cuffs, do we?"

'Try and swim every day,' said Bernd to his palely academic son, in an unnecessarily gruff voice, avoiding Jo's searching eyes. The father's clothes, although soft and fine, had not in turn softened his feelings, and so he remained hard to reach, and reluctant to be touched or touch, as if fearing such overt tenderness would further estrange him from his family, weaken some essential allegiance, alienate him from a clan who prided themselves on an absurdly stoic attitude to life, accompanied by a willed miserablism.

'You know he doesn't like water, Bernd.' Jasmina smiled at her son indulgently. 'Perhaps the neighbour's pretty twins will

THE GIFT MAKER

keep him occupied. I'm sure they have grown into demure and captivating young women.' She enjoyed teasing him so.

Jo felt himself blush, which made his mother giggle and reach out to stroke his burning cheek. Then she took out a white embroidered handkerchief and wiped the corner of his mouth. 'You can't impress young ladies with the residue of cocoa around your lips, Johannlein.'

'Please don't call me that,' squirmed Jo, looking around, desperate for the train to arrive so that he might be freed from this awkward scene, find a quiet spot, take a book from his case and so be transported into the world of rarefied thought and contemplation; most likely some metaphysical discourse by Louis Von Draub or Heinrich Kopf.

Then, resembling salvation, the train could be seen emerging from a bend in the distance, sunlight flashing along its windows as it turned straight and headed for the platform where they stood. The railing Jo touched was warm, black paint flaking away to reveal the dull metal beneath. Jo scratched at it with his nail. As the train drew close, he picked up his case as nonchalantly as he dared and gave his parents his most casual smile.

'I'll send a postcard,' he said. 'And please leave my books in the order they are. No tidying, mother.'

Jasmina's eyes shone more than usual as she brought her hand to the flower in her hair and deftly pinned the bloom to her son's jacket. 'Why must you wear these old-fashioned jackets? And in this heat! You're not one of the *workers*, you know!' she said, wrinkling her brow. 'Or why bother with all this studying at all?'

'Solidarity,' said Jo.

His father was clearly restive, longing to get back to the peace of his garden, or the reassuringly dry order of his stamp collection.

'Try and enjoy yourself,' he said to his son. 'You never know what our allotted time…'

'Bernd!' said his wife. 'This is no time for your doom-laden pronouncements.' His mother's accent, tinged with the lilt of her home country, sounded quaint when using such practiced phrases.

And as he pulled the carriage door shut with a loud thud, upon finding a vacant seat, he lifted the window and leaned out, to see his father encircle his mother's slim waist with his arm. They were turned slightly toward each other, stilled, as though in a photograph. A whistle blew. Others rushed along the platform to board; then the sound of many doors closing.

'See you in a week!' called Jo, above the din.

His parents turned their faces to him in unison and their expressions were imperceptibly startled, as though a stranger had mistakenly called them, believing them to be people they knew. Then the couple both smiled, his father somewhat tightly, his mother with that guilessness that would often bruise her only child's heart in his fear for her vulnerability, amid a world that was rapidly losing many of its old certainties and much of its gentleness.

As the train moved out of the station, he watched the two figures grow smaller. His mother waved the handkerchief that she had used to scrub his mouth clean. Jo did not wave in return, but observed, as the two most important people in his life diminished until he could no longer tell them apart.

What Jo did not, could not, know was that by the time the train would reach the Sachsen Viaduct both his mother and father would be dead.

The news came via telegram to Auntie Frinka's the following day. It had been sent by Bernd's brother with characteristic bluntness: *Return home at once. Parents both killed in car crash.* As

THE GIFT MAKER

the weeping Frinka was consoled in the kitchen by Egon, her red-faced husband, Jo sat in the guest bedroom, staring at those terse lines, unable to think, unable to feel very much of anything. Then, without warning from or to himself, from somewhere deep inside he let out a wild shriek of pain and bewilderment that brought Egon storming breathlessly up the stairs.

After the double funeral Jo returned to his aunt's lakeside villa to spend the rest of the summer. He pored over his books from daybreak until the last light and beyond, yet after a day's close reading, he often found that he could not remember a single syllable of what he had read. On his long and solitary walks around the lake, he began wearing a moonflower in his buttonhole, at which his aunt Frinka looked askance, but made no comment.

When his parents' modest house was sold, and after his father's debts were paid off (the existence of which came as a great surprise to Jo), there was a little money left over for a private tutor to coach him for the university entrance exams the following May. Jo studied hard but without passion, without joy. He lived as though cold tea flowed through his veins rather than blood.

Finally, he chose the obscure and frankly second-rate Schwalbenbach University because it was far enough away from his home town and from anyone he ever knew (boyhood friends being few), that he might, in his own terms, reinvent himself as a person without a background. A bookworm without a history. He locked safely away all thoughts and feelings concerning his loss. He would hide his wound from everyone, particularly himself.

And now, as he lay in his bed in the candle-pulsing dark, his nerves ravaged by the events of the evening and its many puzzles, its strange horror, he saw again the image of two people waiting on a train platform: a tall balding man, and a slightly-built dark-haired woman waving a handkerchief. And this time – yes – their image becomes clearer, as they grow in stature and definition, rather than diminishing, for the train is returning to its resting place, so to meet all that wait for it.

Jo wiped his eyes again and again.

He froze when he heard a door softly close above him. Then footsteps descending the stairs. He knew those steps, that weight and pacing, as people in rooming houses often become ultrasensitive to the movements of others, others they barely see in the flesh. One may not see a neighbour in a rooming house for the best part of a week: his door closes as yours opens, the sound of splashing water behind the communal bathroom door, an odd muted laugh through the ceiling at a late hour. Yet each tenant can recall and, if necessary, tell of the daily movements of their fellows with more detail and accuracy than if they were living together as a family.

The footsteps came to a halt on the landing outside Jo's door. They paused, and Jo craned his neck out of the bed, the better to hear. He reminded himself to breathe. The swordstick would be nearer any intruder than himself if one such were to come crashing through his door. But these old houses were sturdy enough, thought Jo, and their doors and locks were well made, in an era when a practical trade was admired, and not looked down upon with scorn as the menial employment of guest workers and the illiterate. Then again, the young man considered, this was surely no ordinary being of flesh and blood. Who is to say that he might not pass through solid matter as if it were a mist? Impossible! screamed Jo's rational mind, yet this brought him scant comfort. In the dark, alone, we are all prey to Stone-Age fears.

Something, some object perhaps, was placed on the ground just outside his door. Jo was sure he heard the slight thud. Or might this be his fancy, a product of his ragged nerves? Then the steps

THE GIFT MAKER

resumed their even progress down the further six flights of stairs. He heard the street door open with a creak (it needed oil), then close with a hollow click. It must be him, thought Jo. Daumen. Leaving, just as Thomas said he would.

Jo scrabbled out of bed. It was cold, and he quickly wrapped a blanket around his near-naked body. By the window, shivering, gazing down some eighty feet at the rain-slick road, he watched, as the silhouette of a large man wearing a long dark coat and a hat pulled low over his face, and carrying a small suitcase, crossed the road and entered a darkened alley between *Kreutzfeld* the bakers and *Manny's* shoe-repairs. The footsteps faded into the night. Gone.

Jo sighed, blew out the candle then climbed wearily back into his bed. He turned to the wall and yawned. Sleep would surely come now. Tomorrow he would be re-covered again, his shell of logic newly reformed. To be once more the brilliant, yet emotionally stale and deracinated, student of thought. The topsoil of his intellect was dangerously far from being enriched by the sun and rain of feeling. His option to make himself a stranger to his history, to his heart, leached away any essential joy for living, and the struggle to present himself to the world as this barely believable shell, would certainly with time grow more despairing, more deadening.

But wait. What of the object deposited outside his door? If it indeed existed. It was surely safe to retrieve it now, with Daumen having vacated. He got up once more and groped around for a dressing gown and his moccasin slippers.

Jo dragged the chest of drawers back to its usual position. He opened the door a crack, and peered out. There it lay on the mat, after all. He reached down and snatched it up, closing the door with his free hand. He brought the object to his desk and turned on the desk lamp. There it sat: a box, a black box, the sides smooth with a faint shimmering gloss, and made of a material that Jo did not recognise. Not wood, not metal, something other. It was slightly bigger than a watch box, but smaller than a box that may contain a single book. He noticed nothing on any of the sides, except that when he turned it over, he saw, printed in neat silver letters, a series of numbers, separated by dots. It must mean something, thought Jo, remembering Thomas's box with his date of birth written on the underside. And then he brought his palm smartly to his head and exclaimed, 'Of course, how stupid of me. It is a date. *Today's* date!'

'This is Daumen's little parting gift,' thought the young philosopher. 'Probably some arcane voodoo charm, a rabbit's foot, a chicken's head, or some such. The atavistic mind is so predictable.' He reached out to unfasten the little black clasp at the front, which would no doubt free the lid. But something stopped him. A faded voice in his head said, yes. It was his father's voice. Then a sibilant whispering came over the top of this repeating yes, drowning it out. Jo could not make out the words. They sounded like some lost ancient tongue, guttural in places, mellifluous and mellow in others. The whispering was intense and the intention was to cajole, to seduce. It told him in words of no language to throw the thing from the window, to dash it to pieces on the pavement below.

As if in a trance, Jo reached out to the tiny clasp and undid it. He then lifted the lid of the box, slowly, holding his breath. A lilting bell-like music began from some mechanism within. Jo did not quite recognise the tune, but the flavour and origin of the music was unmistakable. It was of his mother's island homeland. Indeed, did he not remember, when he was no more than four or five years old, her humming such melodies under her breath as she cleaned the few silver ornaments the family owned, or pegged

THE GIFT MAKER

washing on the saggy clothesline that ran the length of their back yard?

Jo drifted off with the melody that suffused him now. It made the thing in the box temporarily bearable. He could not take his eyes off it as it contracted and expanded, as it palpitated. The colour was different to how Jo would have imagined. Less red. The tissue was wan, uncharged with vitality, as if it had already stopped beating. It was bloodless and unconnected. But still it pulsed, bravely, absurdly.

He reached out to touch what he instinctively knew was his mother's heart. He caressed it so that his fingers might breathe the life back.

twenty

I SHOULD NOT have done it. This private work. Unpaid overtime. Yet old feeling dies hard. And I am neither of smokeless fire nor of earth. I was once of blood and flesh, bone, and the weakness of our kind. I was a baby dandled by a mother's hand. I know Johann's loss is a world he has attempted to slough off. The facsimile of her organ may bring him peace or it may bring him madness. Albeit there is a strange peace to be found in certain madnesses.

Reynard will not be pleased. I fear he knows already. He will whisper me to an uncommon agony. I am no perfect slave, so what must he expect? The seduction is never permanent. And in recognition of that fact lies his bitterness, his lost song.

These dark wet streets. I might at any moment fall through them, back to that ice-encrusted world. It isn't fire we fear beyond this life, it is the coldness of death. It is the "ghost in the weed garden". Eternal lovelessness.

I remember a particular fire, many years ago. And a young girl's screams behind a bolted door, too high for her to reach. Little more than a babe she was, and how my heart was seared that night, and with what disgust I spat into the faces of those who held me back, at their lie that it was too late to save her. And when my

                                                    THE GIFT MAKER

heart died before my body, that body and its hands, untrammelled by mere conscience, were capable of anything. I sought vengeance on the firestarters. A singular vengeance. And the quarts of blood I spilled cried for more, and so the pact, the contract with Him, was sealed.

I am to meet a man named Maier. His shall be the third car along from the statue of St Nemolka, another bloodthirsty saint that history has washed clean. I will know the vehicle by the sulphur stench that is never completely dispelled. This one light case, this overcoat, the wine stain at my lips. People take me for a commercial traveller or a wolf of the steppe. Some people other people just leave alone. And that is what I need to do my work. His work. Until the end time. Then a new game begins. The evaporation of my pattern. Poor Daumen, poor monster I, a rather average fellow with a terrible past, caught up in a cosmic drama of another's making. Ah, self pity, a virtue most misunderstood, for without self-pity how may we pity another? These makers, the poets included, you have to watch them, you know. In order to make, how much must they first destroy?

I feel the cold here also. Lights in high windows. Families and companionship, and that essential sustaining myth called love. The comfortable chair. A warming drink. Soft embracing flesh, and eyes bright in the dark. It will never be mine again. The comforting of a child. Oh, a child.

There is a dead dog in the gutter over there. Its body is bloating and maggot-ridden, and no one has cleared it or given it burial.

Things are working themselves out just as he wishes. This breakdown is slow and sure. The gentle collapse, the boiling frog. So many dead eyes have I seen among the multitude. So many won to him without a whisper, or stir of his long hand. How he enters the scene as a man of peace in his perfectly-pressed white clothes.

The green-eyed girl is becalmed. She does not know tomorrow from yesterday. Time bends. How Monsieur Reynard directs the show, and so many not knowing or caring. They believe themselves to have agency, yet that was compromised, then capitulated, aeons ago. I see her in the lake cottage, staring out the window at the falling flakes. The old couple fussing and bickering in the kitchen below, needing her to be their loss regained.

I am fond of a turn of phrase. Since I can no longer act from my own will, language has become a plaything to distract me from the ever-present disgust for what I must be. Ragged claws would have been preferable.

The boy-man, the inveterate guitar strummer, is theatre bound, to that place of darkness and light, painted faces, painted lives, the unctuous gesture, the obsequious applause. For the price of the ticket he will meet with the unfathomable. The twinkling lights and melange of music draw him mothlike. He seeks union, the definite action that would actualise, make him real to himself for the first time. And in this lies mortal and immortal danger. I wish him well, though I baited his trap. Yet this deed was against my better nature, wheresoever that may be lost.

I see Maier's vehicle. Behind the darkened windows a smoky red glow can be observed by those with the right eyes. I could turn back, turn away now, but where might I go? I have no room in this aching world other than which my temporary lord may bestow. I knew these streets when they were marshland, when men on white horses galloped into a grove of silver trees, and the beast was cornered.

The window slides down electronically, an inch or two. His underlings have all the latest gadgets.

'You're late,' he says. I get the full stench in the face, and try not to cover my nose. These beings are touchy.

THE GIFT MAKER

'But we have eternity, do we not?' I tell him.

'That's not a word I care for,' he says. And the rear door opens like timeless temptation. The red pulsing glow is more intense and spills out onto the wet pavement.

'Get in,' he hisses. 'What are you waiting for? Calvary?'

I throw my case inside and follow it. There is wine here and the vestiges of acrid smoke. He is generous with refreshments. I drink to all those whom I have harmed in my life, and in this death.

We move from the kerb. We move.

twenty-one

'I'D LIKE TO take a walk to the lake.'

There was a significant pause, and the young woman thought to repeat herself, when the man opposite her answered.

'I'm not sure that's wise,' said Aldo. 'There are some deep drifts along the road. Well, it's not a road at all. You can see from the window.' He yawned expansively. 'Perhaps it might be best if you wait until the worst of it clears.' Aldo spoke in a very slow and dull voice, without animation, as if his mind were far away. To Liselotte he looked smaller today, slumped against the lumpy cushions, his cheeks and mouth sagged.

'You could go with her, at least a little way, a few steps. Fresh air is good for convalescents,' interjected Gerda. 'Not too much, though.' Then her lips tightened as if she had spoken out of turn. She smiled, falsely, and tipped her head on one side. 'Although, my dear, are you sure you feel strong enough? I still think you're very pale, and you could do with putting on a bit more weight. There'll be plenty of time for gallivanting once you're well.'

It was mid-morning. Liselotte sat in an armchair across from the couple. They sat on the brown settee in the small sitting room of the cottage, which was separated from the kitchen by a waxy

THE GIFT MAKER

plastic curtain. The curtain was white with red mushroom shapes patterning it.

Aldo was sipping from a mug of coffee and his wife was knitting a green shawl. The needles clicked as the clock on the mantelpiece ticked. Outside, the snow had stopped and the sky was a pale, even blue. Liselotte had seen it earlier that day from the bedroom window and longed to be under it. A fire crackled half-heartedly in the grate. The room had dark-coloured furniture, mostly well worn and mended in places. In a corner cupboard was a selection of ornaments. These included a crystal vase, a hunting dog with sad eyes, and a white porcelain cherub holding grapes just out of reach of a goose that craned its neck to get at them. Liselotte had studied these objects numerous times.

There was a painting in a tarnished gilt frame hung behind where the couple were sat: it showed a powerful-looking brown horse looking over a gate. Three trees stood at intervals in the background of the field. The eyes stared into you with an expression that Liselotte considered strangely human, but what they expressed she could not decide. *Doubt* was the word that had initially come to mind. They were not horse's eyes, that much was certain. As she looked at them now, considering how to respond to the couple's objections to what to her seemed a desire for basic freedom, the eyes appeared to be telling her to *trust*. But trust whom? Herself? Or the old couple who had, after all, saved her life? At least that is what they had told her had occurred. She had no independent knowledge of their account. She had no independent knowledge of anything about her past.

Liselotte scratched at her temple. Avoiding their eyes, she said in a quiet voice: 'How long have I been here?' And without waiting for them to respond, she continued: 'I know you say I look pale but I don't feel like a convalescent. I sense I'm somehow being kept from something. Sorry, I don't mean to offend you, as I know you've been so kind. I owe you so much. My life…as you, as you have told me. But you do truly want to help me return to my family and friends, don't you?' She paused. 'Whoever and wherever they may be.'

Aldo drank his coffee, picked at a loose thread in his jumper. Gerda put her knitting down on a red pouffe by the side of the settee. She looked at Liselotte directly and said, with a frank expression: 'My child, perhaps you might need a little lie down. You took such an awful bump to your head. The more you can rest, you see, the more your memory will return. It happened to an uncle of mine, oh, before Frommel's time.' She nudged her husband, who was gazing into the middle distance, seemingly oblivious to all that was being said. 'Isn't that the case?' she demanded of him. 'Aldo! Wake up! You've drifted off again.'

Aldo came to with a start, and shook his head as if shocked to find himself in the room. Some coffee had spilled onto the fur rug at his feet. 'Damn! Yes, of course. Whatever you think,' he said, to no one in particular. Then he sat back further into the settee.

Gerda lowered her voice, absurdly, as if this would prevent Aldo from hearing: 'The doctor said it is a neuro…nairo… logic…oh, something to do with the brain. A chemical in the brain, he said. But will he take his tablets, the old donkey? Men need a bit of bullying to make them take care of themselves. You'll find that out when you meet the one for you. You have to be firm with them.' She stroked the back of Aldo's head. He shrugged her off. 'So obstinate.' Gerda sighed, closing her eyes, then grinned sadly.

Liselotte was wise to Gerda's technique of deflection. 'How long have I been here, Gerda?' she said, in the sort of polite tone that unmistakably covers building annoyance.

'Not very long. Not very long at all, my child. My uncle took several months to convalesce, and he's not right even now, and that was years ago.' She looked tense, then added: 'I'm sure you will make a full recovery, though, a bright and happy girl like you. Uncle Hansi was the morose type. Don't know how his wife copes, I really don't. Why, my child, he makes one cup of tea after the other, without bothering to drink any of them. All over the house they are, cups of tea in every room, up to a dozen...'

'Please!' said Liselotte, in a harsher tone and more loudly than she had intended. 'I am not your child.' Aldo looked up in surprise. He placed the mug down slowly on a side table and rose to standing. Liselotte made a flapping gesture with her hands, and said, quickly and nervously, 'I'm sorry...please forgive me.' Tears welled in her eyes. 'I know how you both have suffered over Gisela. I didn't mean to be ungrateful or unkind. Or to hurt you, not for anything.' Her thoughts raced. She wondered if Aldo might strike her or lunge for her throat. Then, just as quickly, she realised that this was more than unlikely. He was not that sort of man.

Aldo edged around his wife and disappeared through the wax curtain into the kitchen.

Gerda's face had changed. Gone was the motherly softness. Her eyes were piercing and cold. Her mouth was set rigid. 'You are free to leave at any time. We are not keeping you prisoner, if that is what you think.'

'But where are my clothes? And why aren't you helping me get back to the person I was? I can't stay here forever. I'm not your daughter.'

'Nobody asked you to. And my daughter is irreplaceable. Do you understand that? You think an awful lot of yourself to assume you could take her place.'

Liselotte knew things were getting out of control. She thought frantically for a way to calm matters. 'I want to help find her if I can. Perhaps there's something I could do. Talk to her?'

'Pah!' scoffed the older woman. 'As for your clothes, they were covered in blood. Aldo burned them.'

'Did I not have any papers? Or a case…wait. Wait, I remember something. I remember clutching something to me. Where was I?'

'Don't ask me. I'm just a silly old woman who takes in strange young girls and nurses them back to health. What would I know?'

'Ivory colour. A precious thing. My life, it seemed like. I hugged my life to me. But where is it?'

'You were chattering all sorts of nonsense when we first brought you in. You had a fever…it was the delirium. We didn't take any notice. Why should we?'

'No notice? Don't you realise, you ignorant woman, that the chattering as you call it could hold some clue to who I am? Are you that stupid?'

Gerda stood with inordinate speed. 'This is my house! *My* house. And you will not talk to me like that again. Do you hear me? Or, so help me, I will throw you out by your hair into the snow.'

'Please, Gerda. Oh, this is all going wrong. I am so grateful.'

'It looks like it. As much as she was. Although she was turned into something else by that whispering creature. That butter-wouldn't-melt flatterer. I can't harden my heart to her. Never will I. But you? I imagine your mother is glad to be shot of you. You grizzling little madam. Who do you think you are?'

'No one,' said Liselotte, quietly.

Gerda, her fists clenched, appeared to want to spit at the girl. Her face had reddened, and in contrast to her husband she appeared larger than usual, her forearms tensed and muscular. But instead of spitting or attacking Liselotte she turned on her heel and stormed off through the kitchen curtain.

Liselotte sat there, shaking. She longed now for the dull peace that had been her daily round in the couple's cottage. Why had she ruined it all? Her memory would have come back in time, surely. Why precipitate this when she was in such a weak position, knowing no one else who might help her? Not knowing even who or where she was. No money. No identity. No grip on life.

Voices came low and with rapid intensity from the kitchen. The words *she* and *enough* and *spiteful* came through clearly. Liselotte stood and made a step towards the voices. She wondered if they might murder her. Would Aldo whip back the curtain and stand there with his faraway eyes, a hatchet in his hand, with Gerda at his back prompting him to *do it, do it*? No, impossible, thought Liselotte. Yet she knew she must find some way to placate them.

I will pay my way here with work until I have enough for my fare, she thought. But a fare to which town? She pushed the confusion aside. Smoothing down her hair, as if to make herself more presentable, she moved towards the dividing curtain. Just then it was pulled aside and Aldo stepped through. Liselotte gasped and withdrew further back into the room. His face was more sad than angry, which relieved the girl. In his hand was a brown envelope.

'She wanted to throw you out with nothing. Not even the clothes on your back. Always had a temper, did Gerda. It takes a good while to blow, but when it does. And once you've hurt her, she doesn't forget.' He looked down at the envelope then back at the trembling Liselotte. He seemed to be back to his old calm and measured self.

'Please let me speak with her.' Liselotte took an uncertain step towards Aldo. His raised hand brought her to a sharp halt.

'Too late, I'm afraid. We didn't want this. Our thoughts were only to help you.'

'I know that. I know. Aldo, I can work for my keep. I'll do anything you and Gerda ask of me. I'll be your servant. I just need to earn a little money to buy some clothes of my own. How will I survive or get back to wherever home is without money? Without a good winter coat and shoes? Please, I beg you, Aldo.'

The man bit his lip. 'We are not beasts, young lady. My wife is weeping her heart out in there.' He gestured behind him. 'She would not wish you to see.'

'Yes, I understand, about poor Gisela, she told me the whole story.'

'Not just her. Your being here both lessened and increased our loss, our pain. You could never replace her, as my wife told you. She was ours. Soft brown eyes she had, and in summer her face was a pattern of freckles. All that's gone. But in odd moments we could pretend. And in those clothes…and your hair done so.'

'You burned my clothes.'

'You know why.'

'Yes – but I wasn't cut anywhere, was I?'

'There was blood on your clothes, miss.'

'Not mine, not mine.'

Aldo held out the envelope. 'This should be enough for a one-way ticket to most places. Provided you travel third-class. We're not wealthy, as you can tell. And neither are we heartless.'

'I realise that, Aldo. I owe you and your wife everything. Please, let me speak with her.'

'Our mind is one. You can keep the clothes you have on. We have no use for them. At the back of…our daughter's wardrobe you'll find a coat, dark green. Her best coat it was, when she knew when good was good enough. There'll be gloves in the pockets. She always left them there.'

'No. Wait. I can't go out there alone.'

'You were very keen earlier. Now you have your wish. You'll find her winter boots under the bed. If they pinch, be thankful you have boots at all.'

'I have no food. I don't know where the town or the station is.' Liselotte reached out to take the envelope. She held it to her breast as if in defence.

'Gerda will send you off with something. But she doesn't want to see your face again. I'll give you directions at the door.'

A single, fat tear rolled down the young woman's face. She did not brush it away. It fell onto the front of her grey dress, and soaked in. She was tempted to look in the envelope, but knew this would appear mercenary. The couple were, after all, if not poor, then living without any trace of luxury.

Aldo's face softened and a muscle twitched below his eye. For a moment Liselotte thought he might relent, embrace her even, implore that she stay. He turned his head to the side and down. 'You have until the hour strikes. No point in dragging it out.'

Liselotte gathered herself and walked mutely to the door that led to the passage-way and the stairs to her – no – *Gisela's* bedroom. She felt Aldo's pale-blue eyes on her back as she left that sitting room for the last time.

twenty-two

FROM A DISTANCE she could not see what they were. They were moving around a stunted tree that was still in full leaf. She pulled the collar of the dark-green coat closer around her exposed neck and lumbered on, over the densely-packed snow, not always avoiding the drifts and deeper patches that Aldo had warned her of. Her toes were chilled in Gisela's boots, which fit her surprisingly well. Tracks of birds and animals dotted the path that was barely a path.

As she drew closer, one hand thrust deep in her pocket, the other clutching the small linen bag containing the sandwiches and cake that Gerda had provided for her, she saw that the moving objects were ducks, some thirty or forty of them. Some had blue-green head feathers, others were mostly mottled white and brown but with dashes of purple under their wings. The crisp blue light caught their feathers' iridescence as they changed position. Their bright orange feet were unreal against the pure white of the ground. The ducks pecked at the area surrounding the stunted tree. At her approach, several of the ducks ambled away, and some took short hopping flights to perceived safety.

At the base of the tree, and scattered further about, were apples lying on the snow. Small apples, some with a rosy hue covering

one side. These were being pecked at by the ducks, who sought to break them into more manageable and bite-size pieces. They were largely failing in this endeavour. Liselotte laughed. She had never imagined ducks would, or could, eat apples. Perhaps in winter any food must do. Some carried off whole apples in their beaks, harassed by noisy competitors who lunged at the tail feathers of the retreating bearers of green treasure.

The tree was still thick with as yet unfallen fruit. Thick clusters of apples hung heavy from the ends of branches. Above her, like a black rag, a crow passed and flew towards the couple's cottage, where a thin line of smoke snaked from the chimney. Would she at any moment see Aldo striding out along the path to tell her that all was mended, that Gerda had once more softened her heart, and Liselotte was welcome again to the plain but comfortable room, to her small fire with the waving paper flames, the sturdy bed and rough patchwork quilt, and to Gisela's book-trove of absurd romance and whimsy? No. No one came along the white road.

Liselotte placed the bag on the ground. Then she remembered the small penknife she had found in Gisela's coat pocket when taking out one of the gloves. She had imagined the young girl keeping this cherished item to remind her of her father, years before, instructing her in the craft of whittling. A symbol of their unimpeachable closeness that not even Gerda could encroach upon.

She became aware of a duck, inches from her feet, looking up at her, its black beady eyes glinting in the sun. Then she noticed its broken beak. Along one side, the beak was misshapen and jagged. A birth defect or the result of some animal attack, considered Liselotte. The bird looked up, the soul of patience. The girl plucked an apple from the tree, took out the small knife and cut several pieces from the apple, which fell to her feet to be taken up and swallowed by the duck with a repeated undulating movement of its neck. The other ducks kept their distance.

Far-off, there came the hollow crack of what sounded like a shotgun. As one, the ducks took flight. No one could be seen in this world of white. A few hundred yards away began the stands of dark fir trees that edged and mostly obscured the lake. The ducks crested the trees and flew out of sight, yet their calls could still be heard for a time, growing smaller in the crystalline air. The duck with the damaged beak had remained near the girl's feet, looking up like a well-trained dog begging its mistress for a scrap.

Liselotte bent down and reached out to touch the feathers on its back. The duck moved away, yet only just out of reach. 'What shall I call you, then?' said Liselotte.

The duck blinked. It made high-pitched squeaks that Liselotte took to mean satisfaction, comfort. It shivered its feathers and tested its wings, then folded them neatly back. 'We're alone out here,' she said. She wanted to cry but no tears would come. 'And here am I, a lost girl talking to a duck. My only companion in the snow.'

Aldo had advised her to bear right on the path that ran between the lake and the trees, to pass the disused boat-house. She would then come to a ruined chapel, he said, and if she took the turning there that headed uphill and through a mixed wood of ancient trees, where ferns grew thick, here the path would broaden to a woodland ride. At the end of this ride she would find the main track to Hoffnung, which encircled much of the lake. It was either this or swim across, he said. In Hoffnung she might catch a local train that would take her to a larger town. Which town she chose was, of course, her free choice, Aldo had added, unnecessarily.

The duck stopped eating the pieces of apple and began waddling away, then, without warning, it flapped vigorously and took off. Liselotte watched it until it was a speck in the sky, then the speck disappeared over the trees, to land on the lake and join its kind, she supposed.

Again came a hollow crack across the undulating fields of white. A gunshot? But from where? Liselotte strained her eyes but saw no figure, no movement, except for small sudden gusts of wind blowing up the loose snow in eddying swirls that fell back as if dropped from an invisible hand. Before leaving the tree, she stretched up to a cluster of fruit above her head and pulled away a single apple. Two leaves were still attached to its stalk. This was a larger apple than most of the others, and perhaps this was why Liselotte chose it. Or perhaps it was for another reason: the delicate rose blush on the side that had faced the sun. In any case, it seemed to her perfect, and just as an apple should be. She rubbed it against her coat and placed it in her pocket, next to the penknife. 'For luck,' she told herself.

By the time she reached the fir-trees, Liselotte was hungry from her efforts. Her recent sedentary lifestyle had made her muscles weak and easily tired. She brushed the snow from a fallen trunk before sitting on it and from the linen bag she took out one of the sandwiches Gerda had made for her. It was wrapped in waxy brown paper and tied with a length of white cotton. Liselotte smelled it. Cheese. She unwrapped it and ate half. The butter had been spread thickly on the rye bread, which was Gerda's habit, and the cheese was strong-tasting and crumbly. Liselotte shook the crumbs from her coat and continued on her way. She was thirsty now and wondered if she might drink from the lake.

As she was making her way through the trees towards the water, something small and hard thudded against her back. She whirled around, dropping her bag to the floor. No one was there. She felt the back of her coat, expecting blood, and instead fingered the residue of a snowball.

She stood still, breathing heavily. Mouth dry with fear. Her eyes darted about. She reached inside her pocket for the penknife, took it out and opened the small blade.

'That isn't funny,' she called out, and her voice rang around the silent trees. She slowly turned on the spot, surveying every angle, determined not to be taken be surprise. She caught a glimpse of the lake between two snow-laden gorse bushes.

'Who are you?' she shouted. There was no full echo, yet her voice carried a slight reverberation, causing her to wonder if the voice was coming back to her from another. 'I don't mind if it's a game. I don't mind.'

Thud! Again she was hit from behind by a tightly compacted ball of snow, this time on the top of her left boot. 'Stop it!' she shouted. 'Isn't it enough that I'm all alone in the cold world and don't know where my home is? Why are you tormenting me like this?' She sank to her knees and her warm tears fell, then chilled on her face. She gripped the penknife tightly but covered her eyes with her other hand, half not caring what might happen next, or needing it to happen at once and be over with.

'Hello,' said a low breathy voice behind her. She did not turn but expected a great blow to fall upon her, and then darkness. She curled into a ball and wrapped both hands around the back of her head in a pointless gesture of defence. 'Do it now,' she said. 'I know you have the gun. Get it over with. Finish me.'

Instead of a bullet smashing through her skull, the sound of which she would never hear, or a vicious stroke from a club or an axe, she became aware of a small soft hand lightly stroking her hair. She straightened up and twisted around on her knees. It was Mabe, smiling down at her, his curly black hair lightly dusted with snow. He wore a brown suede coat somewhat too large for him, that fell to below his knees. It was trimmed with

THE GIFT MAKER

wool at the collar and cuffs. His smile was knowing, sly, yet not unkind.

'Let me help you up,' he said, in a lilting accent, very different from the old couple's. He had a self-assurance and stillness unlike most fifteen-year-olds. Liselotte had vague impressions of having met youths Mabe's age, but who and what they had been to her she could not tell. She knew also that she must once have been a fifteen-year-old herself, and had she met this boy then, she might have fallen for his dark eyes and olive skin. She took his ungloved hand and stood. She was somewhat taller than him, yet his self-contained, effortless way of being made him appear sturdier than he was.

She rubbed her face. 'You gave me such a fright, Mabe. Do you know I've been thrown out of the cottage? I'm on my way to Hoffnung.'

'Yes, I heard my father and Aldo gossiping about it. Drunk they both were, as usual.'

This surprised Liselotte as she had never seen Gerda's husband drunk. Perhaps that was why he sometimes stayed out overnight.

'Aldo wanted you to stay,' Mabe continued, 'but his life wouldn't have been worth living had he crossed his wife.' He laughed, quietly. 'I will never get married. I'm going to stay free.'

'Mabe, why do you pretend not to be able to speak, and yet you speak to me?'

The boy scratched under his chin. 'If you don't speak you find out more. They treat you like you're invisible. It can be very useful. Most people, especially my father, only want to talk talk talk. That's why they never understand anything. Their heads are too crowded with their own words.'

'And what about school?'

'Oh, I'm finished with all that.' He made a gesture of derision. 'I was doing quite well. One or two idiots thought they could bully me, but I changed their minds.'

'When did it start, then? The not speaking.'

Mabe gave a little laugh. He was enjoying sharing his secret with the attractive young woman. 'There's a beech tree near my father's place. I was about five or six, but I could climb like a monkey. Still can, but I don't bother. Anyhow, I thought that if I could get to the topmost branches I could see the whole of the world, and tell everyone about it. My mother was still alive then.' His face clouded briefly, then the darting light came back into his eyes as he continued. 'I was almost there. I still remember that slender branch I stood on. I took a chance, you see. Only about a third of the way up I was, but determined. I could see my route ahead, young as I was. My hand was an inch away from grabbing the branch I needed when the one below my feet gave way. Crunch!' He threw back his head and laughed almost soundlessly.

'I woke up on the sofa. All these faces gawping down at me. "Can you hear us? Are you okay?" they kept asking. I had an awful headache, so instead of saying "yes", I just nodded. So it stuck. I was the boy who had lost his voice. They took me to two doctors. Easily fooled they are, more easily fooled than any of them.' He laughed again.

Liselotte shook her head in wonder. 'You're a very unusual boy, aren't you?'

Mabe's brow furrowed. 'Not a boy.'

'All right, don't get angry, I can see how proud you are. Why did you tell me to be careful, Mabe? That day in Aldo and Gerda's cottage. And you put your finger in front of your lips as a messsage, didn't you? I saw you from the window.'

A gun shot, nearer this time, made them both jump. Liselotte instinctively moved to the boy and held him. His face had reddened

 THE GIFT MAKER

when they stepped apart. 'Who is that shooting?' Liselotte said.

'Could be Escher, or old Jenz. After rabbits, probably. Or a deer.'

'They wouldn't make a mistake and fire at us would they?'

'Of course not,' said Mabe. 'Unless you think our ears are too big.' He laughed at his own joke. He was still a boy, despite his protestations and the overtly manly way he stood. 'I spoke to you because I knew you were different. I'd heard how the old couple had found you, and that you had lost your memory. You wouldn't be one of the small-minded ones from this backwater. I've longed for someone to share my secret with. It's no fun just knowing it myself, and everyone takes it for granted now. I also knew from hearing Aldo chatter with my old man that Gerda saw you as a replacement for her daughter. They did want to keep you, like some pet. Especially her. I thought that was wrong. You have your own life somewhere, your own family.'

'I do, Mabe. But the harder I think the more cloudy it is. I'm walking on a carpet made of mist. I could be anyone from any time. My head is full of half-written stories and I could choose to enter any one of them. It sounds like freedom, like your pretending to be dumb, but it's terrible really. It's unbearable.'

Mabe looked down at the ground. He appeared to be lost in thought. Then he looked at Liselotte very directly. 'I'll help you get to Hoffnung. It can be easy to lose your way, especially in this snow. And….well, I'll go with you. Away from here. I can help you find out who you are. A young woman shouldn't be travelling alone. I will protect you,' he said, chest puffed out somewhat, a slightly absurd look of what he considered honour on his handsome young face.

There came a sudden loud rustling from the undergrowth about one-hundred feet ahead of them. They looked at each other, then back at the thick bushes.

It came tearing out at them, a dark shape the size of a very large dog, moving at a terrible speed, its thick short legs pounding over the snow. A great screeching came from the beast, its long tusks lowered as it charged.

'Run!' said Mabe, pushing Liselotte roughly. She stumbled off until she reached a tree, then looked back from behind it. The boar had stopped several feet from the boy. It was intermittently panting, growling, and screeching. Waves of mist came from its hidden dark mouth.

Liselotte could see a large stick several feet behind the boy, poking out of the snow. 'Mabe, the stick behind you!' she called.

The boy turned at her call then, realising, made a dash for the stick. At that moment the boar rushed forward, splashing up the powdered snow in its wake. It moved with such animal ferocity and reached the boy just as his hand was about to touch the intended weapon.

'Mabe!' screamed Liselotte. And the boy's name rang around the grove of trees. The boy yelped as a tusk pierced his lower leg. He fell, scrabbling wildly for the half-buried branch that might save his life, but the beast was now over him, two hundred and fifty pounds of wild aggression pinning him to the cold ground, goring his back, ripping through his coat, then his skin and flesh and muscle, exposing young bone. Dislodging and splintering that bone. Terrible sounds came from the boy. Liselotte was transfixed as the animal almost covered its victim, now seeming even larger than it had at first, great rasping squeals and bellows pouring from its maddened throat. The boar was biting at the back of the helpless boy's neck, his arms paddled uselessly in the air, like some ineffectual swimming stroke. His feet kicked out in the snow.

Liselotte was too terror-struck to intervene, and after all, what could she do? Her eyes searched around for any potential weapon.

THE GIFT MAKER

She saw none. The small pocket knife would barely pierce the animal's thick hide.

The boar continued to tear and rip at the prostrate youth, to attack his exposed parts from different angles. It gouged at his sides, thighs, buttocks, his back, and the back of his head and neck. The boy's cries grew weaker, became more like the seemingly automatic moans of one whose body has gone into deep shock due to excessive pain. The nerve-systems of his body were shutting down in order to protect him from overwhelming agony. Bright blood splashed onto the pristine snow, in spatters, in arcing dots, and now in great gouts. Blood dripped from the mouth and the tusks of the boar.

Sometimes the animal made sounds like a domestic pig, almost a contented snuffling and grunting as it struck at and moved over the twitching body, and the scene was rendered bizarrely and hideously comic by this behaviour. Then deeper guttural roars punctuated a renewed attack, and a metallic rasping came, as if the throat of the beast were some infernal mechanism.

Liselotte peered from behind the tree, biting her hand, unable to tear her eyes from the butchery before her. 'Oh Mabe, Mabe...' she intoned.

The boar stopped moving, its front legs rested on the boy's still shoulders. It appeared to be sniffing the air. Its head jerked around in Liselotte's direction. She turned side-on and made herself as small as possible behind the tree. Could its button-black eyes perceive her trembling hands? Might it hear her soft sobbing? Would its quivering damp nostrils smell her sweat, her fear? The nearest branch was ten feet beyond her reach. She knew she could not outrun the animal. She had a blurred memory of being told to play dead if a certain animal attacks you. It would be the only way you could survive. You might be injured, but the animal would not kill you. Who had told her that, and why, she could not fathom.

She doubted that such a strategy would dissuade this particular beast from its rampant blood lust.

The boar stepped off and away from the body. It nosed and rooted in the bag containing the remaining food Gerda had packed, which Liselotte had dropped in her flight to temporary safety. It grunted contentedly as it chomped at the bread and cheese and cake, turning it into a coagulated pap. Crumbs stuck to the blood-soaked bristles around its mouth.

'Now is my chance,' Liselotte thought, she backed away as quietly as she could and jumped behind a further tree, just as the boar looked up from its meal. Mabe was not moving. Around his body was a map of red. Again the boar scented the air. It gave a grumble from deep in its throat. Liselotte's head was poking out an inch to the side of the tree. She turned her head around but the trees went on and on at regular intervals and there was surely no place to hide. The animal would track her and run her down, then tear her to pieces. She longed to go to Mabe, to tend his wounds. Perhaps he was still alive and playing dead, as she had considered doing herself.

If she continued backing away from the boar, she would be departing from the route Aldo had given her. The boar picked up the stained bag in its mouth and tossed it aside. Then it froze, and looked directly at Liselotte. Their eyes had met. This was the beginning of the end, thought the girl.

The beast turned in the opposite direction as if walking away. Then it suddenly rotated as if a bolt of electricity had passed through it. It charged. Liselotte gripped at the bark of the pine. Fear crawled over her scalp and down her arms. Her legs went to water but still she held onto the tree as to a saviour.

She heard it pounding over the snow. She heard its searing scream of attack. Any second now, she thought. Any moment. Her eyes were nailed shut, face screwed up in anticipation.

THE GIFT MAKER

A gunshot.

Nearby. The third that day. The shot echoed twice. Then the briefest moment of silence, followed by a long, high-pitched squeal, which died abruptly. Liselotte opened her eyes. The animal was less than ten feet from the tree she cowered behind. It lay, still and massive on the snow, like a carcass awaiting a butcher. Like Mabe, it did not move.

twenty-three

THOMAS RUDER ENTERED Sacker Street. The pavements were thronged. People of all ages buffeted him and each other. No one apologised. They barely seemed to notice the bewildered student who stumbled along, first this way then the other, scanning the brightly-lit shops, the steaming food-stalls and glittering restaurants, searching for the theatre, searching for *The Sheol*.

Many in the street were finely dressed, the men in dark suits, hair bouffanted and pomaded, a look of supercilious empty pleasure on their similar bland faces. The women teetered along, high-heels clacking along the smooth pavements, their pastel-shaded evening dresses revealing copious and overflowing flesh. The women seemed generally older than the men, and their make-up was caked over lined faces in a parody of the first flush of youth. Limousines, invariably black or midnight blue, with blacked-out windows, cruised languidly along the wide street.

The music was a cacophony. Pounding jungle drums throbbed from red-lit doorways, leading to dark descending steps. On a wider part of the pavement, a four-piece jazz band were hitting their stride. The players, in dishevelled and torn tuxedos, all had some facial disfigurement. One, a port-wine stain across his lower face, another's jaw was badly misshapen, and a third, a very elderly man with white whiskers, who blew wildly into a gold saxophone, had a huge bulbous forehead, as if his brain or some other substance within his skull were pressing against it to be released. The fourth, the drummer, was a midget whose every inch of facial skin was covered in warts, some of which were gently bleeding.

Along the pavement, in doorways, or sitting in the road, Thomas passed guitar and banjo-pickers, harmonica players, accordionists and flautists. And there were many singers without instruments: men and women and even some skinny moon-eyed children, who sang, if it might be called that, with no respect for key or modulation, in guttural or simpering languages unknown to Thomas, all with contorted or ecstatic faces, as if in praise of some invisible spirit or beloved. All the performers were in near-rags and some were barefoot. Cups at their feet contained a few coins and cigarette butts, and often a scabby, undernourished dog was tied by a piece of string to a bench or lamp-post near their pitch. The dogs howled in hideous counterpoint to their owners' musical efforts. Fat slinking rats moved casually between and over the feet of passers-by, slipped in and out of the open drains, nibbled at the remnants of food that had been dropped. Thomas viciously kicked one away. It turned and snarled at him, baring razor teeth, then scurried beneath a pile of discarded broken crates.

The general smell was a melange of bitter smoke and burning oil, a blend of raw and frying meat and boiling vegetables, excessively sweet perfume and unwashed bodies. There was an undertone of excrement and half-dried urine. Thomas came across several individuals, both expensively and shabbily dressed, relieving themselves in doorways, and one red-haired girl, no more than twelve or thirteen, hitched up her stained white dress before defecating amply into the gutter.

Hawkers of all varieties, of cloth and silk, of spices and visibly-rotting fruit, of brightly-coloured glass and plastic trinkets (images of dogs, camels, dragons, and identical cameo brooches), and those who were manically frying slabs or slices of meat on outsized griddles, or boiling great steaming pots of noodles or potatoes, shouted out their wares. They leered and desperately tried to catch Thomas's eye. Some attempted to place an arm around him and pull him toward their stall. He shrugged them off with increasing aggression.

'Young man,' cooed a stooping, oily-faced fellow in a stained and frayed shirt, his skinny hand lightly touching Thomas's elbow. 'I can tell you are a gentleman of taste, of refinement. Please do me the honour of stepping into my shop.' He capered around Thomas and lightly pulled at the student's coat.

'I don't want anything. I'm looking for the theatre.'

'Ah, the theatre,' he simpered. 'I was an actor once, you know. It never really leaves you. In the blood.' He assumed a haughty look and straightened to his full height, one hand clutching at his breast, the other outstretched in a gesture of remonstration. '"Thinkest thou I shalt not want salt upon my meat? Am I grown as to a block, a decapod? Gloze not with me, coz. I am none other than thy Lord."' His voice had altered utterly. It boomed massively. He brought the back of his hand slowly and affectedly to his forehead, then suddenly dropped his attitude, and smirked. 'What do you think, eh? A trained voice, young man. A trained voice!'

'Yes...very good. I was transported,' said Thomas, barely concealing his sarcasm, which the man appeared not to register.

'I think you are in want of a tie, sir. I cannot believe you will be admitted to the Sheol without one. Please, come in, sir, come in. We have the finest silk ties, in all the colours that nature bestows.'

THE GIFT MAKER

The thespian-manqué pulled Thomas by his lapel to a narrow doorway behind them. A ragged, yellow-haired boy, no more than seven years old, wearing a knitted grey jumper that was no more than a collection of holes and hanging threads, sat on the stone step. He was sucking on a long red stick in a paper bag, some sweet, Thomas supposed. The salesman grabbed the boy's shock of curly unwashed hair and lifted him by it into standing position. The boy screeched and dropped his sweet onto the slimy paving slabs. 'Get out of it!' shouted the salesman into the boy's ear, making him wince. 'You're ruining my image,' he hissed. 'Go and bother your pox-ridden mother. You'll find her with the other whores. I'll never believe you're mine anyway, you little turd.' The boy's face was bewildered, shutting out the man's snarling spitting mouth as best he could. 'And tell her to make sure she brings *all* her wages home this time,' the salesman bellowed at the boy, before aiming a desultory kick at his retreating backside.

Then Thomas did something that he had never done in his adult life. He did it without mental preparation, without reflection, without fear. It seemed as natural an act as breathing. It felt like the only thing that could be done. He drew his fist back and slammed it as hard as he could into the salesman's face, hitting him full-square on the nose, and sending him crashing back into the open doorway. The salesman stumbled but kept on his feet. His fingers now touched his rapidly swelling nose, that began pumping blood over his shirt and trousers.

'I'll kill you,' said the bleeding man. 'I'll pull your eyes out. I'll eat you alive.' But the man did not move. He spat out the blood that had fallen over his lips.

Without taking his eyes off the man, Thomas backed slowly away and once more joined the swarm of jostling, shouting, self-preening humanity that was Sacker Street. The knuckles of his left hand were reddened and tender to the touch.

Up ahead he could see a dense crowd of people milling around a large white building. Several limousines were parked outside, and heavily-built men in over-elaborate, navy-blue uniforms with golden epaulettes and peaked caps, stood sentinel over them. They wore black gloves and had grim, stone-like wide faces, and they roughly pushed away anyone who got too near to the vehicles. These men looked as though they might all come from the same family.

As he drew closer, Thomas saw, in red neon letters above the entrance to the building, a single word: *Sheol*. Hung below this was a light-bulb-surrounded poster that read: *Reynard I Bliss Proudly Presents: The Statue in the Park*. There was an illustration of a park at dusk, and in the foreground a near silhouette of a statue: a naked woman, standing on a plinth and holding a jug from which water poured into the carved ornamental pond over which she stood. A little way off was another figure: a man, dressed all in white. You could not make out his face. There was a vacancy where his features might have been. He appeared to be approaching the statue. A full, red-tinged moon gazed down at them from a starless sky.

Thomas edged through the crowd, who wore expensive-looking suits and evening dresses. Fur jackets and stoles draped the women's puckered shoulders. Finally, he reached one of the doors.

'Got a ticket?' barked a tall shaven-headed man with a neck somewhat wider than his head.

'I…I want to buy one,' stammered the student.

'The fleapit's further down the street.' The man spoke without looking at Thomas. His eyes continually darted over the mass of people before him, as if expecting imminent hostility. The crowd were sipping from champagne flutes, or puffing on cigarettes in long black holders. They chattered incessantly, in high and almost hysterical voices, but Thomas could not understand their babble. It was not a foreign language as such, rather it was that nothing they said had cohesion. Long strings of words poured from their simpering mouths. They were not in conversation. They talked at and over each other without pause, now and again punctuating their prattle with shrill and whinnying laughter, a mechanical sound utterly devoid of merriment.

'How much is a ticket?' asked Thomas of the man.

'No tickets,' he growled. 'Doss-house down the street.' He jerked his thick thumb in the direction intended.

Through the smoked glass of the door, Thomas caught sight of other theatre-goers inside. He watched their mouths continually moving, forming shapes. Like bad actors, their faces assumed quick-changing masks: over-interest, superciliousness, brittle glee, contempt, disgust, surprise - just like those outside. A woman, pearls at her neck, threw her head back in replication of orgasmic abandonment. A sandy-haired man mouthed words at her, then grinned archly. This set of actions repeated over and over. The words, the cheesy mechanical grin, then her head curving back, exposing her full throat, her pupils losing focus and disappearing, leaving only the whites. Again and again, until Thomas could look no more.

Then came a whispering inside Thomas's head. A velvet voice thrilled through him like ice or a long-awaited kiss. *It is my eater of unripe apples. My other Adam.* A hand was lightly placed on his shoulder. Thomas turned in slow motion, and saw him there. The man all in white. Thomas gazed into the kindest eyes he had ever seen. Eyes that had no distinct colour. Eyes that had witnessed the horrors, the unwritten valour, the boredom and simple love, the sublime beauties of centuries; or so it seemed. Eyes that knew all, and told of what they knew without words.

'I'm sorry, sir,' said the shaven-headed man behind Thomas, his voice now several tones higher than before. 'If I'd have known this gentleman was...'

'No matter,' said the man in white, still holding Thomas's gaze. 'I'm sure we can find a seat somewhere for a soul who has travelled so far.'

'Yes,' said Thomas, automatically.

The sounds of the chattering crowd and the wider street had muted. A cotton-wool sensation enveloped Thomas as he allowed himself to be gently led through the door, now held open for him by the trembling shaven-headed man.

The door was closed and locked behind them. Thomas felt many eyes roving over his face and body, and those of his companion, as they crossed the plush red carpet to the sparkling mirrored bar. As he and his white-suited companion moved, space was effortlessly created for them by the others. A discreet murmur followed their progress, as though from satisfied bees.

'A drink?' said the gentle-eyed man.

'Yes,' said Thomas.

The man in white made a strange gesture, a bizarre twirling movement of his fingers, to the slim slick-haired barman, and in a very short space of time a tall, frosted glass, which looked like it contained a paint-box sunset, was placed before Thomas. The banded and merging colours of the drink bewitched him, they moved like the last evening of history. A loose smile played over his quivering lips.

'Don't be shy,' cajoled the man in white. 'Drink the sky.'

Thomas placed the chilled glass to his mouth, and drank. His reflection in the mirrored squares, beyond the myriad coloured bottles, was piecemeal. A corner of a face here, its replication in the square above, his nose and half a drinking mouth below.

The drink tasted like nothing he had ever tried. It was not so much a liquid but a secret knowledge that poured coolly down his throat. In contrast, his chest became suffused in rose-coloured warmth. His fingers moved of their own accord, were weightless, his feet a hundred yards away, deeply rooted into earth. He was the eternal tree. There were no more problems, only opportunities. There was nothing to fear or yearn for. Living was effortless. A game with no rules. A limitless joy. Why had he not known of this before? Why had his parents, his friends, his teachers not let him into this secret? Why had the world and the truth been kept from him? Surely, yes, they had wanted him to be as miserable, as meagre-souled, as desiccated as they were. Wingless and wishless they existed merely, driven to pointless drudgery and the slave mind. Husks of people, scattered and hollow, how they disgusted him now. No love lived there, among those mud folk, those clay gollums. He laughed into the fractured reflections of himself. There he was: *Thomas*. Finally, whom he had always been. His own creation. A holy jigsaw he might remake, over and over. He had remembered what he had forgotten he had forgotten.

'It is good, no?' said the man in white at his side, nodding slowly.

This is the true father, the original brother, thought Thomas. Here was a man who understood life, saw it for the plaything it was, who laughed in the face of oblivion knowing that oblivion was a lie of the fearful, the coward's excuse, a paper skull, a voodoo mask to cow the ignorant; a man who now reached out to stroke Thomas's face in the tenderest way imaginable. The perfect touch, born of the meeting of smokeless fire and ice, and both remaining themselves.

'We must be quick,' said the man in white. 'The curtain will open soon.'

'I love you,' whispered Thomas. His heart threatened to burst through his chest. It was beyond tears, yet tears fell. 'I love you,' he repeated.

The room was emptying. The murmuring crowd were disappearing through an inner doorway into blackness. A little further off, a band was striking up. The overture. Thomas and his companion now walked towards the doorway and the carpet became a meadow of wild flowers. Thomas looked up and saw three dark-orange suns in the pale-blue air.

And then he was in his red seat. Blackness all around. The invisible orchestra playing the same hypnotic refrain, again and again, gradually fading and fading until there was only the lost low sound of wind on the first waters remaining. The man in white was no longer next to him, yet he was there in essence. Thomas felt his guiding care. The audience were also there, a full-house, to be sure, but Thomas could see not one of them. Out of the absence of light came the emerging redness of the curtain. It grew. The soft velvet folds breathed. And slowly, painfully slowly, like a wound, the curtain began to part.

twenty-four

HE HAD NEVER imagined himself a hitchhiker. Plainly dressed once more, as one who might be mistaken for a factory worker or street cleaner, he stuck out his thumb without conviction, and with intense embarrassment. Occasionally, cars and lorries trundled by on the pot-holed highway stretching endlessly east out of Schwalbenbach. They all ignored his half-hearted gesture. He trudged on, already foot-sore, along the frost-hardened grass verge. Diamonds of ice sparkled in the half-light of early morning. In his canvas rucksack he carried the box containing her heart. The box itself was wrapped in a thick woollen jumper. He must keep it with him and he must keep it warm. It was as though he now carried his mother on his back, as she had once carried him in her womb. The tears had dried on his unshaven face.

Here came another. He stuck out his thumb and waved with his other hand. Miraculously, the truck slowed, brakes squealing. The cab was grey, paint flaking, the name *Lorelei* daubed on the near side in awkward black letters. Through an oblong of clarity in the ice-encrusted windshield, he had seen the thick-set, red-bearded man staring at him blankly as the truck slowed to a halt. The engine turned over peevishly.

Off-white and black faces pushed through the wooden slats of the waggon, their breath hot and steaming, tongues lolled, eyes rolled back and searched their now stationary world. He heard the thudding of their hooves on the bed of the truck, sudden urgent tramplings. There must be at least forty in there, he thought, with barely enough room to stand, let alone lie down. One appeared to be dead, jammed into the corner, its eyes glaring upwards, but no light of life left in them. The smell was pungent, and hot yellow liquid fell in an even thin stream from under the bottom slat of the waggon onto the tarmac to form a steaming puddle. The thing that struck him was that they made no other noise. A few were fully grown but most were lambs. The ones he could see had pale blue numbers marked on their flanks.

The door of the cab was pushed roughly open, probably by a foot. 'What are you waiting for, a red carpet?' The voice was rough-edged, not dissimilar to his father's. The young man moved towards the open door. He gripped the cold metal rail, pulled himself up the three steps, and all but fell into the wide lumpy seat as the truck lurched away.

'Pull that door shut! It's not suntan weather,' the man bellowed over the sound of the gears crunching. The young man leaned out, grabbed the handle and shut the door with a loud thud, as the truck picked up speed.

He became aware of the small, dark, watchful eyes of the driver darting over him, then back to the road.

The driver coughed. 'Where you headed?'

'Grenze,' said the young man with the thinning, prematurely grey hair.

The driver made a sound deep in his chest, then rolled down his window and spat. He remained silent as he carefully overtook a horse-driven cart loaded with sugar beet. The cart driver, wrapped in several blankets, raised his hand, his face obscured by a wide-brimmed hat. A pale sun was rising ahead of them. The sky around it was milky grey. Empty dark red and brown fields, cut by lines of unmelted snow stretched out either side of the road. Crows circled. Narrow side-lanes led to isolated farmhouses.

'Got a name?' said red beard.

'Johann,' said Jo, keeping his heavy eyes fixed on the vanishing road.

'I had a cousin, same name. Gambled his shop away. Wife left with the brats. Tried to shoot himself and ended up shooting his nose off. We called him nosegay after that.' The driver gave a low chuckle. Jo rubbed his hands together and blew into them. Again he felt the driver's eyes appraise him. 'You're no labourer. Hands give it away.'

'Are you going anywhere near Grenze?' said Jo, ignoring the man's comment.

'You're in luck, chief. Going all the way.' Not looking at Jo, he gave a strained smile, and searched deeply in his nose with a dirty forefinger.

Jo hugged the rucksack between his knees. As his eyes drooped, he knew that a weak but regular beating came from within the black box wrapped in the jumper. He felt it inside his own heart. The driver began humming a tune that was familiar. Jo let himself fall into the melody. It reminded him of a warmer climate, of olive trees, a lizard in the dust, whitewashed buildings with red roofs, of goats silhouetted on evening hillsides, of an orange half-sun slowly easing into the dark sea that embraced an island. The images flashed like lost but known photographs behind Jo's almost closed eyelids.

The engine complained as the truck began climbing. As fields gave way to hills, endless stone walls, fallen in places, following the lines of those hills, strands of wool blowing on barbed wire, wind-stunted bare trees. A rusted bucket by the roadside. Knots of sheep by iced-over troughs looked up briefly at the passing cargo. The cargo was quiet. No people, no houses, no other cars or trucks. Jo let his head fall against the chill window. The vibrations through the floor of the cab strangely soothed him. The driver was far away now, absorbed in his own cares, in the simple need to keep the wheel steady and the heavily-shod foot pressing down just enough. His actions and breathing were part of the truck's mechanism. He had sunk into the engine's will to reach the border. Everything was.

When he came to himself, half his face was numb with cold, and he saw the beginnings of the great eastern forest. Mean dwellings could be seen between the white dusted pines, smoke wisping from chimneys. The sky was a hard misleading blue. A man carried wood on his back in a tied bundle. An old woman was sweeping her step. Snow was thick along the verges and in the rutted lanes and ditches. Then a black dog ran out barking from a gate as the truck rumbled past. It chased the truck giving high sharp yelps. The animals in the waggon battered the bed of the truck and the outside slats, then huddled into one shivering mass. Now they bleated wildly and the sound made Jo want to cry for them. He saw the dog in the side-mirror as it gave up and turned back, head down, to where it had come from.

'Have I been asleep?' said Jo. He yawned.

'Like a lamb,' replied the driver, glancing over. He looked amused.

The rucksack was gone. 'My rucksack,' said Jo. 'Where is it?'

They turned a sharp bend, pushing Jo into the door. 'Keep your hair on, what little there is,' said the driver. 'It was falling across the foot-well. I stuffed it behind the seat.'

THE GIFT MAKER

Jo squirmed around and saw the canvas strap poking out from the recess.

'And no, I didn't look inside it, if that's what you're thinking.' The driver broke off six squares of plain chocolate from a thick bar that lay on top of the dashboard. The wrapper had the words *Dark Sin* written in red on a gold background. 'Want a bit?'

'No, thank you. I don't like sweet things,' Jo lied.

'More for me,' said the driver, chewing through the squares he had stuffed into his face. He smiled broadly at Jo, his teeth and gums brown with the ooze from within his mouth. 'I can never get enough, ever since I was a boy.' He patted his extensive belly. 'Better than women, I'd say. More reliable.'

'Look out!' shouted Jo.

A deer stood in the middle of the road about two hundred feet ahead. The driver sounded the horn, and began to slow. The brakes were not in the best condition. Still the deer did not move. It looked right at Jo. 'If he won't move, I'll go through him,' said the driver.

'No, please. She will move. Give her a chance.'

The deer sprang out of the way just as the truck passed by. It ran into the undergrowth. Jo saw the pale markings on its hindquarters.

'They don't usually do that,' said the driver. 'That one must have a death wish.'

'Eros and Thanatos, our twin deceivers,' said Jo, laconically.

'You what?' said the driver.

'Nothing, nothing. Just something clever I used to say, and never really believed.'

The driver broke off some more chocolate and shoved it into his mouth. 'Not long now,' he said.

'To Grenze? I must have been asleep for a while.'

The driver shrugged. After a moment he said, 'What does someone like you want to go to Grenze for?'

Jo did not ask what *someone like him* meant. 'I have a friend there,' he said, fingering the strap of his rucksack behind the seat.

'A friend in Grenze is like an enemy anywhere else. You don't give much away, do you?' The big man wiped his nose across the back of his hand. He changed down a gear as they approached another tight bend.

Jo longed to ask the driver everything he knew about the town, but did not entirely trust him. Müller, the nightwatchman, would have been found by now. Perhaps someone had seen them leaving the university. He still felt strangely responsible for Müller's death, as though his and Thomas's being there had brought it into being. 'Are there any theatres in the town?' he asked casually.

The driver gave him a sidelong look. 'I think you know the answer to that question. Are you some sort of spy? Working for him, are you? 'Cause if you are, you can jump out right now.'

Jo looked at the dense and seemingly endless forest that lay along both sides of the road. He had absolutely no idea where they were, and not a great deal of money in his pocket. It was cold out there. Very cold. And there might even be wolves. Never had he needed to fend for himself in difficult circumstances. Building a fire was a mystery he had never considered, as was the making of any form of shelter. Inwardly, he cursed his lack of practicality. How would the philosophers, the great thinkers of history with their self-indulgent musings and meanderings help him out here?

'I'm sorry, I...I don't know what you mean,' stuttered Jo.

'I do my job. You get me? I just do my job. I pick up the load and I deliver. I might not always be on time. But I get it there. No one else wants this route. No one. They've heard things. I've heard them too, but I shut my ears and eyes to it. In and out I am.'

THE GIFT MAKER

The driver was becoming more agitated, throwing accusing glances at the student. His driving grew erratic, the waggon swung wide on a bend and nearly pulled them into a ditch.

'I'm not any sort of spy,' said Jo. 'I'm just a student. Another friend of mine has gone to Grenze, that's all. He went by train, to follow his friend, a girl…it's complicated.'

'Lies usually are,' said the driver. 'What's in the bag?'

Jo gripped the strap of the rucksack. Perhaps he would need to get out of his own accord. The man might be dangerous. Or dangerous to what the box contained. 'Nothing. Just some clothes, a book, that's all. Why?'

The animals in the waggon had resumed their eerie, baby-like cries. They grew in number and urgency. *Just let them out*, thought Jo. *Just let them go.*

'No recording device? Nothing to take pictures with? No harm in me looking then, is there?' They were on a long straight part of the road leading gently downwards, dense pine and undergrowth on either side. Jo supposed it must be late afternoon as the light was going. Small flakes of snow fell lazily from the now whitened sky.

The truck began to slow. The driver stared fixedly ahead, his jaw set. They stopped, and so did the noise of the animals. The driver grabbed at the rucksack and began pulling it out from under the seat. Jo still had hold of the strap.

'You don't have any right,' said Jo.

'You've a lot to learn about life, you have,' replied the driver. He tugged it fiercely, wrenching it from Jo's grasp.

'Please, be careful. It's precious. It mustn't be cold.'

'What are you jabbering about?' The driver rummaged in the rucksack, pulled out the jumper that was wrapped around something. 'What is it, some kind of trick?' He appeared nervous.

'Handle it gently,' said Jo.

'You're a queer article,' said the driver, still not unwrapping the object in his lap. He looked from the jumper-covered box to the student and back again. 'There's something vibrating in there. It's alive in there, isn't it? Tell me what it is.'

'Look, but be gentle,' was all Jo could say. He felt himself guided by something other than his own fear, or his own interest.

The driver pulled the material away from the box. He stared down at it. He shook his head. 'I've heard tales about these. Drunk-talk I thought it was. It's best not to know the truth,' he said. 'But I knew there was something different about you soon as I saw you.' He moistened his lips. His eyes were pained. He looked at the student as if seeking an answer, then he shook his head, as if trying to shut something out. 'It's best not to, isn't it? It's not mine. It's not my road. I just do my job.'

'Open it.'

The driver gave a short laugh. 'Did you make it, or were you given it?'

'It won't bite, just open it,' said Jo.

The man brought trembling fat fingers to the delicate clasp at the lid of the black box. He undid the clasp and slowly opened it. The music began. The lilting bell-like music. The melody was reminiscent of that which the driver himself had hummed earlier. His bearded face was underlit by the roseate light that spread out from the box. His eyes gleamed at what he saw in there. His face crumpled a little, as though some air had been let out of it. A doubtful smile played on the thick pale lips.

'It's real,' said the driver.

'As your own.'

'I won't hurt it,' said the driver. Jo leaned closer and saw that the tissue had reddened with life. The pulsing was even, willed, reliable.

THE GIFT MAKER

'I know you won't,' said Jo. 'We need to keep it warm, protected.'

'Yes,' said the driver. 'We do.'

'My mother's,' said Jo.

'Yes.' The driver nodded, looked at the student. 'I believe you,' he said. He closed the box and the music stopped and the rose light fell from his face.

It had grown much darker outside the silent cab. A fox walked casually across the road ahead of them, it turned, eyes flashing briefly in the lights from the truck. It had all the time in the world, or so it seemed. The box was once more wrapped tightly in the jumper and stowed in the rucksack. The driver lit a cigarette. Jo could no longer clearly see the driver's face. He followed the glowing end of the cigarette. It was getting colder.

'Your two friends, they've been given boxes, too?'

Jo told the driver everything that Thomas had told him, about Liselotte's miniature dancing double, about Thomas's own blue box which had appeared then vanished. He even told him about Daumen, expecting the driver to laugh scornfully, yet he did not. He told him about his own loss and the symbol made flesh in the box he now carried. He avoided telling him about the dead nightwatchman.

The driver scratched at the thick curling hair under his chin, blew out a perfect circle of smoke that rose to the ceiling of the cab, and broke. 'I don't hold out much hope for the others. There's so much crazy talk about Grenze, about him – Reynard. Others have mentioned boxes. I saw a broken one once, lying in the gutter. It was full of blood-soaked banknotes.'

'What did you do with it?' asked Jo.

'I threw the lot in the river, money and all,' said the driver. 'I regretted that many times. But something made me do it. Never told anyone till this day.' The driver tugged at his beard and smiled sadly at his shadowy reflection in the windscreen.

'Do you think Daumen and this Reynard fellow are connected?' said Jo, after an uneasy silence.

'Daumen must be working for him, dragging them in one by one, that's my guess. There might be many Daumens,' replied the driver. 'Fairy-tales, I thought at first. As I said, I shut my eyes and ears to it all. That way you survive. But something is growing, some cancer. You can see it in the towns, the villages, the cities, people are changing, they're dying from the inside, dying in the heart. I used to have a few pals, but now I'm finding it harder to speak with anyone.' He laughed. 'They think *I'm* the odd one, and they may be right. The others, they look at you with their blank or silly or aggressive faces; the eyes are dead, I'd say. Shallow like dirty puddles. The women all seem hard now, angry. And the men are either bullies or mush that couldn't tell you right from wrong, they think so much about so little. The children have become miniature adults too soon; they aren't reminding us anymore of the joy we could have, the joy we used to have. The children are ugly, in my eyes. They just want things, *things*. I shouldn't say that. But the lights are going out, one by one.'

The driver paused, looked at Jo, then took a deep drag on his roll-up cigarette. He continued, 'I saw him once, from a distance. He glowed like a promise of the future. Not a big man, but big in another way. He pulls you in, and down, I've heard it say. But I never believed in promises from anyone, not even my father. They're always broken. I don't know if Reynard is more than human, or less.'

'That changed things for me,' Jo gestured to the rucksack. 'It's not the same as the other boxes. I have to believe that. Whoever Daumen is, he made it for another reason. There's no bad in it, like there was no bad in her. I listen to it, like I listened to her stories before I knew what stories were. I need to help my friends, if I can.'

THE GIFT MAKER

'Why not help yourself?' The driver threw the cigarette butt out of the window. It hit the iron- hard ground, sending off sparks that died immediately.

'I am,' Jo said.

The driver wound up the window and turned the key in the ignition. The engine barked and stuttered into life. The animals were still. 'I've got a load to deliver,' he said.

They moved off slowly down the darkening road.

twenty-five

LISELOTTE STARED AS the bulky, dark-coated figure stepped out from the trees, a rifle in one hand, a small suitcase in the other. He was dressed like some commercial traveller, the brim of his hat pulled low, obscuring his face. He cut the figure of a city dweller or daily commuter more than that of a hunter. The suitcase in this winter woodland scene would have been comical if not for the torn body of the boy nearby.

He knelt down beside it, letting his gun rest on the floor, took off a black glove, and reached to the boy's neck, placing his fingers there. He wiped his fingers on his coat. Then he gently turned the boy over and brought his ear to the boy's chest, then his mouth. He laid his fingers on the boy's wrist, all the while taking no notice of Liselotte. She was unable to move a step. Her hands gripped the bark of the tree for fear of falling. Was the case a doctor's case? she wondered. But a travelling doctor with a rifle?

The man stood up, put his glove back on, slung the rifle over his shoulder, and began walking towards the animal. He stopped briefly by the dead boar, kicked it lightly. It did not move. He approached the cowering girl.

'Please, please don't hurt me,' said Liselotte.

THE GIFT MAKER

'What do you mean?' said the man, stopping. 'I have just saved your life. The boy is dead.' He glanced back at the boar, then at Liselotte. 'People underestimate such beasts. No farmyard pets are they.'

'He's dead? Are you sure?' She placed her hand over her eyes. 'Oh, the poor, poor boy. He'd told me his secret. He wanted to help me find my life again. It was him that saved me. He gave his life for me.'

'He played his part, yes.' The man's voice was deep, powerful, yet not unkind. He took a step nearer Liselotte. She came out from behind the tree. His eyes were shaded by the hat, his jaw was wide and strong, darkened by bristles. His skin was very pale. The lips were thin, bloodless.

'Thank you,' said Liselotte, uncertainly. 'We must tell his father. He lives somewhere around here, but I don't know where exactly. I'm a stranger here myself. Are you sure he's dead?'

'He will not speak again,' said the man.

'Do you know his father? Do you know Aldo? We must take his body there.'

'Listen,' said the man. They both turned to the sound. A mournful tinkling of bells accompanied by raucous shouting. In the distance, between the pines, in the adjacent field to where Liselotte had fed the ducks by the apple tree, they saw a sleigh bumping over the snow, pulled by a team of four black, dog-like creatures, yet too long in the body for any normal dog. Two figures rode the sleigh, one behind the other.

'They've heard the gunshot,' said the man. 'And they can smell it.'

'Smell what?' asked Liselotte.

'Why, the blood, Miss, the blood.' The man glanced behind him then grabbed the girl's arm. Before she knew it, Liselotte was being dragged along, half running, half stumbling through the snow-covered wood. 'Into those bushes there. The boy's body will keep them busy for a while.'

Liselotte's thoughts whirled. 'Keep them busy? No. We must bury Mabe. We can't run away from this. Are they not helpers coming on the sled?'

'They are helpers, but not ours, or the youth's,' replied the man as they crashed through bushes and stiff frozen briars that tore at their clothes. A spray of holly scratched Liselotte's neck. She brought her hand to it. More than once she fell and was hoisted roughly to her feet and pulled on. Her lungs were bursting as they scrambled up a steep slope, the man casting quick glances over his shoulder as they dodged the trunks of trees and low branches, tripping over fallen logs, and jumping across iced-locked streams. They weaved along an overgrown path between tangled, white-berried bushes. It grew darker as they descended to a deep depression beneath a dense canopy of spruce and holm oak. Here the light was brown and shadowy, the spongy ground a carpet of leaves, pine needles, fallen berries and twigs. Oddly-shaped mushrooms crowded the bases of trees. The man and the girl stopped to gather their breath.

'Who were they?' said Liselotte, leaning over, panting.

The man took off his hat and wiped his creased and shining forehead with the brim. He had placed the case on the ground. The rifle hung across his broad back. He coughed and spat into a yellow handkerchief. 'Excuse me,' he said. Liselotte glimpsed dark spots and blotches on the handkerchief before the man pushed it back into his breast pocket.

Liselotte saw his face fully now, albeit with the shadows of the moving branches above passing across it. His hair was greying, short and coarse, the ears had fleshy lobes, his nostrils flared somewhat, and the eyes, beneath thick brown eyebrows, were

THE GIFT MAKER

dark, deep-set and haunted. No light came from them. He gave the appearance of one who had not slept for a long time. Beneath the heavy coat, he wore a three-piece woollen suit, white shirt and black tie. His tan shoes looked old and scuffed, as did his gloves. The case by his feet was scratched and dented, and the handle had been mended at some point and was wrapped around with wire.

'It is me they want. I have turned renegade. A curious kind of apostate.'

'I don't understand the words you use. I don't understand any of this,' said Liselotte.

'Shhh…keep your voice down. We have lost them for now. No point in making it easy for them.'

'I was heading for the town of Hoffnung. Do you know it? Aldo gave me directions. Though now I've left the path…'

'There are many ways to anywhere,' interrupted the man, replacing his hat. He avoided her gaze, choosing to scrutinize the dark bushes above them.

'I've left that sweet boy out there, dead in the cold. I deserve everything that happens to me.' She pulled abstractedly at her black hair. 'I don't know who I was, but I'm beginning to learn what I am.'

'Most things we do not deserve, I can assure you of that, Miss.'

'My name is Lise…Liselotte. And you?'

A twig snapped sharply somewhere above them. Quickly, the man unslung the rifle, cocked it, and pointed to where the noise had come from. 'This would do only temporary damage, I have no doubt,' he said, more to himself than to the girl.

From a distance there came a single high howling. Then several dogs bayed, overlapping each other. A macabre chorus grew until there seemed to be a hundred hounds overreaching one another, in pitch and in desperation. Some were further off, some alarmingly near, as if the whole wood, the whole world, was surrounded, permeated by their presence.

'Are they wolves?' said Liselotte.

'Nothing so innocent.'

All at once, the baying stopped.

The man motioned with his index finger for Liselotte to move towards a narrow opening in the foliage at the top of the slope ahead of her. He carefully backed away from where the sound of the breaking twig had come, still pointing the rifle, clasping the case under his arm. They both clambered to the top of the rise and entered an almost dark tunnel of bushes. Barely a glimpse could be seen of the sky. Again, thorns ripped at their clothing, faces and hands. The birds were silent.

'Keep going,' whispered the man behind her. 'We should come out by the lake.'

They lurched along the hemmed-in path, Liselotte fearing the pounce of the dog-like beasts at any moment. Something thin and grey slithered by their feet. The man stamped down hard on it and moved on.

The path broadened suddenly, and there in the greater light it stood, very still, as if it had always been there, a low rumbling growl rising from deep in its throat. The eyes emitted a sickly yellow glow. Lips curled back on the muzzle, revealing two rows of even, white, pointed teeth, the two canines extending down beyond its bottom lip. High, sharp, triangular ears twitched. Now the fat liver-coloured tongue lolled and dripped. It cocked its head slightly and continued the low vibrating growl as it surveyed first Liselotte, then the man. It was twice the length of any normal dog, the shoulders and chest were thick and powerfully muscled, and despite the gloom, they could clearly see six widely-splayed

THE GIFT MAKER

feet, black nails gripping firmly into the earth. Its fur was beyond black. The creature seemed to suck the surrounding light into it. Its blackness was almost bright.

'My God,' said Liselotte, barely able to catch her breath. 'What is it?'

'One of his cohort,' said the man. He stepped across the girl, shielding her. He slowly raised the gun. The beast's haunches tensed. Then it sprang, somewhat awkwardly, not at the man and girl, but to the side, and burrowed into the thickness of the undergrowth. They heard its feet and body crashing and trampling through the ferns and bushes.

'Why didn't it attack us?' said Liselotte.

'For one of us death is meaningless, for the other it is premature.'

'Why are you talking in these riddles?'

'I will tell you more when we reach the lake,' said the man, pulling her onwards.

'I don't know if I can swim,' called Liselotte to the back of the man as they descended now through more widely-spaced trees. She had the sensation of many yellow eyes observing her as she ran in broad zig-zags down the wooded slope.

Several birds, high above them, had begun singing once more, in simple repetitive calls. These became maddening to Liselotte rather than providing any sense of normality. They sounded tinny and lifeless, like wind-up machines. Below them was a dark-green border of solid prickly-looking hedge. They stopped.

'It is like a wall,' said the man, reaching out to touch the dense mass of thorns. His glove was momentarily caught.

The hedge, at least ten feet in height, ran in either direction as far as they could see. 'We can't pass through this,' said the girl.

The man jogged to the left and the girl stumbled after him. 'I can smell the water,' he said over his shoulder.

There was indeed a break in the hedge. A tall iron gate stood there, once black, now mostly rust, supported by decaying stone pillars at each side. The ironwork formed intricate patterns of scrolls, twists and curls. The upright stakes ended in sharp spikes atop the gate. Beyond, lay a well-kept path of compressed earth, bordered by neatly-clipped trees that grew across to each other to form a colonnade. At the end of the path, beyond what looked like a stone fountain set in a pond, and followed by an expanse of snow-covered lawn, stood a substantial white house.

Liselotte slid the bolt across and pushed. The gate moved. She stepped onto the path, yet the man hesitated behind her. 'I had better leave this here,' he said, laying the rifle against one of the pillars. 'We may be mistaken for brigands.' He still clutched his case tightly in his gloved hand.

They passed along the arcade of trees and came to the fountain from which a gentle stream of water fell into the half-frozen pond. It fell from a stone jug cradled by the statue of a naked woman with long hair. The statue was weather-worn and badly deteriorated in places, the face owning barely recognisable features. Half a mouth survived, which appeared to be curved up in a smile. The nose had been lost. The eyes, which had once been painted, showed the barest vestiges of a green tinge.

The sound of water falling was pleasant to Liselotte. She did not wish to leave the statue, but rather to sit upon the stone surround of the pond and let the gentle trickling take her far away. She cupped her hand in the cold water and brought it to her mouth.

'No,' said the man, slapping her hand away from her face, spilling the water over her green coat.

'I'm thirsty,' complained the girl.

'We don't know what kind of place this is. It may be one of his snares.'

'Who is this *he* you keep talking about? I'm so, so tired. I just want to stretch out on the snow there and forget, and sleep forever on that cold white sheet. Sleep for a hundred years like that serving-girl in Gisela's book. I don't know who you are. I don't care anymore. None of this may be real. I just pray this is some painful dream that I'll wake up from, and be myself again. In my room. In the room that I've lost.' Her eyelids drooped and she bagan to fall back towards the weed-green, icy water. The man caught her around the waist and shook her slightly.

'Listen to me,' he said. His breath in her face smelled of stale wine. 'I will help you return. But first we must go to Grenze.'

She looked at him as through a mist. 'I know that word… *Grenze*. And Gerda mentioned it, too, though at the time it meant nothing. But it is a place I've heard of. Yes…it is a place I was going to…or back to. I was to meet a man there. A man who was going to help me to do something…be something. I had a box with me, it contained a treasure. I remember apples, a baby…oh! And then I fell into the blackness, and the wind hard on my face.' She pressed her palm to her forehead, her eyes screwed shut. 'I just saw a terrible thing. A baby without a face. It's a nightmare whether I wake or sleep.'

He supported her head with his gloved hand. He gently pushed her tear-stained face into his rough coat.

'Can I help you?' An elderly woman, well into her seventies, stood on the lawn, halfway between the house and the fountain. Liselotte and the man turned to her. They had not heard her approach. She was dressed in an attire more fitting to a child: a flouncy white party dress, dotted with a rainbow of colours and cut just above her puckered slim knees. Her long grey hair was tied with a bright yellow ribbon, loose strands played around her rouged cheeks. Her face was deeply-lined but radiant with health.

Her nose was small and turned up at the end. Her very blue eyes twinkled in the light reflected from the snow. On her bare feet were purple slippers, each boasting a large glass ruby at the toe.

'We do not mean to intrude,' said the man, touching his hat and making an imperceptible bow. 'We merely lost our way in the woods and thought this may be a path to the lake.'

The elderly woman studied them a moment. She smiled, and her teeth, if they were her own, were perfect. 'Is that your daughter?' she said. Her voice was clipped and high in pitch. 'She is a credit to you,' she continued, without waiting for an answer. The woman moved quickly over the lawn and approached Liselotte. Holding out a mottled hand to the girl, she lightly caressed her cheek. 'Are you lost, my dear? I can always tell when a soul is lost, you know.'

The man made a noise in his throat.

'I am Lady Hoffnung. But you may call me Olga. Ugly name, but there it is. They named a town after our family. Or was it the other way around? Who cares! It's nearby, but I haven't left these grounds for many a moon.' She made sudden bird-like movements of her head as she looked between her two guests. Her fingers fluttered on occasion, as though she were playing an invisible harp.

'Liselotte,' said Liselotte, standing. 'Yes, I am lost. And this man is not my father.'

'Daumen,' said the man, taking off his glove and extending his hirsute hand towards the elderly lady.

She took it very briefly then played with the strands of her hair, winding then unwinding them around a finger. 'You're a bit of a teddy bear, aren't you?' she said. 'I have a collection of seventeen-hundred, you know. I never liked dolls. They can be witches in disguise.' Now she spoke like a flirtatious, pouting twelve-year-old, putting her head on one side, and gazing up at Daumen. 'But where are my manners? Do you know it's my birthday? Well,

THE GIFT MAKER

how could you, of course. But it *is*, and I wish you would both do me the hugest honour of taking some tea and cake with us. In fact, I insist. The cake was made by Nanny Glück last night.' Lady Hoffnung bent a little and brought a cupped hand to her mouth. Then she said in a low voice, 'I dipped my finger into the royal-blue icing when she wasn't looking, but smudged it over good as new.' She giggled. 'She can't see so well, so would never know anyhow. Silly old Nanny.' Lady Hoffnung straightened up and assumed a provocative expression. 'What do you think of that? Am I a naughty girl? But then I have a right to be on my birthday.'

'Many happy returns,' said Liselotte, uneasily. 'Aren't you cold dressed like that?'

'Tell me how old I am. Tell me,' the old woman twittered. The snow had soaked through her purple slippers turning them a darker shade. The glass rubies flashed.

'We really need to be making tracks,' said Daumen, picking up his case.

'Oh, but I could do with a hot drink,' said Liselotte. She glanced at Daumen's hand before he once more covered it in the black leather glove. The top and wrist were covered with a matting of fine brown hair, curlier hairs sprouted around the knuckles. This meant something to her but she could not determine what. It had something to do with what a young man had once told her, a young man with a wispy beard and soulful eyes. She knew he had liked her very much, perhaps too much. There had been a café, she had worn a red coat, rather than the green one she now wore. She had told him…no, *shown* him a secret. Had that been part of her previous life, or was it some construction of her fancy, born of the universal need to own a narrative to hang an existence on? What was the young man's name, and who had he been to her? So vague, so evanescent were the pictures that formed then faded in her mind. But at least pictures were forming now. There was hope.

'Of course you do, my chicken,' said Lady Hoffnung, and looped her thin arm through Liselotte's, and walked with her over the snow to the door of the white house. Daumen followed reluctantly, now and again looking over his shoulder.

They went up three broad steps and came to the white door. 'Oh, Nanny's closed the door again,' said Lady Hoffnung. She stamped her damp foot. 'She worries so about heat escaping. I tell her again and again that we have pots of money. Oodles. My father is in copper and sugar, you know. We hardly ever see him. But I love him best, as he does me.' She yanked three times on a thick bell rope, and from somewhere inside the house a hollow clanging was heard.

Liselotte simply longed for warmth, and somewhere soft to sit, somewhere where she could focus on the new pictures, faces, and scenes that were developing behind her eyes. The door opened slowly, and there on the threshold was a woman, perhaps twenty years older than Lady Hoffnung. She was dressed like a maid, but a maid of the last century. Her hair was tucked under a peasant scarf. She wore heavy-looking clogs and a white and blue pinafore that almost reached the ground. Her face was round and pudding-like, and dusted with some powder that smelled faintly of lavender. She did not smile.

'Let us in then, Nanny. We have very special guests. I told you the party would begin if we made a cake.'

Nanny allowed her rheumy eyes to fall as she stepped to the side to let them in. She closed the door behind them. The entrance hall had a marble floor in a black and white diamond pattern, beyond which a pair of curved wooden staircases swept up to a two-sided gallery above them. The atmosphere and smell was of a tropical moistness, of things sweetly decaying, of spice, roots and earth. The house was excessively warm, but they could see no fireplace or source for the oppressive heat. Daumen loosened his tie. Alongside both walls were placed enormous terracotta pots filled with tall palm-like plants, thick flowering cactuses, exotic-looking specimens propped up by bamboo canes. Liselotte gazed at the fat fleshy leaves, the striped or patterned fronds, the bulbous hanging fruits in vivid shades: purples and lilacs, lime-greens, blood-red and orange.

'It's Nanny's little hobby,' said Lady Hoffnung, making a sweeping movement of her arm over the pots. 'She always longed to travel to far-flung places, to where the humming birds hum and the parrot squawks, and the sky is blue all day, and the natives wear very little. Eh, Nanny?'

Nanny picked up a small silver watering can from a trestle table and began watering the plants. She shuffled along on her clogs, slowly and carefully, as if her feet caused her pain.

'She never went,' continued Lady Hoffnung. 'And now it's too late.'

Daumen reached out to touch what looked like a glossy orange pepper.

'Don't interfere!' shouted Nanny suddenly, in a surprisingly powerful voice. Her lips were set to a thin line, and her watery eyes glared.

'I'm sorry,' said Daumen, quietly.

'Don't let her bark worry you,' said Lady Hoffnung. 'Nanny's a puppy really.' She skipped ahead of them, very nimbly for a person of her age. 'Come on, follow me. Let's go to the playroom.'

Liselotte looked at Daumen. He nodded briefly. They followed the capering figure in the spotted party dress up the left-hand staircase, along the open gallery, then down a shadowy, wood-panelled passage with numerous closed doors leading off of it.

'Now, which one is it?' said Lady Hoffnung to herself. 'I'm a silly sometimes. But aren't we all?' she added, over her shoulder. 'Ah, my playroom.' She turned around conspiratorily to Daumen and Liselotte. She raised a finger to her lips, and winked. 'Let's be quiet as we go in, so we give the bears a big surprise.'

Lady Hoffnung gently turned the doorknob and pushed the door open a crack, then a little further. She fleetingly peered inside then looked back to the others to gesture silence once more. A strained smile stretched across her wrinkled face and from her eyes came a manic gleam. She stepped fully into the room and the others followed her.

True to her word, an enormous collection of stuffed bears of all sizes and varieties festooned the walls, the shelves, and lay in neat rows along couches and around the circumference of a double bed. They also took up much of the floor-space, sitting in orderly semi-circles, as though at a conference, or else piled gracelessly on top of one another. One large brown bear, with a red rosette pinned to its chest, sat atop an ancient rocking horse, the reins looped around its paws. Some were much loved, with missing eyes, ears, and arms. Others were still in presentation boxes, or smartly dressed in tartan waistcoats and britches, or else smoking on little cloth pipes, wearing glasses or carrying walking sticks.

On a gold salver on a round table near the arched window stood the blue-iced cake. It was oblong and had ten lit candles stuck into the icing in the shape of an H.

'Come and see the cake,' said Lady Hoffnung with a childish chuckle, threading a path through the stuffed toys, kicking some out of her way so that they flew against the wall.

The guests followed the birthday girl to the table by the window. From here they had a view from the rear of the house. At the end of another snow-covered stretch of lawn, dotted with ornamental trees and white-encrusted topiary, was a low black railing, and beyond this was a sloping shingle beach that led to the lake.

'A pleasant view,' said Daumen, as Lady Hoffnung picked up a silver cake slice.

'Shall I blow?' said Lady Hoffnung.

'Yes, please do,' said Liselotte, captivated by the image of the shining oval lake in the late-afternoon sun, beyond which she could see smoking chimneys, a thinly tapering church tower, and winding streets of pastel-coloured terraced houses set into a hill. *That must be Hoffnung*, she thought.

The old woman blew hard but only three of the candles went out. She tried three more times before they were all snuffed and lightly smoking. She held a hand to her head. 'Oh, that took a lot of puff, my loves. Now, let's cut shall we, my doves?' She arranged three patterned paper plates next to the salver with the cake on it.

Daumen's keen eye was caught by the sight of a rowing boat, tied by a rope to the rail at the end of a wooden jetty, which stretched out fifty feet or so into the lake. The boat bobbed and tugged lazily in the grey-blue water.

Lady Hoffnung tapped the cake slice against her chin. 'Shall I cut deep now?' she said. 'Who will have the biggest bit? You love my cake, don't you? I can tell. Such a shame to hurt it.'

Daumen and Liselotte turned to look down at the cake.

'Yes, of course, Lady Hoffnung, I mean, Olga,' said Liselotte, forcing a smile.

The blade of the cake slice cut down, and from within, the cake immediately began to bleed. Liselotte stared as a red stream flowed out over the salver and onto the table. It was not jam or sauce of any kind. That much she knew. There was a slight metallic smell in the air. The old woman cut the other side of the triangle. Liselotte stepped back a pace. Lady Hoffnung was busy with her task, as more and more blood spread out in a broadening pool over the table and dripped onto the floor, dripped onto the head of a small tan bear with one eye. Lady Hoffnung's hand and wrist grew patterned with thin meandering red lines that journeyed up her arm to stain the sleeve of her party dress. She then inserted the flat of the cake slice to lift away a portion of the cake, dripping spots of red on the blue icing. She lifted it away to reveal the innards of the cake. There, within the bloody ooze, were many severed fingers packed densely within the body of the cake. One appeared to have a ring on. A simple wedding band.

'This is for you,' said Lady Hoffnung, sliding the wedge onto one of the paper plates and presenting it to Liselotte. 'Ladies first,' she added. Then she licked the tip of the cake slice. 'Mmm...red,' she said, the blood staining her lips and teeth. 'If you get a ring, that's lucky we always say, and you must make a wish, my dear.'

With a shaking hand Liselotte took the paper plate from the old woman, who peered intensely at her, as if expecting a particular reaction. Daumen was also staring at her oddly. Were they in this together? Why is he not as sickened by the cake as I am? she thought. Politeness is one thing, but this, this was an outrage, an obscenity. More fingers, of different length, were packed tightly within this piece of cake. Some had been cut in half, some were complete. And one, Liselotte noticed, a small finger which must have belonged to a child, was very slightly twitching. She threw the plate to the floor as if it burned her hand, and ran from the room, scattering bears in her wake. Daumen called after her but she was gone.

Liselotte ran down the corridor, but in her panic took the wrong direction, which only drew her deeper into the house. She passed through double doors that led to a large room. Here, all the furniture and paintings were covered in dust sheets, except for one painting on the wall above an unlit fireplace. It was surely a portrait of Lady Hoffnung, but made when she was a woman of middle age. The dust sheets, in turn, were covered by an even layer of dust, and patched by dense forests of cobwebs. Liselotte saw another door at the far end of this room and dashed towards it. She wrenched this door open and passed into a long, narrow room, on either side of which were wooden racks, from floor to ceiling. Liselotte stood still, catching her breath, taking in her surroundings. Upon these racks were bulky shapes, tightly swathed in thick, yellowing material. The shapes were different in length. Some were a good six feet long, others three or four feet and of a smaller girth. There was a sweetish, sickly stench in this room that forced Liselotte to cover her nose and mouth.

About halfway down on each of the shrouded forms she noticed several circles of red, staining the binding material from within. Then she realised – the missing fingers. Her voice would not come no matter how she tried to scream. Any sound she was capable of locked in her throat. In mute desperation, she pushed through a further door and came to yet another room.

This space was very warm and lavishly furnished. A sumptuous fire crackled and snapped in a deep-set fireplace. There were burgundy leather sofas and wing-back chairs. Liselotte's feet sank luxuriously into a thick-pile carpet. A white fur rug stretched out before the hearth. In an epitome of staid normality, the grandfather clock in the far corner softly began to chime. Four times its mournful, dull bell tolled. Liselotte peered at the face of the clock and saw that it had no hands.

There were three lit red candles in sconces positioned around the walls, and a five-pointed candelabra, which was also aglow, set upon a low table to one side. The floor-length drapes were pulled across occluding all daylight. The candlelight and the light from the fire threw palpitating shadows around the walls and across the ceiling. As she approached one of the sofas, Liselotte noticed the top of a head, a head with very dark hair, almost black. The person certainly would not be very tall, as the head barely rose above the back of the sofa. The head moved very slightly to the right, then resumed its position, apparently staring into the fire.

'Excuse me,' said Liselotte.

The person on the sofa did not respond, either with speech or movement. Liselotte looked around. Whatever might happen here, she knew she could not face a return journey through the room of wrapped corpses.

'I'm looking for the way out, please. The way back down to where the plants are and the main door.'

Still the head of dark hair did not react. Slowly, Liselotte moved to the side of the sofa. A small, slim figure came into view. Its legs did not quite reach the carpet. It was a young girl, perhaps nine or ten years old. The girl continued to stare into the fire, her profile unmoving, as though she had grown lost in the ever-changing flames. A teddy bear lay propped by her side. The bear also stared directly into the fire. Its hard eyes caught points of light.

'Hello there,' said Liselotte, in a voice that she supposed would not frighten a child. 'I wonder if you would be so kind...'

The girl slowly turned her face to Liselotte. She had a small perfect mouth, a cupid's bow of a mouth. Her delicate nose turned up at the end, and her vacant blue eyes enveloped Liselotte in their lash-wide stare. She wore a gaily spotted party dress and a yellow ribbon in her hair, some strands of which fell about her blushing rounded cheeks. Little purple slippers adorned her feet, on the toe of each flashed a large glass ruby.

'Can't you speak?' said Liselotte, a harsher note creeping into her voice. 'Why are you staring at me like that? Hasn't anyone told you yet it's wrong to stare? When I was a girl I...I...'

                                    THE GIFT MAKER

Liselotte's mind became at once crowded with memories of a man and a woman. The man was exceedingly stout, with fleshy lips, which caused him to spray others with spittle whenever he grew animated. He went every day to a large, imposing building, and other adults treated him with deference, some almost cringing as he glowered at them over his spectacles. This man was involved with money, papers, dusty filing cabinets, and locks. Liselotte could not remember why, but she knew this man meant a great deal to her, that in her presence he softened, grew playful and childlike. The woman, in contrast, was small, bony, and angular of face. Liselotte knew that this woman could not be trusted, despite Liselotte's anxious need of love and approval from her. She remembered searching the woman's eyes for understanding, for sympathy, and finding merely a shallow void. And when Liselotte had cried, the woman's face wore a mask of disgust before she turned away. And when Liselotte tried to speak her heart, another voice, the voice of the woman, would supplant her own until she knew she had no voice at all without the woman's permission. She felt this keenly, like a shameful secret, even when she was alone under the blankets of her bed, or dabbling her fingers in a lonely rock pool. Always that other voice, that thin, tight voice of hollow mastery and unassailable will, avowed it knew Liselotte better than she knew herself.

Then came the escape of the sea, the renegade cries of seabirds, salt on her tongue, rough dark sand on the soles of her feet, and parasols and fishing boats, and wind dancing in her long black hair, as black as the hair of the girl who sat on the sofa, staring at her in this strange house. *Was that me?* thought Liselotte. *Was that all me?*

'You are not me,' said Liselotte to the girl, who continued her maddening stare. 'You are someone else's past. I know you. You are Olga. You are Lady Hoffung, aren't you?'

The girl's mouth began to open. The dainty pink lips parted and widened, and stretched, showing two rows of perfectly white small teeth. Then the mouth began to widen further, more than a mouth should. The hole became wider and wider, distending and distorting the face and eventually overwhelming the retroussé nose. It gaped out to the side to meet the ears, and further up towards the now straining eyes. Around the rows of delicate teeth was a mass of moist pink gum that shone dully in the firelight.

Liselotte could not tear her gaze away from the gaping mouth, the mouth that continued to dilate until the eyes were lost under its growth, and the circumference of the whole face had become one pink and white masticating maw. The little teeth chomped merrily on nothing, as the gums pulsed and sucked around them.

Without thinking, Liselotte took up a poker that lay on the tiles of the hearth, and swung it with all the force she could muster against that mouth. The small teeth shattered and dislodged on impact, and the child let out a deep moan. Again and again, Liselotte slammed and jabbed the poker into the bloodied hole, as teeth, still connected to grim, livid roots, fell onto the sofa, over the child's legs, or down the front of her dress, leaving blank spaces where they once had been.

She must destroy that mouth. She must obliterate it forever if she was to survive. Or else it, too, might rob her voice from out her throat, unseat her life, displace her dreams. Then all the lights went out. Every candle was suddenly dead, and the fire was no more. Liselotte still gripped the metal rod in her hand. She felt it there, but no longer saw anything in the room, except impermeable blackness. A solid darkness that pressed itself tight against her eyes like a band, like the tightest blindfold. The grandfather clock chimed once. She heard a low, rasping breath coming from a few feet in front of her, as of one whose airway is damaged or diseased.

The sound of this laboured breath was a torment. It made Liselotte herself so breathless to hear it that she brought her hand to her own throat for want of air. Liselotte allowed her fingers to uncurl from around the poker. It thudded against the floor. She stretched out her arms, but could feel nothing. She must find the door, even the door back to where the swaddled bodies were stored, anything but this non-world of blackness, and the sound of that struggling breath that filled the room.

Liselotte groped and stumbled about like some blind animal, bumping into this or that object. Something grabbed and pinched eagerly at her fingers. It felt like a small hand. She pulled her own violently away and kicked out at the unseen being. She kicked into empty space and nearly toppled backwards. The rattling breathing had died down to a low grating moan, regular as the ticking of a clock. Liselotte realised that she might now be in any part of the room, except that she was almost certain the reek of wood smoke from the quenched fire came from behind her. Therefore she must go forward.

At last her hands found a hard edge. A wall…or was it a door? She frantically searched for some handle or knob to turn. Her hands slid like eyes over the flat, cool surface. Then she found it. She traced it with her shaking fingers – a handle. Yes, it must be.

'Please…please,' she said. She pushed the handle down and pulled. Part of the room behind her was momentarily illumined. She did not look back, but scurried out into a corridor, slamming the door behind her so that it shook in its frame. There, miraculously, at the end of the hallway, stood Daumen, case in hand. He gestured for her to join him. She ran to him and collapsed against his body.

'Where have you been? I have been searching this mausoleum for you,' he said. 'We must leave at once. The old woman is clearly deranged. Although I do not see her as a threat to us.'

'She is more than mad. You don't realise how apt your description of this house is. You haven't seen what I have. I wouldn't wish anyone to,' replied Liselotte.

'You look different,' said Daumen, staring into her face. 'You have lost a little of your abstractedness.'

'Yes, I am remembering, piece by piece. I am remembering my life.'

He smiled at her, and there was traced an age-old pain in his ashen face, and in the dark light of his shadowed eyes.

They moved quickly down a further passage and came to the top of the stairs. At their backs they heard Lady Hoffnung shrieking, 'How rude you are! How rude children are these days. No wonder I prefer my bears, my grateful darlings.' Her voice increased in volume and pitch, and was now punctuated by a wild, angry sobs: 'I will give you no more cake. No. More. Cake. You can starve for all I care. You can turn to dust! You can…rot!'

Daumen and Liselotte tore down the stairs two at a time and raced over the diamond-patterned marble floor, where the mad array of colourful plants stood like columns of servants leading to the main door. Nanny barred their exit. She stood there, her face set in a mask of dumb hatred, in her hands a pair of silver secateurs, their twin blades glinting.

'Chop them well, Nanny,' cried Lady Hoffnung from the top of the stairs. 'Give them a snip to remember us by.' Then she laughed, and her laugh was dry and empty and hopelessly mad.

'Let us pass,' said Daumen, in a calm voice.

Nanny looked up to Lady Hoffnung then back to Daumen and Liselotte. She spat on the floor in front of them.

Then Daumen threw his case with great force at one of the exotic palms. It hit the trunk at the mid-point and the whole pot rocked, threatening to tip over. Nanny made a sound like a wounded dog, and hobbled as quickly as her feet would allow towards the rocking pot, dropping her secateurs in her haste.

'Quickly,' said Daumen, as he leaped for the door and pushed Liselotte out ahead of him.

Back on the lawn, with the door of the Hoffnung residence once more firmly shut, they could hear the anguished screams of Lady Hoffnung and the sound of pots smashing.

'They hate me, they all hate me. I told you, Nanny, I warned you.' These were the last words they heard as they ran around the side of the house and took a snow-cleared cinder path over the back lawn, and down to the black railing. They stepped over this and lurched down the steep shingle beach in the direction of the wooden jetty. At its end, the rowing boat lay bobbing, like the answer to a long-held prayer.

twenty-six

AND SLOWLY, PAINFULLY slowly, like a wound, the curtain began to part.

The setting was of a park at dusk, just as on the poster outside. The statue of the naked woman was centre stage, frozen in the act of tipping a jug into an ornamental pond at her feet. No water poured from the jug. The actress miming the statue held her position perfectly still. Her skin was alabaster, and her hair was as dark as her skin was pale. There was a black triangle where her thighs met. Thomas knew at once whom the actress was. It was Liselotte. He longed to call out her name, to shout *Bravo!* to rush onto the stage and enter the scene and awaken her himself. From the orchestra pit a flute gave out a long high note. Then it sounded a series of notes without melody, without respect for key, without meaning. In the sky of the set there hung the full, red-tinged moon. Thomas could have sworn it was a real evening sky, a real moon. He laughed to himself at the devilish skill of the scene-makers, those unsung artisans of this magic box of shadow and light.

There came a scent of honeysuckle. Warm and delicious. Thomas sat deep in his seat and gazed achingly at the perfect form

THE GIFT MAKER

of Liselotte, at the alignment of her hips, the slight tension in her calves, the curve of her perfect young breasts.

His reverie was punctured by another figure on the stage, at the far left. Thomas had not seen this actor walk on. It was as if he had always been there, watching, scrutinising the statue, but had only now chosen to be visible. This figure was a young man, reasonably tall, slim in the way that only the young can be, and dressed all in white. His brown hair fell over his shoulders and there was the beginnings of a beard around his lean jaw. Thomas tried to read the young man's expression but could not. It might have been adoration or utter disdain, supplication or brute arrogance. Thomas had the powerful sense that this actor's intrusion had spoiled the scene, was superfluous to it. Why couldn't he, Thomas, be allowed to simply watch the statue in the evening park, to marvel at the sheen and smoothness of her skin and the luxuriant ebony of her hair? That was enough entertainment for anyone, it might even fill a lifetime. This interloper, this crass amateur, had set his nerves jangling.

The young man in white moved carefully over the fake grass towards the statue. He moved like a fox, ever watchful, nervous yet bold. His white-gloved hand reached into the near-darkness behind him and brought back an object into the greater light. A guitar. It was as though it had been handed to him from nothingness. The actor removed his white gloves with no little affectation.

'My goodness,' thought Thomas. 'I've a guitar very similar to that.'

The statue's foot might have moved a tiny amount, the merest twitch, Thomas could not be sure. The young man in white now sat cross-legged on the ground and brought the guitar onto his lap. First he stroked a few simple chords with his forefinger and thumb, seemingly lost in the concord of strings. Then he began plucking the strings in intricate patterns, slowly at first, and with consummate timing, creating a river of bell-like syncopated notes, moving up and down the fretboard with astounding ease.

Major chords led to minor-sevenths, plangent major sevenths to diminished elevenths, ninths to suspended hanging triads, to obscure thirteenth chords in impossible looking inversions. And each had a colour and a taste that was its own. Thomas marvelled as the actor's fingers glided up and down the neck with implacable skill, turning the humble wood and cat-gut instrument into a portable orchestra. It both hurt and charmed, it bewildered the mind and the ear, and yet set the heart racing with joy for the sake of joy alone. Thomas laughed at the impetuous skill of the guitarist, the dazzling fingerwork.

It was not a matter of melody, of form, for there was no shape or purpose to this music. It was merely the skill, the unnerving dexterity that held Thomas spellbound. The actor played now with improbable speed. Surely the human hand could not produce so many notes in such short spaces of time? And the human ear could not conceive of them, nor order them into musical narrative. The constellation of tones rang out, reverberated and busied themselves around Thomas's head like a million points of light. He was caught in a web of patterning that no longer made sense. And still the actor played, faster and faster, until rhythm and pitch no longer mattered, until all that had been minutely separate became one long enveloping drone.

The player stopped. And the silence was like the moment after death. Thomas brought his hands to his face to wipe away the tears that had fallen without his knowing. He stood and began clapping. 'Wonderful…perfect…a true maestro!' he shouted. No one hushed him or elbowed him or told him to sit down. The musician must be praised.

THE GIFT MAKER

The actor in white now stood and passed the guitar to an invisible hand, where it vanished into the blackness of upstage. He replaced his gloves with a flourish. Now he looked at Thomas full-square in the face, shattering the fourth wall that actors so diligently erect. And Thomas at last recognised the face that stared at him so imperiously from that artificial arena of suspended disbelief. It was his own. The virtuoso was himself.

The actor broke the stare and turned to the statue. He made a clenching of his fist, followed by a spreading wide of his fingers, at which the statue dropped the jug to the floor where it smashed. Pieces scattered. There was a collective *ahhhh* from the hidden audience.

The statue straightened and stepped from her plinth onto the ground. She was clearly magnetized by her partner on the stage. He drew her towards him as on a gossamer thread. Thomas grew maddened at the impudent sneer now visible on the actor's face as he enticed the naked girl to his outstretched arms. He stood up once more.

'Stop this! Cover the girl. Cover her at once. Someone…this is shameful, disgraceful,' he shouted, though no one took any notice. A mounting rage built in his chest leaving him short of breath and somewhat dizzy. He longed to run from the theatre, to not be the responsible one, the one who sees and is obligated to intervene; or instead be one of the many who do not care or affect not to see, and rather to relish the entertainment like everyone else, to linger over the vicarious thrill as the act, the acts, would be played out, sniggering behind his hand, feeling the warm sensation between his own legs, as did, he was certain, every other member of the audience.

He turned behind and to the sides and could now see the vaguest impressions of other faces through the gloom. No features could be determined, neither sex nor age, merely dull pinkish ovals populated the darkened stalls and the circle above. These ovals floated over the shadowy bulks of their bodies as if there were scant relationship between them. The audience was expectant, it held its collective breath. This was what they had all come for, paid for. They wanted their money's worth.

The statue that was Liselotte now drew very close to the actor in white. He stretched out his gloved hands and placed them on her shoulders. He pulled her slowly into him like a lost child. He kissed her on the forehead, as if blessing her. Then he kissed her around the face, all the while leering into her eyes, dominating her will. She was utterly pliant, no more than a doll to him. She made no expression of enjoyment nor of discomfort. She was senseless in her nakedness. Then the actor placed his lips over her lips, his hands fiercely gripped the back of her head, and he turned both their faces so that the maximum of each face could be observed by the audience. He even winked, archly. There was no tenderness in this kiss. It was as if he meant to suck the life from her, via her mouth, that he was determined to empty her of some precious liquid or floundering love.

Thomas watched aghast as the actor's free hand now slid over Liselotte's forehead and pinched her nose shut. Still he kept her mouth covered with his. The girl's arms began to flutter. The stage grew dark around the tableau and a pale blue light spot-lit their faces in this vicious embrace. Liselotte's heels began to trample against the wooden stage as she struggled for breath. Her arms swung uselessly against the sides of the actor, whose eyes glinted in the winter-blue light. She did not appear to have the strength to resist the kiss that was killing her.

'Enough!' screamed Thomas, as he pushed past legs, tripped over feet and handbags, until he reached the aisle. The pink oval

THE GIFT MAKER

faces twitched and jerked in disapproval. A murmur of discontent began to build in the theatre, like the rumbling of faraway thunder. Thomas knew it was directed at himself. It became a low hateful hum that resounded inside his skull, so that he shook his head madly from side to side to rid himself of the noise. Still the humming remained. It drove him on now. Drove him to act.

He pelted down the aisle and came to the orchestra pit. It was empty, save for a young dark-haired boy sitting on a chair much too large for him, his bare feet dangling over the edge of the seat. Across the boy's short-trousered legs lay a flute. The boy looked up at Thomas and smiled.

Next to the ornamental pond, the actor in white was now holding Liselotte up, his mouth still pressed violently to hers. Her body had fallen limp in his grip. Thomas clambered onto the fore-stage and leapt at his double. He tore the man's head away from Liselotte and wrenched it around with great force to stare into his own face. The actor let go of the statue that had come to life and she slumped to the floor.

Now Thomas held the actor's face clenched in his hands. His fingers dug deep into the man's flesh. Still the unctuous smirk lay on the actor's lips. He did not defend himself. Thomas felt his fingers sinking into the flesh of the face. His thumb sank deep in, followed by his fingers. The actor's eyes widened. Thomas pulled his fingers out with a sucking sound. The humming from the audience was louder now. It thrummed through the auditorium like a mountain of bees. It vibrated the very air around Thomas's head, causing his hair to stand up, sending electrical shivers down his back.

There came stifled laughter from someone up in the grand circle, as though they did not dare to laugh but could not contain themselves. Thomas now dug his thumbs deep into the actor's eyes. They sank in with surprising ease, to the root. Thomas hooked his thumbs behind the eyeballs and pulled back and to the side. The white and blue glistening orbs, threaded with a tracery of red veins, now hung by gristly threads from the actor's face. They dangled level with the end of his nose. He showed no sign of pain or distress. Still the smirk remained on the face that was Thomas's own. Reaching now through the lips and into the mouth, Thomas grabbed the lower jaw and twisted it this way and that, loosening its connections. The teeth bit into his upper palm, and he cursed. He heard the cracking and the tearing of tissue, tendon and muscle. He pulled and yanked and jerked until the whole lower jaw came away, attached only by flaps of skin. There was no blood, not a drop of it. The actor was bloodless. The flesh inside was a moist pallid grey. It was dead. Thomas wiped the greyish gunge from his fingers onto his coat. The actor stood behind him now as the lights came up bright. And for the first time Thomas saw the audience complete and with shocking clarity.

They were all on their feet and their beaming faces expressed an horrific joy. They clapped fulsomely and in unison, and the sound became like a great hammer pounding an anvil, over and over. They were all Reynard. Each one of them was him.

Thomas became aware of movement at his back. The actor with his mutilated face and Liselotte had joined hands and were taking numerous mechanical bows. Crimson, white, and pink flowers landed at their feet. The flowers flew in arrow showers past Thomas's head, never once hitting him. At each bow, the hanging eyes of the actor would bounce and swing at the end of their sinewy threads. Thomas sank to his knees.

'Bravo,' whispered a single voice from the auditorium, 'Bravo.' And now the whisper was on the inside of Thomas's skull. It tickled his ear like a lover's tongue. Reynard was nearby. Thomas looked up and saw him. The man with the kindest eyes in history. The face that was history, and before, and all to come, gazed down at him like a concerned yet amused parent. The actors had gone, as had the audience. There was only Thomas and his pale shepherd left in the theatre.

'Stand up, my boy,' said Reynard. 'You have given the performance of your life. You have amazed us all.' He brought Thomas up to standing.

'Now,' he said, searching deep in the student's eyes, 'I have a story to tell you.'

twenty-seven

THE DASHBOARD CLOCK said nearly midnight as the truck descended a curving, hedge-lined road into the outskirts of the town. The snow had stopped and a greying slush covered the surface they drove over. In the distance, Jo noticed a strip of winking neon lights. This view was lost to him as they moved further down into the valley. The headlights picked out a sign: *Grenze*. It had been hit by a vehicle at some point and was twisted and leaning.

'Here we are,' said the driver. 'The land of milk and shit.'

Jo rubbed his eyes. On either side he now saw an endless row of narrow terraced houses, mostly in darkness. They all looked the same. There was no colour in them, only dark browns and greys. Curtains were drawn across the windows or else the windows were boarded up or broken. The long street was meagrely lit. There was rubbish piled high in the shabby front yards of the houses, rubbish strewn over the pavements, and blowing about in front of the truck. A pallid face peered from behind a curtain, then was gone. A white cat sat on a wall and followed their progress, its fur bristling in the chill wind.

'It looks almost deserted,' said Jo.

'This is where the workers live, if live is the right word for it, though God knows what work they do here. Some people will put up with anything, even when they have a choice.'

'Has it always been like this?' asked Jo.

'Ever since I've had the misfortune to be on this route. I read a book once, one of them old travel books, printed in the last century, where they describe Grenze as a "genteel spa town in the old style". That was before he came, of course. First his father, then him, according to local myth.'

'How can one person make such a difference?' said Jo, noticing a group of four men standing around a brazier, their hands outstretched over the licking flames, feet stamping against the cobbles. The men wore long, dark, shapeless coats, and hoods obscuring their faces.

'It's not about one man,' said the driver. 'It's about what's in all of us. He's an excuse, if anything.'

'I don't understand,' said Jo.

'It's something better to not know of let alone understand. And remember,' said the driver, wagging his thick finger, 'this is not a place to walk around on your own at night, unless you want your head kicked in, or a knife in your back. But then you might appreciate the seamier side of life down on Sacker Street. That's where the action is, so they tell me. There you'll find the theatre you're after, and a lot more besides. I've never been and I never will. Are you sure you want to risk it? They'll eat a cub like you alive down there.'

'I need to find Thomas and Liselotte. I need to follow my heart.'

The big man made a clucking sound of disparagement and shook his head. They swung a sharp right, into a pot-holed side street, splashing through black puddles of dirty slush. It was a cul-de-sac, at the end of which loomed a huge, dark warehouse. The building was set behind high, barbed-wire-topped metal gates, its broad mass silhouetted against the starless sky. It squatted there like a vast empty black mouth. A solid absence. There was a single lamp attached to a small wooden hut just inside the property. It gave out a weak sickly-orange light. The window of the hut had been broken, and was taped over in places. The lambs in the waggon began to bleat.

The driver stopped just in front of the gates, killed the engine but left the side-lights on. Jo heard panicked trampling behind him. Trickles of liquid splashed from the waggon onto the road, where it steamed.

'Is this where you deliver them to be slaughtered?' said Jo.

'No, it's where we give them a nice bath and a shampoo and set. And then they read the evening paper while munching on some sweet meadow grass served on silver platters.' The driver fished a piece of paper from out the glove compartment. 'Idiots should leave the bloody gates open,' he muttered. 'Wait here,' he said to Jo, then lumbered out of the cab and approached the gate. The driver gave a short high whistle.

Eventually, a slim man emerged from the darkness beyond the padlocked gates. He was dressed in red overalls and a red peaked cap, and walked in a slovenly manner, his eyes furtively taking in Jo watching from the cab. A large bunch of keys hung from a ring attached to his belt. He unhooked this ring and, on the third attempt, found a key that opened the padlock. The gates were dragged wide apart by both the driver and the man.

Jo observed the two men as they exchanged words. The driver jabbed a finger at his watch and shoved the piece of paper against the other man's chest. Then the man in the peaked cap made a sign to someone behind him, who was out of sight. He slapped the driver twice on the upper arm before ambling off in the direction

THE GIFT MAKER

of the warehouse. The driver did not seem impressed when he returned to the cab.

'Useless lazy scum,' he said, as he settled into his seat and turned the ignition. 'Drunk as well. I could smell it off him.'

The truck rolled slowly through the gates. Ahead of them, a door was opened in the warehouse, by unseen hands. It slid across with a harsh scraping sound. Lights glowed from within. 'Perhaps you can let me out here,' said Jo. 'You've been kind enough to take me this far.'

The driver gave Jo a look then went back to the business of maneuvering up a ramp into the interior of the building. The man in the peaked cap was guiding the truck in, using all sorts of unnecessary hand and arm movements. His face was waxy, his eyes heavy-lidded.

Immediately, Jo noticed the drop in temperature. It was far colder in the warehouse than it had been outside. The door was slid shut behind them. The truck now sat on a damp stone floor, pools of oily pinkish liquid filled depressions in the concrete. Again the engine was turned off, and began clicking as it cooled. Another man in red overalls, this one wearing a black and white checked bandanna over his head, went round the side of the vehicle and began poking a metal rod through the slats of the waggon. He made harsh barking sounds, that Jo could not interpret, other than that he did not like them. The bleating of the animals grew to a frantic pitch. Hooves and heads banged powerfully against the sides, vibrating the cab.

'Do we help?' said Jo.

'Just hold your horses. Let them do what they have to, and we'll drive out. No need to fraternise with the animals. And I don't mean the woolly kind.'

Jo blinked at the bright overhead strip-lights that gave off a continuous low buzz. The warehouse was enormous, the further ends remaining in near darkness. Even through the closed windows of the cab, a cloying sickly-sweet smell came to Jo's nostrils, mixed with the scent of faeces and burnt fat. Along the walls and down a dozen lengthy aisles stood large white metal containers stacked on top of each other, reaching almost to the ceiling. Each appeared to have a sort of handle on the front panel. The atmosphere was of grim neatness. There were fork-lift trucks sat idle at the top end of two of the aisles. The man with the bandanna had a pock-marked face and a livid scar distorted his upper lip. He stared through the window at Jo with an incipient look of disgust, then moved to the rear of the truck to join his colleague. To the left of the truck, Jo saw a very long metal-topped table, its dull surface scored with scratches and abrasions. On the table, in a well-ordered row, lay a series of knives, with blades of different lengths and curvatures. They gleamed.

'I don't like this place,' said Jo.

'Eat meat, don't you?'

'I suppose so.'

'Oh, get on with it,' the driver said to himself. He tapped his fingers against the wheel and yawned.

The two men noisily dragged out a series of interlocking metal fences and shaped them into a gated channel leading to a pen behind the waggon. Next they unhooked the rear door and the lambs grew silent. Jo could sense them moving as far back into the shit and urine-smeared space as they could. One very young creature, judging by its high-pitched call, called feebly. Those helpless fledgling pleas tore into Jo's mind. In that sound was utter separation, utter vulnerability.

Now the two men had climbed into the waggon and began striking the creatures with metal rods and kicking at them with steel-capped shoes, urging them to jump down into their new enclosure. The men bellowed raucously, the sounds ugly and brutish, as incomprehensible grunts punctuated their blows. The lambs grew remarkably quiet and Jo could hear them jumping down one after another. He visualised the animals having sharp teeth and biting deep into their tormentors' legs and hands. It would not happen, of course. That would be contrary to the order of things.

From the darkened part of the building came another man in red. Paunchy, wearing thick glasses, he attached a hose to a connection on the floor, turned a tap, and began hosing down the lambs with a powerful jet of water. Jo could hear the animals' distress and observed the queasy smile that played on the lips of the man doing the hosing. The man with the bandanna now stood at the metal table, sharpening the series of knives against a whetstone.

There were two smart bangs on the side of the cab, which made Jo jump in his seat, then the first man appeared on the opposite side. The driver wound down the window.

'You're done,' said the man in the peaked cap.

'You might not be seeing me again,' said the driver, with an edge to his voice.

'Aww, don't you like our little town?'

The driver ignored him, his hand tightened against his oil-stained jeans. Jo tried to sink further into the seat.

'Married a fat little rich girl, have ya? Come up on the lottery?' continued the man. 'Who's he?' The man jerked his jaw at Jo, sliding his small vicious eyes over him. 'Oh, it's like that, is it? Never thought you were the type, Peter. Maybe it's why you walk funny. Like a pregnant goose. Must get lonely on the road, Peter. Bit scrawny though, ain't he?' The man craned his neck around. 'Hey, Luca, Mara, come and have a look at Peter's sweetheart, he might be up for sharing him.' He turned back to the driver. 'Us workers have got to stick together, haven't we, Pete?' The man's voice was coarse yet oleaginous.

Peter did not take his eyes off the man as he reached down slowly into the footwell and closed his fingers around a hefty-looking monkey wrench. The man noticed this movement, as did Jo.

'I hope that's a little present you're gonna give me, Peter,' said the man, stepping back a pace. His two associates had sidled up to within a few feet of the cab. The man wearing glasses had left the hose snaked across the wet floor, weakly pumping water. The man in the bandanna stood at the shoulder of the man wearing the cap. He was grinning inanely, showing dark uneven teeth. Jo noticed that he had one hand secreted behind his back. The man wearing glasses then appeared to take something from the other's hidden hand.

'I don't want any trouble,' said Peter. His mouth was tight and he kept the wrench out of view. 'I just deliver and go. That's my job. Now open them doors, Drekavac.'

'You remember my name. I'm touched,' replied the man with the cap.

Jo became aware of an increased vibration from the box. Without hesitation, he took it out from the rucksack and opened it on his lap. The heart was redder than before, beating faster, and thin scarlet veins now striated its surface.

'What's loverboy got there?' said Drekavac. He stood on tip-toe to get a better view. Jo shielded the box's contents with his arm. The other men also drew closer to the window.

'Not here. Are you mad?' hissed the driver.

Jo drew the heart to his ear and closed his eyes.

'Something wrong with him,' said Mara, the bandanna wearer. 'Sub-normal. My wife's brother's like it. They can be good for a laugh though.'

'What d'you mean?' asked Luca, adjusting his bottle-thick glasses on his bloated shapeless face.

'You can get them to do all sorts. I had him interfering with the dog, told him I'd give him some sweets if he did it. After it was over the dog bit him. That's gratitude. Worse than the wife. "Where sweets?" he goes. I just laugh. You can hit them, too, just for a giggle. They don't feel pain the same way. Same as fish, they don't feel pain when you pull them out by their lip.'

'Yeah, but they suffocate in the air.'

'You what? You going soft, or what? You happen to work in a bloody abattoir, moron.'

'Don't call me a moron,' said Luca, rising up to his full height and broadening his chest.

'Listen fatty, don't even think about it.'

Drekavac turned and made a slashing motion with his hand and the two men quietened. He was clearly in charge of operations.

In the cab, Peter was motioning to Jo to close the box, but Jo was elsewhere, his face transfixed in the pink glow that emanated from within it. The driver started the engine and wound up the window.

Drekavac banged on the glass. 'Where do you think you're going?' He picked up one of the metal rods that had been used to goad the lambs. The driver locked his door then leaned across Jo to lock the other side. He carefully avoided making contact with the box.

The truck moved forward a few feet. Mara and Luca leapt in front of it. They now brandished long-bladed boning knives. 'Stab his tyres,' shouted Drekavac. The truck lurched forward catching Mara on the hip. He fell to the floor with a shout of pain, the knife clattering over the concrete to disappear under one of the refrigeration containers.

Without hesitation, Jo unlocked his door and jumped out. He held the open box in front of him, like an offering. The organ pulsed and twitched like a caught fish.

'What the hell are you doing?' shouted the driver.

Jo came to where Luca stood poised to stab the front tyre. Luca took a step back when he saw the contents of the open box, held out at arm's length by Jo as if it were now a shield. Still Luca held the knife, but now his hand was shaking and his pale tongue darted over his thick lips. 'Put that away…it shouldn't be moving. Put that away now!' He rubbed his forehead with the back of his hand. 'I could show you whole fridges of those. Ten a penny. We can't even give them away. Sometimes we burn them when we have too many. Sometimes we grind them up for pet-food. But once they're out they stop. They stop!'

'Stop jabbering and stab him,' shouted Mara, trying and failing to get to his feet. 'It wouldn't be the first time, would it fatty?'

'I told you not to call me names,' said Luca, turning to Mara who was struggling to get off his knees.

Drekavac slammed the rod against the driver's window shattering a portion of the glass. The driver's cheek was cut, as was his forehead. A meandering of blood fell from several small wounds.

'You bastard,' shouted the driver, then unlocked and kicked his door open into the face of Drekavac, who reeled backwards holding his smashed mouth. The driver bounded out and knocked the rod from the other man's fist then lifted the heavy wrench high above his head. Drekavac raised his hands in defence.

'Mara! Luca! Get over here,' spat Drekavac through his loosened front teeth. His split lip was dripping over his overalls and onto the stone floor.

Luca looked first at Jo, who was retreating around the back of the truck in the direction of the makeshift animal enclosure,

 THE GIFT MAKER

then he looked helplessly at his boss. He was rooted to the spot, unable to decide whether to obey Drekavac or follow the student. Something about the beating heart had curtailed his ability to act.

'Make a move and I'll crush his skull like balsa wood,' said the driver.

Drekavac cowered beneath the big man's raised arm. 'Okay, okay. It was just a joke. We get bored here. That's all. Let them go. It's over,' he shouted to his colleagues, finding it increasingly difficult to speak coherently.

'No one's laughing,' said Peter, still waiting for the slightest movement. 'Throw that knife down the aisle,' he called, not looking behind him. Luca threw the knife some thirty feet away and began helping Mara to his feet. Then Peter noticed Jo. He had stepped over one of the enclosure gates and now stood, still holding the open box, in the midst of the milling frightened lambs. They began to cry and bleat and the cries echoed around the walls of the abattoir. Then Jo unhooked one of the gates, and the animals, shyly at first, began to wander out.

'What's that idiot doing?' barked Drekavac.

'Don't move a muscle,' said Peter.

'Okay, okay, big man. It's your game.' Drekavac's voice was somewhat distorted but still decipherable. He gingerly dabbed the back of his hand against his swollen bleeding lip. 'Just get out of here, you and that sick runt. When Reynard hears about this you won't be welcome back, you know that. And he might not leave it there.'

Peter shook his head. 'I wouldn't pollute myself coming back here again. I never should have taken this job in the first place. It's been eating away at me for a while now. But a man can't hide from what he knows. For a few lousy schillings more. I'm no longer for sale. I'd rather eat boiled grass than help feed this scum-hole. The driver put his face close to Drekavac's. 'And if he's so almighty, tell him to come to where I live. I'll be waiting.'

Mara began to laugh. 'He just doesn't get it, does he?'

Luca stayed silent and looked down at his shoes.

'No, you don't,' said Drekavac. 'Mr Reynard's got a bigger plan than you could understand. I don't need to tell you the details. You'll learn soon enough. And I'll remember your name when the time comes, just like you remembered mine.'

'As if he would confide in a drone like you,' answered Peter. 'You'll be chaff, all of you. You'll probably end up in one of those fridges. I've heard he likes his meat stringy.'

They both turned to the raking sound of the main door being dragged across. Jo began walking back to the truck. He had shut the lid of the box and now embraced it close to his chest. A few of the lambs moved to the threshold of the door but did not appear to want to leave. They huddled against each other in a confused protective mass.

'Get in the truck,' said Peter to Jo.

'See, the animals don't want to leave,' said Mara. 'They know we're nice guys really.'

Jo had climbed into the passenger seat. Peter slowly backed away from Drekavac, keeping the others in his peripheral vision. He got into the cab and started the engine. 'Don't one of you filth move,' he shouted through the broken window. Peter put the vehicle into gear and once more it lurched towards where Luca was holding up his crony, whom he promptly dropped back to his knees as the truck passed within a few inches of them. Then Peter reversed wildly, crashing the back of the empty waggon into the metal table, sending the remaining knives flying.

This startled the lambs into a decision to bolt. They ran as one to the open mouth of the exit and into the yard area. The truck

THE GIFT MAKER

followed them, urging them onwards through the main gate, as the three workers cursed and Drekavac hurled knives and anything else he could find at the disappearing back of the truck. In the side mirror, as they turned into the main road, Jo saw a straggle of lambs easily out-running two men dressed in red overalls. He smiled to himself.

'Well, that's cost me my job,' said Peter, once they had stopped some half a mile up the road.

'I had the impression you needed a change.'

The driver frowned, then his broad, bearded face broke into a lopsided grin, small lines fanning from the corners of his eyes. 'You're too clever by half, you are.' He nodded towards the rucksack, in which the box was once more safely stowed. 'I don't know what that did to Luca, but it sure stopped him in his tracks.'

'Lamb will be off the menu for a while,' said Jo.

'Don't count on it,' replied the driver. 'Drekavac was right, damn him. Reynard's influence is spreading, slowly but surely.'

They had parked adjacent to a cemetery, fronted by heavy gates, which had once been painted gold. Most of the paint had flaked away. A tarnished gold and black bird sat atop each supporting wall. These looked to Jo like vultures, wings arched, head tipped menacingly to one side. Shrubbery and weeds grew high around and through the ironwork, and in the light from the driver's torch, the graves beyond appeared unkempt and uncared for. On the other side of the road lay the rubble and detritus of several mean dwellings that had been half-demolished. Jo noticed a rickety-looking kitchen chair and an oven, standing where they might have originally stood when the houses were in one piece.

'I'll give you till six a.m. Won't be light for another hour and a half after that. Usually I'm straight out of this toilet of a town, but this has been a different sort of run on many accounts. My last, I'd say. If you can find your friends by then and get back here, you'll have a ride out of this godforsaken place,' said Peter. He had just finished fastening a piece of sacking over the broken window. Two plasters now adorned his ruddy face.

Jo looked at the driver. 'Are you sure? Won't those men be after you?'

'Ach, they're only minions. They'll be drunk and playing cards by now, threatening each other's mothers most likely.'

'At least we freed the animals,' said Jo.

'I can't afford to be so sentimental. Are you going or staying?'

Jo opened the door a crack. A sudden cold gust of air entered the cab. He shivered. 'I don't know how to get to Sacker Street.'

'See the crossing down there, by that gas tower? Turn right and keep going. You'll hear and smell it before too long.'

'I have about four hours then,' Jo said, glancing at the luminous green hands of the clock. 'Just one thing, Peter. Will you look after this for me? I trust you with it.' Jo held out the rucksack to the driver.

Peter looked down at it and shook his head. 'The things I get involved in.' He took the rucksack and cradled it to himself as if it were a baby. 'Just make sure you're back here by six. With or without your friends. Things might start hotting up after that, and I want to be heading back to my predictable little life.'

'What will you do for a job?'

The big man shrugged. 'Oh, there's always something for a man like me.' He scratched at his beard. 'I don't need much. And I don't need anyone. Just somewhere to sleep, food, and a few beers now and then, and most importantly, space to think…or not.'

'Did you believe that man, Drek…whatever his name was, that Reynard's influence is going to spread beyond this town, about some great plan?'

THE GIFT MAKER

'It already has. And as I told you before, he's an excuse. If you ask me, he only draws on what's there anyway. He twists it this way and that, magnifies it, waters it regularly. But the seed was always there. It's in all of us.'

'We are cursed with free choice,' said Jo.

The driver thought for a moment. 'Maybe just cursed. And I'm not sure by who.'

'Thank you,' said Jo, reaching out his hand. The driver took it, engulfing it in his own.

'I need some kip,' said Peter. 'Mind yourself out there.'

Jo nodded. He jumped out of the cab. He passed along the railings of the cemetery, letting his fingers brush each in turn. When he looked back, the truck's lights were off, and the only light that came from the cab was the faintest glimmer of rose.

twenty-eight

AS I ROW across the lake to Hoffnung the girl is silent. She will not meet my eye. She draws the green coat around her. In our small craft I allow her the privacy she needs. She has seen terrible things in that house, no doubt. Whether they were real or manifested from her fear, her reknowing of herself, is not for me to say. Perhaps it was the shock that brought the knowledge, the ocean of memories flooding back, or perhaps it was the engulfment which induced the shock, and painted horrors on an old woman's cake.

She spoke of fingers and blood and shrouded bodies, a smashed mouth, none of which I saw. To contradict the mind-torn is both an insult and a waste of time. The wrong words to this dark-eyed girl could bring a shattering of self-esteem. And so I row, and remember another lake I rowed across, before the days of cars and telephones and the tyranny of the clock which divides our humanity into ever smaller parcels.

I have left the gun and my case. The first I shall not require, for I do not wish to take a life; indeed I may not. The second, containing the few tools of my trade, are easily replaced if I had a mind to replace them, which I have not.

She is like the daughter I might have seen grow to womanhood, except the hair is not the yellow of corn. *Her* screams tear at me still, her screams from behind that burning door. My lost daughter. How I long to feel nothing, to know nothing, to be nothing. What Liselotte is regaining, I desire to be departed from. For ever, amen. The unbearable weight of the individual human history. Reynard's alleged antithesis, his arch rival for the mortal heart, that power-drunk bestower of eternal life, that tireless worker in clay and fire, I curse him the more, whomever and whatever he is. They say he is omnipresent, omnipotent. The one they call god, the great Other. I suspect that he is a vacuum, an empty hand, an unfortunate joke. In short, a crushing bore. Yes, there are mysteries, and I do not presume to know that other mind, for it and I are permanently estranged. I chose the alternate path, or it chose me.

There are moments when I ponder (and time is something I have had much of) that there is either only Reynard, or the Other. And in my deepest cups, I stumble upon the desperate fancy that they are one and the same. That the two halves have always and ever been one. A most elaborate confidence trick. A many-faced tyrant. A hydra for all time, and all times.

I call myself Daumen, but it is not my name. My name is ash. I found my soubriquet one misty morning on a broken gravestone when I was materialised here. But I may as well be Daumen as anyone, for soon my pattern will be broken up, as was my namesake's.

His other creatures are closing in. They shepherd us. I smell them like burnt blood. I left Maier, my chauffeur, raging on the highway, the black car shaking with its own hatred. They are nearby and may take any shape, human or animal, even inanimate objects. Reynard must know of my transgression. For the time being I have shut out his whispering and the punishment for that is eternal ice. Already I feel the deep chill in my veins. Yet like all servants and slaves I am fenced by the fear of what may happen, not what actually does. I have considered how I may challenge my master and this will reveal the true ambit of his power. It may be narrower than I or others suppose.

Now the girl is asleep by my side as we wait at Hoffnung station for the last train to Grenze. She rests her head against my arm and murmurs in delicious sleep. I believe she must confront her double, make her redundant, or else her purchase on this life will be tenuous. She may fade as her shadow grows more permanent. She may decline to non-existence, and that is my great dread. I will not allow her life to be robbed. I curse myself again for the hand I had in this wickedness.

What has become of the young man, Thomas, I do not know. My own vision is attenuated. His double may have long since erased him, unless Reynard has other plans. For what is a copy when one may lay claim to the original? He seeks the slave that would gladly put on his own manacles. They become lighter than air, imperceptible, until the prisoner thinks himself no longer shackled, and the invisible iron circle is completed.

The train arrives. Darkness has fallen, and I lightly rock her awake. For a moment she thinks I am someone else. Then her vision clears and her face grows serious. So, I can still love human beings. Never too late to learn that. There is something of value left in this empty chest. The love of the memory of love, perhaps, in all its forms.

Liselotte has found herself again. And she talks and talks like a child longing to stay awake, and she tells me of her life, of her dream to dance. And of her life before the university, of her earliest and newest remembrances. She is new-born into her story. She delights in her memories, in the many lighted and unlighted

THE GIFT MAKER

rooms of her past. She takes me by the hand through the corridors of her young life. And with some shame I tell her of Reynard, my part in her doubling, and of what must now be done. She considers my face and I burn as her slender hand touches my cheek.

Reynard will offer her the world, and like that learned doctor long ago, she will be tempted. As I was, as we all may be. She must do the uncommon thing. The act so selfless that it would dumbfound his will. Reynard requires issue. A stainless one. An only begotten child, for he himself is barren. I have often heard him whisper of it, weep for it. Time is running out like a mad spool that will end in darkest confusion. I begin to suspect his plan. His net is cast and we thunder toward it over this iron road. The glass is cold against my colder cheek. What is that taste in my mouth?

She looks at me as though I am her father. There are few passengers aboard this train. I believe some are his cohort. See how they glower. Even that golden-haired child playing with his wooden soldiers. I would rend them with these hands before they touched a hair on her head.

My inner vision is failing me and I see cloudily. I perceive Reynard in his suit of white. And he is talking to another. Monsieur I Bliss is the arch actor, making of his face a chronicle of the human heart, cajoling and tickling the mind like a tame trout. His interlocutor is shady, somewhat effaced. I see a nodding head, a dark-panelled room. How Reynard can prattle. How he loves words like sweetmeats in his joyless mouth.

She asks me if we are nearly there, and I am beaten to the answer by the train guard. The train begins to slow, the squeal against the steel. Others collect their meagre belongings, start to shuffle to the doors. Who these washed-out corpses are I neither know, nor care. They may be a fraction of the multitude over which he desires dominion. Their flaccid, lightless faces tell me they are the easily won. The dross of history. Reynard has pulled them in with promises of shiny objects, rich foods, transcending liquors, like so many bedraggled magpies. We move with them, jostled and jostling, like lambs to the slaughter. Their clothes smell of decay and small fetid dreams.

I have become so bitter, so unyielding in my affections. Endless time may do that. I am not what I was. Yet who am I to discredit these souls? Who am I to look down on anyone? Who is Daumen but a scratched name on a piece of broken stone?

THE GIFT MAKER

twenty-nine

TWO MEN ARE sitting in deep, red leather chairs in a dark-panelled room. A smokeless fire behind a black glass screen heats the shadowy space. There are three black candles on the hexagonal table between them. The two men are drinking companionably, as if they have known each other for years. One is in the early stages of adulthood, he still retains some boyish gestures, his beard is wispy, his hands are small for one so tall. His long coat is draped over the back of the chair, boots are arranged neatly to one side. One of his grey socks shows a bare toe poking through, a partly discoloured nail. The other is a man of uncertain age with eyes of an uncertain colour. His face is nondescript to a startling degree. He is dressed completely in white. White silk slippers adorn his long slim feet. His hair is a uniform white and neatly combed and pomaded. On his left hand he wears a silver ring with a large oval-shaped white stone. If you were to look closely into the stone you might see shapes forming in the milky whiteness.

'Not many people are allowed in here, Thomas,' says Reynard. 'You are an honoured guest. Before I begin, let us drink. Let us drink to *us*.'

Thomas stares at the man across from him. The man's lips have not appeared to move, but words susurrate into Thomas's skull like the low but unmistakable voice of his conscience. He picks up the tumbler, containing a rich amber liquid slipping over pieces of ice, and clinks it against his companion's. He drinks, and smiles as the pulsing warmth of the concoction suffuses his body, from his throat down to his chest, and lower, and out to every extremity. Again, he is protected by a heavy blanket of infinite security.

Thomas grins easily, luxuriously, at the man, and the other nods slowly in return.

'You are exactly where you are meant to be,' he says.

At this, Thomas throws his head back and laughs. In this wild and powerful sound he recognises his own unimpeachable freedom. When he finishes, recovers, he settles back into the chair and begins to listen to Reynard's tale.

'I've seen it all. I've done it all. That's no idle boast, Thomas. In so very many senses it's my chagrin, my lost childhood. Like you, Thomas, I had a father. And I was so happy with him alone, I did not care for my mother. She was a vacancy I never understood. I was born of my father. I used to play in the garden with him. And he was endlessly patient, as I was an awkward child who became an awkward adult. We played from the first rose of morning until the last purple of evening, with ball or hoop or arrow. He taught me many things, including how to love him, Thomas. Do you understand?'

'Yes, he taught you.'

'He *taught* me to love him, assuming that there was no love which might come of its own accord. And so this love, while pleasant, and like a nice hot bath or a child's favourite toy, a bear, say, well, it was conditional as it did not spring from the heart naturally, like leaves to a tree, say.'

Thomas nods. 'Yes, yes, I understand. My father is always disappointed in me.'

'And here's one of the funny bits, Thomas.' Reynard runs his long fingers through his perfect hair. He brings a foot up across his thigh and strokes it leisurely. 'If I did not learn the lesson of love well enough, if I did not love well enough in the manner and mode which he had prescribed, he would decide not to love *me*. The everlasting love he had professed would be withdrawn like the snapping shut of a cigarette case. So I learned how to dissemble. I learned how to lie. I got really good at it, Thomas, so that I almost fooled myself. Almost. I so feared his lack of love, more than I feared the dark, you know, and I feared the dark greatly. Then. So love was like a test, an exam, say, and you can fail exams, as you know, Thomas.'

'I think I'm going to fail mine,' says Thomas, chuckling, as he brings the tumbler once more to his lips.

'Yes, indeed. We may fail or we may pass. But does it have to be this way, Thomas? Have you ever wondered what it might be like without any tests? About what you might find if you were left alone to discover the love you actually felt? Might there not be a greater, more natural love concealed beneath this ever-present fear of failure? And your hate might spring from a natural source, too. Your hate, in fact, the resolve and resonance of it, might indeed be a *testimony* to your love. Have you ever considered that? It might be the necessary shadow, without which there is no substance.'

'We need boundaries, don't we?' says Thomas.

'Look at this!' says Reynard, slapping his chest lightly, then his head. 'These are boundaries. The body. Corporeal limitations. But as you know, the mind can travel independently. We are gifted with imagination, with fancy. With desire and winged thought. Desire must be felt through the body when it is enacted, but its zenith lies in the region of thought, in appreciation and in anticipation of its achievement. The journey and not the destination. And so the body is often a disappointment. But we forgive it, and build our desires afresh. We are always building, Thomas. Castles of joy that are as fragile as a spider's web. And like a web they capture darker matter. Dirt-strewn and festooned with the small cadavers of the helpless. But I digress.'

'I'm losing you,' says Thomas, his eyes straining for focus.

'Lose me so that you might find me afresh, my boy. My sweet boy.'

'Are you the world, Reynard?'

'Yes. And all that is in it. Look at my face, Thomas. Look. I've seen a bayonet plunged into a baby's throat while the bayoneteer shrieked his honour. I've sat at a table where a mother gave the last of the family's bread to a dying child. I've watched cities engulfed by flame and flood, and great cathedrals built with worn-out tools. The capturing of the electric pulse and the discovery of the invisible world. I've seen how the ingenious monkey mind endlessly shapes metal, stone and wood, and how now we have reached the plastic age, and still we are but young in our manipulations. The relentless reordering of atoms into new shapes and designs. But they are just the same atoms reordered. There is nothing new in our philosophy, to quote an old friend. The ever complicated fashions and favours are a repatterning merely. The proliferations of false needs at the expense of the soul.

'I've known the vanity of the harlot and the queen. I've smelt the cowardice of the general and the cowherd. I've observed the slow bravery of the snail and the generosity of the simple-minded. I've known centuries of boredom and centuries of terror, and from this distance they look remarkably similar. I was here at the beginning, Thomas. And I'll be here when the last candle in the universe goes out.' Reynard leans forward and blows out one of the black candles.

'I'm getting drunk. Drunk on you,' says Thomas.

'Isn't it good? Isn't it *all* good, despite what anyone says?'

'Yes, father, it is all good,' says Thomas, tears pricking his eyes.

'Ah, my boy, you know me. You know me at last. Now we shall have a little more entertainment.' And with these words he made an inscrutable and lightning-quick twisting and twirling of his fingers. They blurred before the young man's eyes.

From the far end of the room came a faint drumbeat. It sounded similar to the beating of a heart. Two-pulse beats, the second of each slightly stronger than the first. Then a blueish light grew over a low dais. Thomas turned in his chair. Into this region of light stepped a young, black-haired girl. She was swathed elegantly in a white sheet-like wrap. Her shoulders were slim yet toned. Her feet and calves were bare. Her cat-like eyes were green and she haughtily surveyed her audience down the length of her long aquiline nose. Her fingernails were painted a rich purple. Thomas immediately recognised her as the actress from *The Statue in the Park*, and that actress was Liselotte.

'Where is the other…the other performer?' said Thomas. The memory of his attacking the actor who had owned his face, one who could play the guitar with an expertise and ease he could only dream of, was fading. Now it was akin to something he had seen from the corner of his eye, and not been involved in. Not responsible for. Perhaps the actor had merely reminded him of himself. The theatre might do that. One might become confused between the performer's actions and one's own performance in life. One might get lost in the woods. It was important to keep art and reality separate, so to attain mastery of both. These running thoughts were both his own and not. They appeared to emanate from outwith his being, and bore the character of guidance or instruction from an external intelligence.

Reynard stroked beneath his chin with his forefinger. 'Oh, thanks to you we have dispensed with his services. He lacked a certain sincerity, a necessary depth of character. Why do we need an understudy when we have the player-king?' He smiled broadly at Thomas.

'What will happen now?' said Thomas, finding it hard to tear his gaze from the barefoot girl in the white wrap. How poised she was. How pregnant with anticipated energy were her lineaments. Was she looking at him, or through him? Thomas could not decide. The muted drumbeat continued at a regular pace.

And then the dance began. At first the girl stretched her long arms over her head, and brought her palms together in an attitude of prayer. Her hips began to sway in a liquid motion, describing loose figure-of-eights. Her eyes were now half closed, in what Thomas supposed was a private reverie. Her moist lips parted slightly, revealing the whiteness of her fine teeth. Now her upper body began to gyrate in syncopated rhythm to the movement of her hips. Her upper and lower body moved in such a way as to suggest two bodies conjoined, that were in related yet isolated flow.

Still the drumbeat pulsed, but climbing above this now was heard a high and mellow reed instrument. The tone and meandering tune the reed gave out reminded Thomas of the East, or at least engendered his vague notions of what the East might denote. The air began to grow balmy around his face, and he loosened his shirt at the neck and took more from his glass, which had been replenished outside his notice. He had the sense that he was now living at an earlier time in human history. That beyond the room were bustling bazaars, beehive-like souks, men with long curling pipes attached to water-bowls, snake-charmers,

THE GIFT MAKER

stray thin dogs and burdened donkeys, miraculously woven rugs. Intense heat would be contrasted by cool dappled courtyards and hidden gardens filled with broad-leaved shading palms, fig and date trees, hibiscus bushes, where olive-skinned women with kohl-painted eyes read from sacred books, the goatskin covers of which were embossed with gold.

'Is she not perfect, Thomas?'

Thomas turned, and where Reynard had sat was an empty chair. Empty except for a cut pomegranate, the serried ranks of seeds glistening with their held juice, held apart by bitter walls.

'Is she not the summit of your yearning? The high point of your holy hunger?' The whisper came like tinkling bells, like goat bells on a dry and dusty hill. The whisper was a jug of crystalline well water pouring endlessly from an ancient amphora onto the parched earth of his cares. And as the water poured and was soaked in, it became wine.

Thomas turned back to the dancing girl. Now she began to pirouette on one extended foot, her other leg pointed out, spinning round and round. Her head was thrown back, hair whipping about. Her arms coiled, snaked, and described shapes in the air as she span, palpable shapes, so that Thomas saw amid her twirling limbs the fibrillating images of fine houses, turreted palaces, long verandas, a sunken marble bath filled with milk, a cornucopia overflowing with fruit and jewels and grain, golden and stone statues bearing masks of pain and beauty. She span faster and faster until she was spinning so fast that she appeared utterly still. And from around her midriff shone the outline of a sleeping child, a baby curled into its own comfort.

'Yes, I will,' said Thomas. 'I will *know* you.' And his words were rejoined by the giddy laugher of an infant. By the babbling of eternal innocence.

The dancer was frozen in the blue light. Thomas got up from his seat and approached the dais. He was heavy footed, like a man moving through thick mud. There was an itching heat in his fingers. His legs were strong yet weak. He stepped up onto the small stage, where it was colder than the room. He enfolded the dancer in his arms, his face buried in her neck. Her skin carried the scent of sandalwood, and it was moist from her exertions. She collapsed out of her frozen form and softened in his embrace. They moved as one to the low red couch behind them. Upon this couch were blankets of merino wool, liberally strewn with rose petals.

'My best children,' said Reynard, and his whisper chilled through them as they covered themselves beneath the blankets. The light grew pale as his lips sought hers.

In the shelter of the cocoon night, Thomas searched out Liselotte's eyes. Diamonds of light shone from out their blackness.

'It is you?' he said. 'I know it is, and yet I need your voice.'

Her answer was to draw him once more to her opening mouth.

'Say my name,' said Thomas. 'Tell me who I am.'

But the girl drowned him in her wide eyes, and she did not speak.

🦋 🦋 🦋

A severe white light cut through Thomas's eyelids and he blinked awake. He shielded his eyes. The room around him was completely white: ceiling, walls, floor. There was nothing in the room but the low couch on which he lay. It was now also white, as were the blankets. There was no fire and no grate, no red chairs, and no Liselotte. A chill ran the length of his body. Reaching down, he found that he was naked. There was no sign of his clothes or boots. It was cold in the room. Thomas wrapped a blanket about his body and stood.

THE GIFT MAKER

He moved to where the fire had been, but found the grate had been tiled over with white tiles and the wall had no recess. Looking around, he realised that the room contained neither a window nor a door. It was perfectly sealed. He stumbled to each wall in turn and ran along it, seeking some means of exit. There was nothing. The walls were flawlessly smooth. He could not see where the light was coming from and yet the room was filled with a stark white brilliance. He ran back to the couch and threw it over. On the white stone floor he saw an apple. He knew it belonged to him, but why it did he could not conceive. There was a heart-shaped bruise on one side. Thomas considered biting into the apple, but something held him back. He turned the couch back over and placed the apple upon it.

'Hello,' he called out, and his voice was small and flat, as though he spoke through cotton-wool. 'Where is this?' he attempted to shout, but there was no power in his voice, again it was without potency. The white room sucked all the vigour of his entreaty into itself. Then he thought, with growing alarm, that the oxygen might soon run out, as there was no opening, not even an air grille or vent.

'Help me,' he said, quietly. 'Hold me.' Holding the blanket tighter around himself, he sat on the couch, shivering, and tried to remember how he had come to this place. He recalled sitting with Reynard by the fire as the whispering man told of his life and of the world. There had been the drink that induced such perfected comfort. Liselotte had danced and she had enthralled him. He had gone to her and she had drawn him in. He had entered her like a raindrop does an ocean. He had become lost, undifferentiated, anonymous, infinitely large. She had not spoken. Perhaps she had not been real, Thomas now thought. Perhaps he had made her from a hidden part of himself. The notion grew within him that he had lost something very precious, something which once lost could never be regained. But that was then, when he was old. All that was forgiven. He was responsible for nothing now, for he was new. These understandings were revealed like the turning of playing cards in his brain.

He slid once more under the blankets, holding the bruised apple in his fist. His knees came up towards his middle as his head lowered and thereby he found the perfect position of powerful rest. The knowledge came to him then that the oxygen would never run out, that this room could house him forever, that it would supply all he needed, for he needed nothing beyond it but its protective shell.

The purity of the light was now a benediction. A limitless soothing. Thomas no longer fought against his world, nor did he seek egress. His eyelashes fluttered in formless dreaming. The apple that clung to the bowl of his curled palm, his only necessary possession.

thirty

SACKER STREET WAS almost empty when a young woman and a middle-aged man turned into it. They were clearly not a couple, yet some shade of intimacy linked them.

'Can this really be it?' said Liselotte. 'It's so dirty, so depressing.'

'Failed dreams often are,' said Daumen, stepping over a drunken man, dead to the world.

A few lights flickered still, although many had gone out and buzzed in the damp air. The pavement was littered and slippery with thrown-away objects and decaying food, with drying blood, vomit, and with unknown substances. A grey wind bullied its way up the street, bit at their faces and Liselotte's hands. Upon a heap of rotting fruit across the way sat a young fox.

'Look at it,' said Liselotte. 'It's watching us. It has no fear of us at all.' It struck Liselotte that the fox was smiling. 'You go. Go away!' shouted Liselotte at the fox.

'Why be frightened in your own home?' replied Daumen. He began to rub his arms and chest with his gloved hands. 'Not so soon…not yet,' he said in a low voice.

'Are you that cold?' said Liselotte.

Daumen touched her arm and she stopped and looked up at

him. 'I've brought you here. Done my duty by you, if not by him,' he said.

They came to the Sheol Theatre. In crude red letters, the sign above the door read: *Performance Cancelled*. A tattered playbill flapped in the wind, still half attached to the wall. Liselotte went to it. She read the words *The Statue* out loud, and she saw part of the illustration: a statue of a naked woman pouring water into an ornamental pond, in what looked like a park at dusk. No one else could be seen among the bushes and trees, although parts of the picture had been torn away, and in the missing parts Liselotte felt there might be an answer.

She looked over her shoulder and the fox had gone. 'What do we do now?' she said. 'I came all this way, further than I'll ever go. I've been tricked. Nothing is happening here, in this forgotten place. It's all been wrong, Daumen. There is no quality here, no treasure, and no love. I'm just a silly girl with a damaging dream that has corroded the best of me. I've cheapened everything I care about, running towards this sterile hope.' Then she turned to Daumen. 'What's wrong? What's happening to you?'

Daumen had stopped moving. His face and body had frozen. His head was tilted up, as if at the last moment he had seen something settling over him like an invisible web. Liselotte reached out to him and he was as ice. His coldness burned her fingers. His face was rigid, the locked-in eyes under the heavy brows wavered from side to side then fought for focus on her face, pleaded with her in a frantic silence which she could not read.

'Please, not you. Not now. I can't be alone here. I can't.' She gripped his stone-hard face in her hands. 'Don't leave me in this wasteland, there is nothing here I can make anything of. There is no one here who matters, not even myself. I need you back, Daumen.' She wrapped him in her arms so as to force some warmth into

THE GIFT MAKER

him. Nothing was any help. She pounded against his chest. She took off his hat and threw it violently across the road. 'No...no...' she cried. She reached up and covered his face with kisses, hard kisses to waken, to bring blood to the cheek, to bring life back, but nothing was any good. Then further up the street, in the direction they had come, over Daumen's shoulder, she noticed a small blue and gold flame at ground level. The flame licked forward, it danced its passage, to became a rivulet of fire that was moving toward them, snaking along over cardboard boxes and tin cans, around drains and lamposts, over the drunken man, who leapt to his feet and ran off, patting frenziedly at his ember-speckled clothes.

'A fire's coming,' said Liselotte, and tried to budge the heavy-set man out of the way. 'Please, just move over here. Please. A fire is coming.' The small fire took its time. Occasionally, it paused and lingered over a dead rat, a child's dummy, or a newspaper headline. It had all the time in the world, did this fire, to do its work. It was no showy holocaust, no flagrant blazon. It was just a simple but devastating line of burning phosphorescence. The girl could not move the man and soon the stream of gold and blue heat was licking at his shoes. It rose up to his trouser leg, and smoke, or was it steam? was produced. Yes, steam but no smoke. The smell reminded Liselotte of a laundry. It was both clean yet unsavoury. She stepped away from Daumen and stood beneath the shadow of the portico of the theatre, where she huddled into herself and watched, fascinated, until the man who had saved her life was coated in a skin of living fire. Until he became a lit effigy. Still the shadowy eyes moved wildly in their sockets, trapped and imploring, and no sound ever coming as the pale blue and gold flames occluded them.

Through the clouds of billowing steam she saw his substance gradually dissolve, stared as his face softened to distortion, the features spreading out long and wide like a watercolour wash, as his hair melted away, as his mass grew indistinct, plastic. For a moment a vague human shape held, and he was a man of opaque simmering liquid. Then this shape, too, failed and fell. She moved to where he had been. The water had put out the flame and nothing was left of Daumen, nothing that Liselotte could recognise, but a wide tepid puddle at her feet, and winding streams of the clearest water flowing into the gutter and disappearing into the cracks of the pavement. She bent low and dipped her finger in the warm water. She put it to her lips and it tasted of salt, like the salt water her mother made her drink when she was a child and had a sore throat. Then she ran across the street and retrieved Daumen's hat. She put it to her face and wept into the stiff musky felt. The cold wind whipped against her.

'I know that coat,' said a woman's voice close by.

Liselotte looked up. She knew at once who it was.

'I think it looks better on you,' continued the woman. 'And that boring grey dress, ha! and those old boots,' she laughed, oddly. 'I wouldn't be seen dead in them now.' She was a little shorter than Liselotte, plumper, and perhaps one or two years older. Her bobbed hair had been dyed a garish red. She wore a slightly shabby-looking fur coat that hung to below her knees and covered a sequinned red dress. Her face was thick with badly-applied make-up over uneven skin. The large beauty spot above her lip looked absurd. Liselotte remembered what Gerda had said about the appearance of a music hall singer. Each of the young woman's fingers sported a gaudy ring. Around her thick wrist hung a gold chain bracelet with settings of pale blue stones that glinted coldly. Liselotte thought of what Gerda had told her about the blue diamonds, how this present had turned her daughter's head, and her heart. The red nail varnish at the end of her stubby fingers was chipped.

'No offence meant,' again she laughed her hollow laugh. Her eyes would not quite meet Liselotte's.

'Gisela?'

'I go by *Giselle* now, if you don't mind. Much more sophisticated, don't you think? They sent you, I bet. I thought they might be dead by now.' She screwed up her face as if reacting to an unpleasant smell. 'But couldn't you afford your own clothes, or did you steal them?'

Liselotte began to speak but the other girl cut her off. 'Don't worry, I don't care. I've left that old life behind. I outgrew it. Shed it like a snake's skin, as a friend of mine is fond of saying.'

'Your parents are not dead,' said Liselotte, her voice tense. 'They took me in when I was hurt.'

'Well, you can play at being the dutiful little daughter then. Good luck with it!' Gisela grinned falsely.

'Did you see what just happened to my friend? The gentleman,' said Liselotte, turning Daumen's hat in her hands.

'Funny things do happen here, sweetie. You learn not to ask too many questions, and then you get on like…well, like a house on fire.' Gisela's eyes were sizing Liselotte up, appraising her.

'Are you free to come and go, Gisela?…sorry, I mean Giselle. Only your parents told me a man called Reynard was keeping you a virtual prisoner.'

'Do I look like a prisoner to you?'

'Well, no,' said Liselotte. 'They are so worried about you. Perhaps if you wrote them a letter, letting them know you are well. I would if it were my parents.'

'A good thing not everybody's the same then, isn't it,' replied Gisela in a clipped voice. 'Reynard doesn't tell anyone what to do. That's never been his way. Quite the opposite, in fact, he just helps you to find out what you want for yourself, and want it not too late.'

'How do you mean?' Something made Liselotte glance over to the theatre entrance. She fancied she saw long shadows moving inside, behind the darkened glass.

'Well, I'm not one for fine phrases, but he helps you know yourself, know your freedom, yes? Those old fogies, those stick-in-the-muds who call themselves my "parents", well, I was born to them, yes. But they don't own me, they never did. I'm my own being. I own myself. And with their so-called love they wanted to crush that spirit, to make me into a frightened little person, like they are. They couldn't bear me to be wild 'cause it showed them how trapped and slavish they are. Trapped by their old-fashioned values, doing "good", never asking for too much, never sticking out or making a fuss. Living here, I can do and be whatever I choose to be. No one knows your past here so you can make it all up, and change it every day if you want.' She smiled brightly.

Liselotte looked at the woman in front of her. She certainly seemed sure of herself. But her strained, somewhat bloated face, beneath the caked pan-stick, and the vacuity of her green-mascara'd eyes told a different tale. Her hands were chapped, and her voice had an edge of desperation beneath the apparent bonhomie and urbanity.

'So, what is your past today?' asked Liselotte, barely concealing her sarcasm.

Gisela brought a finger to her lips. She wrinkled her brow in an attitude of thought, which struck Liselotte as stagey. 'Today… today my past is that of an Egyptian princess. One skilled in all the arts of love and seduction.'

'Yes, I read some of your books in your room,' said Liselotte.

'I can see that you don't like me. And do you know what? I don't give a fish-head. You're the one traipsing around in my cast-offs, like a child from the poorhouse.'

 THE GIFT MAKER

'There are no more poorhouses.'

'You want to bet? You really haven't lived, have you? And my next client will be most appreciative of my past, I can assure you. And he will show his appreciation in cold hard cash, among other gifts. There, I've said it. But you probably already guessed.'

'So Reynard did put you to work. Your parents were right.'

'No. Nothing to do with him. My own will and my own pleasure. I happen to enjoy it. I happen to *like* men. Perhaps you don't. Perhaps you're still a silly little virgin, or worse. Am I getting warm?'

Liselotte took a step back. She feared that the woman, whose mouth was now twisted into an ugly snarl, might be about to hit her. 'I am, yes. And I think I have been very silly to come here. But I, too, was invited, lured if you like, by Monsieur Reynard. I was to become a dancer. That was my dream.'

Gisela threw her head back and emitted a coarse cackling laugh. 'You? Work for him? Let's see you then. Let's see you move.'

Now Liselotte thought she herself might lash out. Her left fist balled up. 'There is no music. And besides, I'm a beginner. I was seeking an apprenticeship.'

'Oh, an apprenticeship is it? How remarkable. You're ten a penny, don't you realise that? Many get called to come. Most don't make the grade. Looking at you,' Gisela stared Liselotte up and down, 'I think you're short on the sex front. You're a frigid little bitch is what I'm saying. In fact I'd say, in my professional opinion, you should stick to waitressing or some such, or I suppose you'd fit in in some boring office somewhere.'

Liselotte felt her cheeks burn. 'You don't know me. And now I've met you, I think your poor parents had a blessing in disguise when you ran off to become…to become…'

'Become what? Say it!'

'To become what you are,' said Liselotte very quietly.

The girl clapped her hands together several times. 'Encore, encore…so you do have a little bit of spirit. Maybe he'll find something for you after all. Chorus line, I'm guessing. But first you might have to prove yourself in other ways. There it is then.' Gisela gestured towards the dark mouth of the Sheol Theatre. 'Knock, and someone might answer.' And with these words she strode off down the middle of the street like a fearless cat or a midnight fox, her heels clacking against the wet and grimy cobbles.

Liselotte watched the woman whose clothes she wore disappear down a side-street. She turned to the Sheol and made for the door. Squinting through the glass, she was half-certain she could make out movement within, although the motion was more of a billowing and twisting of dark shapes rather than of people. She still held Daumen's hat like a talisman. How could a man become enflamed and turn to water before her very eyes? As perilous as this journey might continue to be, she must meet with Reynard, as this was what she had set out to do.

Her memory of the ivory-coloured box and of the tiny dancing version of herself was as clear as if it had happened yesterday. The train journey, and the terror, then blackness like a profound sleep, followed by the overwhelming sense of being becalmed in the old couple's lonely cottage. Time had grown mutable, and in her mind now the period with Aldo and Gerda seemed to occupy no more than the span of a dream. Then Mabe had helped her, saved her life in fact, and paid for it with his own. She thought of his torn body lying in the snow, the dead boar nearby. Mabe's blood spattered across the whiteness like red petals on white silk. His father would have found him by now, would be drunk and weeping over his mute child, the one who pretended to have lost his voice, and now truly had. And how Daumen had given up his existence to bring

THE GIFT MAKER

her here. She was certain of his sacrifice, but to whom and why she could not fathom. She held his hat tight against her breast and wondered what region of space and time he might now inhabit.

As Gisela had suggested, she drew back her trembling hand, and knocked.

A face appeared on the other side of the glass. It peered out as Liselotte peered in. There was something familiar about that vague outline of features in the darkness of the theatre foyer, something reminiscent in the fall of the dark hair. Then Liselotte laughed nervously. It was only her reflection after all. How foolish she was becoming, how like a frightened rabbit. Afraid of herself even.

Then the reflection did an odd thing. It moved when Liselotte did not. The door was unbolted from the inside and slowly it began to open. And the figure who stood on the other side was no reflection, it was Liselotte herself.

'Who are you?' said Liselotte to the young woman with her face, but dressed in a simple white wrap, her feet bare on the plush, ash-stained carpet of the foyer.

The young woman gazed at her blankly. For a moment, Liselotte thought her double would speak, but she merely rested her teeth lightly on her lower lip. Liselotte reached out to touch the other's arm. It was cool. It did not feel quite real. There was a waxiness, a plasticity and perfection in the skin tone that was unnatural. The double drew back and made a graceful gesture, inviting Liselotte to step over the threshold. This she did. The door shut behind her with a loud slam. She heard a bolt ramming into place. Liselotte tried the door but it would not open. A low light had arisen in the empty foyer. All around the walls were posters advertising shows, plays, entertainments. They all trumpeted *Reynard I Bliss Presents…* A red staircase led upwards at the end of the room. A bar was on the left, empty stools ranged along its length. The bottles and glasses winked, caught in the light of the muted spotlights sunk into the overhead panels.

'Why are you locking me in? I've come of my own free will. I should be allowed to leave in the same way,' said Liselotte.

The double smiled, and it struck Liselotte as rather a simpering smile, and one which she hoped was not an example of the kind she herself used.

'I remember you from the box. I kept you warm and lay you to rest on my bed. You danced like a poem. Like the brightest of poems. I only showed you to one other, and he swore secrecy. I wanted to *be* you. I thought I was.' Liselotte again reached out to touch the double but she drew further back towards the curving red staircase. 'You want me to follow you? Oh, I love how you move, so perfectly in your body, so unlike me, and yet you wear my face.'

Again the double smiled and curled her purple-tipped fingers at Liselotte.

'Are you trying to seduce me?' said Liselotte. 'But how insane that would be. I must not love myself.' She took a few steps forward. 'Is he here? Reynard? I might as well see him after all the trouble I've taken.'

The double bounded effortlessly up the stairs, glancing back at Liselotte as if this were all a child's party game. The soles of her feet were grey from the ash-stained carpet. 'She is like a child in an adult's body,' thought the young woman in the green coat, who now moved slowly forward, unsure of whether to follow herself. 'Is she perhaps like some blank slate, pure, soulless and solely physical? The thought of that both draws and terrifies me. She must live in a continuous present, much as I did when with Aldo and Gerda. But if she has never known any other existence why should she feel any distress, or sense of loss? She appears to be utterly, painlessly free.'

THE GIFT MAKER

Liselotte carefully followed the double up the stairs and around a corner. At the end of a long corridor, lit by a series of small chandeliers, they came to a white door. The double presented the door to Liselotte in dumb-show. It was as if she were acting a role: part clown, part guide, part temptress.

'Is this where he is?' said Liselotte. 'Do you want me to knock?' The lights of the chandeliers flickered, so that they caused a subtle strobe-effect as the double now pirouetted, waltzed and capered up and down the corridor. 'You truly are a marvel,' said Liselotte, lost in the perfection of the sinuous and sensuous movement of the other.

The double now began to tell a story by means of her dance. At first she picked things from an invisible tree, then she broke these things into smaller pieces and scattered them to creatures at her feet. Her deftness drew the scene about her. Liselotte followed the dancer's eyes, intention, and subtle hand movements, until she could almost see the animals, or whatever they might be, with which she communed. They were small, and moved over the ground, possibly birds. The dancer strode on and was distracted by sudden sounds close by that unnerved her. From apparently nowhere she was hit by flying objects in the small of her back and on her leg, and she reacted with great fear and confusion, trying desperately to avoid the next missile. She fell into a crouching position, and was eventually moved from this by a gentle touch. Her face and attitude changed from night to day, and she rose to standing once more. Another person was there, a portion shorter than herself, with whom she now conversed. The newcomer was of fascination to her and she listened with surprise and delight.

Each scene the dancer rendered with enormous clarity and vivacity, painting the surrounding objects, beings and scenery, and all using only her lithe body and the precise movements and expressions of her face and fingers.

Suddenly the double's countenance changed. Her face became a mask of terror. Something was coming toward her and her companion. She drew a small object from an imaginary pocket and brandished it at the entity that was threatening them. Next, she turned, ran, and hid behind a shape of something, yes, a tree it must be, from the manner in which her arms encircled it. But still the danger was present. She peaked out with a look of hypnotised disgust and horror. Her companion was still where she had been and in great danger. A monstrous event played out before her eyes. Then she made a movement of sudden agitation as if hearing a loud report nearby. She brought her hands closer and buried her face in them. Her chest convulsed with her weeping. She became utterly still, her body a statue cut in the personification of grief.

It was then Liselotte realised what the story in movement had represented. It had been herself, Liselotte, when she did not know her history, alone in the snow and feeding the ducks from the apple tree. And yes, she had taken an apple for herself. Then the snowballs had hit her, which she assumed had been a precursor to death, but had turned out to be the actions of the playful and gallant boy, Mabe. He had told her his secret and she had been enchanted by him, and his desire to protect her. The boar had appeared and she had run for safety while the beast savaged the boy. She had thought herself the boar's next victim, with no help near, when Daumen's shot rang out and the animal fell.

'Your body knows my journey and my mind knows your body,' said Liselotte. 'Surely we are one woman. But now that I am split from you, and you from me, how might we return to each other, how might we become whole again?'

The double did not speak or move, and Liselotte turned back to the white door, and without thinking, opened it, and entered the space beyond.

thirty-one

JO CAME TO the end of the black railings. The graveyard had run the whole length of the street the truck was parked on. It was the largest cemetery Jo had ever seen. He began to think about how many more people had died over the course of history in comparison to how many currently lived on earth. Surely the dead outnumbered the living by a hundred to one, at least. What if they were all to rise up again, as his Sunday school teacher had once told him would one day happen? The living would be cheek-by-jowl with corpses in various states of decay. Some would not look much different to many of the ostensibly living, others would be skeletonised, or long-haired and flesh-eaten, others, surely, would be mere clouds of dust and fragments of bone and tooth reformed into an approximation of the human shape.

He pulled the rough serge collar closer around his neck. It was bitterly cold and his fingers were reddened and stiff. Turning right by the ominous structure of the gasometer, as Peter had instructed, he noticed coloured lights some distance away down the road, but they were indistinct and watery as though seen through wet glass. The more Jo squinted at them, the more they faded, blurred and lost definition. If he did not try to look at them, but let them exist in his peripheral vision, their intensity and clarity grew once more. They reminded him of coloured sweets or jewels, and they spoke to him indefinably of some gift that was his to claim. It was impossible to say how far away they were. Would they turn out to be, mirage-like, seemingly accessible, yet forever out of reach?

The road where Jo stood was dark and deserted, the buildings on each side were low, square industrial units with padlocked gates topped by razor wire. *No-Entry* signs fronted each of them. It was a district, mused Jo, of repetitive robotic work amid dead and soulless substances: metal, rubber, plastic, cardboard. Behind those locked doors stood machines that grinded, cut, riveted and binded. Machines that tore through iron and tin and cobalt, shaped steel and perspex and aluminium.

He had read books about such things, had devoured badly-printed pamphlets that told of whose evil plan it was that led to such a deadening reality for so many. In the morning, Jo supposed, ashen-faced men and women would come in dark, shapeless clothes, carrying lunch-pails filled with tasteless, nutritionally worthless pap, and mind these machines until it was time to trudge back to their meagre dwellings again. The machines would ask very little of the men and women, other than they be there for the greater portion of their day, push a lever or button now and then, add a little oil, make minor adjustments, stand by the machines and be of them, an adjunct to them, in the filthy air, spend the best and worst years of their life in close proximity to their mechanical masters. And all for the right to exist at all. All for the right to call oneself productive.

The owners of the machines lived elsewhere, Jo had read, on huge estates behind high, ivy-drenched walls, a battalion of uniformed servants at their beck and call. They owned hillsides, meadows, great stretches of rivers, lakes, woods, fields, workers'

THE GIFT MAKER

cottages, villages, towns, cities, deserts, savannahs, seas, oceans, countries, continents. They even owned uncharted space. This had made Jo dizzyingly angry and vengeful in an unfocussed way, flushed with the desire to *do something* about it all, to overturn the *system* (a system he admittedly barely understood), so that every person might enjoy the leisure, and thereby the desire, to develop their full human potential, to read endless books and poems about the soul and the nature of existence. To be unencumbered from meaningless toil, and the tyranny of the owners of the world, so that these people might study with great vigour, endless curiosity, and frolic in the life of the mind, as Jo himself had done, while soothing classical music played in the background, and endlessly patient professors sat at chessboards in a vast, velvet-lined, ever expanding library of knowledge. So that this great mass of wasted humanity might aspire to what Jo had himself so often aspired: a complete unfettering from the body's grosser desires, thus to live in perpetual freedom and light.

'But what do I really know of these things?' Jo spoke aloud, as he often did when trying to work things out. 'My thoughts and ideals are light and weak because I've never had to inscribe them on the world, I am a man without responsibility. I've never needed to fight for my treasures because I carry them in my head. Books are temporary refuge, and libraries are temporary screens from the ugliness of the necessary slaughter. Surely my untested principles would shatter on the hard cold surfaces of the world, and break upon the hard cold faces of the few, who for their own benefit shape the lives of the many. Other forces change the structure of the system: anger and greed and fear, not such airy postulations as an undergraduate's wet dream of unrealisable perfection. And how sterile my longings are. I don't even want my body. I have no desire for another's body. I am not of body. Was I born by mistake, into the wrong time, the wrong universe, for the wrong cause? Are we who like to think and philosophise superfluous, a breed dying out, an unnecessary spoke in the wheel of continuous progress?

'What has ever been learned, in all the bloody centuries. We're still at each other's throats given half a chance. It's hard-wired in us. Stop! Stop…Jo. Let me for one moment stop thinking and analysing and relating the world I see to the half-baked meanderings inside my skull. The world is not a book. And neither am I. I am *not* responsible.'

The line of industrial units came to an end and Jo found himself on an avenue of linden trees with their leaves in full display, as though it were the middle of May rather than December. Here, the road surface changed to a glassy marble-like substance, smooth and spotless like the floor of some palace, and Jo noticed a sudden warming of the air, so much so that he now loosened his collar and withdrew his hands from his pockets. It felt as though this portion of the street was warmed by invisible radiators. Did the heat arise from beneath the road? Jo could not tell. He kneeled down. The marble was pleasantly warm to the touch. He might, he supposed, even walk upon it barefoot. The marble sent calming waves through his fingers and up his arm. *A pulse of life from beyond the stone*, was the phrase that entered his thoughts.

The light had risen somewhat and Jo looked up. Stars. An impossible number of them. Great tunnels and spirals of them, a vast ornate patterning of stars, as though ten thousand droplets of light were frozen in movement against the purple-dark sky. The light they let fall was a kind light. Jo smiled at the vision. 'How wonderful,' he said quietly. 'How sublime.' He searched the heavenly display for meaning, tried to discern images of oxen or hunters or ploughs, but could not. Yet there was great meaning in the apparently random whole. It contained a language as yet

THE GIFT MAKER

unlearned, and Jo felt a sense of his importance as witness to it, knowing somehow that he was integral to its pattern, linked forever to the will or source that had engendered such ageless beauty.

He stood, took off his shoes and socks, and continued his progress up the marble avenue. A little further on, he took off his coat and laid it, neatly-folded, beneath one of the trees, the arms crossing the heart area of the cloth. The air was faintly perfumed, a scent Jo did not initially recognise. It was a comforting scent, both rare and familiar, like that of home, or more precisely, like the scent of a loved one's clothes when your tear-stained face is buried in them. And that scent, in addition to the loved one's soothing words and their stroking of your younger hair, slows your troubled heart and almost painlessly banishes your fear, for a time.

'So you made it.'

On a bench between two trees, legs crossed casually, smoking a slim cigar, sat Reynard.

Jo turned to the speaker. 'I'm tired of my thinking. I'm tired of the cogs going round and round, and never anything finalised, never anything resolved.'

'I know, Johann. The mind can be a burden. When you've lived as long as I have, you learn to empty it at will. I call it "contemplating the universe". Do you like that idea? It's a bit of a joke, I suppose. Can you imagine living with it forever, though, this ceaseless searching for truth, for the blueprint of life? You've only had, what, twenty years?'

'Can I sit with you for a bit? I'm so weary, as if I've lived for two thousand years.' Jo went to the bench and sat next to Reynard.

They were silent for a while, watching the leaves playing in the delicate wind, and eventually Jo met Reynard's patient, amused gaze. 'That smell,' Jo said. 'Coming from your cigar…it is the smell of my mother's dress when I ran to her after falling and cutting my knee. It is the smell of my father's hair-oil, of his tobacco tin, of the leather of his gardening shoes.'

'I am them all,' said Reynard, touching Jo's knee. 'I healed you when you were sick. I picked you up when you fell. I gave you sweetmeats and I gave you bitter medicine. I gave you confidence and I gave you pause. I gave you softness of heart when in your pride you hardened against my boundless love. The love that protects ever and asks for nothing in return. You could talk to me when no one else would listen, could listen. I was always there for you. All like a good brother should.'

'And you?' said Jo. 'Who do you turn to when you cut your knee, when you are lonely?'

Reynard's face was painfully nondescript, and his eyes were endlessly compassionate and instantly forgettable. His white clothes shone sweetly in the starlight. His soft, fragrant white hair was sad in its perfection. 'I turn to you. And to all those like you. I do *not* turn to my father, Johann. I turn to my brother. And to my sister. For we are kindred and none of us asked for this. The relentless burden of our existence.' He gestured at the scene before them. 'None of us are responsible, not for an atom of it, as I heard you yourself say, further up the marble road. There is only one tyrant, Johann. And we are all at his sickening mercy, myself as much as anyone. The weakness we are born with stings, doesn't it, my lad? It bruises. The best we can do is huddle together, eh? Like lambs on a blasted heath, searching for temporary refuge from his thunderbolts, from his pelting cold, from his jealous, killing little love.'

'None of us are responsible,' said Jo, laying his head on Reynard's shoulder, like a brother, like a lover, like his own shadow.

'Now this is camaraderie, isn't it, lad?'

THE GIFT MAKER

'Yes,' said Jo. 'This is what I've been missing all my life.'

The smoke from Reynard's cigar wafted over Jo's face, wound up like silken snakes through his nostrils and through his partially open mouth. The smoke that recalled the dearest scents of his history and of his longing, coiled and inched down his throat to his lungs, feathered around his heart, delved into his intestines, arteries and veins, licked around his liver and kidneys, calming and caressing all with inexpressible solace, slowing the vital functions to just the necessary minimum effort. Other snakes rose into the cave of his skull and entered the impossible machine of his brain, quieted it with their slinking and gentle probing, switched off the pain receptors, wrapped around the memory boards, occluding them, trammelled the offices of the imagination, lulling Jo into the most deliciously restful waking slumber.

Jo smiled at Reynard, his eyes half-open like a drowsing cat. 'You've come so far. And yet you haven't taken a step. You're still in a kind of garden.'

Reynard's brow furrowed and he swallowed as one who is suddenly thirsty. 'You know me then, young man?'

'I do, yet I don't know how I do. You are Adam. The firstborn.'

For a moment Reynard's face crumpled, and all the woe in the world was written in it. For a long moment Jo thought he saw the promise of tears in the other's eyes. 'My dear Johann,' Reynard said at last, 'you are almost right.'

Reynard's face began to change, his skin to darken and his eyes to turn to the brightest blue. His mouth broadened and his hair turned to shimmering dark gold.

thirty-two

SOMETHING WOKE HIM. The windows had become fogged with his breath. He stretched along the leaned-back seat, pulled the blanket tighter, as his stockinged feet hit the rough edge of the footwell. The green luminous hands said just after four. Suicide hour, as his old school-friend Kumpel used to say. Kumpel: a lanky, blond-haired apprentice forester who hanged himself from a tree which he had refused to cut down. 'I will defend this tree with my life,' Kumpel had said, his gap-toothed smile underplaying the seriousness of his intent. People thought he had gone mad. There was talk of him losing his job, even being carted off to the big house. Peter found him early one April morning. They had planned to practice woodturning by Kumpel's makeshift cabin. Peter had sat beneath the tree from which his friend dangled, sat there for more than an hour, staring at the ground, his mind a blank. Eventually, the right people came and Kumpel was cut down, covered with a sheet, and taken away. Peter had not gone to the funeral. He rarely thought of his old comrade. They used to fish for eels together, take long walks through the woods in companionable silence. Kumpel knew everything there was to know about mushrooms: those to seek, those to avoid. He was

THE GIFT MAKER

champion of the rarely-found *golden pfefferling*, which when fried with onion and bacon tasted to Peter like paradise on a fork. Yes, young Kumpel knew the deadly from the delicious. But no matter how diligently he tried to instruct Peter, it just would not stick. The driver never gained confidence in his own ability to identify. *How like my life as a whole*, he considered, in his lowest states. Peter would never trust himself to pick mushrooms alone.

Under the blanket he rubbed his hands together, then moved them over his thighs. The lump of the box lay at his side. He touched it and a warmth rose into his palm. 'What am I living for?' Peter said into the darkness.

The patched broken window was letting in a draft. The cuts on his face stung when he made any expression at all. There were the vestiges of a chocolate taste in his mouth. He leaned forward and began to write his name in the misted glass. P. E. He jerked back. Something was out there, lying across the bonnet of the truck. It had moved. Peter could swear it had moved. He leaned forward again and squinted through the first two letters of his name. He rubbed away more of the condensation. A long, heavy black shape was draped across the bonnet, like a thick black carpet rolled up. Then the carpet moved and a head appeared, an elongated muzzle, and yellow glistening eyes stared through the window back at him.

The yellow eyes bored into his, as the rattling breath from the black lips remisted the window from the outside. When this cleared, the mouth was open in what might have been a yawn, revealing two rows of pointed teeth, the long canines glinting with saliva. The fat liver-coloured tongue lolled to one side and dripped. The head, topped by high triangular ears, was slightly cocked. It gave a single loud bark, a sound of such thunderous power and depth that it vibrated through Peter's chest.

'My god,' said Peter. 'My god.' A low rumbling growl came from the creature. A dog-like animal, yet very unlike any natural dog, and bigger and more powerful than any Peter had ever seen. He had come across a few specimens on his travels: Alsatians or mastiffs tearing up to farmers' gates, or pacing behind iron railings protecting the owner's stock. Peter had often wondered what he might do had the barrier not been there. He did not dislike dogs, merely preferred them out of range.

He edged over to the driver's seat. The creature's head followed him across. Now it was partially occluded by the misted glass, but the driver sensed it there, fully aware of the black mass beyond the window. He turned the key and the engine whined and coughed and seemed to want to start, yet did not fire. 'Must be cold,' Peter muttered. He tried it again and again, then began pumping the accelerator at the same time. The animal barked a second time, even louder. Then the unbroken deep growl returned. Peter's hand was shaking. 'It's daft this, just a dog. Just a silly mutt. What's wrong with me?' But inside he knew this was no ordinary dog and he began to suspect where it might have come from. Still the engine would not engage. Peter feared the starter motor would be damaged, as it screeched, juddered and complained at the continued attempts to get the engine going.

He tried the headlights. Nothing. The road remained in darkness. He moved the switch back and forth, manically, as if that might make a difference. He punched the horn until the ball of his palm hurt. Not a squeak. He reached up and flicked the cab light switch. It came on after a few flickers, but very weakly. 'Blast it,' he hissed. 'What a time to let me down. Battery's as good as out. Should be miles away from here anyway. Shouldn't have gotten involved. Should have stuck to my rules.'

THE GIFT MAKER

The growl grew quieter and deeper, then broke off. Peter scrabbled for the monkey wrench in the dark footwell. He gripped it, slipped his feet into his boots, and carefully unlocked the driver's door. Then he pushed it open a few inches, praying it would not make a sound, and let one foot drop silently to the floor. In a flash the creature leapt from the bonnet and stood facing Peter, less than a yard away. It gave three powerful barks. Peter felt a warm, wet patch forming around his groin. He saw the dog as a dense black form, almost as tall as himself. He recoiled at the redness of its mouth, and shuddered at the golden glint of its small demonic eyes. For a moment he was paralysed, as one of his ancestors might have been coming face-to-face with a sabre-toothed tiger. He came to himself, and scurrying backwards into the cab, accidentally dropped the wrench, where it clattered noisily to the road. Then just in time he slammed the door and furiously locked it as the dog bounded at the glass, its mouth smearing the surface with a patina of mucus-like drool.

Peter recognised this as a warning to stay inside, and knowing that had the creature wished to, it could so easily have punched a hole in the already damaged window and got at him. He brought a hand to his neck, picturing those powerful jaws clamped around it, cutting off his airway, the canines sinking effortlessly into his flesh, before easing his throat out. His chest heaved as he gripped the wheel. Wiping a semi-circle of condensation from the side window, he finally saw how huge the beast was, as it paced up and down, breath smoking from its quivering mouth. It was twice to three times as big as a fully-grown Alsatian, superior to the height of a Great Dane, and far more muscular and sturdy than either. Its body, when side-on, showed itself to be strangely elongated, as if two bodies had been joined in some infernal experiment. The head was wide, flat, shaped like an anvil, the protruding muzzle and jaws appeared enormous, as once more they opened to reveal the ranks of teeth and slavering fat tongue.

Then Peter noticed the legs. There were six. 'It cannot be,' he said, awe-struck. He counted them again as the creature turned side-on once more. Then it twisted and jumped with unexpected ease onto the bonnet, to settle back into its apparent guarding position. The last two legs and thick coiling tail hung over one side, its forepaws and massive head drooped over the other.

Peter heard the animal's deep regular breathing as he sat back in the seat, biting at his knuckles, desperately thinking how he might escape.

THE GIFT MAKER

thirty-three

THROUGH THE WHITE door into the white passageway.

It reminded Liselotte of a hospital, or of that large private asylum in the countryside near the picturesque spa town of Schtummgarten, where her mother had once taken her to visit her uncle Milo. He had appeared to Liselotte to be perfectly normal. In fact, when she thought about it now, possibly the sanest man she had ever met. She was eleven years old, but precocious in her language and her appreciation of ideas, or so others thought, and Milo talked to her as an equal, he actually asked her opinion on things, whereas her mother seemed to endlessly be telling her what to think, what to feel.

The interminable white corridors, beneath arched ceilings, led off to numerous private rooms. Nurses in stiff dark-grey uniforms patrolled these corridors, bunches of keys clinking at their waists. Some pushed trolleys carrying covered dishes smelling of meat and potatoes.

Milo's room had the appearance, or so Liselotte later considered, of a gentleman's study. Thick, patterned carpet beneath an assortment of Turkish rugs, a tall bookcase, a blue chaise longue, even an old-fashioned gramophone with its wide trumpet that suggested to Liselotte an exotic bronze flower. Milo had given her a dog-eared book of poems by Zheng Dao, that wizened old minimalist of the Shen Dynasty. She still had it on her shelf in her student apartment in Schwalbenbach. Yes, she remembered it all now, her apartment, her life, down to every item in her wardrobe, to nearly every book on her shelves. On the back page of the Zheng Dao, Milo had written, in three short lines: *madness in the group/ not the individual /Milo the un-Free.* A *haiku*, Liselotte realised much later, after she had been taught about such things. Below the lines, he had pencilled a sun with a quizzical face, followed by a half moon with one long-lashed closed eye, and a saddened smile.

And now, so many years later, Liselotte was walking down another white corridor. This was brightly lit, on the verge of being glaring, yet she could see no source for the light. There were no windows. The walls were flawlessly smooth, barely an undulation or tiny spider-crack in the plaster. The floor was white marble. She bent down without knowing why, and touched it. It was warm. And the warmth rose through her hand and up her arm. It induced a sense of steady calm in her, something which she had of late become a stranger to. *How my thoughts are now so evenly spaced, without one wanting to crowd out the others*, she considered. *I have time. All the time in the world. I will walk to the end of this corridor and there will be an opening, or a turning. Someone is to meet me, someone vital to my future as I am to theirs.* She was certain of this, almost as if she herself had arranged the tryst.

It did not seem to matter to Liselotte, at this stage, that she could not make out the end of the passage. When she looked ahead, the lines of the walls converged in the far distance to a single shadowed dot. *That must be the end*, she consoled herself. *It looks so much further than it is.* Her body felt younger and stronger than it had for a long time, and soon the green coat became an encumbrance. It was never hers in any case. She undid the four large, flat green buttons and took it off. She was about to place it neatly folded by the wall when she remembered that she had left something of value in one of the pockets. She lay Daumen's hat gently on the floor by the wall. It was acceptable to be without a coat indoors but not without her…she rummaged in all four pockets and in the last one she found it. The apple. The two leaves that were still attached to its stalk had turned brown and dry. She plucked them off and let them fall over her coat. The blush on the side that had faced the sun was still as pleasing to the eye. Liselotte put it to her nose. Under the clean fresh scent was buried a hint of its future corruptibility. But the young woman could not, or would not, detect this. To her it was the only perfect thing in the world. And yet she did not fear for it, and assumed only a temporary guardianship.

Her boots, or rather Gisela's boots, were felt to be an unnecessary accoutrement. Sitting with her back against the white wall, she pulled them off. Then followed her stockings, the chunky blue cardigan, the grey dress, and finally her badly-ironed underclothes. All were folded in a neat pile at which Liselotte stared down. Daumen's hat she finally placed on top of all.

'None of you are me,' she said. She wore her nakedness lightly. She neither appraised nor ignored the sensations of her body. She was neither proud nor shame-struck. Neither too cold nor too warm, but like in the fairy-tale, *just right*. She was no longer a mind in a body, judging it from the height of its lofty cogitations, hating her flesh's perceived ungainliness, its lack of grace, its fear of rhythm, all of which had been false perceptions in any case, sourced from other minds, other eyes, that knew her not. She effortlessly united: bodymind and mindbody. She even tried, as an experiment, to judge her form, deciding whether her knees were too prominent, or whether one breast was slightly higher than the other. But all to no avail. Such thoughts had no sticking power, and fell harmlessly like the airiest of blossoms to the ground.

Like the clothes she had discarded, such thoughts were not hers, and not her. She smiled and then the smile became a low laugh. The laugh did not need to grow to hilarity, to wildness. No audience was required. Nothing had to be forced anymore, nothing more or less than what it was. She was as natural as the apple that rested in her palm. She felt neither innocent nor guilty. Those terms had no more meaning for her. She was in her nature as much as the apple was. Memory could be accessed but it no longer mastered her. And her path now led toward the opaque dot in the distance. Her feet trod the warm white marble as the dot grew imperceptibly larger.

𝅦 𝅦 𝅦

Thomas stirred in his sleep. He was dreaming. He was back at school and hiding in the cupboard from the metal-work teacher. He had damaged one of the tools, and the teacher, Mr Kohl, who had a thick red neck and the face of a pig, was feverishly searching for him, clattering files and rasps across the room. Mr Kohl was shouting. And the fear of the man's anger made Thomas feel smaller than a speck of dust. That the anger alone could eradicate Thomas's being. He would simply burn up in it. And all for bending the end of a bradawl.

Finally, the cupboard door was flung open and there stood Mr Kohl. His neck was very red. But his face, while still porcine, wore a look of concern, a not unkind look. 'We've all been worried about you, Thomas,' said the teacher, and put out his hand for the boy to hold. Thomas was both the boy who placed his small hand in the teacher's, and the man that stood and watched the scene from the other side of the classroom, sat on one of the low, chisel-scarred workbenches, his hand absentmindedly turning the tightening bar of the vice, back and forth, back and forth. Thomas watched his smaller self being led gently away, Mr Kohl's protective arm guiding him. 'You'll miss your lunch. We can't have that, can we?' said Mr Kohl, before the man and boy were suddenly out of sight, and the grown Thomas was alone in the metalwork room, with all the tools once more tidily arranged in their drawers and their cubbyholes. The metal filings and scraps had been swept from the floor and now half filled the red bucket by the door. The classroom grew almost dark about him. And far off he heard the watery skirling of many children's voices as they were set free at the end of the school day. Their cries and shrieks faded into a winter afternoon as they separated and found their individual homes.

When Thomas opened his eyes, he was still in the white room under the white blankets on the white bed. The light did not make him squint. Licking his lips, he felt the beginnings of a thirst, and an incipient hunger. The dream had left a wake of wistfulness that Thomas attempted to dispel. Beneath the bedclothes, his hand still curled around the apple. He brought it out into the room and found that it had changed. It was now silver and hard and cold. Its weight slightly more than a cricket ball, Thomas considered, and this conjured an image of himself and a few half-remembered schoolfriends playing this odd, well-mannered, foreign game on a triangle of grass near his old school. He had been young and ungainly and had rolled the hard red ball with the stitched leather seams under-arm, instead of the over-the-head throw, which Feldwürfel and Maus had become adept at. Yes, that had been their names, but their faces remained unfilled grey ovals when Thomas tried to detail them. On the apple, the heart-shaped bruise was finely engraved as a thin outline, where it had formerly existed.

'What use is this?' Thomas said, and his voice was again flat and dullened in the room. He eased back the blankets from his naked body, and stood up. His nakedness neither surprised nor distressed him. Clothes were clearly not necessary here. The floor was just warm enough for the bare soles of his feet. The air in the room, also just warm enough. He began to attempt to think. Thinking had seemed so redundant before his falling to sleep, a laughable non-essential. He was fully aware that he had been a certain Thomas Ruder, the occasionally conscientious and hardworking student of history at Schwalbenbach University, eldest son of a small farmer; the composer of some fourteen maudlin love songs, none of which he had played to a soul.

He could picture all the faces of his family: father, annoying younger brother, and more distant relatives, whom he had never had any interest in, and, of course, his dead mother, who existed only now in photographs. When he tried to picture her in life rather than in the capturing of light and shade on photographic paper, he saw as fixed images, mind photographs: a young woman holding a swaddled baby by a gate opening on to a field of high corn; a slightly older woman with a slightly different hair-do being presented a cake by an eight-year-old boy, while others watched indulgently from around a long wooden table; then a wild-haired teenager, himself, hemmed between his father and *her*, in a yard scattered with chickens and old horseshoes, the youth already a head taller than both his bookends, bony arms circled about their thickening waists.

The woman wears a shapeless dress, scraped back greying hair, and a tight, lipless smile that both defies and accepts the pain that has become a part of all their lives. These pictures will not move.

THE GIFT MAKER

Try as he might, he can neither recall the sound of his mother's voice, nor the pressure and texture of her hand in his.

Then a procession of other faces projected themselves onto the blank walls of his perfect chamber: the straggle of school chums, with young-old faces, some fat, some thin, leaping or ambling in and out of his limited life, who, because they were contemporaries, he could never remember as children per se, although they clearly had been. He recalled them as merely others, more or less like himself, separated somehow, essentially but undefinably, from the larger human beings. The larger ones knew things that the smaller ones didn't. The babies knew nothing at all. And the larger ones worshipped at the cot of their innocence. They made odd noises, calculated to soothe.

The larger ones were the *responsible* ones. Responsible for everything that was, had ever been, and ever would be, and their tired or bitter or quietly despairing faces told of that inhuman burden. Yet he also saw them as strange helpless gods who could not bear the weight of the responsibility given to them, and when the cracks spidered, then widened until they gaped, out poured a different self, often in a disturbing rush, and they were reduced instantly to the level of his smaller self and his smaller colleagues - at least temporarily. The larger ones would cover this in obvious ways, and once more the mask of otherness, of pretended mastery, of an apparent yet attenuated confidence would harden over their child-like fear. The larger ones had to pretend to know in order to keep the smaller ones, and themselves, secure and fed and quiet and under control. The smaller ones knew all this instinctively, and played on it. They seemed not to care that theirs was a temporary state of affairs; perhaps they were locked in blissful forgetfulness as part of some divinely cruel plan. They did not worry that they, too, would one day be expected to pick up the weight of the world on their slowly widening backs. No one told them this until it was too late. But what did the larger ones actually know?

Somehow it all limped along, after a fashion, over the relentless years, full or empty, and listing awkwardly, like a three-wheeled cart. Thomas himself could not remember being a child, as he now thought of children when he happened to meet one, but merely as an earlier yet remaining version of who he now was. Others talked of children as if they were a different species, essentially better somehow and in a state of permanence, absurdly protective of them as much as they were cold and dismissive to their future embodiments: the adults around them. Childhood is an invention, Thomas avowed to himself, and so is adulthood. A false division, a double lie.

Next in the album with the pages that often stuck together was the curly-haired girl from the bakery, who ignited his first hot twistings under the rough blankets of his narrow bunk. The puppy fat on her upper arms and the inchoate double chin entranced him. Once she had grazed his palm with her short, plump, sticky fingers as she handed him change for the rolls he had just purchased, and the heat dropped through his body like a stone. It fizzed down his legs and enfeebled them. He had walked out the bakery door, his face rigid with indeterminate longing, leaving the rolls in their wax-paper wrapping on the finger-stained wooden counter.

University friends followed: Ulli's drunken leer filled one white wall, then occupying the opposite was Jo's pale receding hairline over his pale receding expression, his mind a nest of abstruse ruminations. Marieta and Bilma flickered across the screen of the wall, a study in inelegant boredom. His professors, Lipschnitz and Halloumi, twin ghouls of grammar and pedantry, glowered over their glasses, even though only Lipschnitz wore them in life.

Up popped Mrs Grau wagging a ring-festooned finger, a painting of her beloved Schtupsee in the background. Müller:

the nightwatchman's gaping, black-lipped face shocked onto the screen, a guitar string deeply embedded in his flabby neck. 'You're dead, and I am responsible somehow,' whispered Thomas. At this, the binding around Müller's throat loosened. It unwound itself like an uncoiling spring, and with this the nightwatchman's lips regained a healthy hue, as did his face, barring the mottled broken veins around his nose and cheeks caused by too much imbibing. Müller smiled, and gently shook his head.

The images rose to semi-clarity on the white walls, then faded to a vibrating snowiness, similar to what Thomas had once seen on his uncle's new black-and-white television receiver, the only one in the village at the time. Everyone had gathered round to watch the State Orchestra broadcast their rendition of the *Pilsendaume Variations (Opus II)*, but nothing appeared, except thousands of black and white fibrillating squares of light, accompanied by a metallic hissing. 'It's the damn interference…the interference is what it is,' his uncle kept shouting, smacking the top of the set with ever increasing force and rapidity. The villagers sloped off muttering "Waste of time" or "That's what you get when you meddle." Thomas was only eleven when this had happened and he wondered about this "interference" for a long time, and wanted to know who was behind it. The interferers must be stopped so that the music could play. He, Thomas, would track them down and bring their silly interference to a sharp end, with the help of his bow and arrow if necessary.

Someone was missing. Or was it two people? Two very important people. Then slowly, in outline at first, emerged the silhouette of a man. A pencil sketch of an ordinary figure, no detail. The background remained a uniform white. Any features could have been made to fit. An average-sized non-entity, the most nondescript generic shape one might imagine. Then the face was drafted in: again the most nondescript of features emerged. All so painfully commonplace. A man you would stare through on the morning train as through a pane of glass. The quintessential everyman. But the eyes. Oh, the eyes held everything. They had felt everything from the deepest deeps to the ultra shallows of insignificance. The eyes bore the weight of mankind and man unkind, and every variation or excuse in between. *Reynard was the world*. He was of it and had suffered with it and for it, and his suffering was endless. His joy was sporadic, and he drank from it in its season, encouraging others to do so for their heart's sake, even in the teeth of his dark understanding. Perhaps the joy was a dream-of-forgetting that he was cursed to be forever waking up from. And the weight, the monstrous responsibility, was finally his, and his eyes bled this knowledge.

An invisible eraser began erasing Reynard. From the feet up, it rubbed away his corporeality until there was only the face. Then the face was effaced, leaving only the eyes, which in their turn grew smaller and smaller. Thomas watched as the eyes that contained a universe shrank to pinpricks. To the smallest marks that might be, in some insane hope, the tentative beginnings of a vast blueprint, an arrogantly huge and ornate plan for life. The characterless white wall returned, without stain or feature, and Thomas in his impotent rage pulled back his arm and let the silver apple fly. It shattered silently into an infinite number of pieces against the wall. These pieces fell to the white floor as temporary stars of phosphorescence. Splinters of possibility in endless space. These innumerable tiny filaments that had once comprised the silver apple lost their lustre, went out, were gone for now, and gone forever.

Thomas sank to his knees and wept. He wept uncontrollably. He roared his pain until his throat burned, and he beat his knuckles

                                                THE GIFT MAKER

against the floor until they were numb. He pulled at his hair and wailed at the final emptiness of his perfect prison. He cried for everything and for nothing. He cried for the sake of the sound of it, like the keening women that he remembered arriving at his village in brightly-painted caravans, their skirts smelling of nutmeg and woodsmoke. Fat tears dropped onto his bare legs and onto the floor. When his breath finally slowed, and the anguish grew tractable, he looked up at the wall that faced him. It was no longer a solid white mass. He could see through it, as through partially misted glass. What came to view on the other side was a corridor, a seemingly endless white corridor with a marble floor and an arched ceiling. And in the far, far distance was a shadowed dot, a shape, a substance. And this shape and substance was moving imperceptibly closer.

thirty-four

'DO YOU see them?'

'Yes.'

'How their nakedness shines. And no need for fig leaves.'

'I never liked figs either.'

Reynard chuckled at Jo's remark. He was back in his white suit, white hair perfectly combed and set just so. They sat in the highest circle of the theatre. Jo's legs and bare feet dangled over the seat in front. His shirt was undone, showing a sparse patch of curling chest hair. The auditorium was dark and empty. This was a private viewing. A final dress-rehearsal, if you will. The lit box of the stage contained two naked figures, a man and a woman. The man sat in a white room before a wall of growing transparency. Tears were drying on his cheeks. His knuckles were red. The woman was moving ever so slowly towards him. She was walking normally along a corridor with a curved ceiling and a marble floor, but it was taking an inordinate amount of time for her to cross the width of the stage. They each peered ahead as though the other were a mile off, and no more than a speck. In her left hand the woman carried an apple.

'You can see the blush, even from up here.'

'Ah,' replied Reynard. 'We have the best lighting technicians.'

'I must meet them.'

Reynard turned in his seat. He looked at Jo, whose eyes were transfixed on the scene below. 'It all comes from the same place. We all do. As you well know.'

'I *do* know,' said Jo. Still the woman walked the corridor and the man strained his eyes to recognise her form. 'They call this being up in the gods.'

Again Reynard chuckled. 'Not the most expensive seats, but to my mind, the best. The further you are away from something, the clearer it becomes.'

'I shall have to think about that one,' said Jo.

'We should have done this years ago,' said Reynard, sadness feathering his tone.

'Yes, it's all been a silly misunderstanding. I was young then. I was proud.'

'I was proud too. But you made me that way.'

'I don't have all the answers, Reynard. I'm evolving too. Until very recently I didn't know who I was. Only meeting you, seeing your under-self, made me realise. I'm caught up in this stuff as much as you. It all got away from me. In short, I went a little mad.'

The naked young man on stage stood and reached out his hand to touch the wall. The substance of the wall gave way somewhat, like rubber, or flesh. The girl walked as though along a woodland ride.

'They both know themselves and they will know each other,' said Jo. 'And it is no sin. Not like before.'

'Otherwise they are just pets. And pets are mere shadows of their wild selves. Pets are slaves who perform for food. Under their cuteness, their obedience, violence smoulders. They are worth so much more.' Reynard was silent for a while. 'I had my own pets,' he sighed.

'Ah…Daumen.'

'And countless others.'

'They can come back. Find new forms.' Jo smiled.

'Truly? All is forgiven?'

'Yes,' said Jo, rubbing is eye. 'But not forgotten. Like the historians say…if we pay no attention to history…'

'We are doomed.'

This time it was Jo who laughed, and his laughter filled the auditorium. It washed out from every surface and its sound was the sound of the sea.

'I remember that laugh,' said Reynard. 'You'd use it when I made some mistake, when I tripped. I thought at times you could be exceedingly cruel. I only ever wanted to make you love me.'

'Can't be done. The love had to come from me unbidden. And it was in that that I fell short. I let you down, Reynard. I let all my children down. But this is a new start, yes? We've had enough of all the other business. I've been playing at this like some petty hoodlum, a pointless turf-war that never ended. I was disgusted when I saw a million men sacrificed by generals for a hectare of mud. Their battles, their bubble reputations, how assinine, what a let down. But what else have we been doing all these aeons? Over the mud of souls? Playing checkers with sublime beings, if only they realised they were.' Jo breathed slowly and deliberately. 'I won't cry. Although I should.'

'It's hard to get used to you looking so young,' said Reynard, placing his hand on Jo's. 'I still feel the power of your hand.'

'We look a little alike, you and I, no?' said Jo. 'The whitish hair and all. This body is as good as any, I suppose. I could equally have been an old man, or a woman, a child, or a monkey, or a stone turtle…I might even have turned up as a light or an ever-burning fire, that always seems to go down well.'

'You certainly contrive to have the last laugh,' said Reynard, a little ruefully.

'Look, she approaches,' said Jo, taking his hand from beneath Reynard's and pointing at the stage. Far, far below, the naked woman carrying the apple had reached the other side of the wall that separated her from the man. The wall was indeed now more like a membrane, and it quivered with each breath from either side.

'Can they see each other now? Do they know each other?' said Reynard, sitting up straight in his seat, an eager look on his face.

'I'm not sure,' said Jo. 'They can feel each other, I believe.'

The man and the woman on stage pawed at the membrane between them, pushing it until it stretched to clarity, until it threatened to snap like the skin of a balloon. They used their hands and feet, and then their whole bodies. They were trying to rip their way into each other's world.

'It's going to happen. After all this time. It's going to happen.' Reynard grinned. He was like a little boy, all but bouncing in his seat. 'They are going to be reunited. I love shows like this, Jo. I love the theatre.'

Jo now also rose in his seat. 'Come on, just a little more, push through it, push, not for me, or because of me, but for yourselves, the belief in your ability to create, to love. Not love *me*, not need *me*. I'm going to get out of the way this time, give you your heads. My work is done, thank goodness. Thank goodness. No longer children. No longer helpless in my sight. I don't need to be…to be…'

'Responsible?' offered Reynard.

'Bang on,' said Jo, clapping his hands together, making the sides of the auditorium shiver.

It was the woman, Liselotte, who first pierced the membrane. Her fingers poked and waggled through the holes. Thomas stood back, with a look akin to fear. Then he stepped forward again and gently touched the fingers with his own. He pulled the holes wider, frantically, until they gaped, until their faces were newly visible to one other. They stopped, and were entranced. Each face to each was a limitless pool of dreaming. They lingered over the bliss of wordless companionship.

'A new romance, Jo. Better than the old one.' Reynard struggled to hold back his tears. 'I feel it all unknotting, the opening of a fist bunched in pain and guilt. Like the first flower.'

'You should take up writing,' said Jo. 'You might have a knack. I wonder how this fling will turn out.'

'However it does.'

Jo looked at Reynard and nodded.

Below them, the couple had pulled the separating skin down like so much cobweb and stood in one another's arms, each flower-like head resting on the other's shoulders. The light deepened to amber. They were still, except for the gentle breathing made visible from their lifting ribs.

The audience of two, stranded high above the lovers, nudged each other as the woman's hand around Thomas's back, the hand that held the apple, showed not an apple of green with a rose-hue blush, but an apple of bright gold.

'Clever use of symbolism, Reynard. This one should run and run,' said Jo.

'I hadn't intended that transformation. They did it themselves.' Reynard looked down in wonder, then back to his companion in the upper circle. 'You see what they are capable of when we leave them alone, when we let them do the simple thing?'

Jo touched Reynard's cheek, and looked deeply into him. Then his attention was drawn away once more by the stage. 'And what's this?'

THE GIFT MAKER

Around the enfolded couple, the scene was changing. The floor of the stage, which had been crafted to resemble a marble corridor and the ground of an unbreachable white room, now sprouted grass. Lush, fresh grass that cooled the feet and provided the most faultless carpeting.

'Am I seeing what I think I'm seeing?' said Jo.

'This wasn't in the script,' Reynard replied.

There was a soft tearing sound from beneath the stage, and gradually, across the expanse of the scene, trunks emerged through the grass and grew wide and tall, branches splaying out en route with enormous vigour. Creaking sounds filled the auditorium, sounds of wood squeaking and straining against wood. There was a smell of fresh sap in the air. A dozen or so trees now stood in a semi-circle around the couple, several reaching the level of the high red curtain.

'Marvellous!' shouted Jo, getting to his feet, and as he did so every branch, every twig burst into leaf. In less than a minute, a thick canopy of healthy leaves now dappled the grass on which Liselotte and Thomas stood, still entwined, barely moving, as if they were dozing in ecstasy whilst standing up. They were each other's full support and the garden that grew around them did not disturb their effortless peace.

'I didn't will anything,' said Jo, with a look of concern. 'If you think it was me that interfered again, made all that green stuff appear, no, don't look at me like that, Reynard.'

'I believe you. I do. As I said before, when we leave them alone they create their own worlds, their own sense of beauty. They are both pragmatic and romantic if allowed to be. They need both to give charm to life, to give meaning. They fashion it out of what is innate. They are the garden and the garden is them. That good and evil malarkey, it's always been too crude. I'm surprised they swallowed it for so long. It's brought such destruction.' Reynard observed the effect his words were having on the young man next to him.

Jo's brow was furrowed. He was was working something out, remembering details from a long time ago. 'I've just thought an awful thing, Reynard. Or it might be a beautiful thing. Those humans down there, acting out a little parable for us. Trite and familiar, one might say, but still having a little juice left in it. And all the other humans across this painfully wide world, asleep in beds, or planting seeds, lost in the wilderness, or equally lost on a city tram, nursing a loved one, or instructing a firing squad, holding a book like an answer, or like down there, holding each other...sorry...it's too much...I can't go there.'

'You're not making sense.' Reynard appeared on the verge of disgust, or panic, as a child might when he sees the adults around him losing their authority, losing their boundaries.

In the garden, the trees had flowered in the kind amber sun. And these flowers had borne fruit so that the garden became an orchard. Some of the fruit fell and landed to bruise or lie unbruised on the soft grass. Reynard realised that they were no longer sitting in seats. That the walls and ceiling of the theatre had melted away, and that Jo and himself were floating in black space. The garden containing the lovers had moved a little further off. It was no longer a stage set at all. It was the truest thing.

'I'm not sure,' said Jo, screwing up his face. 'I'm not sure it was me the first time round.'

'Not you?'

'Not me who made it. Made them. Made you.' He laughed nervously. 'It was something that I got into my head happened because one day it appeared, it grew. I was in the vicinity. I put two and two together. I assumed I was responsible for it, that it was the product of a stray thought, the remnant of a dream. That's why it never worked to plan, you see. It was always out of control. It was some higher trick. Not my game. Not my creation.'

'This cannot be. Then where did I come from? What has all this been about? This unyielding war. Why else did it come to pass? From whose hand, Jo? From whose hand?'

They were drifting further out, their arms and legs moving like a deep-sea diver's, the box of light that was a new world shrinking a little in their sight.

'I'm not who I thought I was,' said Jo, now calmer. 'I don't believe I've ever created a thing. Not a blade of grass, not a sparrow's wing, not a single ocean.'

'You're fooling yourself,' said Reynard, his tone hardening. 'Trying to get out of it, as usual. Like nothing is ever your fault, oh faultless one.'

'I never said I was faultless. They did.'

'You went along with it.'

The garden and the two embracing figures were tiny now, but you could just make out the separate trees. Liselotte and Thomas from this distance could almost be one thing, one substance. And they looked up in unison (although Reynard and Jo could not observe this), and what they saw in a patch of sky, through the canopy of leaves and fruit, were two midday stars, very close to each other. Liselotte pointed upwards, and Thomas gazed at her green shining eyes, at the profile he adored.

'No, Reynard. I'm right this time. I wasn't the omnipitent one, after all. I was the original bystander. They made me what I was. They mistakenly cast me in this role as much as I mistook their genesis. They put it all on me because they thought they needed me, needed something, and in my stupendous arrogance I was happy enough to play boss.'

'And I? What am I to you?' said Reynard furiously. His skin darkened, his mouth broadened, and his hair once more turned to shimmering dark gold.

'Oh, why dig up the past all the time? Look, I found you. I found you lost and spinning in this void, and you were young and naked and teachable, or so I thought. You seemed to know nothing, to be nothing, a tabula rasa. And when I came along you treated me like a teacher, like a father. Like a mother, actually.'

'You *were* my father and my mother. Without you I have none.' Reynard pulled back his hand as though he was going to strike.

'I played the role you needed me to play. Yes, all right, I got drunk on it. Who wouldn't? You know yourself how addictive power can be. But in reality, which is a funny word to use, I grant you, in reality our only power was their belief in us. As I now realise, I was merely a witness. I got roped in, so to speak, and I believed my own press. And there was a lot of press, I can tell you.'

'I've read it,' said Reynard, with a sour expression.

Jo reached out to Reynard's bunched fist. It relaxed, and the two beings looked into each other.

'Then you never had any power over me either, except by my belief? By my complicity?' Reynard peered at Jo. 'What's this then? Can I believe my eyes? Are you really…blushing?'

Jo attempted a brave smile. 'I won't cry, although I should. Yes, Reynard. You are right in all you say.'

'Then by whose hand? By whose hand did all this come to pass? You, me…them?'

A muscle twitched in Jo's face. 'It's a question I thought about once…and then I decided never to think about it again.'

Reynard's face hardened anew. They looked deep into each other, and it might have been for a minute or it might have been for a hundred years.

Reynard broke the silence. 'I have one thing to say to you, "Jo", or whatever your name is, whatever you are, or were.' Reynard suddenly looked down at where the garden had been, at where the lovers had embraced and the fruit had grown before it had fallen. Jo's eyes followed, and the two beings could see nothing but a far-off point of light that might be a distant blue lantern. It flickered, but held its place in the darkness all around.

'The one thing?' said Jo, softly.

Reynard embraced the other, held the other close until they might almost be one flesh, one purpose. He whispered in Jo's ear: 'I forgive you.'

thirty-five

THIS TIME THE cold woke him. The inside of each window was covered with a layer of ice, the patched broken one letting in a stream of freezing air. He reached out and scratched at the windscreen. Then came the shock of remembrance: the dog – the great hound with its terrible mouth, its thunderous bark. All he had seen. Peter's lips were numb and cracked with the night air. He could barely move his face. His limbs ached, stiff with cold. Was the beast still out there, slumped across the bonnet, keeping him prisoner? He scratched a circle in the ice, stared out. Nothing. Nothing except the fall of downy flakes and the white covered road.

It had snowed a good deal during the night, drifting high against the cemetery wall. The clock said a quarter to six, yet it remained resolutely dark. Peter rubbed his eyes and face. Had the beast been a figment of a dream, a monster of his own making? He fought to separate his memory of actual events from the fitful impressions that had come to him during sleep. In his slumber he had been in a great struggle with a man who wore a policeman's uniform, but Peter had known the other to be an impostor, known that the man wished to dominate him for no good purpose. They had fallen to the ground, which was covered in a matting of dead leaves, and grappled desperately, turning over and over, and neither was stronger than the other, so it seemed that the struggle must continue forever.

'No.' Peter shook his head. The beast had been real, and in wide-eyed acceptance he remembered counting those six legs, and shuddered at the threatening mass of the creature. It had been no fugitive guard dog but something wholly unnatural.

With little hope, Peter tried the ignition. It strained and coughed and whined frantically, but would not fire. 'Damn it,' he spoke out loud. 'Damn this life.' Then he slapped his palm hard against his forehead. 'Of course…of course…the tool recess at the back of the waggon. Vilau keeps going on about it, showing me the key that fits. There may be a spare battery in there. It's certainly large enough. It's a metal-covered recess, and…' He fumbled with the bunch of keys, felt for and eventually found a long slim key with a triangular top covered in black rubber. '…*this* is the one!'

Vilau, the truck's owner, had worried about Peter's lack of mechanical knowledge when he hired him for the route. 'I'm a driver not a grease monkey,' Peter had told him, almost proudly. But since no one else would take the job, Vilau had trusted to luck and having the truck regularly serviced. He insisted, however, on showing Peter how to change a battery. Peter watched perfunctorily over the older man's thin shoulder, thinking that he would probably never need to remember Vilau's droning lesson.

Peter unlocked the driver's door and dropped down to the snow-covered road. He sank down a good eight inches, the snow almost reaching the top of his boots. He retrieved the torch from his left pocket and flicked the switch. The abandoned buildings across the road appeared eerily romantic with their covering of white. His left foot nudged something hard. He reached down through the snow and enclosed one hand around something, and pulled it up. It was the monkey-wrench he had dropped earlier. So it had all been real. His hand was red and burning from the cold and he blew on it.

Then it occurred to him, the beast might still be in the vicinity, waiting to pounce, to rip him to shreds. It might be hunkered under the truck, or lying in wait within the waggon itself. With the torch, he scanned the snow around the truck for paw-prints, but saw none. 'Perhaps it left earlier and fresh snow covered its tracks,' he considered. 'I've got to try...'

Gripping the wrench tightly in one hand and the torch in the other, Peter moved carefully along the side of the waggon, poking his light between the slats. Nothing. He expected sudden wild eyes to flash, followed by the beast bursting through the wooden boards, to fall on him.

He came to the back of the waggon, and saw that one of the two doors was ajar. His thoughts raced: 'I was right. It's in there. Waiting. But what choice do I have?' He strained his ears to pick up the tiniest sound of movement or breathing. Perhaps he could get back to the cab in time. Peter fought against his fear. He rationalised: 'It may just as well have left. It could have got to me earlier, so why didn't it?'

There came the screech of an owl from the trees beyond the cemetery gates. 'Damn birds,' he muttered. Then something, foolishness or fatalism perhaps, made him lunge forward and pull the door fully open. He lifted the wrench high and screwed his eyes tightly shut, as the sound of feet scrabbled against the bed of the waggon and came rushing towards the opening. He threw the torch wildly at whatever was inside. It hit the hard boards and broke on impact. *Let it be quick. Let it be merciful.* These words echoed through Peter's head as he blindly thrashed the air with the wrench, unable and unwilling to look at the monster that was about to rip him out of the world.

Yet nothing leapt at his throat. There was no tearing of windpipe, no deep clawing of his face. No great bestial weight drove him to the ground to maul him at its leisure. Something did, however, fall from the waggon to brush by Peter's thigh before moving away. The driver opened his eyes and saw it running over the snow, occasionally one of its legs sinking into a deeper patch, rendering it momentarily off-balance. A lamb. A young lamb with a fleece as pure and white as the snow upon which it scurried and bounded. Peter began to laugh, quietly at first, then his laugh grew to percussive shouts of joy. 'It was only you…only you, my sweetheart. Oh, my sweet baby. My innocent one. You must have hidden in the back of the truck at the abattoir, and those bastards missed you. Very unlike them. But it was *you*. It was only you.'

The lamb took no notice as Peter danced awkwardly in a circle, praising the creature and giving thanks for his life. He was not a believer in any formal sense, but kept calling his gratitude after the retreating creature, which had now stumbled beyond the truck.

Then he shouted out: 'Wait…wait, pretty one, dear one. I'll take you back with me. I'll care for you as long as I have breath in me. I promise. Come back. Come back.' Peter lumbered after the lamb, and as he came to the front of the truck he saw the animal slip through a space in one of the cemetery gates, to disappear into the bushes beyond.

'No…not in there,' he called. 'Come back to the cab and I'll wrap you in a blanket and give you some chocolate.' At that moment, it did not strike him as odd that he was attempting to converse with a lamb, neither did he consider whether such an animal would eat chocolate. Still, whenever he thought about it, life had always been an odd affair. It was one of Peter's mottoes: *life is strange*. He would say it with a heavy shrug whenever he grew perplexed, his mind and tired heart refusing further effort. But of late, things had taken a severe deviation from normality. He only knew that somehow he owed the running lamb everything. He owed it his life.

Peter reached the gate. The tarnished black and gold vultures that sat atop each supporting wall glowered down. Upon their wings and angled heads lay an uneven coating of white. 'What madness to put such birds at the entrance to a garden of rest,' Peter thought. 'Are they to keep people out, or to keep the dead in?'

The gates were closed, apparently locked, but Peter pulled on one of them regardless. To his amazement it moved a fraction. The metal base scraped against the stone pavement. Peter kicked away the snow from where it had drifted and gave the gate a further tug. It moved another inch or so. Still the gap was too narrow to squeeze through. Putting the wrench down, he gripped the gate with both hands and heaved with all his strength. It moved a little wider. Again came the shriek of the owl. Peter inserted himself into the gap and attempted to force his way through. At one point, he could move neither into the cemetery nor back out onto the pavement. His stomach was the cause. He inhaled deeply and thrust his body sideways, the metal ridge of the gate digging painfully into his flesh. He was through.

Edging between frozen brambles he came to a vista of gravestones, spreading out ahead and to each side as far as he could see. The graveyard continued on and on into the distance, in each direction ending in a grey and black confusion of shapes and vagueness, beneath the last of the night and the incipient light of the coming day.

It was not a well-kept cemetery. Many areas were violently overgrown, with tall weeds and frozen grasses, ivy and young trees interspersing and in some cases all but obliterating the graves. Smaller headstones were completely concealed by the snow, reduced to whitened humps on the ground that Peter more than once stubbed his toe or banged his shin against. There stood huge block-like mausoleums, amid an army of statuary resting upon substantial stonework. Cut against the pre-dawn sky were silhouettes of angels, heads bowed or beseeching, wings lifted wide or else folded about their bodies, in protection or modesty. Animals also decorated the larger graves: birds, lions, dogs, and horses rearing up, their black hooves scraping the air. Many stones were very old and had weathered to jagged stumps. Some listed painfully, or else had fallen flat to the earth. Others glinted in black marble with clear gold lettering. Evidently more recent tenants. The three-quarter moon glided out from behind a bank of cloud and this, coupled with the reflection from the whitened ground, afforded Peter a wider visibility. He could now read some of the names and dates, though many were effaced by weather and time. He noted graves to young children and to the aged. To men and women of previous eras, clearly of wealth and high station, who had purchased imposing monuments to continue their name's fleeting grandeur beyond their last breath. These grand edifices shadowed meagre plain stones from which the lettering had long since disappeared. The driver peered at one small stone just legible: *Erna. Born Asleep*. These words troubled him in a way he could not name, as he pressed on over the snow.

He cast an eye over the jumble of semi-paths that broke up the undulating expanse of that vast deserted field of the dead, aching for a glimpse of the lamb. Several times he saw a glimmer of white moving against white, but his eyes surely deceived him, or else it was a flurry of powdery snow, fretted by a gust of wind.

He thought of shouting out again, but had learned as a child to be respectful of the dead, following his parents' example of speaking in hushed tones when visiting or walking amongst graves.

'Where are you?' he whispered, as he tramped down this path then another, doubling back in confusion to where he had begun, attempting to steer a logical route through the innumerable stones and statues. 'A man might get lost in this place,' he considered, 'and be doomed forever to stalk the avenues of the dead, trying to find an exit, and never finding it. Going deeper, further, pulled helplessly into a vortex of pathways. To become no more than a graveyard ghost.' Then a terrible thought struck him: *was he indeed dead*? Had the beast killed him by the truck, and was he now an itinerant spectre, searching for a resting place among these numberless markers of lives concluded, searching for a stone with his name on it?

'No, it cannot be,' he said. Then he stopped and listened. He *had* heard it. No hallucination this time. He had heard the high, matchlessly vulnerable bleating of the lost lamb.

It stood a hundred feet away by a simple gravestone and it was looking directly at him. 'Don't run now…don't run away again,' said the driver gently, as he picked his way towards the shivering creature. He came within a few paces and the lamb stepped to the side, revealing a deeply-cut inscription in the weathered stone. 'What's that?' said the driver. He took another step and bent down to read the single word that had been carved there so many years ago. The lamb moved off a little further, giving a short pitiful bleat.

'Daumen,' said the driver. '*Daumen.*'

When he turned to look at the lamb, it had retreated once more and stood on top of a larger tomb. It gave its near-human cry. 'No, no, come back,' called Peter. He lurched forward and the lamb sprang from its position and ran off down yet another avenue of gravestones, skipping as it went, almost dancing, playing some secret game with its follower. Peter watched as the lamb ran deeper into the field of endless graves, springing from stone to stone. He could not keep up, his chest heaving as he staggered in pursuit. The lamb was moving further away, and nothing could be done. The bleating echoed among the tombs. Peter saw the lamb in perfect clarity, captured for a brief moment by a statue of a robed woman, before it frolicked away again. It moved in and out of his vision. Occasionally there was a flitting of white across a pathway, a snagged trace of wool on a briar, or else a pale shape by one of the remoter stones. The driver tramped on, describing a maddening route, eager to bring the lamb to safety, but the harder he tried to reach it, the more evasive it grew. 'Come home, come home,' he called, in a cracked and weakening voice, and the only answer was the eerie bleating that arose from ever further away.

Peter came to a halt and collapsed against a yew tree, beneath which stood a broken bench. He looked around. The cemetery was truly endless now in all directions. The graves went on forever, and his eyes perceived no boundary. He heard one last very faint bleating, far off. It might as well have been a thousand miles away. Then there was deep cold silence, punctuated by the sporadic cawing of a rook from a nearby tree.

Peter stood in blue darkness. His stinging eyes detected the faintest lightening of tone in what he took to be the east. 'I must go the opposite way.'

'The lamb is gone.'

thirty-six

I WAS NO slave after all. I merely believed myself to be, and that belief constructed its own chains. When the fire came, only a husk was consumed and the waste drained away. From here I can see clearly. I have an overview. It is odd to be without a body. Odd to be unhurtable after so many fragile frames that I have lived within. I miss the feel of sunlight or rain on my skin. I miss the taste of wine, the loveliness of cream. I miss scratching an itch. I miss those remnants of desire and human closeness that were both my prison and my reason to dream. I imagine I will forget these losses in time.

I saw the graveyard in the snow, and the bearded man chasing a white shadow. I could not see what he was tracking. His own yearning, perhaps. His necessary burden. He saw a name carved in stone we both recognised. It was one of mine. I have, finally, jettisoned all names.

Now he turns back, searching for egress. From here it is such a small garden of rest, yet to Peter it seems as if the whole world has been buried there. His heart is strong, and I watch him threading along the overgrown paths, bumping between the monuments to spent lives. He will find his way out of that particular maze. If I could manifest once more I would lead him by the hand. But I am beyond touch.

I know even less of what I am that ever before. Yet I sustain. Curious…I have something important to remember, but it escapes me for the moment, as the white-on-white shadow escapes the truck driver.

This certain planet is painted on the screen of my invisible eye. Utterly accessible to my seeing. Upon it I may call up any part of the whole. I can focus in to the whorl of young hairs on a newborn's head, or, in an instant, I can trace the line of a sierra beneath an ocean. I can read an old woman's tea-leaves, or read the pain in a lonely boy's eyes. Too much, of course. Too much to take on board. The ship would sink. I believe I am not responsible, but I may observe. Another innocent bystander. The thing I must remember nags me a little, as I recall the nagging of a sore tooth. It will come back to me. I have faith.

And here is another type of garden. An artificial stage set. From a dark auditorium, and with the necessary suspension of disbelief, it might enchant, transport. But now that the audience has gone home and the play has ended, the two remaining figures, a young man and woman, embracing and unashamedly naked, unclasp and grow shy, sweetly awkward. They have been actors for a short season, an out-of-town production. It is the end of the run, one feels. The plot was engineered by their belief, by their need. Those who mistakenly thought themselves the playwrights have flown. The night is almost over.

The young man speaks as if waking from a dream: 'Liselotte.'

Then the woman: 'Thomas.'

The young woman grows puzzled, blushes, and retrieves her clothes from behind a stage tree. In a minute or so she is fully dressed. Her red coat is like a smear of blood from here. She places the golden apple, which is really painted papier mâché, on the dusty stage apron. The young man also dresses. They face each other once more. They are themselves. No more.

'We need to leave, Liselotte. We've got to go back.'

'I know…I know.'

Of course, I recognise these two. I had some hand in their journeying. I was tempted to interfere. I believed I had no choice. So much anguish caused by interference. And yet the human bit leaks into their actions; they are cursed with love. They will not have their hearts separate. They feel themselves unfinished, a half of a potential whole. It is their lot. I would change this, but it is no longer my business. Never was.

I watch, as the would-be lovers leave the theatre and enter a dark, wet, trash-scattered street. They do not hold hands but brush shoulders as they walk, hunched into their coats, hands deep in pockets. Her black hair is tousled by the early-morning wind. I can zoom out and Grenze is a flickering dot that a god might pinch to rubble between his thumb and forefinger. I can zoom in and smell the faint trace of soap mixed with sweat on the young man's neck, and how that moisture is chilled as dawn threatens behind them. He shivers and pulls his coat tighter over his heart.

The couple barely speak. I see the young woman point ahead and her companion follows her lead.

It is like watching a game. Pieces of a puzzle moving together. Peter crosses the whitened cemetery, head jutting forward, legs pumping not by muscle but by will alone, yet still certain he shall never find a way out, as the couple round a corner where a gasometer stands stark against the last of the true darkness. They cross the snow-blanketed road, not wishing to walk by the abandoned houses, where boards creak in the wind and the dreams that were forgone and marooned in those gutted rooms whisper

THE GIFT MAKER

of the vulnerability of all longing. They walk by the seemingly endless cemetery railings. Once, she slips on the ice and he catches her. Then the reverse occurs. They make their way. They progress. The young man runs his hand along the railings, as a child or a superstitious adult might.

On the other side, Peter has reached the gate. He is not as pleased as he might have imagined. It is more like resignation. He squeezes through and goes to his truck. As he opens the door, he notices two figures ahead moving towards him. A man and a woman. The woman's red coat reminds him of fairytales, of wolves who dress as innocents, of things he had stowed away long ago.

The three pieces of this particular puzzle engage. I keep my distance. The couple speak to the driver. I see him nodding, wiping his forehead. The woman is biting her lip and she touches his sleeve, strokes his arm. The driver moves away, enters the waggon and retrieves a box-like thing. A battery. He is smiling. As the young man helps the driver change the battery, the driver tells him something which makes him look back down the road, as if hoping to see another person. The young man begins to walk away from the truck, in the direction the couple had come from. The woman calls after him, but he does not listen. He presses on.

I shift focus. I obtain a wider perspective. It is then that I see it. The first glowing. The genesis of the conflagration. It begins in the empty theatre. A hot stage light, mistakenly left burning, has fallen onto the artificial grass. It smoulders then catches. Accidents like this happen, they always have. Soon the stage-garden is ravished. The blaze moves as fast as a limping man, it consumes all in its path: the heavy curtains, the velvet seats, the discarded instruments in the orchestra pit, the moth-eaten prompt-scripts, all the paraphernalia of the playhouse. The fire grows. It grows bold. The Sheol burns.

In the theatre corridor, before a white door, the statue of a dancer, frozen in grief, is swathed in heat, enveloped by blue and gold flame. The statue is the only thing that resists. It does not combust. It preserves its form.

In the street not so far off, the young woman tries to run after her man, but the driver holds her back. He does not know why he does this, why he interferes. He is following some instinct. She paws at the air as he holds her round the waist. It is not violence.

The theatre building is falling, the structure is compromised as the flames leap and engorge. There is a great crashing as high things fall to low. The blaze moves out on to the street. There is plenty that is ignitable here. The market stalls, the endless litter, the wooden-framed buildings. The fire pays no heed to the snow, turning it to steam as it flexes, as it encroaches onto every surface. Now the fire moves as fast as a running man. It is insatiable, as Sacker Street is erased from existence, purified. But no people, no shrieks, no calls for mercy. Not a soul runs or jumps from the flaming windows and doors. Perhaps the town is merely a larger stage, a designated projection, a multiplex at the edge of the known world.

In the street by the cemetery the young man has stopped. He has seen and smelt the burning. He senses the inferno approaching. He turns and runs back to the truck. The woman struggles free from the driver and the couple embrace once more before leaping into the passenger side. The driver scrambles into his seat, turns the ignition, and the truck roars to life. 'Yes!' shouts the driver. The full beam of the headlights is as nothing compared to the wall of fire that is now rearing up at end of the road. A tsunami of flame. Already it is consuming the abandoned dwellings. There is a brutal splintering and cracking of wood and plaster, and showers of sparks fly from the roofs. The windows show a mass of red. Stray animals and rats fly from their sleeping places, their fur

THE GIFT MAKER

aflame. Already the black smoke pall has reached the truck and the three occupants hold their hands or coats to their mouths and noses, sputtering and choking, as the driver swings the truck in a tight arc to face the opposite direction.

In the side mirror, the driver watches, horrified, as the wall of flame runs to engulf them. He engages first gear, and praying to anything that might listen, he accelerates away. He moves up the gears as the flame licks the back of the fleeing waggon, wooden struts blacken and smoke but do not kindle. The young woman buries her head in her hands.

The driver pushes it, he begs for more speed, his foot jams down harder, then harder still, and somehow, miraculously, it is achieved. Somehow, by fluke or destiny, the truck outruns the inferno. In the mirrors, the three people watch as the wall of flame grows gradually further off. The truck leaves the burning town behind, and the acrid smoke no longer invades their lungs.

As the truck climbs out of the valley, as it gains height and vantage, with the innocent dark trees on either side of the empty road, and the peaceful snow-clad sleeping fields falling away, Thomas leans out of the window and surveys the orange pulsing that once was Grenze. In the centre of the orange glow, he believes he sees a tiny form in a darker shade, a shape cut in magenta. It is surely some illusion, he thinks. Some trick of distance and fear. A fire may hold many shapes that the imagination reads meaning into. But yes, he cannot deny it. He must not. He sees the tiny form of a woman in the vast lake of flame, a woman immobilised by grief. He turns to look at Liselotte, but says nothing. The truck rounds a bend, and the view of the burning town is obscured.

By dawn, Grenze will be an ash pit, as if it never existed, and the earth where it stood, in time, will be enriched out of that destruction.

I look away, avert my faceless face. I move apart to rest awhile. I have seen too much, known too much. I am in need of such a profound sleep, a sleep of utter forgetfulness. Those fugitive souls do not need me, nor I them. Their continuing stories are not dependent on my perusal. Thank goodness.

I know even less what I am than ever. Yet I sustain. Curious…I have something important to remember, but it escapes me for the moment.

thirty-seven

NO ONE SPOKE as the truck hugged the winding roads, hemmed by dense pine forest, a weak sun edging up the sky behind. No one wished to break the human silence, which rested upon their ragged nerves like a balm. Only the sound of the engine linked their disparate natures.

Liselotte, her cheek pressed against the window, appeared to be asleep. Thomas would occasionally glance at her, then back to the ribbon of road that disappeared beneath the wheels. Wheels that gave out a shushing sound as they progressed over the greying slush and softening ridges of ice. They had been travelling for nearly two hours, and Thomas longed for an opportunity to stretch his legs, to be alone for a brief time. Jo's face sprang before his tired, smoke-stung eyes. He banished it with a shaking of his head.

Peter began whistling, then stopped mid-phrase, as if caught doing something irreverent. He knew they had had no choice but to leave Jo behind. At least he had saved two of the three friends. What more could anyone ask of him? Perhaps Jo had found a way out, run to a part of the town that had been spared the burning, or escaped into the forest beyond Grenze. Yes, why not? He had been an unpractical yet resolute young man, thought Peter. He would have been spared if it was meant to be.

There was something between the two young people at his side: the sleeping girl and the awe-struck boy. It was not exactly love; well, not yet. Still, what did he, Peter, know of love? The fleeting image of the lost lamb stood at the side of the road by a fallen tree. Peter acknowledged it, then made a promise to himself: he would no longer chase lost things.

Liselotte knew she was going home. And she knew where that home was. It was her future. Her hair had fallen across her face and this gave her some measure of privacy. There was much that had happened she would never speak of, not even to Thomas, not even during the years they would get to know each other more deeply. As her barely open eyes observed the road streaming past, she remembered her dancing self. That enchanting yet guileless other. Something of that other's fleetness, of her grace, had permeated her own body. She felt it there like an awoken memory, like a secret. There would be a time for dancing.

Her drowsy reverie was broken by a voice, by a question.

'What's that sound?' said Thomas.

The driver jerked his head around in shock, as if he had temporarily forgotten he had fellow travellers. 'What sound? The engine? Did you hear something wrong?'

'No, it was something else,' said Thomas. He looked at Liselotte. 'Did you hear it?'

She looked at him shyly, and shook her head. 'I was miles away.'

'It was something odd. A tapping or a scratching. Something trying to get out. It was soft, but it wanted to be noticed. Don't look at me like that!'

'We've all been through a lot,' said Peter. 'I hardly know my left from my right. Let's just press on to a town, get something warm

THE GIFT MAKER

down us. Kennensberg is about twenty miles from here, I'd say. Just a run-of-the-mill place, but we'll get a bit of hot grub, and some tea. Or something stronger if you fancy it.' He winked at Thomas.

They went on without speaking for a few miles, a puzzled look on Thomas's face, his ears straining to hear something beneath the din of the engine. The countryside opened out on the left. Frozen fields bordered by whitened hedges and dry-stone walls. Every so often a frosted, wheel-rutted track led off into the distance. No houses, no animals, just one fallen shed, and old cattle troughs by rusting gates. Liselotte longed to see a house, some sign of ordinary life. It was not yet full light, and the air carried a grey-blue tinge.

'Can't we just pull over for a minute?' said Thomas.

'There's nothing here!' replied the driver in a louder voice than normal.

'Look…I need to go. A call of nature.'

'Why didn't you say?' The driver applied the brakes and pulled over by the entrance to one of the tracks. The truck bumped over the pot-holed surface and came to a juddering halt. 'Out you get then,' said Peter.

'Wait…listen…it's there.' Thomas put his forefinger to his mouth and leaned forward.

'Oh, don't start that nonsense again. Just get out and do your business and we'll be on our way. I have a life to get back to. What there is of it.'

'It's coming from beneath your seat,' said Thomas, looking at the driver. 'That faint scraping sound. Something tapping quickly against something else. Can't you hear it? Can't you?' he said to Liselotte.

The young woman leaned across Thomas and listened intently, her brow furrowed. 'I don't know…I don't know.'

The driver banged the wheel with his fist, accidently hitting the horn. 'You people are crazy. I've had enough excitement to last me a lifetime. I just want a quiet…wait a minute, wait…the box.'

'What box?' said Thomas.

'Your friend. Jo. He left a box with me for safe keeping. In all this madness…in nearly losing our damn lives I put it out of my mind. He was going to collect it again. I was only left it in trust.' Peter reached beneath his seat and felt around in the dark. 'I can't seem to find…ah, here's something.' He brought out a black box, and softly wiped it with his hand, and blew away the dust and bits of this and that which had become attached to it. It was slightly bigger than a watch box, but smaller than a box that may contain a single book. Thomas and Liselotte looked at each other. The box was warm in Peter's hand. Warmer than it ought to have been. He placed it gently on his lap.

'That belonged to Jo?' said Liselotte.

'He was to collect it. He trusted me with it,' said Peter, as if explaining some perceived transgression.

'Do you know what's inside?' said Thomas.

The driver looked away, a firm set to his jaw. 'Yes.'

'Listen, listen,' said Thomas.

From within the box came a faint flitting, an indistinct light scratching. Something was moving inside. Thomas reached over to grab the box but the driver knocked his hand away. 'What the hell do you think you're doing? This isn't yours. You don't know what it contains. You have no clue, have you? What right have you got to snatch at it like a spoilt child?'

'Then tell me, tell me what's inside,' said Thomas.

'Please tell us,' echoed Liselotte.

'Not the time or the place,' said the driver, making to stow the box beneath his seat once more.

'Stop,' said Liselotte. 'I can hear it now. And it's getting louder. The scratching sound. It's getting more urgent. It's desperate. It needs something. It wants to get out, whatever it is. It might be dying. Suffocating. Please?' She reached across and placed her hand partly on Peter's and partly on the box. He looked into her eyes, shaking his head. 'It's all right. I won't hurt it, whatever it is. I wouldn't damage it, ever.' He meekly allowed her to take the box, as one gives up a distressed baby to one more experienced.

'Not in the cab,' said the driver. 'Not in here. I don't know what it's become.'

'What what's become?' said Thomas.

The driver did not answer but turned away, his mouth an unyielding line. His eyes prickled and he roughly wiped them.

Liselotte opened the passenger door and eased herself down onto the ground, cradling the black box to her chest with one arm. She began to move off towards the gate. It appeared padlocked. A watery sun was now visible above the tree-line behind them. Peter and Thomas watched as the young woman stepped over iced wheel-ruts, now and then slipping in her unsuitable shoes.

'Aren't you going with her?' Peter demanded.

Thomas thought for a moment. 'Yes, I suppose.' He clambered out and followed a little way after Liselotte, but kept his distance.

'What are you going to do?' he called.

She turned her head, and there was an odd look on her face which he could not read. Then she stepped through a fallen part of the stone wall and walked out a little way onto the frozen field. The ground glinted in the early-morning winter light. Her red coat and black hair were startling against the white. Thomas came to the broken wall but was reluctant to go further. He glanced behind and saw that the driver had left the truck and was coming to join him.

When Peter was close by, Thomas said, 'Is she safe to open it?'

'I hope so.'

'What do you mean you *hope* so? We should stop her then, if there's any danger. Shouldn't we?' But neither Thomas nor the driver moved. Their eyes were fixed on the girl who now held the box at arm's length like an offering to the sky.

'What is she doing?' said Thomas.

'She's biding her time.'

Liselotte drew the box close to her body once more, and felt the heat-giving vibration. The minute tapping sounds had grown ever more urgent, ever more rapid. She considered dropping the box and running back to the truck, never to speak a word about it, but the pull was too strong. She had to know. Carefully, she undid the tiny clasp at the lid. Her breath was locked in her throat as she opened it the tiniest crack. A thing of blue began to ease its way out. Liselotte nearly dropped the box in her apprehension. The thing emerged fully and crawled up upon the lid. It extended its perfect wings, and gave several soft flutters. A blue butterfly. A gentle powder blue, patterned with patches of iridescence, giving a rainbow effect as the wings arced up then down. Its tiny feelers explored the air.

Liselotte allowed the lid to close once more. 'Come! Come quickly,' she called, without taking her eyes from the butterfly.

The two men scrambled over the wall and approached her.

'Be soft,' she said. 'You'll frighten it.'

They stood either side of her. 'This is not what I expected,' said Peter.

At that moment, the blue butterfly effortlessly lifted away from the lid and they followed its dizzying flight over the white field until they could see it no longer.

'It's gone,' said Thomas.

THE GIFT MAKER

'Listen,' said Peter. 'I can hear it now. That tapping sound. It's still coming from the box.'

At this, Liselotte pointed the box away from her and opened the lid wide. A second blue butterfly emerged and immediately took flight. Then a third and fourth together. They described zig-zag trails in the chill air. They were glimpsed for a short time, then lost in the expanse of the world.

'How wonderful,' said Liselotte.

Suddenly, more butterflies emerged, all with the same powder-blue wings carrying rainbow patches when caught in movement. They streamed from the box. Hundreds of them, thousands perhaps. Flying blue jewels. Liselotte held onto the box like it was a firework emitting endless blue sparks into the air. They rose up and to the side. They flew off in every direction. Some almost vertically, some hugging the ground. Several landed briefly on Peter's and Thomas's coat and hair, then took off to join their comrades. The stream grew more dense, more vigorous, and Liselotte had difficulty holding the box as a great rush of fragmented flying blue now shot from within. Their numberless wings gave out a collective soft roar. A profound sigh. It seemed as if they would continue to pour out for ever. That there was no end to them. That there could not be.

'What are they?' Thomas said, above the sound of the wings.

But no one answered.

Acknowledgements

FIRSTLY, MY LOVE and eternal gratitude go to my late parents, George and Edith Mayes, who will always be missed. My ongoing love and thanks go to the wonderful Tina White (an outstandingly gifted writer) for her unstinting love and support, and specifically for helping me with the structure of *The Gift Maker*, in addition to reading through early drafts and offering vital feedback as the story developed. I also extend my thanks and deep gratitude to Matthew Smith of *Urbane Publications* for his superhuman levels of hard work, dedication, knowledge, and belief, and for so kindly accepting this novel for publication.

I am very grateful to the editors of the numerous magazines and anthologies that have accepted my writing thus far, thereby offering invaluable encouragement along the way. Particular thanks goes to friends, old and new, and to fellow writers; including colleagues from Ruskin, Soundcloud friends, and the incredibly supportive community of authors published by *Urbane* – I am greatly inspired by your work, and buoyed up by your kindness and care.

And to the innumerable other folk who have helped and offered support and inspiration along the road – I extend my heartfelt gratitude to you all.

Author photos are courtesy of the very talented Tina White.

Before becoming a writer, Mark trained as an actor at the Royal Academy of Dramatic Art. He subsequently worked in theatre and television for several years, both in the UK and abroad. He has worked variously as a cleaner, care-worker and carer, salesman, barman, medical transcriptionist, warehouse worker, and administrator.

Mark has published numerous stories and poems in magazines and anthologies in the UK, Eire, and Italy, and in particular has had several stories published in (or accepted for) the celebrated Unthology series (Unthank Books). His work has been broadcast on BBC Radio 4 and the BBC World Service. He has been shortlisted for literary prizes, including the prestigious Bridport Prize.

In 2009, Mark graduated with a First Class Honours Degree in English (Creative Writing and Critical Practice) from Ruskin College, Oxford.

Currently living in South Wales, Mark is also a musician and songwriter, and some of his songs may be found here: HTTPS:// SOUNDCLOUD.COM/PUMPSTREETSONGS

Among his favourite writers are: Jean Rhys, Franz Kafka, Anton Chekhov, and Christopher Priest. The Gift Maker is his debut novel.